THE OATH SAGA

VOLUME ONE

WHISPERING WIND

WRITTEN BY: KARLIE MAVRE

A.K.A. CO-AUTHORS

KARIN REEVE
&
LESLIE MARVIN

To my son, Javon Williams, who has been so gracious throughout this entire process, never once have you complained about the numerous hours I have spent on the computer writing. Your love, patience and encouragement has kept me on track and focused to keep growing and chasing after my dreams. You are my heart and happiness. I love you to the moon and beyond.

To my family who has encouraged me during this adventure, your unwavering faith and support means so much. I love, and thank you.

Last but not least, my friend and co-author, Leslie Marvin. Thank you for your willingness to walk beside me on this journey. There is no one else that I could imagine doing this with. I am eternally grateful that God placed you in my life. In you, I have found a sister - friends and family forever.

ʕ•ᴥ•ʔ

To the love of my life, Jeremy Marvin, you have been my solace and my rock for twenty-two years. Without your love and encouragement, fulfilling this dream would not have been possible. To my boys, Kyle and Nicholas, you are both the light of my life, and being your mom is my greatest joy and accomplishment. I could not be more proud of the fine, upstanding young men you have become.

To my family, your absolute faith in me and encouraging words mean more than I could possibly say. This has been my dream since childhood, and you had no doubt that I would accomplish it.

To my partner in crime, Karin Reeve, I'm so glad that fate steered us in the same direction. This story would never have come to fruition without your driving force and dedication to see it through. You kept me grounded and focused. It's astounding to witness first-hand how your mind works and this story is a testament to that and to the great team we make. The Dynamic Duo is alive and well and will persevere! Thank you for being you! You are the only one that I could have done this with. No matter the miles apart, you will forever be a true friend and family.

Acknowledgements

We would like to thank those who supported and believed in us, as well as those we met along the way on this journey.

First the Ottawa Writers' Guild of Kansas, what a wonderful group of creative and supportive souls we found in you. And to our group's fearless leader, Dave Burns, who encourages all of us to be the best that we can be. Thank you!

David Thompson, thank you for the interest you have taken in our project and the support you have provided.

Carter Bowman and Javon Williams, thank you for your creative efforts. Your futures look bright.

To our beta readers, Tina Albers, Bethany Hofmeier, Debbie Folsom, Emily Rayson, Kelly-Ray Shepherd, Shelby Jordan, Shawn Reeve, Paula Reeve, Stephanie Surber, Diane Speer, Baylee Parkison, Emily Moore, Christina Reeve, Charlene Reeve, Nick Marvin, Jeanne Bickerstaff, Sam Holtwick, Natasha Seymour and those who wish to remain anonymous, thank you for taking the time to read our book and complete our questionnaire. Your feedback was greatly appreciated as well as humbling. Again, thank you.

TABLE OF CONTENTS

PROLOGUE

August 19, 1999

Gracyn Knight stood in front of the bathroom mirror smoothing night cream on her perfectly flawless face. She studied her reflection carefully, looking for any sign that she was starting to show her true age. Satisfied that not a single laugh line was visible, she smiled. At fifty-four she still looked like she was in her early twenties. Her blonde hair cascaded half way down her back in natural waves. Piercing green eyes, still sharp as ever, stared back at her. Her love often told her he could get lost in the depths of those eyes. Turning to the side, she surveyed her flat stomach before tilting her chin up to make sure the skin there was not starting to sag. Happy with the whole image, she put the cap back on the jar of cream, flipped off the bathroom light and walked into her bedroom to find her husband smiling from their bed.

"I don't know why you bother with that stuff," Theron joked with her. "You haven't aged a day in thirty years."

She crawled into bed beside him. "And I don't plan to."

"You are as beautiful as the day I met you," he whispered, kissing her softly. He saw the worry come into her eyes as he pulled back. "What is it?"

Gracyn bit her lip. "Do you think we did the right thing? They are so young."

"Don't worry, Gracie. It will be just fine."

"But a fish? Maybe we should have gotten them a puppy or a kitten, or even a hamster. Fish die so easily. They're already attached to that thing. Your daughter wanted to kiss it goodnight," she stated, referring to their two-year-old.

Theron chuckled, "That's my girl. If the fish dies we will just get another one. They will never know. Trust me, Sweetie. Remember the joy on their faces today when we let them pick it out at the pet store? A fish first. Maybe in a few years we can consider a kitten, but for now a fish is the perfect low-maintenance pet."

"You're right." She sighed, laying back and snuggling into his arms. The elation on the faces of her children had made her heart swell when they had picked out Ralph, the ugliest gold fish in the bunch. Her son's eyes had filled with pride as he carefully cradled the plastic bag on the short ride home. Both children had hovered around the table, taking their turns placing the aquarium decorations inside before it was filled with water. Once Ralph was released into his new home they had watched for hours, laughing as he came to the top to grab a bite of food. Her babies were happy. She just prayed that Ralph lived a long, full life. They were too young to learn of death.

Pulling his wife close, Theron dropped a kiss on her head before reaching up to shut off the bedside lamp. "Goodnight, beautiful Gracie."

She smiled into the dark. "Goodnight, my love."

ഇൽഇൽ

"Are you awake?" the little boy whispered to his sister in the darkness.

"Yes."

"I want to go play with Ralph," he said.

She rubbed her eyes and sat up. "Me too. But Mommy doesn't like it when we get out of bed."

"We'll be quiet. Come on."

Her bare feet touched the floor as she gripped her brother's hand. Together they made their way silently down the hall and to the main floor. Creeping on their tippy toes they snuck into the kitchen toward the table that held the aquarium, climbing up on chairs with quiet giggles. In the soft glow of the aquarium light the children looked for their fish.

The little boy pointed to the glass and gave a childish laugh. "Look at Ralph! He's floating!"

His sister grinned and watched the fish lying on its side on top of the water. "He's funny!" she said in her sweet little voice.

They both watched quietly as the fish continued to float, motionless. After a few minutes the little boy whispered, "I think Ralph is sick."

With a trembling lip and tears in her eyes the little girl cried, "We have to help him. Maybe Mommy can give him some of that yucky medicine she gives us when our tummies hurt."

The boy bit his lip, much like his mother. "You wait here. I'll go get her."

With her chin propped on her hands, the little girl sat and watched the aquarium as silent tears tracked down her face, waiting for her brother to return with help. She heard feet coming down the stairs. Wanting to soothe her pet, she reached out a finger as her brother and parents came into the room.

Gracyn watched as her daughter's finger traced over the side of the dead fish. Her heart leapt into her throat when its gills fluttered before it flipped upright and began swimming about. The little girl laughed and clapped her hands in delight, unaware that her parents had locked terrified eyes on each other.

Theron nodded at his wife before bolting out of the room and up the stairs. Gracyn knelt down beside her daughter.

"Did you see that, Mommy? Ralph was sick, but he's all better now."

She pulled her into her arms, trying to calm the tremors coursing through her own body. "Yes, Baby. I saw it." Tears pooled in her eyes as she picked her daughter up and sat down, motioning for her son to join her. He climbed into her lap and she held both of her children tightly as the tears flowed.

"Don't cry, Mommy," her son whispered. "Ralph isn't sick anymore."

"I know, my sweet boy," she sniffled. "I know. I need you both to listen very carefully." Her children looked at her, love and trust shining on their faces. "Daddy and I love you very much. Promise me that you will always remember how much we love you, no matter what happens."

"I promise," her son answered, squeezing her tight.

With a trembling lip the little girl said meekly, "I promise too, Mommy." She laid her head on her mother's chest, listening to her beating heart.

As her husband entered the room Gracyn said to the children, "It's time to go back to bed now. Ralph is just fine. You can see him in the morning."

Theron reached down and took his son in his arms and carried him up the stairs, Gracyn following behind with their daughter. They tucked the children in and kissed them both goodnight before making their way back to their own bedroom.

Once the door was securely shut, she collapsed to the floor, her body jerking with wracking sobs. Theron engulfed her in his arms and held her, fighting to keep his own tears at bay. They sat, intertwined for what seemed like an eternity, before she whispered, "How?"

"I don't know, Baby. She's too young. Maybe the fish wasn't dead," he suggested hopefully.

"We both saw it. It was dead, until her finger touched it. I don't know if I can do this." Her voice broke with fresh tears. "Why, why does it have to be our little girl?"

"Shhh," he soothed as he ran a hand down her hair. "We don't have a choice. It's the only way to keep them safe."

She reached up and kissed her husband, her heart shattering into a million pieces with the knowledge that, after tonight, she might never see him again. Their lips remained fused for several moments. "I can't say goodbye to you," she whispered.

Theron's voice trembled as he placed his hands on her face and looked into her beautiful green eyes. "We'll be together again. I promise. As soon as it's safe, I'll find you." He kissed her gently.

She threw her arms around him and buried her face in his neck, breathing in his enticing scent, wanting to commit it to memory. "They're asleep," she stated. "It's time."

They stood, hand-in-hand, and walked down the hall to the children's room. Once inside, Theron sat on his daughter's bed and held her tiny little hand in his. Her angel face was soft in sleep. Tears streamed unashamedly down his cheek as he leaned over and placed a tender kiss on her forehead. "Daddy loves you, my sweet baby girl. I hope some part of you will always remember that. Be safe, be happy."

Gracyn sat on the edge of her son's bed and ran her fingers softly over his brow. She took in every detail of his face, so much like his father's. With any luck he would grow into a handsome young man. She prayed with every fiber of her being that she would be able to see that beautiful face again. Leaning down she placed a tender kiss on his cheek. "I love you," she whispered. "You are my heart, forever and always."

She stood, walking across the room to pick up her sleeping daughter, cradling her in her arms, patting her back when she murmured. "It's okay, Baby, go back to sleep. We're just going to take a little trip."

Theron followed them out of the room and down to the garage. Once the little girl was safely secured in her car seat, Gracyn went into her husband's arms once again. She struggled hard to keep the tears in check, not wanting their last moments to be filled with her blubbering sobs. They held each other quietly for a long time before she finally pulled away.

"The bags are in the trunk. The envelope of cash is in the glove box," he instructed. "Be careful. Don't take any unnecessary risks. I need to know that you'll both be safe."

"And what about you?"

"We'll leave within the week. Don't worry, Love. We will be fine. You are the one that needs to keep a close eye out. They will be coming for her. It's just a matter of time."

"They will have to go through me first," she stated, striking a chord of fear into his heart.

He pulled her back into his arms. "I love you, Gracie. Don't ever forget that. I'm going to do everything in my power to find a way for us to be together again. Stay safe and under the radar until I do."

Tears tracked down her face as she whispered, "I love you. Take care of our boy." She leaned up and kissed him softly before getting into the car.

Theron hit the button to raise the garage door. After starting the car she rolled down the window, pulling his hand to her cheek as he gripped it in his own. His thumb wiped away a tear as he leaned in to kiss her once again. "Remember me, Gracie."

"Always." She gave him a watery smile as she rolled up the window and backed out of the garage.

He watched as she pulled out of the driveway and drove down the street. The taillights flashed a final farewell at the stop sign before he lost sight of them. Pushing the button to close the garage door, he collapsed onto the cement floor, pulling his knees up to his chest and curling his body into a tight ball. As the sobs came unabated, he thought of his wife and daughter. His heart wanted to believe that he would be able to hold them again one day, but his head was telling him that this might have been their final goodbye.

After several minutes he pulled himself together and went back into the house. Entering his children's bedroom Theron looked at his daughter's empty bed one last time before crawling in beside his son. Pulling his child tightly against him, he laid there for several long hours before drifting into a fitful sleep with his wife's beautiful face in his mind.

CHAPTER ONE

August 2013

"Are we almost there?" Taryn Malone yawned, looking out the car window into the inky darkness.

Sensing her daughter's apprehension over the move, Ilya glanced over. "Another thirty minutes or so and we'll be home, Sweetie."

The distant lights of a small town caught Taryn's eye. "Is that the place?"

"No, we have a place south of here."

"Of course we do," she grumbled, pulling her light brown, honey colored hair into a ponytail.

"Taryn, I think you're going to like this place much better than the last."

She shot a doubting look at her mother before turning her head to gaze out the window again. As they passed through Williams, Arizona, she took in every visible detail. She raised her eyebrows as they passed under the arched iron sign declaring the town as the gateway to the Grand Canyon. Could it really be true? After a lifetime of nothing but corn and wheat fields, was it possible that she was this close to something that majestic and beautiful? Of course she had heard of the Grand Canyon, she had even seen it on television and in magazines. Never had she dreamt that she might be able to actually see it up close and personal. That is, if she was truly out from under lock and key as her mother had expressed.

Sighing, she studied the quaint little town. It certainly looked warm and inviting in the soft glow of the streetlamps. Pristine buildings housed eclectic shops selling everything from general store merchandise to handcrafted jewelry. Each street corner was abloom with colorful flowers in large ceramic pots. When they passed by a diner boasting the best cherry pie this side of the canyon, Taryn let herself get lost in a moment of weakness as a glimmer of excitement fluttered in her chest. Longing to be part of something, anything, weighed heavily on her young shoulders.

She continued to stare out the windows as the terrain changed from small town to towering ponderosa pines and aspen trees. As they drove deeper into the wooded area, she began shifting from side to side in her seat, her anticipation at a fever pitch. "Just around this curve and we'll be home," Ilya smiled, taking her daughter's hand in her own. "What do you think?"

She looked out the window, trying to make out the house in the darkness. "It looks bigger than the last place. But it's too dark and secluded to see anything," she replied, pulling away in disappointment. Once they were parked she jumped out of the SUV and headed to the hatch to get her bags.

"Taryn, why don't you turn on the lights for us?"

"Really?"

"It's one of the perks of not having neighbors," Ilya nodded in the direction of the house.

Fighting to subdue her excitement, she shrugged her shoulders casually. "I suppose." With a smile in her eyes, she turned to face the darkened structure. Holding her left hand out, she exhaled slightly and the lights throughout the entire house turned on. "Is this for real?" she laughed. Before her stood a two-story log cabin with gray stone detailing. The lights burning through the large glass windows showcased a wood and tempered glass entry door with lead detailing, a wraparound porch and full walk-out basement. The house was enormous, and so completely different from the small bungalow they had left behind.

Ilya grinned, "So what do you think?"

"Did you forget to tell me we won the lottery or something?"

"No, Taryn. I just think it's time for a change…for both of us."

"Well this is definitely going to be a change," she exhaled, feeling as though she had stepped into a dream after leaving their cozy, two bedroom, one bath, thousand square foot home in Galatia, Kansas. "You said this would be different. That it would be better. I don't understand how going from the middle of a wheat field to the middle of a forest is better."

"You know why it's important that we keep a low profile, Taryn."

"As if you would ever let me forget." She rolled her eyes again before following her mother up the porch steps.

Once inside, she looked around, surprised to find the house already furnished, and in a way that suited her mother perfectly. A beautiful stone fireplace adorned one wall of the great room, stretching all the way up to the second story ceiling above, with a comfortable looking couch and love seat in a deep forest green strategically placed in front of it. An ornately carved mantle decorated the stone, making the fireplace even more magnificent than the ones she had seen depicted in her mother's decorating magazines. The flat screen television hanging above the mantle brought a secret smile to her face. It was definitely a step up from her little nineteen inch boxy television that had sat on her dresser before. On the floor in front of the furniture was a shaggy, cream-colored rug that looked soft enough to curl your bare toes into it.

To the left of the great room was a massive kitchen that dwarfed the one from their home in Galatia. This kitchen had dark cherry cabinetry and shiny granite countertops that seemed to go on for miles. The appliances were gleaming stainless steel and top of the line. A large island dominated the center of the room and was equipped with a small prep sink on one side and barstools on the other. Taryn was sure they would be able to fit a whole army in that kitchen and still have room to maneuver and cook.

"Well, what do you think?" Ilya asked, setting a box on the kitchen counter.

"It's beautiful, Mom. Which room is mine?"

"Up the stairs and third door down the hall."

She headed up with her backpack on one shoulder and a large duffel bag in hand. Opening the door, Taryn could not contain her excitement when she spied the full-sized bed with a lime green comforter, hot pink pillows and a large, brightly colored letter T hanging on the wall above it. A computer desk sat against one wall, with a wrought iron vanity on another. In the corner of the room, a large pot held a small plant struggling to survive. As she brushed her fingers over one of its tiny leaves the plant started to grow, quickly filling in the empty space.

Laying her bags on her bed, she continued to explore her room, laughing in delight as she opened a door and found a large walk-in closet. There was no way she had nearly enough clothes to fill even one of the racks, but she loved it anyway. The closet itself was bigger than her entire bedroom back home. This was home now, she told herself. Galatia would soon be just a distant memory.

As she tried the other door she found her very own bathroom. Her mouth formed into a perfect circle as she took in the huge whirlpool tub and separate glass shower big enough to hold ten people. It had river rock walls with a marble bench on one side and a large rain shower head hanging in the center. Eight other jets were placed strategically to hit a person from every direction. Apart from the luxurious shower, dual sinks lined one wall with a massive ornately framed mirror positioned above them. The beautiful bathroom, a closet larger than her old bedroom, and a room perfectly decorated for a teenage girl had her sighing in content, letting the stress of the move flow away, if only for the night.

Deciding she wanted to try out the massive shower, Taryn unpacked quickly. After taking her time and letting the hot water work out the fatigue of the drive, she put on a pair of shorts and a tank top then headed downstairs to tell her mother goodnight.

"I've warmed some water. Do you want a glass of tea before bed?"

"No thanks, Mom. I'm going to turn in if you don't need my help."

"It's been a long day, Taryn. Go ahead and go to bed. We can get everything else out of the SUV tomorrow."

"Night, Mom. Love you." She gave her a hug.

"I love you too," Ilya replied, watching as her daughter headed back up the stairs. Taking a sip of her tea she sent up a silent prayer that the decision to uproot them and move here had been the right one.

ಬಂಛಬಂಛ

Seventeen-year-old Larkin Taylor woke early and ran his hands through his dark brown hair, before standing to stretch his muscular frame. At six foot, three inches, he was tall and lean. Though there were still a few days left before school started back up for the fall, waking early was a usual routine on mornings when he was readying for a run with his friends. After grabbing a quick bite to eat he knocked on his dad's bedroom door. "Hey, I'm going out for a run with the guys. I'll be back in a little while."

His father opened the door. "I need you back by noon, Son."

"No problem." Without batting an eye, he rushed out of the house and released a howl. Immediately, his call was answered back by three of his pack brothers. He grinned, heading into the tree line before shape-shifting into his favorite form, a large black wolf.

As he ran through the forest with lightning speed, one-by-one his brothers joined him. Kellan James, a brownish wolf, pulled up on his left, Gerrick Skye in muted gray to his right, and Thorne Adams, sandy colored, covered the rear. The group ran the mountain for two hours before stopping to shift back into human form and catch their breath.

"So what's the plan for tonight?" Thorne asked. His blue eyes twinkled as he thought about the best way to spend their last weekend before school started again. Running his hands through his short cap of blonde hair, he waited for one of his brothers to chime in.

"Whatever we do, we have to include the girls this time," Kellan laughed, as he flexed his muscular arms. His chiseled body made most of the girls swoon, but his wavy brown hair and striking green eyes were his real claim to fame. Underneath that strong exterior lay a heart of gold, though he did everything he could not to let it show and ruin his bad boy reputation. Who wanted to be thought of as the gentle teddy bear, when you could be the big bad wolf instead?

Gerrick, the pack member with the shortest fuse, patted Kellan on the back and smiled. "They won't forgive us if we ditch them two Saturday nights in a row, Brother." His crystal blue eyes sparkled with merriment. He had an exotic quality about him, made only more prominent by his jet black hair and caramel-colored skin and Native American heritage. Most referred to him as a pretty boy, and he had the suave attitude to match.

"We'll let them choose what we do. That should make up for last weekend," Larkin suggested.

Gerrick chuckled, "Great. I can see it now. We are going to have to suffer through some lovey dovey chick flick."

"That's the price of having babes in the group," Thorne sighed.

"Dude, don't forget one of those babes is my cousin."

"Take it easy, Ger. You should know by now that I'm into Dagney," he retorted.

Kellan rolled his eyes. "Nalani wouldn't be into you anyway, Thorne. She's still carrying a flame for the bird boy."

"Shut it, Kellan," Gerrick warned.

"Shut it or what?" he taunted, knowing how easy it was to get Gerrick riled.

Gerrick tackled him to the ground and the pair began to wrestle about while Thorne and Larkin watched in amusement. After several minutes, Gerrick finally surrendered, knowing he wasn't anywhere close to besting Kellan just yet. The two laughed as they joined their friends relaxing in the shade under the trees.

After an hour spent talking sports and girls, they decided to head back. Shifting into wolf form, they raced through the woods. Larkin pulled back, allowing Kellan to take the lead, pushing Thorne forward, while he pulled up the rear.

Soon he found himself lagging behind, distracted by a strange feeling in the air. Finding himself for the first time with no desire to stay with the pack, he changed course and let instinct guide him.

৪০৫৪৩৪০৫৪৩

Taryn gave her mother a kiss on the cheek before leaving the house to explore the surrounding woods. With a heavy heart, Ilya watched as her daughter stepped off the back deck and disappeared into the trees, alone for the first time.

Enjoying her first real taste of solitude, Taryn let down her guard, allowing the power inside of her to flow freely, unobstructed by her mother's constant restrictions. Walking down a small path, still uncertain if all of this was real or just a dream she had yet to wake from, she took in every minute detail from the trees to each blade of grass and tiny pebble she wandered past, saving it to memory. Her heart soared as she breathed in the tantalizing scents of the forest. She could feel the presence of life teeming around her, from the plants to the animals that made the forest their home. A sigh escaped her as she allowed herself a small glimmer of hope that just maybe this tiny little place on Earth would finally be her forever home.

ഇൽ ☙❧☙❧

Just a short half mile away, Larkin continued running through the woods, slowing for a moment when he caught the scent of something overwhelming and powerful. Stopping, he tried to make sense of the smell. Sniffing the air, he let out a whoosh of breath as his feet were knocked out from under him. With Kellan's face inches from his own, the friends slid several feet down the mountain while shifting back into human form.

"What the hell?" Larkin growled, shoving him off and glaring angrily.

"Relax guys," Thorne intervened, stepping between the two, one hand pressing against each of their chests trying to put distance between them.

"Why did you break away?" Gerrick asked with concern.

Confused by the scent still lingering in the air, and the fact that he seemed to be the only one affected by it, he answered, dazed. "I don't really know, but we should head back."

Gerrick shrugged his shoulders and gave a quick glance to Kellan and Thorne. This was the first time since the friends had started running together that anyone had dared to break away from the pack mid-run. Deciding now was not the time to press the issue, he shifted back into wolf form as his friends did the same.

Larkin ran with full speed back towards his house, leaving his pack brothers struggling to keep his pace. When he emerged from the tree line near his home, his father, Maxym Taylor, who was working on rebuilding an engine, looked up, immediately noticing that something was off with his son. He stopped what he was doing and went to him.

"How was your run?"

"Fine," Larkin stated plainly, distracted by the burning presence in his stomach. Walking to the spigot, he twisted the knob and placed his head under the running water to help cool down as he took the occasional swallow.

"Did something happen?"

"It's nothing."

Knowing his son had inherited his stubbornness, he decided it was best to keep the peace and change the subject. "Let's grab a bite to eat in town. Afterwards, we can work on your jeep."

ഔഗ്ഔഗ്

When Taryn walked through the French doors at the rear of the house, her mother let out a sigh of relief. She had managed to work herself into a frenzy of worry over the last hour and a half with her daughter not safe by her side. "So, how was it?"

"The woods are spectacular," she beamed.

"Are you hungry?"

"I'll grab a sandwich or something later."

Looking at her daughter with nothing but love, Ilya's heart warmed at seeing how happy she was for once. "I have to run into town to buy some groceries. Would you like to join me?"

Taryn stopped dead in her tracks and looked warily at her mother. "Are you sick or something?"

"Taryn Delany Malone, do I look sick?"

Fearing she had hurt her mother's feelings, she explained, "No, mom. All I meant was that you haven't let me go grocery shopping or into any store with you since I was…well I can't remember the last time."

Ilya patted the cushion beside her on the couch. "Sweetie, please come and sit with me." Hesitantly, Taryn moved towards her and took a seat. She grabbed her daughters' hand and squeezed it gently. "You're special, Taryn. So special that I've had to make decisions, tough decisions, that you didn't necessarily like or agree with."

"I've heard it all before," Taryn mocked, irritated by the thought of another lecture as to why she should hide away from the rest of the world.

"I know. I'm sorry, I'm not saying this right. Please give me a chance."

Taryn rolled her eyes, expecting their conversation to take the same direction as they always did. "By all means, please do go on." Her voice dripped with sarcasm.

"For not having been around other kids, you sure do seem to have this whole teenage drama thing down perfectly," Ilya smirked. Noticing Taryn's less than amused facial expression, she cleared her throat and tried to explain her intentions. "What I'm trying to tell you, Taryn, is that…is that maybe I've had it wrong all of these years. Maybe I've sheltered you too much in the past."

"And maybe I should drive you to the hospital. You really are sick," she responded, placing her hand on her mother's forehead in a mock attempt to check for fever.

"I'm being serious, Taryn. Even mothers can make mistakes." Her eyes locked on her daughter. "Everything I have ever done has been to protect you. Right or wrong, I can't undo it. But you are growing up so fast and I'm afraid the next time I blink you will be a grown woman. As much as I want to, I can't keep you under lock and key forever. We moved here for a fresh start. Letting you have a little bit of freedom is just one small step in preparing you for adulthood."

Taryn's eyes were huge as she took in her mother's face, looking for any signs that this was just some dreadful practical joke. When she saw nothing but sincerity staring back at her, she gave a hesitant smile. "Just how much freedom are we talking about? Do I get to attend public school? Go to dances and sporting events? Hang out with friends?"

"We'll talk about it," Ilya promised. "I want nothing more than for you to be happy, but you have to promise me that you won't ever forget how special you are and that being special can have grave consequences if you can't control your emotions."

She rolled her eyes. "I know, Mom. I've only heard this a million times. Can we go now?"

Ilya smiled and engulfed her in a fierce hug. "I love you, Sweet Girl. More than you will ever know."

"I love you, too…Now let's go!"

Laughing she stood up and held out her hand, pulling Taryn to her feet. Placing an arm around her daughter's waist, she led her out the door.

೫೦೧೮೩೫೦೧೮೩

Walking through the automatic sliding doors of the local grocery store in Williams, Taryn was elated by the sensory overload that was occurring within her. Fresh baked breads from the bakery on her left permeated the air, the delicious smells causing her stomach to grumble with hunger pangs. A long glass case held a large variety of special occasion cakes, elaborately decorated with frosting in a multitude of colors, some so intricate that she thought it would be a shame to eat them and destroy the beauty.

A little further into the store, she gasped in delight as they reached the produce section. Every fresh fruit and vegetable a person could ever want was artfully displayed in bins and cooler cases. The vibrant colors and smells of the berries and melons made her mouth water.

"Taryn, please stay close," Ilya patted her daughter on the back, taking note of the ear-to-ear grin she wore. She couldn't pull from memory a time when Taryn had smiled so widely. Taking a deep breath, she kept her anxiousness at bay and let her baby girl enjoy the experience as she pushed the cart down the produce aisle.

Taryn followed soon after her. Finding a small bin containing Honey Crisp apples, she placed several in one of the plastic bags and put it in the cart, grinning at her mother. Ilya returned the gesture, relieved that things were going far better than she could have ever hoped.

After going down every aisle at least once, with Ilya pretending not to notice when something that was not on her list managed to make it into her cart, mother and daughter finally made their way through the check out. She watched in apprehension as the young man sacking their groceries smiled incessantly at Taryn, trying to engage her in brief conversation. Even though social interaction with a boy was new to her, Taryn played it cool, flashing a casual smile and giving him a slight shoulder shrug in response before walking nonchalantly to the exit.

"I can help you, Ma'am." The boy took the cart laden with their groceries and began pushing it towards the exit.

"Thank you, but please don't trouble yourself. We can manage," Ilya responded politely, knowing full well his true intentions were to seek out her daughter one last time.

"Oh, it's no trouble, Ma'am," the boy smiled as he continued to push the cart.

Deciding it would be best not to make a scene, she followed the sacker and her cart full of groceries. As they neared the vehicle the young man began making small talk, asking if they were tourists or if they were new to the area. She smiled at him while he continued gazing in the direction of her daughter.

"We just moved here," Taryn answered, ignoring her mother's admonishing look.

"Are you going to school here in Williams?" the young man persisted.

"No," Ilya quickly interjected.

"What my mother means to say is that we still haven't decided," she smiled, with a biting undertone to her words. With that said, she slid into the passenger seat of the SUV and waited for her mother.

ഇൻഗ്ഇൻഗ്

A few blocks away, Larkin and Maxym Taylor were enjoying their lunch at the Desert Rose Cafe. After devouring two cheeseburgers, a large order of fries and washing it down with a cold soda, Larkin sat back in the booth and waited for his father to finish his lunch.

"You want to talk about it?" Maxym asked, sensing his unrest.

"There's nothing to talk about," Larkin sighed heavily, weighted by inner turmoil. Whatever he had felt this morning during their run had continued to linger deep inside of him, consuming his every thought and putting him on edge. He hated shutting his father out, but how could he explain what he didn't understand himself? Sending his dad a pleading look, he willed him to let the subject drop.

Maxym studied him for several minutes before giving him a small nod and sliding out of the booth. While his father went to the register to pay, Larkin walked towards the doors, completely lost in thought. Grunting, he bumped squarely into his former best friend, Keiryn Falcon. Keiryn was tall and muscular, but Larkin still had at least twenty pounds on him. His blue eyes were striking in his face framed with blonde hair. Known as the play boy by all the girls, Keiryn had a witty sense of humor and a sharp tongue to match his short fuse.

"Watch it," Keiryn growled.

Too distracted to care, Larkin pushed past him and headed to his father's truck, sliding into the front seat and staring blankly out the window. Keiryn watched in confusion, surprised by his lack of response considering the two of them butted heads as often as possible. Shaking it off, he settled into his favorite booth and waited for his own father to show.

After paying their bill, Maxym started toward the doors, nodding as he locked eyes with Keiryn. Well versed in the order of things, Keiryn returned the simple gesture, cautious not to show any disrespect.

"How's your father doing?" Maxym asked.

"He's good, Mr. Taylor. I'm expecting him anytime."

Tapping his fingers on the wood partition between the booths, he sighed. "Tell him I said hello."

"Sure thing, Mr. Taylor," Keiryn answered.

Maxym nodded one last time, before heading out to his truck.

As his father slid into the driver's seat, Larkin glanced at him briefly. "Dad, do me a favor and drive by the grocery store before we head home."

"Is there something you need?" He could see the distracted look on his son's face.

Larkin shook his head. "No. I guess I just need a little extra time to let my food settle before we start on the jeep, so let's take the scenic route."

As far as excuses went, that was a doozy, Maxym thought. Shrugging, he drove out of the café parking lot and headed through Williams before returning home.

ഇൽഽൽ഻

Teigan Falcon opened the door to the diner and stepped inside. His tall, muscular frame was accented by his choice of dark washed denim jeans and fitted grey t-shirt with dark boots. He had short, wavy, dark blonde colored hair that parted perfectly off to one side showcasing his beautiful blue eyes. Looking over his shoulder he saw the familiar truck pass down the road. "Was that the Taylors?"

"Yeah. Mr. Taylor says hello," Keiryn nodded from the booth.

Teigan settled into the seat across from his son. "Did you and Larkin talk?"

"Nope, but he did bump into me and then acted as if he didn't know who I was. Rude as ever too, since he didn't bother to apologize."

"That seems strange, considering how attuned to everything he tends to be. He must have something heavy weighing on his mind, especially if he is willing to pass up a chance to butt heads with you." Teigan paused, waving the waitress over to take their order. "I hope someday the two of you can get back to being friends."

Keiryn immediately went on the defensive. "How can you say that after what he did to me?"

"It's been what, five years? You were just children, Keiryn, innocent children. He was as surprised by what happened as you. You're going to have to learn to let it go."

He shot his father a look of indignation. "He could have killed me. It'll be a cold day in hell before I forgive, and even longer before I forget."

Teigan studied the angry look on his son's face. Larkin had been a touchy subject ever since that fateful night where the bond

~ 22 ~

the best friends shared had been torn into irreparable pieces. Both of the boys were too stubborn to look beyond what had happened. Regardless of how many times Teigan and Maxym had tried to push them together, to get them to talk it out, the pair remained locked in their feud, unable and unwilling to let bygones be bygones.

Deciding that he wanted to enjoy a peaceful lunch with his son, he gave his order to the waitress and turned the conversation to talk of sports and the upcoming first day of school.

ഇൠඝഇൠඝ

Ilya leaned against the counter watching as Taryn sat on a barstool eating a turkey sandwich and a honey crisp apple. "I'm really proud of the way you handled yourself earlier."

Taryn looked over her shoulder and smiled widely. "Proud enough to let me go to school?" she asked, biting her bottom lip.

Shaking her head, Ilya walked over to her daughter and cupped her chin in her hand. "Let's see how the next few days go. Then we'll discuss whether or not you can attend public school."

Taryn pulled away and sighed loudly, annoyed by the answer her mother had given her. "I'm going for a walk."

"Why don't you stay and we can go for a swim in the pool?" Ilya suggested, wanting to keep her daughter close.

"Maybe later," she replied, walking towards the door.

"Please, Taryn. Can we talk for a moment?"

Turning on her heel she looked at her mother and rolled her eyes. "About?"

"That boy at the grocery store, he was flirting with you. Did you realize that?"

"Mom!"

"Well he was. And I have to say, he was rather handsome."

"Okay, I am going for that walk now. When I get back I hope you have all of this nonsense out of your system." Taryn retorted, as she pulled the door open.

"I know you thought he was cute too," Ilya called out just before the latch secured.

Rolling her eyes again and shaking her head at her mother's silliness, she took off down the stairs and wandered into the woods.

ಏಞಏಞ

"Could you hand me that wrench?" Maxym asked, holding his hand out to receive the tool. When there was no response, he stood up and glanced around, looking for his son. Walking outside of the garage, he saw him standing several feet away from the doors, staring off into the tree line. "Something on your mind, Larkin?" When he still didn't get an answer, he placed his hand on Larkin's shoulder, distracting him from his thoughts only momentarily. "What's going on with you today?"

"I don't know," he answered, his eyes never shifting from the woods.

"Are you going to help with your engine?"

"Dad, I'm sorry. I have to go."

"Go where?"

"I don't know, but I have to run," he replied, knowing there was nothing he could do to fight the urge that was pulling forcefully on his insides. Before his father could object, he sprinted to the trees, shifting into wolf form and running as fast as he could towards whatever was calling to him.

He ran nearly two miles before something stopped him in his tracks, causing him to paw at his nose as it burned with the familiar and alluring scent from earlier. Whatever it was, he could sense that it was extremely close this time. Cautiously, he stalked through the woods still in wolf form, following the overwhelming fragrance.

With his defenses heightened, he inched closer. The burn in his nostrils made its way down the back of his throat, pushing him near the edge of insanity. The scent was so fragrant, so appealing that he knew whatever was behind it was saturated with immense power. Camouflaged only by the shadows cast by the thick bunching of tree branches overhead, he laid in wait with bared teeth, waiting for it to step into the tiny clearing lit by the rays of the sun.

The hair on the back of his coat stood up straight as the creature passed between the bases of two large trees giving him a glimpse of the outline of its small frame. With his heart racing wildly inside his chest, he struggled for composure while waiting for a better look.

"Hello?" Taryn called out, sensing she was no longer alone in the woods. With her back to Larkin, she stepped into the light of the sun in the small clearing and called out again. "Is anyone there?"

He heard her sweet voice, but thought that it must be some form of trickery. Releasing a low growl he stepped forward, approaching the girl.

Turning around, she saw the large black wolf standing only a few feet away. "Oh, hello there," she smiled.

He stood in wolf form, drinking in her lovely face. Her honey colored hair flowed in loose waves down to the middle of her back. The light, naturally tan color of her skin accented her rosy pink lips along with her beautiful emerald green eyes. Eyes that were all too familiar to him. Stunned, his legs gave out, sending him abruptly to the ground.

She bent down only a few feet away from him, her voice full of concern. "Are you alright?"

Internally, Larkin spiraled downward emotionally. His instincts were conflicted, as a part of him screamed that he should jump to his feet and run while the other side shouted for him to stay. The latter won out as all four of his legs were still rendered useless from shock.

"Are you hurt?" Taryn asked, inching closer, holding her hand out to him. An instinctive growl slipped from his mouth causing him to bow his head in embarrassment. "No one is going to hurt you." Calm sincerity rang in each word. Slowly she placed her hand in front of his snout.

Larkin sniffed at it, much like a dog would do. Her scent was utterly intoxicating, causing another wave of emotion to surge through his body. Lost in the melodic tone of her voice, he somehow managed to get to his feet.

"Looks like you're fine," she smiled, standing upright.

He watched as she began to walk away, conflicted by the urge to follow after her and his instinct that she was trouble. Unable to resist, he trailed behind her, mindful to keep his distance, trying to lessen the impact of her powerful scent.

ᘒᘎᘒᘎ

Taryn walked through the woods, unaffected by the company of the large black wolf. Larkin watched her carefully. Every movement she made was exceptionally light and graceful as she navigated the terrain with ease. "Well Big Guy, this is where we part ways," she sighed, acknowledging the wolf. "My house is just through those trees. I'm quite certain my mother wouldn't approve of me bringing home a wolf. Maybe I'll see you again tomorrow," she shrugged, talking to the animal as if he could understand her.

Larkin stalked carefully through the trees, moving close enough to the house to see that she had made it inside safely before heading back towards his own home. As he began to run his mind recalled the events that had transpired in the woods, mulling each one over until he reached the edge of the trees leading into his back yard.

Shifting back into human form, he entered his house, immediately heading to the kitchen. Opening the refrigerator door, he grabbed a bottle of water and chugged it down.

Maxym walked in and sighed with relief when he found his son home. "Gerrick and Nalani stopped by looking for you earlier," he stated, noting his son wore a tense and troubled expression.

Larkin tossed the empty bottle into the sink and placed his hands heavily against the countertop. "Dad, she's here," he exhaled.

"Who's here, Larkin?"

"The girl from my dreams. She's real, Dad, and she's living only a few miles away," he blurted out, with a terrified look on his face.

CHAPTER TWO

The revelation that his son had just shared struck a chord deep inside Maxym's chest, making his worst nightmare come true. "Are you sure? You're positive that it's the same girl?" he asked, with panic lingering on each word. Knowing this girl was, without a doubt, behind his son's troubled demeanor.

Larkin ran his hands through his hair and looked to his father with pained eyes. "Her face has been etched into my memory since I was twelve. So yes, Dad, I'm sure it's her."

"Did she see you? Did the two of you talk?"

"She saw me, but I was in wolf form."

"When she saw you, was she afraid, Son?"

"Not even a little bit."

Maxym paced between the kitchen and the dining room, thinking carefully about what they should do. "You have to stay away from her until we can figure out what this all means." When there was no answer, he lifted his head and looked at his son. Larkin's expression said it all. "You have to stay away from her, Larkin. Tell me that you understand it's for your own good."

Larkin shook his head and shrugged his shoulders. "I'm not going to be able to do that, Dad." It hurt him to defy his father, but he couldn't comply with the request. "Something about her calls out to me. I can't ignore it, even if I wanted to."

Maxym's jaw pulled up tight, fighting back his own emotions as he watched his son struggle in turmoil. "When you saw her, Larkin, what did you feel?"

His eyes filled with emotion as he thought back to that moment. "Everything, Dad. Before I saw her face, I was ready to destroy her. But now…now that I've seen that sweet face, all I want is to protect her, to wrap her safely in my arms, be there for her whenever she needs me, and to keep her safe."

"Safe from what?"

"Anything or anyone that might pose a threat to her."

"And what about right now? What do you feel?"

"I'm angry, but I still want to be near her," Larkin stated urgently, looking out the kitchen window, back to the woods.

"What about Gerrick, Kellan and the others?"

"What about them?" he growled, walking outside.

"A girl who is all alone in the forest but isn't afraid of a wolf can take care of herself, Son," Maxym tried to reason.

Throwing his father a frosty scowl, he headed to the detached garage.

"Hey, Larkin. You about ready for tonight?" Kellan asked, walking up from the driveway.

"You guys should go without me."

"You're staying in?" Thorne shouted from the car.

"I have some stuff going on," he nodded in the direction of his dad, who was standing on the back porch watching them.

"All the more reason to hang with us," Kellan retorted, patting his friend on the back.

"Give us a minute, fellas. I need a moment with my son," Maxym called out. Larkin walked back over to his father. "Look, go out with your friends tonight. Have a good time and let me see what I can find out about the girl. We'll talk about it in the morning, after you've had some time to clear your head."

"Whatever," he answered heading inside to change his clothes.

When he walked back out the door, his father placed his hand on his shoulder. "Try to have a good time tonight. We'll talk about the rest in the morning."

Maxym watched as Larkin got in the car with Thorne and Kellan. Once they were out of sight, he went inside and made a few phone calls trying to find out anything he could about the mystery girl that no longer haunted his son's dreams, but now walked amongst them.

80CX80CX

"Taryn, dinner's ready," Ilya called out from the bottom of the staircase.

"What are we having?"

"Come down and find out," she grinned, walking back into the kitchen.

Taryn strolled in, wearing a swimsuit with a large towel wrapped around her waist.

"What on earth do you think you're doing? I've told you the desert is cooler at night.

"Yes, but you also said there are perks to living in the middle of a small forest with no neighbors for miles," she retorted, kissing her mother on the cheek.

"So you plan on making our pool into one big hot tub?"

"Something like that." She took a seat on one of the barstools. "Dinner smells delicious, Mom."

Shaking her head in mock exasperation, Ilya smiled, "Alright, we'll eat, clean up and then we can go for a swim."

80CX80CX

Taryn placed the last plate back in the cupboard and smiled anxiously at her mother.

~ 30 ~

"Go ahead, Sweetie. I'll be there in a moment."

Excitement teamed inside her as she quickly headed out to the pool. She stopped to dip the toes of her left foot in. Instantly, the water in the pool began to bubble and the temperature rose twenty degrees.

"Taryn Delaney Malone, how many times do I have to tell you to use your hands?" Ilya scolded her daughter.

"At least one more," Taryn laughed before jumping into the warm water. She smiled, breaking the surface. "Come on in, Mom. It feels amazing."

"I'm sure it does. But seriously, Taryn, you have to remember to use your hands. What if someone would have seen you?"

She sank to the bottom of the pool, drowning out her mother's voice. When she thought it was safe, she resurfaced only to find her still waiting. "I know you get tired of hearing me tell you, but it's for your own good. There are people like us who would find what you do unnatural. I just don't want to give them a reason to take you away from me."

"You worry way too much, Mom. When's the last time you've seen someone else like us?" she argued.

Ilya started to reply, but was interrupted by the sound of the doorbell filling the air from the open French doors near the pool. Concern quickly set in. She wasn't expecting company until tomorrow. "Taryn, I'm going to see who is at the door. Do me a favor and stay out here. And no more funny business."

Immune to her mother's concern and constant worry, she rolled her eyes and began swimming laps.

Ilya walked inside, closing the doors behind her, hoping to keep her daughter out of sight. As she moved closer to the door, she braced for the unknown. "Who is it?" she called out, sensing the power pulsing just on the other side.

"Maxym Taylor. I live a few miles from here and I was trying to help my neighbor find her dog." He held up a leash in front of the glass portion of the door.

Inhaling deeply before opening the door, Ilya positioned herself to block his view into the house. "Hello."

Maxym was taken aback by the beautiful woman on the other side. Her long brown hair was pulled up into a messy bun with ringlet curls spilling haphazardly out. To say she was beautiful was truly an understatement. She had the face of an angel with her flawless, alabaster skin and full pouty lips. Her slender frame was accented by the short jean shorts and turquoise tank top she wore. Apprehension and concern danced in her jewel toned green eyes. For a moment he forgot why he came. Pulling himself together, he cleared his throat. "Good evening, Miss. I hope I'm not intruding, but I've been driving around for the past hour and noticed the lights on up here. It's been a long time since this place has been occupied."

Ilya studied him coolly. The man was incredibly handsome with his wavy dark hair and hazel eyes that sparkled with mild curiosity, and something else she couldn't quite put her finger on. He was well over six foot tall, and his body was fit and chiseled. Another place, another time, she might have given him a second look. "You said you were looking for a dog?"

"Yes, my neighbor lost her border collie. She's an elderly woman and that dog means the world to her so I was trying to help out."

"I'm sorry, but I haven't seen a dog today."

"Maybe someone else in your family saw her," Maxym suggested.

She studied him for a moment before continuing. "Give me a moment. I will go ask my daughter."

"Gaias. You're a Gaias, right?" Though he knew he might be taking a risk, pushing her too far, too fast, he was desperate to find answers to help his son.

A flicker of fear passed through Ilya's eyes, and her stance went from casual to full on alert as she pulled the door tighter to her, effectively barring him from seeing even the smallest detail inside. Gaias were a powerful people who possessed special abilities, unlike ordinary humans. She cursed herself for not being more cautious. Of course he would know she was a Gaias. Being able to sense each other's powers was an ability that they all possessed. She had felt his power pulsing even before she had opened the door. It was becoming glaringly obvious to her that she had been living under the radar for far too long.

She stared at him, taking note of the innocent curiosity shining in his eyes. Nothing about him was threatening, but still she remained cautious. "Skin-Walker?" It was common knowledge that the majority of the male Gaias population had the Skin Walker gene, but since he was standing at her door uninvited, the need to know as much as she could about him made her voice the question aloud.

"Yes. I'm sorry about that. I didn't mean to catch you off guard. We normally have a heads up when someone new moves into the territory," he explained.

"I was unaware that I had to inform the Gaias community of our arrival."

Maxym laughed, "Of course you don't. I only meant that we have a pretty tight knit community here in Williams. And since it's a small town, word tends to travel fast. I'm sorry. It was not my intention to offend you."

"Apology accepted. May I ask what form you prefer?" Her curiosity was getting the better of her.

"Most in this area prefer the wolf. It helps us blend in if we are seen by normal humans."

"Interesting." She studied him closely. "Snakes might have been a safer bet."

Knowing he was being baited, Maxym tipped his head in acknowledgment. "Nah, they aren't nearly as fast, and it wouldn't be much fun to be carted off by some hungry bird." He gave her a disarming smile. "If it's not too much trouble, I really would like to know if your daughter has seen the dog. It belonged to my neighbor's husband. He passed away this last winter. The dog is all she has left of him. It's very important to her."

The sincere look on his face made her sigh. Deciding she had to make good on her promise not to keep Taryn under lock and key forever, she opened the door and gestured inside. "Follow me." She introduced herself as she led him through the living room and out the French doors leading to the patio.

While treading water in the center of the pool, Taryn watched as they approached. She took note of the worn leash that the stranger was carrying before glancing towards her mother.

"Taryn, this is Maxym Taylor. He lives a few miles south of here. Mr. Taylor, this is my daughter Taryn."

She swam to the edge of the pool and carefully studied the man dressed in faded blue jeans and a black v-neck t-shirt. Nice to meet you, Mr. Taylor."

Maxym locked his eyes on her and struggled to look away, uncertain of exactly how he felt about this girl who had been haunting his sons' dreams for the past several years. "It's nice to meet you, Taryn. Your mother says you were walking through the woods earlier. You didn't happen to come across a stray dog when you were out there, did you?"

"No, Sir. Nothing out there but me and the trees today," Taryn fibbed, keeping her eyes locked on him.

"Well I guess I'll let you get back to your swim, Taryn. Thanks for your time," he nodded, before walking over to speak with Ilya. "Mrs. Malone," he started.

"It's Miss, and please, call me Ilya," she interrupted.

Maxym smiled before starting again. "Ilya, thanks for your help and let me be the first to welcome you to Arizona. This is a great place to live and raise children, especially like ours."

She arched a brow. "You have children?"

"I have one son, Larkin. He's seventeen and will be a senior this year at Williams High School. I suspect he and Taryn will cross paths then," he surmised, knowing in reality that they already had.

"I haven't decided if she will be attending public school or not this year. Gastyn Wylder is coming out tomorrow afternoon to meet with us and discuss options for her."

"Gastyn's a great teacher and the kids' really seem to like him. He has a knack for helping each one embrace their strengths as well as enhance their weaker areas," he encouraged her, taking one last look over his shoulder at Taryn. "I suppose I should let you get back to your swim. It was a pleasure meeting you, Miss Malone."

"I'm sure we will see you around," Ilya smiled, closing the door. She leaned in against it, waiting until she could no longer sense his presence. Letting out a sigh of relief, she headed back towards the pool. They had passed this first test with flying colors. She could only pray that the others yet to come would be so easy.

ಐೞಐೞ

After watching a movie in Flagstaff, Larkin, Kellan, Gerrick and Thorne, along with the female members of their pack, Nalani Skye and Dagney Abbott, set up camp near Cataract Lake. The friends were joking around and having a good time, with the exception of Larkin, who had been distant much of the night. Unable to get the vivid image of his dream girl's face off his mind, he sat quietly while everyone else celebrated the last weekend of summer.

"Earth to Larkin," Nalani joked, poking him in the ribs as she sat down next to him on a log near the campfire. She shared the same caramel-colored skin, intense blue eyes and dark hair as her cousin, Gerrick. Her face was flawless with perfect cheek bones, and long, thick eye lashes that cover girls could only dream of. Stunning was the word most often used to describe her physical characteristics. She had a quick wit and a short temper, and prided herself on being able to give any sailor a run for his money where vocabulary was concerned.

Larkin didn't respond as he continued to stare distractedly at the flames as they danced on the logs.

"Seriously, Larkin, what's going on with you?" Gerrick hollered at his friend.

When he still didn't respond, Kellan placed him in a sleeper hold and pulled him from the log. His eyes went dark as he pushed to his feet with relative ease, flipping Kellan onto his back. "What the hell, man?" he shouted, taking a few steps back as the rest of his friends looked at him with surprise on their faces.

"Larkin, is everything alright?" Dagney, a petite red-head with fair skin and a smattering of freckles across the bridge of her nose, asked, showing concern for her friend.

"Look guys, I thought I could do this tonight, but I can't. I've got to go," he replied, walking away.

Kellan followed after him, trying to smooth things over, thinking maybe he had pushed him too far. "Larkin, wait up," he called out. Larkin slowed and looked back at his friend. "I'm sorry, I was just messing around. I didn't mean to upset you."

He stopped and placed his hands atop Kellan's shoulders, leaning down and looking him in the eye. "I know. I just have some stuff going on at home. I need you to look after them while I work this out. I'm trusting you with our family."

"You can talk to me about whatever it is that's bothering you."

"Look, just take care of them and I'll be in touch." Larkin shifted into wolf form and took off in a dead sprint, desperate to see the girl's face again, to reassure himself that she was indeed, real.

Placing his hand on Kellan's back, Gerrick watched his pack brother fade into the darkness. "What was that about?"

Kellan shook his head and shrugged his shoulders. "I'm not sure, but we can check on him tomorrow. Whatever it is, he's been somewhere else all day."

৪৩৫৪৩৫

Outside the Malone residence, Larkin watched the girl and her mother as they headed back into the house after finishing their swim. Still in wolf form, he crept as close as he could without being detected, observing her through the windows as she ascended the open staircase and disappeared from view.

After a short while, she came back down the stairs, freshly showered and wearing her favorite pair of gray sweatpants and a white tank top. She curled up on the couch next to her mother and laid her head on her shoulder.

"What did you think about our guest from earlier?" Ilya inquired.

"I don't know. He seemed nice, I guess," Taryn yawned.

"Did you notice anything particular about him?"

"What? How he was checking you out?"

A wide smile formed on Ilya's face as she thought for a moment. "That's not what I was talking about, Honey. Did you

~ 37 ~

notice anything different about him…say different than the young man at the grocery store earlier today?"

Lifting her head from her mother's shoulder she leaned back to look her in the eye. "Only that he's more age appropriate for you to date," Taryn retorted, bursting into laughter.

"Ha, ha, very funny, young lady," she replied, pretending to be annoyed by her daughter's interesting take on events. She pulled her head back to her shoulder and kissed the top of it. "Tomorrow I have a friend stopping by for lunch. I need for you to be on your best behavior, understand?"

She rolled her eyes before releasing a heavy sigh. "I won't make a sound."

"No, you misunderstood me. He's coming to see us both."

Taryn lifted her head off her mother's shoulder and scooted away from her. "Seriously?" she asked, surprised when Ilya nodded in acknowledgement. With the feeling that something was definitely awry, she furrowed her brow. "Okay, that's it. Who are you, and what have you done with my mother?"

"It's like I told you before, this is a change for us. Maybe I kept you too sheltered from the world and I'm trying to make it right now."

She gave her mother a wary look, wondering what was really motivating her willingness to consider change after living so many years hidden away. "I'm going to call it a night, Mom. I'll see you tomorrow." Taryn stood and walked past her, towards the stairs.

"I love you, Taryn."

"Love you too, Mom."

ೞ୦ଓೞ୦ଓ

Once it appeared that both Dream Girl and her mother had gone to bed, and enough time has lapsed for both to fall to sleep, Larkin shifted into human form and crept closer to the house. Carefully, he squatted down, then bounded upward, landing softly on the roof near the girl's bedroom window. Giant waves of emotion swept through him as he peaked through the glass. Awe and wonder were warring with trepidation and anger, causing an overwhelming battle in his head, making him stumble into the window. She stirred briefly, but drifted off quickly once again. He sighed in relief as he watched her.

Her honey-colored hair cascaded out on her pillow like a halo that framed her beautiful face, currently relaxed in a peaceful slumber. That face had been etched in his mind for the last five years. Though she could be termed petite, she didn't come across as frail. Her fearlessness at encountering a large wolf in the woods had made her appear courageous and bold. He would give anything to be able to wake her up and have those gorgeous emerald eyes look at him once again.

He lost track of time as he stood still, never taking his eyes off of her while struggling with the emotions that continued to stir within him. Try as he might to decipher each one and analyze its meaning, it was no use.

"Larkin?" His father's voice came from below. When he finally turned his gaze downward, Maxym continued. "Please, Son, come home with me and we can talk about this."

"I need to stay here," he insisted, turning back to watch the girl.

Maxym took note of the continued state of turmoil his son was in and tried to reason with him, knowing it would not be easy. "Her name is Taryn Malone. She and her mother arrived here in Arizona late last night," he offered, in an attempt to sway him to change his mind.

"Taryn?" He repeated, the name rolling off his tongue with ease, piquing his curiosity as the weight on his chest lifted slightly.

Taking advantage of finally having his son's undivided attention Maxym tried to bargain with him to get him to accompany him back to their house. "If you come home, we can discuss what else I know."

Torn by his need to stay close to Taryn and his desire for answers, he looked back through the window at her sleeping form, framed in the light of the moon. With a small sigh he gave in and jumped from the roof, landing a few feet from his father. "We need to hurry, so I can come back."

"Okay, Son. One step at a time though."

With a nod the pair shifted into wolf form and raced back to their home. Struggling to keep up, Maxym watched as Larkin disappeared ahead of him. When he finally arrived home, he found him anxiously pacing the living room floor.

"You want something to drink?" Maxym asked, heading into the kitchen. Larkin released a loud sigh, expressing his impatience, knowing his father was trying to stall. "When did you get so fast?" he inquired, trying his best to settle his son before sharing what he had learned.

"How did you know where I was?"

He took a long drink from his glass of iced tea before replying. "Your friends were worried after you took off without an explanation. So Kellan called to check in on you."

"And what did you tell him?"

"Only that you had some things going on. But I am glad he called. I think there are a few things we need to talk about."

"I'm waiting," Larkin prompted, desperately wanting to know whatever it was his father had found out.

"Have a seat and we'll talk." He motioned for him to take a seat at the dining room table. "Her name is Taryn Malone. She and her mother, Ilya, arrived late last night. They are Gaias."

"I already knew the last part. Where has she been?"

"I don't have all of the details, Son. But I suspect they've been off the radar for a long time."

"Why do you say that?" Larkin leaned forward in his chair.

"Her mother was pretty on edge when I showed up. She definitely isn't used to having people stopping by unexpectedly," he explained.

"Did you talk to Taryn?"

"For a moment."

"So what did you think of her?"

"She's a very pretty girl, Son."

"Yeah she is," he agreed, sitting back in the chair absentmindedly while images of her angelic face played through his head.

Maxym would have loved to tease his son for such an admission. He couldn't recall ever hearing him say a girl was pretty, let alone appearing to get lost in thought about one. Worry and concern settled in the pit of his stomach when he saw the forlorn look on Larkin's face. "She's sixteen years old and there's no sign of her father being in the picture."

"Yeah, it was just she and her mother tonight."

"She's meeting with Gastyn to get his thoughts about Taryn attending school this year."

"Why wouldn't she attend school? If she's only sixteen, surely she hasn't graduated already." A sickening feeling surged through him at the thought of spending his days in school without knowing where she was or what she was doing.

"I'm sorry, Son. I don't know why there is an issue with her attending school, but I have a theory."

Larkin looked at his father, waiting for him to continue. When he remained silent he lifted his eyebrows. "Well?"

"It's just a theory, Larkin. I'm probably grasping at straws."

"Please, Dad."

Maxym sighed and ran his hands through his hair, much like his son would do. "I think they've been in hiding. Likely living in a community where no other Gaias resided, blending in with the human society and trying their best not to draw attention to themselves."

"What gave you that impression?"

"The look of fear that came into Ilya's eyes when I mentioned being Gaias. She looked like she wanted to bolt then and there. As I said, it's just a theory, but if I'm right about any of it, they could be dangerous."

"Or they could be in danger," Larkin interjected, placing his hand over his heart as a fierce longing to protect her at all costs surged through him.

Maxym studied his son for several moments. "I don't know why she has been haunting your dreams for the last five years, and until I do, I would feel a lot better if you kept your distance from her."

"I can't. There is something inside me that is pulling me toward her. I don't know how to explain it."

Trying his best to squash the fear that roiled in his stomach, Maxym nodded. "I can't keep you chained here in your room, although it's what I want to do to ensure your safety, so instead I'm going to ask you to make me a promise." Larkin lifted his eyebrows in acknowledgement as Maxym continued. "Promise me that you will be careful. If you find out something that might put your life in danger I need you to tell me. We will handle it together. And don't shut your brothers out. Our bond as Skin Walkers runs deep. They can help you, especially if you don't feel like you can let me in."

"I'm sorry, Dad. I'm not trying to hurt you. I wish I could explain what I feel, but I don't understand it myself right now. I promise I will be careful and if I find out anything that you need to know, I'll tell you."

Knowing that was the best promise he was going to get from his son, Maxym engulfed him in a strong hug. "Stay here tonight, please," he added when he felt Larkin stiffen against him. "She's safe in her own bed. You can go to her in the morning if you must."

He sighed. "Alright, for tonight," he responded, making no promises for the nights to come. "Good night, Dad."

"Good night, Son. I love you."

An hour later Larkin struggled to fall asleep, tormented by thoughts of Taryn's sweet face. He wanted desperately to know what it was about her that called to him, but there was nothing solid he could put his finger on. Finally his body gave in to exhaustion and he drifted into a deep sleep, groaning softly as dreams of her plagued him for the first time in several weeks.

⁕⁖⁕⁖

Taryn woke before the sun rose to explore deeper into the woods near her new home. Not wasting a minute, she made her way up the mountain. The sound of sticks breaking caught her attention. Smiling slightly, she acted as if she didn't know the black wolf was following closely behind her.

Continuing her walk, she came across a section of the forest that had been scarred by fire. With pursed lips, she took in the area where the campfire had burned, obviously unattended. It had spread from the small circle of rocks that had been placed to contain it, into the dry grass and trees beyond, causing blackened devastation in its wake. Her heart ached at the sight of the dead earth surrounding her. Kneeling down, she grabbed a handful of the barren soil and let it empty slowly between her fingers.

Standing, she closed her eyes for a moment before she began to walk through the ruined woods.

From ten yards back, behind a burned out tree stump, Larkin watched her. When he began to creep behind her, he suddenly found himself unable to move as he took in the unbelievable scene unfolding before him. Taryn walked forward carrying a water bottle in one hand and a walking stick in the other, the once damaged and desecrated woods began to heal and fill with life as she passed. Trees, that only moments before had been stripped of their bark, began to bloom with leaves rich in color. He jumped back as grass pushed up beneath his paws and vines and flowers emerged and appeared to trail after her.

Larkin's mind spiraled, trying to make sense of what he had just witnessed. A whimper escaped his snout, in lieu of a human gasp. She couldn't have. *It wasn't possible*, he argued inside his head. But he had seen it with his own two eyes. She had restored the broken forest without as much as a wiggle of her finger. How was that possible? How could she perform such a magnificent feat without letting her power flow through her hands? In all of his life he had never heard of such a thing. Was she truly a Gaias, or was she something entirely different, something unique? He continued to watch her in awe, as the forest came to life around them.

"Good morning," Taryn called out, looking over her shoulder at him. "I was hoping to see you again."

Gazing at her beautiful face, some of his emotional turmoil subsided, allowing him to breathe easier. While she shouldn't have been able to do what she had just done, he was not afraid of her. She was an Ontogeny, a grower, and an enigma who could project her gifts without using her hands. There were some that would be threatened by her incredible power, but not him. The overwhelming need to protect her and keep her secret safe took root deep inside of him.

Taryn moved on with an amazed Larkin trailing close behind, no longer worried about hiding in the shadows. She stopped for a moment and placed a finger to her lips, directing him to stay quiet. Pointing with her other hand, she knelt down and watched as a small heard of white tail deer grazed several feet away.

He found the look on her face baffling. Her eyes widened in wonder and her mouth moved into a perfect smile of joy as she watched the simple act, one that he gave little thought to. After observing for several minutes, they quietly moved on, continuing to explore.

ഇരുന്നു

Two hours later Taryn's home came into view. She took a seat under a tree and rested against it while Larkin laid down a few feet away. "Thanks for walking with me," she sighed before taking a drink of her water. "I wish I could stay out here all day with you, Big Guy. But my mom has a friend stopping by for lunch today and she's going to let me meet him." Larkin's pointy ears perked up as he listened to her speak. "I know it's silly, but I'm actually pretty nervous about it. With the exception of Mr. Taylor just last night, she hasn't let me meet anyone new in well, forever…and now I'm supposed to last through an entire lunch with a stranger."

He could sense her sadness and hear the uncertainty in her tone. Feeling the urge to wrap his arms around her in comfort, he whimpered softly.

"I'm afraid if I do something wrong, she won't let me go to school," Taryn sighed again, this time with silent tears rolling down her cheeks.

Almost instantly, a gentle rain began to fall. She remained sitting, unaffected by the cool water. Larkin moved closer to her, pushing his snout against her arm until she lifted it and draped it around his neck. She ran her fingers through his soft, silken coat and looked into his eyes. Hers, no longer marred by tears, looked affectionately upon him.

"Thanks," she whispered, placing both of her arms around his neck and hugging him. When she released her hold, the rain stopped and the sun's rays filled the sky along with a rainbow that glistened overhead. "I have to go," she stood and straightened herself up as she headed toward the house. Walking past the pool, she glanced back over her shoulder and smiled in his direction, mouthing the words, "See you later."

𝕾𝖢𝕾𝕾

Larkin raced home, his paws barely touching the ground as he flew through the woods, shifting into human form seconds before he burst through the tree line. Running inside, straight to the kitchen, he gulped down an entire pitcher of water to quench his thirst.

"Good morning," his father greeted him from the dining room table. Noticing a less tense, almost joyful look on his son's face, Maxym decided to rib him a little. "I guess I don't have to ask where you've been all morning."

"She's amazing, Dad." A ridiculous, love-struck grin shone on his face.

"Why do you say that?"

Larkin opened his mouth to respond, but stopped short when he realized he couldn't tell his father about what he had witnessed her doing in the forest. No matter how accepting he had been in the past of things that were anything but normal in their secret world, he couldn't trust anyone else with her secrets. "She's a real nature lover. And let's just say, nature seems to love her too," he grinned, thinking back to how she had restored the forest without the use of her hands.

"Well I'm glad to see you're doing better, Son." Maxym patted him on the shoulder. "I have to admit, you had me worried yesterday."

"You don't have to worry. She's not going to hurt me."

Maxym gave him a curious look, wondering what he had meant by that last statement, but Larkin gave nothing away. "So what's your plan for today?"

"I'm going to sleep for a bit while Wylder is over there. I figure he should be gone by two this afternoon, then I can go back to see her." He was completely oblivious to the look of concern that returned to his father's face.

Maxym didn't argue. It was apparent to him that there was something far deeper taking place between his son and the girl, and the last thing he wanted to do was alienate Larkin when he needed him the most. While Larkin headed into his room and fell back onto his bed, his head filled with nothing but thoughts of Taryn, Maxym went outside and began working in the garage.

ಐಅಐಅ

"So this friend of yours, what does he do?" Taryn inquired as she finished setting the dining room table.

"He's a teacher at the high school in Williams, and his name is Gastyn. You aren't nervous are you?"

Taryn shrugged her shoulders casually. "Why would I be nervous, Mother? I mean after all, it's not like he's the first guest we've had for lunch…in like…oh that's right…never," she retorted sarcastically.

Ilya walked over to her daughter and placed a hand on her shoulder. "Taryn, I know this is a lot for you to take in, and it's not all going to be easy, but it is for the best. Before I can let you go to public school, I have to know that you can handle yourself and keep our secrets." She placed a kiss on her daughter's forehead before turning to walk away.

~ 47 ~

Irritation churned inside Taryn's chest as her mother's words struck a nerve. All of her life she had followed her instructions, trusted every decision she had ever made without question, even when those decisions had broken her own heart. She swallowed down her emotions just as she had done a million times before, but just as in more recent times, a small amount of that burn stayed present, lingering inside of her.

As she was about to say something, a knock sounded on the door. "Are you ready, Sweet Girl?" Ilya asked, flashing a reassuring smile.

"Let's get this over with," Taryn sighed audibly.

Giving her daughter a no-nonsense look, Ilya headed to the front door and warmly greeted the man on the other side. "Hello, Gastyn. Please, come in. You haven't aged a day in the last twenty years."

"I could say the same to you. The place looks great, Ilya. I like what you have done with it." He pulled her into a quick hug before the two continued chatting as they made their way into the dining room. Gastyn stopped abruptly when his eyes landed on Taryn. "Well, hello there. You must be Taryn," he smiled, studying her.

"Hello, Gastyn, is it?" Taryn asked, looking him over. He reminded her of the teachers she had seen portrayed in movies, young and handsome. His shoulder length, jet black hair set off his olive skin and made his vibrant blue eyes all the more alluring. Kindness and mild curiosity twinkled in those eyes as he continued to study her at length. He was lean and tall, almost imposingly so, but he had a gentle smile.

"That's Mr. Wylder to you," Ilya corrected her.

"No, it's alright. Please, call me Gastyn," he interjected. "Thank you for having me over today, Taryn."

She locked eyes with him and smiled politely. "It was my mother's idea."

He raised his eyebrows, admiring her spunk.

With a nervous laugh, Ilya said, "Let's eat."

CHAPTER THREE

As they finished their meal, the casual conversation started to wane. Taryn began to stand, ready to clear the dirty dishes from the table, but Gastyn reached over to touch her hand. "Please sit, Taryn. The dishes will wait." Hesitantly she agreed and sat back in her seat. "Do you know what I am?"

"My mother says you're a teacher at the high school."

"Yes, I am a teacher, Taryn. But try to see beyond what she has told you about me." He leaned in closer. "What am I?"

She studied him for several moments. "You're our guest?"

"Look deeper, Taryn. What do you see?"

Her eyes darted between Gastyn and her mother, full of confusion. "You're a man?"

"Hold out your hand and close your eyes."

At a complete loss, she looked only at her mother.

"Do as he asks, Sweetie. Everything will be okay."

Cautiously, she complied.

"Clear your mind, Taryn. Let go of what you have seen, and what you have been told. Open yourself up to what you are feeling deep down. When you can feel it, let me know." Speaking softly and with control, he placed his hand above hers, careful not to physically touch her. He pushed out a small amount of power from his hands and let it fall against her palm.

With her eyes closed tightly, she tried desperately to feel whatever it was she was supposed to, but it was no use. She felt nothing, and was beginning to think he was trying to make her look foolish.

Gastyn looked to Ilya, who sat, watching anxiously. She knew he was testing her ability to recognize others who possessed powers like her own.

"Do you feel it now?" he inquired

"Feel what?" Taryn's voice was full of frustration.

He forced more of his power onto her palm and waited for her response. After thirty seconds without any reaction, he began to cut his power on and off, creating a pulse-like effect against her skin.

"What is that?" she giggled, feeling a faint tickle against her palm.

"Exceptional!" He exclaimed, prompting Taryn to open her eyes. "You really have no idea, do you?" Amused, he settled back in his chair.

"Did I do something wrong?"

"No, Baby Girl, you didn't do anything wrong," Ilya answered. Seeing how on edge her daughter had become, she took a deep breath before continuing. "Remember last night when I asked if you had noticed anything about Mr. Taylor that was different than the boy at the grocery store?"

"Yeah, sure. What about it?"

"Do you also recall your comment about when was the last time we saw someone like us?"

"What are you doing, Mom?" A hint of panic laced her words as she inclined her head slightly in Gastyn's direction.

"I need you to stay calm," Ilya cautioned before nodding to Gastyn.

Returning Ilya's nod, he turned to Taryn, seeing her look of apprehension. In an attempt to put her at ease, he raised his hand and directed her to look towards the small arrangement of flowers in the center of the table, pulsing the muscles in his hand. On cue the arrangement tripled in size, nearly spilling out of the vase that held it.

Taryn's eyes sparkled as an elated look washed over her. "You're one of us."

"Yes, Taryn, Gastyn is like us," her mother affirmed.

"What else can you do?"

"Not so fast, Taryn. I've shown you something, now it's your turn to show me."

Looking to her mother for approval, she recalled the warning she had given her time and time again. *Never let them see the full extent of your powers, it will give you the advantage.* Ilya nodded for her to go ahead, but gave her a look of caution.

Standing at the sink, Taryn filled a glass with water and carried it over to the table, setting it down in the center. She took note of Gastyn's curious expression as he looked at the simple glass. Holding her hand inches from her chest, palm facing away, she slowly extended her fingers. The water rose and hovered two feet in the air, still holding the shape of its former container. She glanced at him, trying to gauge his reaction.

"Very good, Taryn," he acknowledged, not exactly impressed.

Ilya sighed heavily, knowing she was about to remove the lid on a box that she wouldn't be able to put back on. "Go on. Show him."

"Are you sure?" Taryn asked, unable to believe her ears. Ilya bit her bottom lip nervously while giving her a nod of encouragement. Slowly spreading her fingers, the water expanded causing him to move forward in his chair, watching closely. "Now you see me, now you don't." Taryn arched her brows before flicking her wrist. The water dispersed in the air filling the house with a dense fog.

Ilya waved her hands and cleared away the fog directly around the trio. Gastyn wore a surprised expression.

"That is amazing, Taryn," he praised. "Could we go outside and do it again?"

"Clear the house Taryn," Ilya directed.

With another slight flick of her wrist, the fog in the house emptied out. Gasping in astonishment, his eyes widened as he saw the dense fog lingering outside each window. Rushing to the French doors, he opened them and stepped outside. Mother and daughter could hear his delighted laughter. "How far is the blanket?"

"Two and a half miles north, just shy of Williams and two miles south. It stops to the east about fifty yards from our drive way and a half mile west," Taryn replied casually. Waving her hand, the blanket disappeared as quickly as it had come.

Gastyn rushed back inside and looked at her in wonder, shocked when he spied the water sitting back inside the glass, exactly as it was before. "Amazing."

"You should probably go for a walk now, Sweetie. I believe Gastyn and I have a few things to discuss," Ilya nodded.

"That we do, that we do," he agreed, still in awe, marveling at Taryn. "That we do."

😊&#x3

Once Taryn was out of sight, Ilya turned to Gastyn, who sat shaking his head. "I told you she was special."

"You know, Ilya, I've seen a lot in my one hundred fifty years but I've never seen anything like that from someone so young. I know Elders who struggle to have such control..." he stated, still trying to come to grips with what he had just witnessed. "How long did it take her to master that skill?"

"Once," she divulged, walking over the couch.

"Surely you must be kidding!"

"Taryn was eight-years-old when she became upset with me for not letting her go outside to play. I told her it was for her own protection as we couldn't risk anyone like us seeing her. She took one look at a pitcher of water sitting on the kitchen counter and that was it. She blanketed three counties in a dense fog, just like you witnessed today," Ilya shared, settling into one of the corners of the couch. "She's exceptionally smart and intuitive, and it seems that all things come naturally to her."

"Eight-years-old, it's unfathomable," he stated incredulously, taking a seat in the opposing chair. "When I spoke with you on the phone a few weeks ago, I had no idea what you had meant when you referred to her as being special. I have to ask you something, Ilya, and I need you to be honest…she was holding back, wasn't she?"

Silent tears streamed down her cheeks as she buried her face in her hands. "Yes."

Moving to her, Gastyn took a seat and placed his arms tightly around her. "You're not alone anymore. You don't have to carry this burden by yourself. I want to help if you'll let me."

"I don't know if I can risk it, Gastyn. She's all I have."

"Ilya." He took her hands in his. "I remember the first time I saw you. You walked into my classroom a scared little girl, unsure of the powers that were awakening inside you. With my help you found a safe environment to channel them, and explore the potential of those powers, and you learned to control them. I can help your daughter do the same. Do you trust me?"

She nodded as fresh tears streaked down her face. "She's different, Gastyn. If others find out, she could be in danger."

"I saw moments ago just how special she is. Her secret will be safe with me. It is my job, as a teacher of Gaias, to hone her abilities and to help her understand the responsibilities that come along with having great power. I promise you, she will be safe with me."

She studied his face, seeing only sincerity shining in his eyes. "I'm trusting you with my baby girl. I've never trusted anyone else with her before. Please don't make me regret it."

"You have my word, as your former teacher, but more importantly as your friend," he promised. "Tell Taryn I said goodbye, and that I would like to have a one-on-one meeting with her on the first day of school. I will make arrangements with the office. There will be certain things she will have to hide in order to appear like the other students. I'll make certain she doesn't attract unnecessary attention to herself."

"Thank you, Gastyn." She wiped her tears away. "After Maxym Taylor showed up on my doorstep last night I thought I had made a mistake in coming back here."

"Maxym Taylor is harmless, Ilya. He's a Skin Walker and a good man. You've been living in seclusion for far too long. I hope you can learn to relax now that Taryn will be under my tutelage."

"Me too." She gave a shaky laugh, standing when he did to give him a hug. "Thank you again. Taryn is going to flip when I tell her she gets to go to public school."

"It will be a delight to actually have a student who looks forward to attending to school," he chuckled. "I'm only a phone call away if you need anything. Perhaps I can work with her one-on-one a few evenings a week. It may be helpful since she has a lot of catching up to do with the other Gaias children in her class."

"Whatever you think is best. Goodbye, Gastyn."

"Goodbye, Ilya." Leaning in, he kissed her on the cheek before walking down the steps and entering his car.

Ilya watched as he drove away. Wrapping her arms around her waist, she fought off the chill that coursed through her, realizing it was too late to turn back now.

ᏃᏓᏃᏓ

On her solitary walk through the woods, Taryn took note of the worn out path off the beaten trail. Deciding a little adventure was just what she needed, she changed course and began to follow it. Crouching down she studied the dirt track, observing the myriad of paw prints running through it, prints that looked much like the ones her little wolf friend would make. She smiled as she thought of the large black wolf she affectionately called Big Guy, and released a sigh of relief at the realization that she had a friend, albeit a furry one.

After meandering along the trail for two miles, studying the plant life along the way, her body became attuned to the sudden breeze pushing through the trees. An electric charge in the air had the hair on her arms standing on end like hundreds of little stick pins. It was coming. She could feel it bearing down on her. In a panic, she began to race down the path as fast as she could, trying to stay ahead of it. As the winds grew stronger, she could see the trees thinning out ahead of the trail. Pushing down deep, she willed her feet to move faster as she continued to fly over the path, praying that safety could be found at the edge of the forest.

ᏃᏓᏃᏓ

"Thanks for sticking around and helping out with the engine for the Jeep." Maxym grinned at his son. "We should be able to get it back in tomorrow so that it will be ready for your first day of school."

"It was either help you today or have you drive me to school indefinitely."

Wiping his grease covered hands on an old towel, Maxym looked towards the opened back door of the garage where Larkin was standing. "Whatever the reason, I'm glad you're here."

"Sure, dad," he replied, barely hearing his father's words, distracted by something in the air.

"Looks like it's going to rain," Maxym stated as he placed a hand on Larkin's shoulder, noticing the distant look on his son's face. "What is it?"

"She's close by." Taking a deep breath, he filled his lungs with her intoxicating scent. Before Maxym could reply, a young girl flew through the tree line at a dead run. "It's Taryn!"

"What is she doing here?" Maxym sighed, considering the possibility that maybe she was as drawn to Larkin as he was to her.

"I, I don't know. But something's wrong." He took off sprinting in her direction.

Taryn saw the boy running towards her and waved her arms at him, frantically. "Go back, it's not safe!" Unconcerned for his own safety, Larkin continued forward, seemingly oblivious to danger in the air. "Get back inside, it's coming!"

He stopped, sniffing the air and trying to pinpoint the unforeseen danger she spoke of. Seeing her palpable fear put his back up, yet he could sense nothing out of the ordinary. "What's coming?"

She grabbed his arm as she approached, trying to pull him with her, but he stood rooted to the spot. "We have to go." A look of absolute terror shone in her beautiful green eyes.

"There's nothing out there," he replied calmly in an attempt to soothe her.

Just then, static electricity filled the air, causing her hair to stand on end. He watched, fascinated by the way it floated off her shoulders to frame her head like a perfect halo. "It's too late," she cried, backing away from him. He reached out to touch her, but she pulled away. "Run!" She took off in a dead sprint in the opposite direction, trying to put distance between them. Thunder rumbled overhead, followed immediately by a crash of lightning that struck the ground only inches away from her.

The powerful bolt sent her body soaring into the air. Larkin jumped into action, catching her in his arms just before impact with the ground. With adrenaline coursing through his veins, and a single-minded purpose to keep her safe, he raced toward the backdoor of the house that his father was holding open. Lightning struck the ground, seeming to chase after them. Barely missing another powerful bolt, he stepped through the door with her in his arms. The wood planks of their porch smoldered from the strike that had missed his feet by mere inches.

"Are you okay?" Maxym asked, as Larkin carried a trembling Taryn into the living room.

"I'm fine. Are you hurt?" he addressed her as he placed her carefully on the sofa.

She looked from father to son with wide eyes. "How did you...I don't understand. You saved me."

Maxym studied her for several moments trying to comprehend why she would ask such a question. She was a Gaias, after all. She had to know that male Gaias that possessed the Skin-Walker gene were exceptionally fast and agile, yet she seemed to have no clue. Maybe her senses were weak and her mother had not told her that he was a Gaias also after his visit last night. It was the only explanation.

Larkin cleared his throat and shot a meaningful look to his father. "Adrenaline. Are you hurt?"

"No. I'm perfectly alright, thanks to you." She glanced to the other man. "Mr. Taylor, right?"

"Nice to see you again, Taryn. This is my son, Larkin. What were you doing out in the woods so far from home?"

Glancing back at the son, she could not help but notice how beautiful he was. His hair was dark and thick, and it framed his face in a way that showcased his perfectly chiseled features. The intense hazel eyes were boring into her like a hawk, as if he were trying to see into the very depths of her soul. She had no doubt that she was the cause of the brooding look that was currently plastered on his handsome face. He could have easily walked straight out of a movie screen with the striking perfection of his tall muscular frame and dangerous good looks. "I was exploring the woods behind my house when I found a trail that looked interesting, so I followed it. I didn't' realize I had wandered so far from home until I felt the wind pick up and the air change with the coming storm."

Maxym nodded, "There are dozens of trails running through those woods. You're very lucky you didn't happen upon a different one. I would exercise caution in the future. People have gotten lost out there."

"Yes, Mr. Taylor. I'm very sorry to intrude. If I could just wait out the storm, I will be on my way as soon as it has passed." She flinched as a large crack of thunder shook the windows.

"Dad," Larkin's eyes stayed locked on hers. "Why don't you call Ms. Malone and let her know Taryn is here and that she's safe? She must be worried."

Noticing the intense look on his son's face, he complied. "Of course. I'll be just a moment." He stepped out of the room, leaving the two of them alone.

"Thank you for saving me out there, although you should have listened to me and ran. You could have gotten yourself killed."

Larkin was silent for a moment. "What was that?"

New panic began to set in at his question. She could not answer. It would only draw unwanted attention to herself, something her mother had cautioned her about countless times in the past. She knew by the firm set of his shoulders and the determined look on his face that he would not rest until he had an explanation. Without batting an eye, she replied, "An electrical storm. Any good science book will tell you one of the warning signs is the hair on your body standing on end. It's from the electrical charge in the air. You can feel it, and when it happens you better find cover quick." She was not exactly lying, but she was not giving the absolute truth either. She hoped it was enough to appease him.

"You're welcome," he responded to her earlier thank you.

She studied him from her seat on the couch. He was around her age but appeared to have a worldliness in his eyes that most teenagers lacked. She found it intriguing, and there was something that she could not quite put her finger on, a familiarity that should not have been there. Tilting her head to the side, she eyed him. "Have we met before?"

The surprise, mixed with trepidation caught her off guard as Larkin shook his head. "Not that I recall." Relief ran through him as his father came back in to the room.

"Taryn, your mother is on her way to pick you up. Can I get you anything?"

"No thank you, Mr. Taylor. Though, I appreciate the offer."

Sensing his son's sudden unease, he turned to Larkin. "Why don't you go dig up an umbrella and watch for Ms. Malone. We don't want her to get soaked when she arrives." Larkin shot his father a grateful look before taking his leave. "So," Maxym continued, "Are you looking forward to the first day of school?"

"I've been homeschooled up until now. My mother hasn't decided if she wants to continue with that. Did you find the dog?"

"The dog?" He hesitated for a brief moment. "Oh, my neighbor's dog. No, I'm afraid she's still missing."

"That's a shame," Taryn replied. "I'll definitely keep my eye out for her."

"Taryn!" Ilya cried as she walked into the room, "Are you alright? I was so worried." She pulled her daughter off the couch and into a tight embrace.

"I'm fine, Mom."

"What were you thinking, wandering so far from home?" A solitary tear streaked down her cheek.

She rolled her eyes, although her stomach was churning from causing her mother pain. "I'm sorry. I was just exploring. I didn't know it was going to storm."

Keeping her arm around her daughter, she turned to Maxym. "Thank you for taking her in. I truly appreciate your generosity."

He inclined his head, noticing the stiffness in the delivery of her words. He could tell she was sincere in the meaning, but the fact that she had to say them to him seemed to be grating on her. "You're welcome. I'm glad she found us. That storm would have been a dangerous one to be caught out in."

She maneuvered Taryn ahead of her, steering her towards the kitchen. "I'm very grateful. We'll get out of your hair now."

Taryn looked around for Larkin, intending to thank him again, but he was nowhere to be found. As she reached the back door she turned. "Thank you again, Mr. Taylor. Please tell Larkin I said thank you as well." The sight of the burn mark on the porch had her swallowing the lump of fear in her throat as she stepped wide of it, her mother trailing in her wake.

Maxym watched from the doorway as the two ran through the slight drizzle still falling from the sky. Once they were safely in their SUV and heading down his driveway, he shut the door and went to find his son.

₧ω₧ω

Taryn sat quietly on the ride back to their house. The stiff set of her mother's shoulders and the pursed lips were a telltale sign that she was angry. She deserved the anger, but it wasn't as if she had set out intending to get caught in a storm. It was quite the opposite, in fact. She hated storms. Ever since she could remember, the sound of the thunder accompanied by lightening had terrified her. The raw power emanating from the raging skies shook her to her very core. They were magnificent and beautiful and terrible at the same time. And though she couldn't explain it, she felt like each one was trying to seek her out.

Ilya remained stony faced as they pulled into their driveway. Her heart had dropped into her stomach when she heard the first clap of thunder and realized that Taryn was not back. She had spent thirty minutes mentally searching the surrounding woods, trying to feel the presence of her daughter, but she had come up empty. The phone had rang just as she was getting ready to trek off into the forest. Now that she had her back safe and sound, she was ready to kill her.

Following her mom into the house, she helped herself to a glass of juice while she waited for a different kind of storm to unleash its fury.

"You could have been killed!" Ilya raged, looking at Taryn with an accusing look. "What were you thinking?"

"I'm sorry. I didn't know it was supposed to storm."

"Why were you so far from home?"

"I just lost track of time. I didn't realize I had gone so far until it was too late." She tried desperately to fight back her tears. Tears that were streaking down her cheeks not only because she was sorry for causing her mother so much worry, but more due to the thought of things going back to the way they were, never being able to go outside except on rare occasions, and always with her mother by her side.

When Ilya saw how truly sorry her daughter was for all of the worry she had caused, her tone softened. "Oh, Sweetie, I know it wasn't intentional. You've never been out of my reach, where I couldn't feel you before. I've never been so scared in my entire life." She wrapped her arms around her daughter, hugging her tightly. Taryn sobbed against her mother's shoulder. "It's alright, Taryn. You're safe," Ilya consoled her.

"I know I'm safe, but…"

"But what?"

"Did I screw up my chance of going to a real school?"

Realizing just how set her daughter's heart was on attending, her own heart swelled with joy knowing she could give her this one thing. Taking a deep breath, she laid caution and concern aside. Cupping Taryn's chin with her hand, she tilted her head so she could look into her eyes when she broke the good news. "About that…" she sighed theatrically. "After speaking with Gastyn earlier, he and I both think it would be best…" The tension was clearly mounting in the teen's eyes. "Well, we decided that it would be best if you…attended public school here in Williams."

After taking a minute for her mother's words to sink in, she bounded from the bar stool, wrapping her arms tightly around her, and shrieked with excitement. "Thank you, thank you, thank you!"

"Okay, okay, settle down. I get it, you're excited but…there are a few things we have to discuss before you can go to school,

Young Lady." Taryn's excitement stalled immediately, afraid her mother was going to insist on going with her. "If you're going to go to a public school, we're going to have to go school clothes shopping to buy you a new wardrobe."

Not at all what she had expected to hear, Taryn's jaw gaped open for a moment as she absorbed the good news. "Please tell me that you're not messing with me, or that I'm dreaming or something like that."

"I'm not messing with you and you're not dreaming. You're going to be a Junior at Williams High School. And you're going to do great," Ilya beamed proudly.

ఴఁ౩ఴఁ౩

"Larkin," Maxym called out to his son.

"In my bedroom," he replied, staring at the screen on his laptop, where he had sat for the past half hour watching the weather radar loop over and over again.

"That was pretty intense earlier." When he received no response, Maxym took a seat next to Larkin on the bed. "What it is?"

"This doesn't make any sense." Larkin pointed to the screen. "I'm checking the weather radar for activity in the past hour. The storm that just blew through here, it's not showing up anywhere."

"Are you sure you're not just missing it?" Maxym insisted, turning the laptop so he could get a better look. He watched as the radar looped again, an uneasiness settling in the pit of his stomach when nothing appeared, causing his unrest with the girl to grow immensely.

Larkin turned to look at him, his eyes full of confusion. "How is this even possible?" Maxym sat quietly, certain that he could not offer a plausible explanation. "It was real, wasn't it?" He shook his head yet again. Tossing the laptop aside, he rushed downstairs and

~ 64 ~

opened the back door. Staring at the three foot wide hole in the wooden deck, he looked to his father who had trailed behind him.

"Looks like it was plenty real to me, Son," he sighed heavily. "I guess we'll have to go into town tomorrow to pick up some lumber to replace those boards. I hope you will find time to help me with that as well as finishing up on your jeep."

He nodded in acceptance. After all it was Taryn who had brought the storm, quite literally, to their doorstep. Stepping back inside, he went into the living room and collapsed onto the couch. Her lingering scent surrounded him as he inhaled deeply.

His father took a seat in the tan recliner. "When you ran out to help Taryn…what did she say to you?"

"That we should run because it was coming. Then her hair started floating around her head from the static electricity and she said it was too late." Larkin told the story, appearing to be reliving it play-by-play. "Then she tried to run away."

Even though he hadn't been right there when it had started, Maxym could see her terror, even from a distance. "You said her hair floated around her head. What about your hair, did you feel the static electricity?"

"No. Everything was perfectly normal. I didn't feel anything until I caught her after that first lightning strike."

Listening to his son describe the events, he considered the possibility that she had been trying to protect him from the storm. And it had been very obvious that this had not been her first encounter with such a menacing display of the elements.

"I know this is going to sound crazy, Dad, but I think the storm was after her, chasing her down or something."

"No, Son, that actually sounds about right. What do you say we light up the grill and have steak for dinner?" Maxym suggested, hoping to distract him.

"She was really scared, and it was strange how she acted like she had no idea what we are." More confusion settled on the teen's face.

"She's home safe with her mother, and I suspect that woman would kill before she let anything happen to her," Maxym reasoned. "I'm going to get the grill started."

ೞಉೞಉ

Under a blanket of darkness, waiting for the sun to make an appearance, Larkin stretched while carefully balancing on the Malone's roof. After moving over to Taryn's window, he took a long look inside, watching as she slept. His mind played back the scared look on her face over and over again, making him cringe at the thought of her ever being in danger.

He continued to watch over her for thirty more minutes until the sun's morning rays pierced the sky. As she began to stir, he nimbly jumped to the ground and gave one last look up to her window, before sprinting into the trees to shift into the black wolf that would carry him home.

ೞಉೞಉ

Ilya warmed with joy as she took in Taryn's wide, brilliant smile and the excitement shining in her eyes as they settled into the SUV. "Are you ready for today?"

"Yes." She was trying hard to contain her excitement, though she seemed to be failing miserably. Her mother steered the car east on highway forty, away from Williams. "Where are we going?"

"Since you need a whole new wardrobe before you start school, I thought we should go to the mall in Flagstaff."

She sat, recalling the numerous times in the past that she had dreamt of going to a mall. Every time she had asked, her mother had always told her no, saying it was too much of a risk to go out in such a public place. Shrugging off the disappointment she could

~ 66 ~

still taste from just the memory alone, she flashed her a smile before looking out the window.

When they finally arrived at the mall, the pair made their way to the main entrance. Once inside, Taryn looked around in awe as she took in everything from the stores and décor to the large number of people. The building was two stories high and each floor was filled with a myriad of shops selling everything from clothes and jewelry to furniture and eclectic knick knacks. Large potted plants thrived under the sky lights placed strategically throughout the ceiling, allowing natural light in. People laughed and chatted merrily as they bustled about carrying their bags from store to store. For her, it was a sight she had only dreamt of seeing. It was everything and so much more than what had been portrayed on the big screen.

"Pretty cool, huh?" Ilya asked, sensing a hint of apprehension from her daughter.

"I suppose it's alright." She tried hard to appear playfully casual, but inside her stomach was full of fluttering little butterflies. "Where should we start?"

"Why don't we take a walk through and then you can decide. Just remember, Sweetie, no funny stuff here."

"I know." She rolled her eyes, having heard the warning at least a million times before.

Strolling through the main level, Taryn spotted the escalator providing access between the two levels. She had seen them on television, but this was her first glimpse of one in real life. Eager to try it out, she stepped on the moving stairs with ease. Her heart soared in delight as they carried her up to the second floor. Stepping off, she looked around, enjoying the birds-eye-view she now had of the inside of the mall.

"So where are we going first?" Ilya asked, realizing her daughter seemed to be far more captivated by the people than the stores.

Glancing around, the brightly dressed mannequins in a store called Elsie's Boutique caught her eye. "Let's start there."

Ilya looped her arm through hers. "Shall we?"

Grinning ear-to-ear, they made their way into the store. Taryn's senses were pleasantly assaulted with all of the bright colors and textures of the fabric. She ran her fingers over a silky blouse in bright orange adorning a white mannequin.

Watching the wonder in her daughter's eyes, Ilya was delighted that she could finally give her this, a sense of normalcy. As much as it terrified her to let Taryn be a typical teenager, it was the right thing to do. She had to believe that, because the alternative was too unbearable to think about.

ༀଔༀଔ

Maxym placed the final nail on the deck repair while his son carried the damaged boards and put them in a pile near the garage. Next they began on the jeep, hoping to finish before the day's end. After an hour had passed, Larkin became restless.

"Go ahead, Son. You should check on her."

"Thanks, Dad. I'll be back in a little while." He ran toward the tree line, shifting the second he was protected from view. He raced to the part of the forest where he could usually find Taryn and settled down to wait. After twenty minutes had passed an uneasy feeling settled in his stomach, as he was unable to catch even a hint of her scent in the air. She should have been there by now. Going on the assumption that she must still be at home, he ran in that direction, desperate to quell the longing feeling in his chest.

Approaching the large, two story log cabin he noticed there was something off. The sensations that normally filled him when she was near were absent. He stalked around to the front of the

~ 68 ~

house to find their white SUV wasn't where it was always parked. Shifting back into human form, he looked inside the large living room windows at the back of the home. When he saw nothing there, he stepped back before leaping onto the roof, and looking inside her bedroom window. The bed was made, but there was no hint as to where she or her mother might have gone.

With an empty feeling inside his chest, he shifted back into the black wolf and headed home.

ଧଓଃ୫ଠଓ

"Where's Larkin, Mr. Taylor?" Kellan asked, noticing his friend was M.I.A. from the bar-b-que he, and the rest of the pack, had been invited to.

Maxym patted him on the shoulder. "Larkin should be here in a little while." He couldn't help but notice the questioning look Kellan and Thorne shared.

Gerrick's truck pulled up with Nalani and Dagney chatting away in the passenger seat. The girls jumped out and walked around to the back. Lowering the tailgate, they lifted a large cooler packed full of soda and bottles of water and began carrying it towards the house.

"Hey, Ladies. Can I help you with that?" Thorne offered, while looking dreamily at Dagney.

"Just because Dagney and I don't possess the genes you boys do, doesn't mean we're the weaker sex," Nalani snapped.

"Whatever, Nalani. I was only trying to be a gentleman," he moaned, knowing Kellan and Gerrick were watching and likely enjoying his suffering at the hands of the angry one.

Once the girls set the cooler down, Dagney approached him. "Thanks for the offer," she smiled, before walking back to sit by Nalani.

"I don't know what you see in him," Nalani hissed.

"He was only trying to be nice."

~ 69 ~

"Only because he's hot for you."

"Look, Nalani, I get it. You're angry, but you really need to talk to Larkin about it and stop taking it out on Thorne."

"I'm sorry, Dags," she sighed. "Thorne's a good guy and he's sweet on you."

Dagney smiled at her friend, pleased that she thought Thorne was interested in her. The girls made their way inside to help Maxym with the food while the guys sat outside discussing Larkin's absence.

ℰ℟ℭ℥ℰ℟ℭ℥

"So do either of you know what's going on with Larkin?" Gerrick asked, taking a soda from the cooler.

"No, haven't seen or heard from him since he left the campgrounds Saturday night," Kellan responded, rubbing the back of his neck.

"I don't get it," Thorne chimed in. "Ever since he broke away from the pack the other day, it's like he's been somewhere else. I mean, he sat through that silly chick flick Saturday night without saying a word."

"His birthday isn't for another five months, so I don't think it's the final phase that's bothering him," Gerrick offered, referring to the eighteenth birthday when all Gaias inherited their full powers.

"No, I don't think it has anything to do with phasing. But something is definitely wrong," Kellan surmised.

Looking to the tree line, Thorne smiled seeing Larkin emerge from his normal point of entry. "Well look what the cat dragged in."

The three stayed seated, waiting for him to get close. "So glad you could join us," Kellan ribbed his friend. Larkin walked past them as if he hadn't even noticed they were there.

"That was rude," Gerrick grunted as the screen door banged shut behind him.

CHAPTER FOUR

Walking through the kitchen, Larkin gave his dad a look, causing Maxym to follow him to his room. "What's wrong?"

"They're gone," he grumbled, taking a seat on his bed.

"So she wasn't home. Maybe they went to Williams to pick up groceries or something."

"Her scent was weak. They must have left shortly after I came home earlier."

Taking a seat next to his son on the bed, he placed a comforting hand on his shoulder. "Son, you can't expect them to stay home all of the time. I'm sure they'll be back later," Maxym paused, looking for any change in his expression. "Look, everyone's here and I think you owe it to them to give them some of your time as well." He waited for a response, but soon realized that his son was lost inside of his own head. "I know this girl has your head in a mess, but you need to remember that when sides were chosen, those kids down there, they chose you, and you need to honor the pact. Taryn and her mother will be home later and you can see her then. But for now you need to get downstairs and spend time with your brothers and sisters."

Knowing his father was right, Larkin relented. "I need to shower and then I'll be down."

"Then I'll leave you to it and we will see you downstairs shortly."

Keiryn Falcon and his friends, Eben Carter, Jonesy Blake, Dalen Graham, Bency Porter and the twins Bentley and Hadley Love walked through the Flagstaff mall, joking around as they went.

At six foot two inches, with blonde hair and blue eyes, Keiryn looked like your typical high school jock, however he was anything but. Instead of focusing on sports and dating the head cheerleader, he spent his time with his pack brothers and sisters running the forest or soaring through the skies in his preferred form, the hawk.

His pack brother, Eben Carter, was muscular in stature, with dark skin and hazel colored eyes that suited his suave demeanor. He was affectionately known as the "chick magnet" since all the ladies seem to flock to him, due to his striking good looks and charming personality.

Dalen Graham, the jock of the group, enjoyed playing sports and excelled at each new one he tackled. But his passion was football, soccer and skiing, whether it was on the snowy winter slopes or the warm waters of Lake Powell. He was tall and fit with shaggy black hair and jet blue eyes.

Known as the runt, Jonesy Blake was small in stature compared to his pack brothers. He had blonde hair and blue eyes that were enhanced by his black-framed glasses. There appeared to be nothing exceptional about him on the surface. He was just your average teenager who didn't have any incredible talents. All his life he had felt like a misfit, never really belonging, even though he was an accepted member of Keiryn's pack.

Bency Porter was tall and willowy, with curly dark hair that cascaded halfway down her back. Her violet colored eyes were full of intensity and could show a myriad of emotions. Due to her bi-racial heritage, her skin was a few shades lighter than her pack brother, Eben. Affectionately known as the freak of the pack, she wore the title proudly. She was one in about every ten thousand female Gaias that had inherited the Skin-Walker gene.

Rounding out the group, identical twins, Bentley and Hadley Love, had long, straight blonde hair and gray eyes. They were short and petite and loved all things boys and shopping. In true twin fashion they could finish each other's sentences, a fact that some found cute, and others found annoying.

"I can't believe we have to go back to school so soon. It seems like we just started summer vacation a few days ago," Eben whined.

Dalen sighed in agreement. "No more late night runs. My parents will probably make me be home by nine."

"We still have the weekends," Bency interjected, trying to see the bright side.

The twins laughed and said in unison, "You just like to run with the boys."

"Whatever! You two are just jealous that you didn't get the freak gene."

Twining their arms through Bency's, the twins carried on their conversation about one thing all the female pack members had in common, a love for looking at cute boys, Gaias or not.

"Ugh. Could you please keep your opinions to yourself," Dalen implored when he overheard the words "cute butt".

"Is someone feeling a little neglected," Bentley razzed, sticking her tongue out at him.

"Girls," he muttered, turning his attention back to his brothers.

The group stopped at the food court and sat down at a long table to share three orders of loaded nachos.

"I hear you ran into the black dog the other day. Anything interesting happen?" Eben asked, hoping for all of the bloody details.

Keiryn shrugged his broad shoulders nonchalantly. "Not really, I don't think he even noticed I was there."

"Sounds like he might be coming down with rabies," Dalen laughed.

"Couldn't happen to a nicer guy," Eben added. Bency threw him a frosty glare. "Don't go getting all righteous on us now, Bency. They aren't part of our family and haven't been for a long time."

"Whatever," she growled, before turning to the twins. "There's a shop downstairs I want to stop by. You game?"

Bentley and Hadley smiled at one another before turning back to their pack sister. "Of course!"

"See you losers later," Hadley smiled as they walked away.

Deciding they had nothing better to do, the boys trailed behind them, standing outside the shop checking out the kiosks with cell phones, sun glasses and mechanical helicopters while holding their sisters' purchases as they moved on to the next store.

"Now all I need are some cute sandals to go with the dress and I will be all set," Bency stated as the girls emerged from the last store on the lower level.

Looking at each other, they all three said in unison, "Soleful!" Ignoring the groans from their pack brothers, the trio looped arms and headed back to the center of the mall to catch the escalator to the second floor where their favorite shoe store was located.

As they all stepped on the moving staircase, they could immediately sense the presence of another Gaias. Looking around, Keiryn's eyes fixed on a pretty girl who had just stepped onto the opposing escalator, heading down to the main level. Her long hair, the color of warm honey, and striking green eyes captured his attention, causing him to stare blatantly as he passed her. She appeared not to have noticed him. When he reached the top he stepped off quickly and moved through the crowd, keeping his eyes locked on her retreating form as she headed towards the exit carrying several bags.

Noticing how his friend was eyeing the girl, Dalen took the opportunity to tease him. "Looks like she isn't interested, Lover boy."

Once she was out of sight, Keiryn turned and pushed past Dalen. "It doesn't matter. It's not like she's from Williams or anything."

ଛୠଔଔଔ

Placing their bags in the back of the SUV, Ilya looked at her daughter. "You had enough or do you think you could handle going to a few more stores?"

"Since we're already here in Flagstaff, it only makes sense that we continue." Taryn was absolutely in love with the idea of more shopping.

Wrapping her arms around her daughter, she squeezed her tightly. "You're doing great, Sweetie."

She shrugged off her mother's embrace, insulted by the words. "What's that supposed to mean?"

"I'm sorry. I didn't mean anything by it. I only meant that it seems you have been doing this your entire life."

"Whatever," Taryn stated coolly. "Are we going to shop or what?"

Deciding to drop the subject in hopes that they could continue to enjoy this day of firsts, Ilya smiled, "Let's go."

ଛୠଔଔଔ

"Hey, Larkin." Dagney gave him a big hug as he finally joined them. "You had us worried the other night when you left."

"Sorry, Dags. I just have a lot on my mind and needed time to work it out," he replied, squeezing her gently. "Hey, Nalani."

"Hey, Larkin," Nalani smiled and gave him a hug. "You'd better get out there and spend time with your brothers. They tend to be lost without their fearless leader around."

He cringed on the inside at the word fearless. He had felt anything but fearless since realizing Taryn was real and not just an image from a dream. As he walked out the door, he was greeted sarcastically by his three friends.

"Oh, so glad the great Larkin Taylor could grace us with his presence," Gerrick jeered.

"Are you going to be here with us today or do you plan on being off somewhere else?" Kellan added, waving his hands around his head playfully as though he were pretending to be lost in space.

He shrugged his shoulders and sighed loudly. "Your turn, Thorne. Go on, let's hear it."

Thorne placed his hand out for Larkin to take. "I'm just glad to have you back, Brother. I brought the football. Anyone up for some catch?"

The boys spread out in the field and began tossing the ball back and forth. Larkin and Kellan were on one side with Gerrick and Thorne on the other. After a few friendly tosses, their true competitive nature began to emerge and their friendly game of catch turned serious.

Larkin tossed the ball to Thorne as Gerrick tried to intercept. Though Gerrick was faster, Thorne was much more limber and easily evaded him on the first throw. Thorne threw the ball back to Larkin, who was gifted with speed, agility and strength. He also possessed a greater perception to anticipate his opponent's moves before they made them. Feeling as if he was cheating somehow, he tried to suppress the latter gift to give Kellan a chance.

Maxym and the girls lounged on the porch, watching as the two teams battled for bragging rights. Gerrick finally out maneuvered Thorne and won the ball. Knowing how intense Kellan could be, Larkin put on a good show, allowing him to catch a few balls.

"Looks like the past few days have made you soft," Kellan ribbed before tossing the ball back to Gerrick.

Gerrick looked to Kellan and signaled. Running closer to the tree line, he leapt twenty feet in the air, grabbing hold of the football and one of the trees, before letting out a celebratory howl. Getting ready to jump down, he turned to look at his friends and noticed something strange.

"What is it?" Gerrick called out when he saw his baffled expression.

"What happened back here?" Kellan asked Larkin.

"What do you mean, what happened?"

"I mean there are a lot of large black circles in your yard." Jumping down from the tree, he walked over to one. "I wouldn't have noticed them if I hadn't seen them from above. What are they?"

Larkin swallowed hard, realizing Kellan could see where the lightning had struck the earth in the freak storm that had passed over the day before.

"What is it?" Thorne and Gerrick inquired simultaneously.

"I don't know exactly. But whatever they are there are a few more over there," Kellan pointed in the direction that Taryn had started to run. "Then there's a nearly perfect line leading up to the backdoor." He followed the circles he hadn't been able to detect earlier while at ground level. "What happened here?"

Larkin's muscles tensed while he tried to think of a plausible excuse for the strange occurrence. Maxym, who had nearly six decades of perfecting excuses, cleared his throat and offered one that no one would doubt. "I was in the field yesterday working on honing my weaker powers and let's just say, it didn't go so well."

"Is that what happened to your deck?" Dagney inquired, motioning to the new boards.

"Yes, Dagney, that's right," Maxym sighed, pretending to be embarrassed. "Look, sometimes you get it right the first time, sometimes you don't. Sometimes you should recognize your limits, and yesterday I found mine."

Content with his explanation, the group went back to having fun and relaxing. Larkin sent his dad a grateful look, acknowledging the slight nod he gave him in response.

⁕⁓⁕⁓⁕

"Taryn, I don't feel much like cooking tonight. How would you feel about grabbing a bite to eat at the café in Williams?" Ilya asked.

"Sounds fine," she replied casually while the voice inside her head was screaming a sarcastic, *"Are you sure that's a good idea? After all, I might not be able to handle it."*

Pulling up outside the café, Ilya grabbed her hand. "Look, Taryn, what I said earlier, I didn't mean it the way it may have sounded. I truly hope it hasn't ruined what I intended to be a very special day for you."

"The yogurt from that shop isn't really holding me over anymore and I'm starving. Can we forget it and move on?"

"Sure, Sweetie. Let's go eat."

Mother and daughter headed inside and picked a booth towards the back of the café. Taryn ordered a cheeseburger, fries and a banana milkshake while her mother opted for a grilled chicken salad. Deciding to let the resentment go, she smiled as they both enjoyed their meal, discussing the numerous outfits she had purchased.

After finishing, Ilya paid at the register while Taryn perused the small dessert case that sat on top of the bar area. "Something catch your eye?"

"No, Mom, just looking," she smiled, too full to eat another bite.

As they made their way down the aisle, Keiryn and his friends entered the front door of the café, pushing and laughing as they filed in. Dalen stopped and sported a mischievous grin when he spotted the girl from the mall, knowing Keiryn would likely flip out when he saw her again. Ilya threw the young man a look of caution after noticing the way he looked at Taryn.

As the last to make his way inside, Keiryn stopped and held the door for the pretty brown-haired woman trying to exit, not noticing the shadow trailing behind her.

"Thank you," a lilting voice said.

He turned. "You're wel...welcome," he stuttered, caught completely by surprise as he stood staring at the girl that had captured his attention earlier in the mall. After a brief moment, he smiled back at her as they both lingered in the doorway, locked in a shared gazed.

"Taryn," Ilya called out, realizing she had lagged behind.

With her eyes still locked on the boy holding the door for her, she stepped forward as he moved to step out of the way. She gasped when he brushed lightly up against her, agape at the physical spark, white in color that filled the air between them.

"Sorry." A blush bloomed across her cheeks, absorbing the awe struck expression on his handsome face, ready to explain that the spark was caused by static electricity if he asked. Unable to speak, Keiryn stood there and continued to stare at her pretty face.

She curled her mouth into a shy smile before stepping outside to join her mother in the SUV.

As Ilya watched her daughter buckle her seatbelt, she took note of the extra sparkle in her eyes. "He was very polite and handsome." She nodded in the direction of the boy currently staring out the door of the café.

Glancing at her mother, Taryn only smiled before looking back. She could clearly see him watching them as her mother put the car in reverse. Unable to tear her eyes away, she lifted her hand in a slight wave, noticing his eyes never strayed from her until the SUV maneuvered out of the parking lot towards their home.

ଓଔଓଔ

Keiryn watched from the window as mother and daughter drove away. "You going to join us or what, Lover boy?" Dalen teased from the large booth the group had claimed.

"You guys go ahead and order. I'll catch up with you later," he replied, distracted by the white SUV that was growing smaller in the distance. There was something inside him that urged him to follow and to find out more about the girl named Taryn.

Rushing to his blue truck, he jumped in and headed in the same direction. Unable to get a visual on them, he pulled off on a side road and parked along the ditch. After exiting his vehicle he took a look around, ensuring that he was alone. Knowing he had to act quickly, he shifted into a large hawk and took to the air in order to get a bird's eye view of the surrounding area and the roads.

After a few minutes of soaring through the sky he spotted the white SUV. Swooping down to get a better look, he saw Taryn talking animatedly with her mother as they turned off the paved road and headed west, towards a thick tree line. He soared over the trees and watched as they pulled up close to a large log home.

Landing deftly on a tree branch, he watched as the pair exited the vehicle and took numerous shopping bags out of the back hatch. He listened to their conversation, his heart leaping with excitement as he heard the mother divulge that they had been school clothes shopping all day. Hopeful that the girl, Taryn, would be attending Williams High School, he flew around to the rear of the house and observed them through the large windows as they made their way inside. The pretty girl with the light brown hair and captivating green eyes demanded his attention. For the next hour he watched her intently, never once losing interest.

Keiryn grew anxious when she disappeared upstairs for several minutes, finally returning clad only in a black bikini with a towel draped around her shoulders. He continued to watch as mother and daughter made their way out the French doors leading to the pool. Afraid they might sense his presence he gave an internal sigh and took flight, hoping he would be able to see her again soon.

ഇരുൽ

"I'm so full," Thorne whined, rubbing his stomach.

"No one told you to eat three burgers and half a slab of ribs," Nalani chided.

"Oh leave him alone, Nalani. He's a growing boy who's only trying to catch up with the rest of us," Kellan laughed.

"In that case, he'd better get another plate," Gerrick tormented knowing how easy it was to rile him when he was being teased about his smaller stature.

Dagney walked up behind Thorne and tousled his hair with her fingers. "Don't pay them any mind. They're just jealous you know." Looking up in her direction, he flashed an affectionate smile. She started to return the gesture but her cheeks grew warm when she realized that everyone was watching them. "So who's going to help clean the kitchen?" she asked instead, hoping to distract them from the bright blush blooming on her cheeks.

Instantly, the air filled with groans and excuses. Nalani shook her head at the boys, who had already started disappearing from the deck area. Looping her arm through Dagney's, they headed inside. While the girls cleaned, the boys went into the garage to help work on Larkin's engine. After twenty minutes their sisters joined them, watching from a bench in the garage while the brothers laughed and called each other names.

While his pack worked, Larkin could feel his attention span starting to diminish. He knew there was only one thing that would make the hollow feeling inside go away. He needed to see Taryn, to assure himself that she was indeed safe and sound and back in Williams. Part of him feared that his father was right about their past. There had to be a reason they had lived off the radar for so long, and maybe the storm yesterday had been enough to cause Ilya to take her and go back into hiding. He hoped like hell that he was wrong. She had consumed his dreams for so long. He could not lose her now after just finding out she was real.

No longer able to keep himself restrained, he pushed past Gerrick and Thorne without a word and left out the rear door of the garage. "Larkin?" Maxym called out.

"I'll be back." He never glanced towards his father and his friends.

Sprinting to the tree line, he shifted into the black wolf and took off in a dead run towards Taryn's home. The urge to see her spurred him onward. He dug deep and pushed himself harder, not stopping until he arrived near the edge of the yard at the rear of the Malone's home. Carefully he stalked in the shadows, searching for any sign that she had returned. Relief flooded his body when she emerged from the French doors.

He watched her as she moved to the edge of the porch and looked up at the crystal blue sky for a moment before glancing into the woods. Larkin's heart skipped a beat as her eyes locked on him.

Surely she can't see me, he thought to himself, as he stepped further back in the shadows.

With a softened smile, she continued to stare at him as she placed her fingers in the back pockets of her shorts and rocked gently on the balls of her feet. After a quick glance over her shoulder, she stepped off of the porch and walked towards him. Anxiously he waited for her to join him away from her mother's view.

"I didn't think I'd see you today," she smiled.

Taking a seat on the ground a few feet away, she leaned back against a tree. Larkin watched in amazement as the small tufts of grass with tiny purple wild flowers came to life in her presence. He sat listening to her sweet voice as it calmed the emotional storm that had gripped him all day.

"We went to Flagstaff today, to buy school clothes and stuff. It was pretty cool considering it was my first shopping trip that I can remember, with the exception of the grocery store in Williams," she shrugged, stretching her legs out.

Larkin tilted his head to the side. If they had bought school clothes that could only mean that she would be starting school with him on Wednesday. He felt the giant weight of unease lift at the thought of her being in such close proximity to him throughout the day.

"I don't get it. One day we are living in the middle of a wheat field in Kansas, and I'm never allowed to venture out or talk to anyone, and the next we're going to the mall and even out to dinner at a café." She released a long sigh. "I have to admit, after that storm chased me down yesterday, and then her having to come pick me up at the Taylor's home...I didn't think she would let us stay here for even another minute."

Taryn patted the ground hoping that he would come and sit next to her. Instead a deep growl rumbled in the back of the black wolf's throat. "What's the matter?"

Larkin stood, his fur bristling as he caught the scent of another Skin-Walker closing in on them. Not wanting to expose himself to her for what he really was, he bounded off into the woods intent on tracking down the intruder before he could get near her.

Crouching down, he laid in wait, hurling himself on top of the brown wolf who crept by. They wrestled about, snarling and growling for a moment before shifting back into human form.

"What are you doing out here, Kellan?" Larkin demanded of his brother.

Kellan rubbed his neck and shot him a frosty look. "I was looking for you. You've been acting really strange the past few days and I figured it must have something to do with whatever it was that caused you to break away from the pack."

"You shouldn't have followed me." He could smell Taryn's intoxicating scent getting stronger. Realizing she had followed after him, he ordered Kellan to go. "You need to leave. Go back to my house and wait for me."

"Not without my brother."

"You need to go right now."

"I'll go…only if you come too."

After a brief internal struggle, Larkin nodded, knowing it was the only way to get Kellan away before she found them. Shifting into wolf form, he sprinted back towards his house with Kellan following closely behind. When the burn of her sweet fragrance weakened, he sighed with relief, knowing both his secret and Taryn were safe, at least for the moment.

Bursting through the tree line behind his house, he shifted back into his human form as Kellan did the same.

Sensing his friend, his brother, was hiding something, Kellan moved in on him. "What's going on with you?"

"Let it go," Larkin warned.

"No, I won't," Kellan grabbed his shoulder, trying to make him stop. Larkin shrugged away from him, fighting desperately to keep his anger at bay as the rest of the pack formed an audience around them. "You owe me an explanation, Larkin. No, forget that, you owe all of us an explanation."

Larkin stalked past Nalani and Gerrick without so much as a glance in their direction. "Fine, if you're not going to tell me what's going on, then I'll just have to go back into the woods to find the answers myself."

A burn instantly surged through his body and his eyes grew dark at the sound of Kellan's threats. His instinct to protect Taryn took control, fearing she would unknowingly expose her secrets to Kellan, just as she had done with him while in wolf form.

"I wouldn't do that," Larkin warned his friend.

"Then tell us what's going on," Kellan demanded, walking towards him.

"It doesn't concern you." His tone grew darker with every syllable as his nostrils flared and his muscles tensed.

Maxym stepped between the two boys standing nose-to-nose, knowing neither would back down. "Everyone needs to take a step back. Larkin, Kellan, you're brothers. You both need to calm down and realize that sometimes we all need a little space." Noting the darkness in his son's eyes, it became clear to him just how deeply he was connected to Taryn. "Larkin, I need you to go inside the house."

"Dad, I can't do that."

Placing a gentle hand on his son's tense shoulder, he looked him in the eye. "You need to go to the house, Son." Shaking his head, Larkin turned and headed inside, but not before shooting Kellan a look of warning.

"Mr. Taylor," Kellan began.

"Kellan," he interrupted. "I need you to back off of him for a little while." Turning his attention to the group, he tried to calm the worry he saw on each of their faces. "I know this isn't easy, watching one of your own struggling like this. But Larkin's going to be fine, he just needs more time before he's ready to open up about what's going on right now."

"Larkin isn't thinking about leaving us, is he?" Thorne inquired, causing Gerrick and Nalani to gasp.

"He's our brother, Thorne. How could you say such a thing?" she admonished.

"Back off, Nalani," Dagney growled. "Thorne only asked what the rest of us where thinking."

Maxym saw the unrest tearing away at the group and tried to reassure them. "No one's leaving the pack. He just needs a little time and space." Looking around, he saw the concern shining through more than anger. "Tell me you guys can do this for him."

Gerrick looked around at his friends and saw the apprehension written clearly on their faces along with resignation. Speaking for them all, he nodded, "Yes, Mr. Taylor, we'll give him some time."

Inclining his head in acknowledgement, Maxym gestured the group toward the driveway. "Kellan." He pulled the boy aside. "I need your word that you're not going to go back into the woods for the next few days."

"Oh, I wasn't really going to go back in, Mr. Taylor. I was only trying to get him to tell us what's going on. But if you say he's going to be okay, then I'll take your word for it."

Maxym patted him on the shoulder. "Thank you. Everything will be alright, I promise."

Kellan smiled and sprinted toward his friends.

Watching until the group was out of sight, Maxym started toward the house to find his son.

ಬಂಚಬಂಚ

Keiryn returned to the Desert Rose Café just as his friends were finishing their meal. "What's up, Keiryn? Where did you run off to?" Eben asked as his friend squeezed into the already packed booth.

"Nowhere particular," he shrugged nonchalantly, even though his mind was full of mental pictures of the girl from earlier.

"Oh, I know exactly where Lover Boy flew off to," Dalen grinned smugly. Keiryn shot him a futile glare. "Our little friend here just chased after that girl and her mother."

Rolling his eyes in mock exasperation, Keiryn smirked as he listened to Dalen's commentary, even though every bit of it was the truth. He sighed as every pair of eyes at the table slowly turned to him.

"So let's hear it. What did you learn about this girl?" Eben prompted.

"Her name is Taryn. It looks like she and her mother just moved here recently. There were still some packed boxes in the living room. No sign of her father."

"Did you talk to her?" Bency asked.

"Nope, just flew by," he yawned. "It's my job to check out people new to town to make sure they don't pose a threat to us. That's all I was doing. Can we talk about something else now?"

When a few silent moments had passed, the conversation resumed around the table. Keiryn was grateful that the subject of the new girl had been dropped. While the group discussed their plans for the evening, he finished his meal. After settling up the bill at the counter they filed out of the café and climbed into Dalen's SUV. As they pulled out of the parking lot and headed towards Keiryn's house, he looked out the window, thoughts of Taryn fresh in his mind.

ೞೞೞೞ

"Larkin, where are you , Son?"

"On the couch," he mumbled through the pillow resting over his head.

"We need to talk about what happened out there between you and Kellan."

"What about it?"

"What had you so upset with him that it would cause your eyes to go dark?"

"What?" He sat up on the couch, giving his father all of his attention.

"Son, your eyes went dark... just like the last time you changed."

Confusion flooded Larkin's mind as he tried to remember the exact moment his father was referring to. He could not pinpoint it, leaving him fearful of what could have happened if his dad had not told him to go inside. He sat with his head between his hands, exhaling forcefully. The image of Keiryn's face from that fateful day five years ago burned in his mind.

"I don't understand. It's been almost two years since I last turned."

"We should call Gastyn and ask him to come over." His father sat down beside him.

Larkin nodded in agreement, fear heavy in his eyes.

ೞೞೞೞ

Larkin disappeared into the darkness, leaving his father and Gastyn to discuss whatever it was they would not say in his presence. Anxious to feel the calm that only Taryn could provide to him, he thundered through the woods towards her house. When he arrived, he watched from a distance, noticing a change in her

~ 89 ~

demeanor. She appeared distracted, pacing about as her mother talked to her.

For the next hour he observed her as her behavior became more edgy, fighting the urge that consumed him, the one telling him to go to her and comfort her. The secret he was keeping from her was tearing him apart. As much as he wanted to help her, he knew it would upset her if she found out that he was the wolf that she had been confiding in over the past few days.

Before turning in for the night, Taryn stepped outside on the porch and scanned the woods around her home as if she were looking for something. Even in the black of night, her eyes caught his, causing her to smile widely. A look of contentment settled on her face before she returned inside, instantly placing him at ease.

After kissing her mother goodnight, she rushed upstairs to her bedroom and looked out the window in his direction. This time she waved and blew him a kiss before getting ready for bed.

An hour later, after Ilya had gone to bed, Larkin shifted back into his human form and claimed his normal spot outside her bedroom window.

Looking in at her while she slept peacefully, several thoughts passed through his mind. Thinking back, it was almost as if she had been distraught until she had seen him standing in the shadows watching her. Could it really be that his rushed disappearance earlier had worried her enough to upset her? He considered the possibility as a ridiculous sized grin broke across his mouth. It was quickly replaced by a frown when he realized it was not really him she had been happy to see. She had been waiting for the large black wolf that had accompanied her in the forest over the past few days. Frustration set in as he contemplated how and when he could break the news to her, and what would happen when he did. Would she freak out? After all, she didn't even know he was a Skin-

Walker, and something told him she didn't even know such things existed.

Playing numerous scenarios over in his head, he decided that he would tell her during their walk in the morning. Laying it all out in the open was the best way to move forward. Content with his plan, he positioned himself carefully on the roof and fell asleep.

ಬಂಗ್ಯಬಂಗ್ಯ

As the sun broke the morning sky Larkin yawned and jumped to his feet, realizing that Taryn was already up. Trying to remain unseen, he waited for her to go into her closet before jumping down quickly and sprinting towards the trees for cover. Once he was out of sight he shifted into wolf form and waited for her to join him.

In a matter of minutes she bounded from the French doors and in his direction. "Have you been waiting long?" she asked upon approach. Shrugging in response to his silence, she walked past, running her fingers through his thick black fur before scratching the top of his head.

He quivered under her touch and his tail began to wag. When he realized that he was giving in to the typical canine response, he shook himself, trying to brush off her hand no matter how much he enjoyed it.

"What's the matter? Is someone too much of a macho wolf to be scratched?"

Walking deeper into the woods, Larkin followed closely behind, trying to find the perfect moment to reveal his true self to her. Another half mile passed before he mustered up enough courage. She took a seat under a large tree. Settling in next to her, he mentally started the countdown in his head. Three, two...

Just before he reached one, a shrieking sound pierced the air. Taryn immediately jumped to her feet and raced towards it. He pushed ahead of her, concerned for her safety as she neared the

~ 91 ~

area where the horrific cries were emanating from. She bumped solidly into him as he stopped abruptly.

Less than ten feet away a frantic bobcat shrieked as its leg lay mangled from the teeth of the metal trap it had stepped in. She tried to move past the wolf, but he pushed back, intent on keeping her away from the injured animal. Even though the bobcat was not huge, he knew a hurt and scared animal meant a dangerous one.

"Stop that!" He froze at the seriousness in her tone, allowing her to breeze past him and closer to the injured creature.

"No!" he barked, cursing his wolf form, knowing she did not understand what he was trying to say. Not that she would have cared anyway.

"If it were you stuck in this trap, you'd want someone to help you," she scolded before turning back to the bobcat. "There, there. No one's going to hurt you."

Larkin whimpered as she moved closer, but stopped and stood utterly amazed, noticing the bobcat was calming down as she continued to speak in her soothing voice. Could it be that she was also an Influential? It was the only explanation as to why the injured cat stood perfectly still. She had to be using her gift of Influence to keep him calm.

"I only want to help you." She now stood less than a foot away. Bending down to the animal's level, she reached out to touch him, causing Larkin to growl. She shot him a cautioned look, with an unspoken command not to interfere.

"I need you to lay down, my friend," she whispered to the bobcat. Larkin watched in awe as the animal did exactly what she asked of him. With nothing, not even the slightest twitch of a muscle, the jaws of the trap sprang open and she gently pulled it away. "I know it hurts right now, but I'm going to make it better."

Larkin was even more in awe. She had to be an Imperium as well, if she could so easily release the trap. How was it possible that a sixteen-year-old Gaias could possess so many abilities, and have such amazing control over each one? What she was, what she could do, had to be unprecedented. Never in the history of their race had there ever been anyone quite like Taryn.

He moved in closer to get a better look at the animal's gruesome injuries. When he saw its leg, he realized that it was barely attached, hanging by a thread of muscle where the metal jaws had bit through. The bobcat continued to lie still while she hovered over him.

She placed one hand on the injured leg and the other on the thick grass beneath them. Larkin's amazement quickly turned to confusion as he watched the grass around them begin to brown and crumple into dust.

"There, good as new," Taryn smiled, pulling her hand away from the cat's leg.

Larkin's eyes stayed fixated on the animal. *It wasn't possible*, he thought to himself, blinking to take a second look.

"Go on, now. But be careful out there." The animal rose on its four perfect legs and bounded away from them. As soon as the bobcat was out of sight, she turned to the barren ground beneath her feet and gazed at it apologetically.

His heart raced inside his chest as his mind spiraled out of control, trying to grasp what he had just witnessed. She had absorbed the life from the plants below to heal the bobcat. *How was that possible?* He screamed loudly inside his head. A Healer had not been born in hundreds of years, and those that were had been destroyed the moment their gift was known. After witnessing what he had just seen, there was no way for him to expose himself to her now.

"I guess we need to do something with this awful thing," she nodded in the direction of the trap. Larkin watched as she carefully picked it up. Pursing her lips together, she studied the mechanical monstrosity as the wolf looked on, taking in her every move, no matter how subtle. He continued to watch her, wary in the knowledge that she appeared to be a Healer. The revelation should have compelled him to run as fast as he could in the opposite direction, but he found himself rooted to her side, unable and unwilling to walk away.

"Whoever left this out here will be back to get it, no doubt. I think I'll just take it home." With a simple glance the jaws closed, no longer posing a danger to her or any animal.

After lugging the heavy trap back to her house, she dropped it next to a tree and took a seat. "Thanks for walking with me, Big Guy." She ran her fingers gingerly through his fur. Sitting back against the tree, she pondered about tomorrow. "I wish you could go to school with me. It would be nice to have someone familiar with me on my first day, but don't tell my mother that, otherwise she'll insist on accompanying me." She ruffled his fur again before resting her head against him.

Larkin snuggled beside her, torn by everything that he had discovered and his ever growing affections for her. Despite what she was, he couldn't help but enjoy the moment and the realization that he brought comfort to her. She might hate him tomorrow if she found out his secret, but for today, it didn't matter.

℠...

After parting ways with Taryn, he rushed back home needing time to sort through what he had witnessed. Running as fast as he could, he made it home in record time.

"Morning," Maxym greeted him as he walked inside the house.

"Hey, Dad." He could see the tired look upon his father's face. "Everything okay?"

"I didn't sleep very well last night. But I'm heading out to work on your jeep. I'd like to finish it off today if at all possible."

"Give me thirty and I'll be out." His father was holding something back from him but he was too distracted at the moment to care.

Getting a drink of water from the kitchen, he watched out the side window as his father walked into the garage. Once Maxym was out of sight, he slammed the glass down on the counter and ran into his father's office. Quickly scouring through the shelves of books, he found the one he hoped would provide him with more of an insight on Taryn and her many gifts.

Flipping through its numerous pages over and over again, his search yielded nothing. He sighed in frustration, knowing he would have to wait until school started and Gastyn allowed them into his personal library. Protecting her and her secrets was his main priority. His desire for answers would have to take a back seat for now.

ಬಂದ್ಬಂದ್

"So who's this girl Dalen was talking about?" Teigan inquired of his son as they ate dinner.

Barely aware that his father was talking, Keiryn's mind was lost in thought, recalling the electric pulse between him and the girl he knew only as Taryn, as he pushed his food around unconsciously on his plate.

"Larkin's stopping by later. Is that alright with you?"

"Sure," a distracted Keiryn agreed.

"Really? It's okay if Larkin Taylor comes over?"

"What? No! Why would you even ask?" he scowled, irritated by the thought.

"I was asking about this girl I overhead Dalen talking about. But I guess I know all that I need to about her, seeing how distracted you are. I assume it's her that is on your mind?"

Keiryn sat back in his chair and smiled brightly. "You should have seen her, Dad. She's so beautiful. Her long brown hair, gorgeous green eyes and wow, her smile is…well, it's perfect."

"Another pretty face," Teigan rolled his eyes.

"Oh no, Dad, you should have seen it when she walked past me. As we brushed against each other there was a visible spark. She's more than a pretty face, she's incredible."

"More than a pretty face, huh? Whatever she is, you need to be careful until you know what she's doing here in Williams, and if she already belongs to another pack," he cautioned. "So does this incredible girl have a name?"

"Taryn," he sighed with delight, finding happiness in the way her name rolled easily off his tongue. "Hey, I'm going over to Eben's for a little while to hang with him, Dalen and Jonesy…if that's okay with you."

"That's fine. Just be home at a decent hour. I don't want you exhausted on your first day of school."

Keiryn patted his dad on the shoulder as he headed to the door. "Love you, Dad."

"Love you too, Son."

Walking out the back door of their home, he shifted into a hawk and flew off to meet up with his friends just north of Williams.

೮೦೮೮೮೦೮೮

"It's about time you showed up," Dalen grunted in Keiryn's direction.

"What's wrong with you?" Keiryn asked.

"He's just mad because his parents told him he has to be in by ten," Eben smirked.

"Shut up, Eben," Dalen growled.

Keiryn walked over and placed his arm around Jonesy's neck. "You ready to run tonight?"

"Sure, I'll try to keep up," Jonesy shrugged.

"You doing okay, Jonesy?"

"Yeah, I'm good."

"Okay then boys, let's do this."

The brothers began to shift into wolf form, Keiryn into a large white wolf with crystal blue eyes. Eben and Dalen were both shades of gray while Jonesy's wolf form had a reddish hue. After Keiryn released a long howl, the brothers thundered off into the woods.

Keiryn took the lead, while Dalen had his left flank and Eben his right, leaving Jonesy to pull up the rear. Dalen tried forcing the pack to move faster, but Keiryn kept a steady pace in order to allow Jonesy to keep up with them. As Dalen tried to move past him, he released a low growl and snapped at his friend causing him to fall hesitantly back into place.

They ran for the next two hours before returning to Dalen's house. When they arrived, an angry Bency was waiting for them. "How could you guys?" She walked past each one, giving them the same frosty glare. "It's the last run of summer vacation and you left me out."

"It's my fault, Bency. I didn't think about what it would mean to you," Keiryn explained.

"Shut it, Falcon. I don't need your pity after the fact," she seethed, stomping around. When she stepped in front of Jonesy, she stopped and turned to him. "I expected this from them, but not from you. You know how much it sucks being left out, and yet you agreed to run without me."

Jonesy hung his head low, guilt obvious on his face. "I'm sorry, Bency. We shouldn't have left you...I shouldn't have left you."

She looked him up and down, taking pity when she realized that on the inside, he was her mirror image. As much as she hated the thought of them leaving her out, she understood it was worse for him when it happened because he was a guy and should have been able to keep up with the pack. They left her out simply because she was a girl, regardless of her freak gene.

She smiled and punched him lightly on the shoulder. "Walk me home?"

"Sure, Bency."

Wrapping her arm through his, they headed towards the woods. "Later losers," she smirked.

With Bency and Jonesy out of sight, Keiryn and his friends breathed a sigh of relief.

"Wow! For a minute, I thought she was really going to let the poor kid have it," Dalen laughed.

"Better him than us," Eben confessed.

"Easy guys, you know it has to be hard for her. What we did tonight…it wasn't right. We shouldn't have left her out," Keiryn stated, seeing a remorseful look pass between his brothers. "Look, I'm going to head out. I'll see you guys in the morning."

Shifting back into the large hawk, he began his flight home. Along the way, thoughts of Taryn's pretty face and that intense spark between them filled his head. Deciding he had enough time to fly by her house, he headed south of Williams. When he arrived, he perched himself at a perfect level to see in the many large windows.

She and her mother sat on the couch, watching a movie. Whatever it was had both mother and daughter laughing often and loudly. His heart warmed while watching her. Seeing that she was still there and happy, he decided it was time to go home and spend some time with his own father.

ಬಂಛಿಬಂಛಿ

Keiryn awoke the next morning from dreams filled with Taryn's smiling face. He sprinted out of bed, deciding to do a quick fly by her house just in case she didn't show up for school. Stepping outside, he shifted into hawk form and took flight, soaring high above the trees, anxious to see her again.

Flying overhead, he gaped as he spied Larkin jumping down from the roof. Assuming the black dog must have just came from her bedroom window, Keiryn perched himself high in a tree and watched the scene unfold. Larkin rushed into the woods with her peering out her bedroom window a few seconds later, smiling in the black wolf's direction.

It can't be, he thought to himself. Try as he might to deny it, what he had just witnessed struck him to the very core. Taryn and Larkin were dating and the dog had just snuck out of her bedroom window after spending the night with her.

Anger consumed him as he pieced it all together, the girl who had taken over his thoughts was dating his sworn enemy. All too soon his anger began to turn to fear. Fear that Larkin might do to Taryn the same thing he had done to him five years ago. He knew he couldn't let that happen. He needed time to think and formulate a game plan. With a melting pot of emotions stirring inside of him, he took to the sky and flew back home.

CHAPTER FIVE

"Good morning, Son." Exhausted, Larkin nodded at his father. "Go take your shower, breakfast will be ready in ten." Maxym took note of the dark circles under his son's eyes.

He did as his father asked. Several minutes later, he emerged freshly showered and dressed for school. "So today's the big day," Maxym smiled.

"Big day for what?"

"You'll get to hang out with Taryn. Not as a wolf, but as a man." Larkin's eyes widened and a heavy sigh passed his lips. "Did I miss something?"

"I can't go to school, Dad."

"Now, Son, you agreed that if I let you go to her house at night, you would still go to school. That was the deal and you can't renege on it now."

"No, no, no. It's not that. I can't let her get close to me."

Maxym rolled his eyes, irritated by his son's teenage angst. "I thought that's what you wanted, to get close to her?"

"You don't get it. The other night when she showed up here, she thought we had met before. I can't be near her in human form or she'll know it's been me this whole time."

"You knew you were going to have to tell her at some point. So why not today?" It was very clear his normally calm and collected son was having a panic attack. "Breathe, Son. Just breathe."

Larkin listened to the words of his father and let his voice calm him. Taking deep breaths in and slowly exhaling, he finally settled down.

Maxym gave a small sigh of relief as he watched his son overcome his internal struggle. He sat a platter of scrambled eggs and bacon on the table and took his seat, watching Larkin as he took a small scoop of the eggs and two strips of the bacon.

With his stomach still in knots, he took a couple of bites before taking his plate to the trash and scraping the leftovers inside. After rinsing the plate and putting it in the dishwasher, he grabbed his backpack that was hanging on the back of his chair.

"Thanks for breakfast. I'll be home right after school."

Watching his only child walk out the door with the weight of the world on his shoulders, Maxym dumped his own breakfast in the trash and began to clean up the mess. He hoped that Larkin's obsession with the Malone girl would be short lived. Seeing him in so much turmoil was a pain no father wanted to bear.

৪০৩৪০৩

"Mom, hurry up or you're going to make me late," Taryn yelled from downstairs, anxious yet terrified, for her first day of school.

"I'm coming. Give me a minute," Ilya replied, walking down the staircase. Looking her daughter up and down, she smiled. "Out of all of your new clothes, this is what you decide to wear?"

"Is something wrong with the way I look?" Taryn began to panic, looking down at her denim shorts, blue tank top and plaid button up shirt.

Walking over to her daughter, Ilya placed a hand on her shoulders. "I was only teasing. You look great, Taryn."

"Don't do that!" Taryn rolled her eyes before glancing toward the windows, hoping to catch a glimpse of her wolf friend to help settle the butterflies in her stomach.

"We'd better get going. And remember, if you need anything, or if anything should happen while I'm not there, you need to find Mr. Wylder."

"Yes, mother," she rolled her eyes and sighed.

Smiling, Ilya planted a kiss on her daughter's forehead as she fought the unsettling feeling in the pit of her stomach.

Taryn turned on her heel and grabbed her backpack off the kitchen island before stalking outside. Releasing a sigh of her own, her mother followed.

৪০৫৪০৫

Outside on the front steps of the school, Keiryn and his friends leaned against the railing while the other students walked around them.

"What's up with Keiryn?" Eben whispered to Dalen.

"I don't know. But if you're smart, I wouldn't ask him," he warned, arching a brow.

The rest of the friends sat quietly, not wanting to push Keiryn over whatever proverbial edge he was standing near. Soon a familiar white SUV pulled up to the curb causing him to shift uncomfortably.

৪০৫৪০৫

"Now, Sweetie, if you need anything, anything at all, just find Mr."

"Alright, I get it already!"

"I'm sorry, Taryn, but this is new for me too. I'm not very good at letting you go." Tears of happiness and dread streaked down Ilya's face.

"Stop it, Mom, before someone sees you," Taryn shrieked. "If you want me to blend in and not stand out, then you need to get yourself under control. It's not like there's any other parents crying while dropping their teenagers off at school."

"I know, Baby Girl. But this is a first for me. You'd better get out of here."

"Love you, Mom," Taryn smiled as she stepped out of the vehicle.

"I love you, my precious little girl."

Ilya sat parked at the curb until her daughter turned around and shot her a pleading look to go. When the white SUV finally pulled away, she gave a huge sigh of relief.

Turning, she stood for a moment studying the brick building before her. Large lettering above the entrance doors proclaimed it to be Williams High School, home of the Wolverines. As butterflies danced in her stomach, she began walking toward the double doors leading inside, hoping to blend in with the other students that were bustling around her.

೫೦೦೮೩೪೦೮೩

"Look who we got here. She should put you in a better mood, Lover Boy," Dalen smirked. Keiryn shot him a frigid glare. "Or maybe not," he conceded, with his hands up in surrender.

Walking towards the stairs, Taryn noticed the group of teenagers milling about, happy when she saw a familiar face. Stepping up onto the first step, she made eye contact with the boy from the diner and flashed him a brilliant smile. When he only stared back at her, his face lacking emotion of any kind, her smile began to fade.

Maybe public school wasn't such a good idea, she thought to herself.

Adjusting the strap on her backpack, she kept walking up the remaining stairs with her head held high, looking straight ahead.

Once inside, she quickly forgot about the strange behavior of the boy outside. Lockers adorned the walls along with a large bulletin board, already covered in various fliers advertising try outs and sign-ups for different clubs and groups. The hallways were teeming with students of varying ages and looks, all laughing and chatting as if they hadn't seen each other in years. Looking them over while walking towards the office, she ran straight into a large group of boys and girls.

"Hey, watch it," one of the boys hissed.

"I'm sorry," she apologized, looking up at him and his friends. Even though she'd never gone to school before, she knew from watching many television shows that these must be the popular students. The way they were dressed, and their superior attitude, made it hard not to notice.

A dark haired boy placed the back of his hand on the chest of the boy she had bumped into and pushed him away. "Please excuse my friend, he forgets his manners sometimes."

Taryn looked around and noticed the group starting to close in around her. A feeling of warmth began to run throughout her body. *Stay calm*, she repeated in her head over and over again trying to force it back down.

"I was just on my way to the office to check in. With it being my first day and all," she smiled politely at him.

"Well then we'd better let you get checked out...I mean in," he offered stepping aside, motioning for the rest of them to move out of her way as he looked her up and down.

"Thanks."

"Miss Malone, I'm so glad you made it," Gastyn greeted, shooting the group surrounding her a withered look. "Follow me. We have some things to go over before your classes begin."

"Good morning, Mr. Wylder," she sighed with relief.

"Let's step back here and we'll get you settled." He escorted her through the office and back to a small conference room. Once the door was closed behind them, he offered her some advice. "You should probably steer clear of that particular group of kids,

Taryn. They tend to stir up trouble, and that's the last thing you need if you want to blend in."

"Yeah, I guess my mom would frown upon me getting into trouble."

"That she would," he laughed in agreement. "Now let's get down to business. Your powers shouldn't be used during the school day for any reason, unless it's in my classroom and under my direction. These first few days of school, I'm going to have you read through some of the books from my personal library to get you up to speed on the Gaias history and culture."

"Gaias?"

Studying her face, he realized Ilya had done more than just keep her sheltered, she had kept the girl in total darkness. "It's what we are, Taryn. It's what you are."

"Good to know," she shrugged, trying to hide her embarrassment over not knowing such a basic bit of information.

"I don't want you to stress about it, Taryn. Your mother says you're a quick study and extremely bright. With a few extra hours of one-on-one study with me, I suspect you'll be up to speed on the need to know by the end of the week."

"There will be others in your class?"

"Yes, I have several pupils under my tutelage currently. They are a good group of kids for the most part. I believe you will blend in just fine."

৪০৪৩৪০৫৪

"The bell is about to ring. Shouldn't we head inside?" Jonesy inquired.

"Not just yet," Keiryn smirked, watching as Larkin finally pulled into the parking lot.

"Dude, you know I'm usually down with whatever you have planned. But my parents would kill me if I got into a fight on the first day of school," Dalen admitted.

"There isn't going to be a fight. I just want to make sure the black dog knows he's not as sly as he thinks he is," Keiryn declared.

Larkin and his friends headed up to the entrance of the school and noticed Keiryn and his pack eying them. "What's that about?" Gerrick nodded in Keiryn's direction.

"I don't know," Larkin shrugged. "Anyone gone running in their territory?" The group shook their head in a collective no.

"If the bird boy is looking for trouble, I have plenty," Gerrick smiled wickedly.

"Seriously, Gerrick, grow up," Nalani growled, throwing her cousin one of her famous angry glares.

Knowing there was no way he could handle being forced to stay away from Taryn eight hours a day if they were to get expelled, Larkin interjected, "It's the first day of school and we're not getting kicked out, sent home or otherwise. If Keiryn and his pack are looking for trouble, let them find it elsewhere."

Happy with Larkin's decision, Nalani stuck her tongue out at Gerrick, who in turn, shot her a mocking glare to mimic one of her own.

"All right you two," Dagney intervened. "I think he also meant no fighting amongst each other."

As Larkin and his pack passed, Keiryn stood with his arms folded in front of his chest and stared blatantly at him. Larkin stared back, giving him a wink, hoping to throw him off of whatever issue he was having.

"We need to talk," Keiryn stated coolly.

"Not today, we don't. We have an assembly to get to and it looks like the last member of your pack just arrived," Larkin smirked, nodding in the direction of the girl being dropped off at the curb.

While the rest of Keiryn's pack groaned, unhappy to see that Adalia Moore had returned for yet another year of school at Williams, he never took his eyes off of Larkin. Larkin pulled the door open and held it, making sure all of his family made it into the school without incident.

ဆလ္ဆလ္

Inside the auditorium, the students settled into their respective sections according to grade level or preference. Larkin looked towards one of the side doors, sensing Taryn's presence as she walked in. He smiled while he watched her standing to the side, looking around for an open seat. His eyes fixated on her face as she bit nervously on her lower lip, stirring more unfamiliar emotions within him.

Suddenly, a strange look passed over her face and she turned, looking straight at him. Her mouth curled up on one side, into a cautious half-smile. Needing to maintain distance between them, he nodded casually at her then turned to join Kellan and Thorne's conversation. When he sensed she was no longer looking in his direction, he turned his gaze back to watch over her once again.

Keiryn observed the exchange, while most of his friends chatted amongst themselves, finding it interesting that Larkin didn't run over to join his girlfriend.

An astute Eben chuckled as his brother glared daggers in the black dog's direction, while glancing occasionally at Taryn. "So earlier, it was all about the new girl?"

"This is between me and the dog," Keiryn growled, keeping his focus on Larkin.

ဆလ္ဆလ္

"Hey there, new girl," Douglas Scott called out, waving to Taryn from the middle section of the auditorium. She looked at him and instantly recognized the sacker from the grocery store. "I have an extra seat over here if you're interested."

~ 107 ~

Taryn sighed with relief, glad to find someone welcoming at the school. She made her way over to him. Larkin instantly tensed, causing Keiryn's attention to turn towards her. "Thanks," a grateful Taryn smiled to the familiar boy.

Both boys sat on opposing sides of the auditorium and watched as she took a seat next to Douglas. Keiryn's eyes darted constantly back and forth between Larkin and Taryn. His anger and concern regarding her relationship with the black dog, as well as his jealousy that even Douglas knew her better than he did, only intensified his brooding moodiness.

Before Taryn and Douglas could say anything more, the principal took to the stage and began his annual presentation. His words fell on deaf ears where Larkin and Keiryn were concerned. Each one remained focused solely on Taryn, neither happy that she was sitting next to Douglas. Not because he posed any threat to her, but more because they both wanted to be in the seat next to her, having her smile beaming at them.

ဢၢဢၢ

When the assembly came to an end, Taryn stood and looked at her schedule. "I can show you where your classes are," Douglas offered.

"That would be great. I haven't a clue where I'm going around here."

Larkin followed them out of the auditorium, with Keiryn slipping out behind him. He listened casually to Taryn's conversation.

"Wow, horticulture? I didn't take you for a plant loving kind of girl," Douglas smiled.

"It just goes to show you shouldn't judge a book by its cover. Thanks again for pointing me in the right direction…" she paused.

"Oh, Douglas, my name is Douglas Scott."

"Douglas Scott. I am Taryn Malone."

Douglas' smile turned awkward, and an apologetic look laced with a hint of apprehension came over his face. "Oh, I'm sorry. I didn't realize you were one of them," he sighed, nodding to Larkin and Keiryn lurking a few feet away, pretending to study the bulletin boards. "I guess this is where we part ways. Welcome to Williams."

Confused by what had just occurred, she looked toward Larkin, irritated when he intentionally looked away to avoid making eye contact with her. Turning to Keiryn she found him looking at her with more confusion than her own. Unsure of what was causing both of them to behave so strangely, she walked into her first hour period and tried to shake it off.

ಬಂಡ೩ಬಂಡ೩

"Taryn Malone?" the teacher questioned.

"Yes," she replied with a blush in her cheeks while the eyes of all the students were bearing down upon her.

"There's an empty seat next to Mr. Blake, if you wouldn't mind taking it so that we may begin."

Jonesy Blake smiled widely in her direction and pulled out a chair for her to sit in at his desk. "Hi." He pushed his thick black framed glasses back into place.

"Hello." She studied him briefly, confused by the warm feeling coursing through her as she took in his face. Though she couldn't put her finger on it, she had a lingering sense that there was something different about him.

For the next thirty minutes, the teacher read over the syllabus and informed the students that they would need to choose partners for the numerous class projects that would be taking place over the course of the school year.

When the bell rang, the room quickly emptied out while Jonesy and Taryn were still sitting in their seats. "Would you like to be partners?" he asked nervously.

~ 109 ~

"Definitely!" Taking a quick glance around the room, she introduced herself to him and hoped that he wouldn't take off like Douglas Scott had.

"I'm Jonesy Blake. Are you a sophomore or a junior?"

"Junior. What about you?" she asked as they began to walk down the hall.

"Junior," he sighed. "What's your schedule look like?"

"English, Math, Science, Horticulture and…"

"Wylder's class, right?"

She stopped abruptly in her tracks. "How did you know that?"

Seeing her concern, he quickly covered. "It was on your class schedule. I noticed it when you sat it on the desk."

"Oh right. Of course."

"Jonesy Blake," Dalen called out from down the hallway.

"Friends of yours?" she inquired, noticing that the guy that yelled for Jonesy had also been at the café the other day, as well as standing outside on the steps when she entered.

"Jonesy Blake," Dalen shouted even louder.

"Look, I'd better go. But I'll see you later, alright."

ഇൽൿഇൽൿ

"What are you thinking?" Dalen asked, giving Jonesy a slap to the back of his head. "Keiryn's already in a mood. What do you think would happen if he knew you were chatting up his girl?"

"He already knows," Keiryn interrupted. "Jonesy, you and I should talk." He pulled him into the closest empty room. "What did she say?"

"Nothing much. We just talked about her class schedule."

"Is she in Wylder's class?"

"Yes. But there's something different about her, Keiryn."

"What? Did you see something? Did she do something? Was she with Larkin?" he demanded.

~ 110 ~

Jonesy gently shook his head no and looked up at Keiryn, who was towering over him. "No, it's nothing like that. It isn't anything specific, but she's just different. I thought maybe you could back off until we know what it is."

Keiryn fumed, irritated that he didn't know anything more than he had an hour ago about the girl. Before walking out the door, he punched the wall, creating a gaping hole in his wake.

Shaking his head and sighing with his own frustration, Jonesy followed him out of the room and headed to second period, hoping that Keiryn's sour mood would pass sooner rather than later.

ഇൻൽഞ്ചഇൻൽഞ്ച

At lunch time, Taryn waited for her turn in line. She was fascinated as she watched the students around her. Each one seemed to know exactly where they fit in. It was easy to pick out the various cliques. The jocks and their popular girl following were congregated at a long table in the center of the room. A group, who were obviously the studious nerds, had a table at the back of the room where they all hovered around with their calculators and notebooks, furiously working away as they ignored their lunches. The misfits, she could only assume, as each one had a unique look about them, occupied a table close to the lunch line. Finding her eyes drawn to Larkin, she caught him staring at her, but just like earlier in the morning, he turned away when she looked in his direction. He and the group he seemed to favor sat at their own table in the far corner of the room.

Across the lunch room, Keiryn watched her and Larkin while his brothers and sisters ate and talked. As Taryn continued to look around, her eyes landed on his. Though he didn't look away, she could feel the chill exuding from him. Her eyes moved on to Jonesy, hoping for a warm welcome, but he was looking away from her, listening to a pretty girl sitting at their table.

Taking her tray, she walked over and sat at the only empty table in the cafeteria and began picking at the food on her plate.

"So does anyone know who the new girl is?" Nalani inquired, referring to Taryn.

"Nope, but she's hot," Gerrick smiled.

"I second that," Kellan echoed, high fiving his brother.

A low growl that only his pack brothers could hear escaped Larkin's throat. "Watch what you say about her."

"Whoa," Thorne laughed. "You don't like this girl, do you?" The cautionary glare that Larkin sent his way more than answered his question.

"It's about time," Kellan and Gerrick both agreed.

"I think it's sweet," Dagney giggled. "I mean, you've never so much as dated, let alone had a girlfriend. Do you want me to go say hello?"

"No, stay away from her."

Unaffected by Larkin's moody behavior, she tousled his hair while taking a seat next to him. "She is awfully pretty. Would it really be so bad to go say hello?"

Larkin looked briefly at her before turning back to watch Taryn.

"She isn't that pretty," Nalani disagreed, irritated when she noticed how Keiryn only took his eyes off the new girl to stare at Larkin. "She looks like trouble."

"You don't even know her," Dagney interjected.

"She's right, Cuz. This girl could be our best chance to balance out the ranks around here," Gerrick mused, considering the possibility that she could serve as their seventh member.

"As long as she's nothing like Ada. If not, then I say we should try to recruit her," Thorne agreed, referencing his dislike for Adalia Moore, who they often referred to as Ada.

"You're already inviting her into our pack and you don't even know what she can do, if anything at all," Nalani hissed.

Larkin's mouth began to open in retort, but he was quickly silenced by a burning sensation deep inside his chest.

⋈ദ⋈ദ

"Why are you sitting here all alone?" the mouthpiece from the group she had ran into earlier in the morning asked, taking a seat next to Taryn as his friends filled in around them.

"I'm the new girl, remember? I haven't really had the time to make friends."

"I'm James and these are my friends," he stated, waving his hand nonchalantly through the air. "I'm the quarterback here at Williams."

"How nice for you."

"Word is, you moved into the old Dolyard home south of here. That place is like a palace compared to the dumps that a lot of people around here live in."

"It's alright I suppose," Taryn shrugged, growing uncomfortable with the direction of the conversation. Even though social interaction was new to her, she had no trouble sensing that James was obviously spoiled and entitled.

As she started to stand, James reached out and ran his fingers through her hair, twirling a strand around the tip. "Don't go," he objected.

Larkin jumped to his feet, rushing towards her as Keiryn did the same.

"Don't touch her," Larkin growled.

"Leave her alone, James," Keiryn echoed.

"We were only talking," James smirked, inciting Larkin's protective instinct even further.

Keiryn's heart paused when he saw the change of color in Larkin's eyes. Knowing firsthand what followed, he quickly

~ 113 ~

intervened by snatching James up from his seat, trying to give Larkin a second to realize what was happening. "I've got this, Larkin. You need to take a walk." Larkin's nostrils flared, but in that split second, he could feel the change coming over his body and understood what Keiryn was trying to prevent. Needing some air and space to calm down, he fled out the side door of the cafeteria.

Back at Larkin's table, Kellan could not help himself. "I think we just found the answer to what's been going on with our boy," he laughed, not grasping the full extent of what was driving his brother mad.

All of the other football players stood, ready to come to James' defense, but quickly sat back down again when both Larkin and Keiryn's pack joined them, surrounding the table.

"Is there a problem here?" Gastyn thundered throughout the lunchroom.

Keiryn released his hold on James.

"Miss Malone, are you alright?" Gastyn asked.

"Yes, I'm fine. Although I never realized that cavemen still existed," she fumed, blushing with embarrassment.

A smirk formed across Nalani's exotic face, happy to hear the new girl didn't appreciate a knight in shining armor.

"Does she sound like anyone we know?" Dagney smiled to her sister, who rolled her eyes with irritation.

Taryn excused herself and headed out the same door Larkin had, trailing in his direction, but it was no use. He was long gone, leaving her with more questions than answers to his strange behavior.

"Taryn," Gastyn called to her.

"Yes?"

"I wanted to check on you and make certain you were okay."

"Outside of being utterly humiliated, I'm fine." Pursing her lips together, she looked at him with worry flooding her eyes.

"I think it's best if you don't mention what happened during lunch today to your mother," he suggested. "Would you walk with me to class?"

"Sure, Mr. Wylder."

He studied her as they walked, taking the long way to his classroom. "The two boys in the cafeteria, did you know them?"

"I met Larkin Taylor the other day, for like a second. I saw the other boy at the café in town a couple of days ago. So no, I don't really know either of them."

Stopping in the hallway, Gastyn turned to face her. "I want to ask you a question, and I want you to be one hundred percent honest with me. Can you do that?"

"If I am to be honest with you, then I can only promise maybe."

"You're mother has taught you well to protect your secrets. Did she ever tell you who taught her?" Genuine curiosity rang in his voice.

Feelings of disappointment stirred deep inside her, realizing her mother had only told her of experiences but never of a person by detail or name. "No."

As much as Gastyn wanted to tell her of Ilya's time in his classroom, to use as a common ground, he thought better of it after recalling how she had questioned what a Gaias was. "We'll leave that discussion for another day. But what I am curious about is if you felt anything throughout the day, when you passed people in the hall or were in class."

She was thoughtful for a moment, thinking back on the morning. "There was this one guy, Jonesy Blake, from my horticulture class. There was something about him."

"Have you ever experienced anything like that before? Perhaps when we met," he inquired, intrigued that she could detect something within Jonesy, the weakest out of the two packs he currently taught.

Looking as though she was recalling specific moments from memory, she finally turned to him. "Nope, only Jonesy."

"Fair enough."

The two began walking and soon were standing outside the threshold of his classroom door. "Are you ready to meet others who are like you?"

Taryn swallowed hard, fearful of what she might find on the other side of the door, and more, who she would find. "No time better than the present."

Gastyn opened the door and stepped aside to let her take it all in. The room she had expected to be so very different looked exactly like the other four classrooms she had already been in earlier in the day, but this time she noticed some familiar faces looking back at her. Larkin and his group of friends, along with the boy from the diner and his friends, including Jonesy Blake, all turned their eyes towards her. A girl whom she hadn't noticed before with white blonde hair, shot a scowl in her direction leaving her to wonder if she had managed to offend her somehow without even knowing. A young boy with sandy blonde hair and bright green eyes, who looked barely in his teens, gave her an angelic smile. Feeling like all eyes were locked on her, gauging her every move, she stepped further into the room.

"Everyone, please take a seat," Gastyn directed. Larkin's group sat on the left side of the classroom while the diner group took the right, including the white-blonde haired girl. The young boy joined Larkin's group, though he looked unsure if he should be sitting there. It was clear in Taryn's mind that there was a definite division among the two sides. After a few moments of indecision, she took her seat.

Smiling curiously at Taryn, Gastyn asked, "Miss Malone, could you please tell me why you chose to sit on the floor when there are plenty of empty chairs?"

"Well, it's clear from what I have seen today, as well as when we walked into the room...there are two very distinct groups here. For me to sit in any of the seats on the two rows to my left or to my right might be interpreted as choosing sides. I belong to neither."

He studied her carefully, as did the other students in the room. Amazed at her perception, he smiled and turned to the rest of the students. "Class as you can all see, we have a new student. Please welcome Taryn Malone." Gastyn called out each student's name for introduction. Each one acknowledged her with a nod or politely curious smiles, with the exception of Adalia Moore, who continued to shoot glaring daggers in her direction.

"Now that the introductions are out of the way I would like to have everyone, with the exception of Andyn and Taryn, go into the back room and wait for me."

"Looks like you have some reading to do before playing with the grownups," Adalia smirked as she walked past Taryn.

"Move it, Ada. You're holding everyone up," Gerrick growled.

"Shut up."

"Don't pay her any mind. She's petty and hateful most of the time," Dagney smiled, placing her hand gently on Taryn's shoulder.

Once everyone else had cleared the room, Gastyn gave Andyn and Taryn their first assignments, consisting of reading from his personal library, before he left them to join the others in the back room.

Taryn's book was as basic as a book could be, but she didn't mind since she apparently knew nothing about her people or their culture.

"So, you're new to Arizona?" Andyn inquired.

"Yep. It hasn't even been a week yet," Taryn replied, taking in the boy's sweet smile, shaggy blonde hair and green eyes. "How old are you, Andyn?"

"Twelve years and three months."

"So how is it that you're in a high school taking classes?"

Looking at her like she was crazy, he laughed. "Where did you live before Arizona, at the bottom of an ocean?"

Taryn leaned back in her seat and laughed at the irony, knowing that there probably wasn't much difference between the bottom of the ocean and how she and her mother used to live back in Galatia.

"What book are you reading?" Not seeing an actual title on the book, she held it up instead for him to see. "That book is like Gaias for Dummies," he chuckled. Taryn blushed with embarrassment, placing the book flat on the table. Sensing that he had offended her, he quickly tried to lessen the sting. "Not that you're a dummy or anything. I was just messing with you. Mr. Wylder used his Influential powers to convince the teachers and principals that I am better suited here in his class for the gifted instead of a regular classroom."

Taryn pondered his words, 'class for the gifted'. Desire to know more surged inside of her, but before she could ask any questions, Gastyn walked back into the room.

"How's the reading coming along?"

"Fine, Mr. Wylder," Andyn assured, answering for them both.

He smiled at the blonde haired boy with fondness. "Andyn, it's time for you to go in and find Kellan. He's going to work with you for a little while."

The boy's face lit up with enthusiasm. "I'll see you later, Taryn," he called out, heading for the door.

Once alone, Gastyn sat down beside her, deciding it would be best to offer some insight on the two groups. "You know, they used to be a single unit, running and learning together since most of them were seven years old. It's customary when a young Gaias moves to the area that they will generally become part of a pack. With our current situation being what it is, it will be up to you to decide which pack you want to belong to."

"So I'm supposed to choose a side?"

"Essentially yes, you would pick one or the other. But there's always the possibility that you won't be accepted by either. Adalia is a testament to that."

"That explains a lot," she mumbled under her breath. For a moment she sat quietly, thinking about having to make a choice. Surely there were other alternatives. "Mr. Wylder, what if I don't want to choose a side?"

Surprised by the question, his forehead wrinkled as he pursed his lips. "Well I suppose it's possible for a Gaias to remain a single unit, or to begin their own pack. But I must tell you, Taryn, there's a certain amount of loyalty and safety that comes from belonging."

"I understand. Is my mother part of a pack?"

Taking his time to formulate an answer that she could understand, he chose his words carefully. "Yes. However, when a Gaias enters their thirties their need to run with a pack lessens. The pack loyalty and bond remains unchanged, but it is not essential for them to stay in close proximity as they grow older and start their own families. Haven't you ever noticed the tattoo on her right shoulder?"

"Yes, but she would never tell me what it meant."

"The tattoo appears somewhere between the ages of eighteen and twenty-two, when an individual becomes a true member of a legitimate pack. The tattoo is symbolic and anyone who bears the same mark is bonded together for life."

"Thank you for being honest. It seems my mother has kept a lot from me."

Changing gears, Gastyn turned his focus back to her studies. "I need for you to get through as much of this book as you can before the end of the school day. Once everyone has gone we will go over any questions you might have."

He left her to her reading and joined the students in the other room. Taryn flipped through page after page of the book that he had provided her. As she read about the history of the Gaias, she eagerly consumed the information, absorbing every word, needing to know everything she could about who she truly was. She could feel a burn in her abdomen, brought on by irritation that her mother had kept all of this from her. It was clear that the other students in the class had been raised with this knowledge. Anger simmered just below the surface as she thought about how her life could have been different if she had been given this information before. Knowing she had to keep the anger in check, she took a breath and pushed it deep inside herself. The anger could wait for later when she was safely at home, not in a school full of unsuspecting students.

“ㄗㄷ”

A few hours later the final bell rang, signaling the end of the school day. The door leading to the back room opened and the students began to trickle out a few at a time, until Gastyn followed them. Seeing Taryn seated at his desk, he walked over and stood behind her.

Kellan emerged carrying a smiling Andyn on his back. Stopping near Gastyn's desk, Andyn slid off before looking up at him mischievously. "Go on, Little Dude," Kellan prompted before taking a step back, as if he were waiting for something spectacular.

"Taryn," Andyn said, looking up cautiously at Gastyn then back to her.

"Yes, Andyn?"

"This is for you." He took a pencil from his back pants pocket and handed it to her.

She took the pencil and looked it over thoughtfully. "It's a pencil. Thanks."

Nervously, he glanced back to Kellan. "Go on, Dude. You can do it," he encouraged him.

Turning back to her and the pencil she was still holding, he lifted his hand and focused. His eyebrows squeezed together in concentration. With a flick of his wrist, the yellow number two pencil turned into a miniature prickly cactus.

"Ouch!" She winced as its many sharp points pierced her flesh. Dropping the plant, she looked up and could see the horror on young Andyn's face. Knowing a cactus is not what he had intended to turn the pencil into, she started to speak, but he turned on his heel and fled the classroom in embarrassment before she could get a word out.

Barely able to contain his laughter, Kellan approached. "Sorry about that. The kid was trying to give you a desert flower…not a cactus," he assured her before walking out the door and bursting into uncontrollable laughter with Gerrick and Thorne by his side.

"Are you alright, Taryn?" Gastyn asked, taking her hand into his own in order to remove the needles he had seen sticking out only moments ago. Much to his surprise, they were no longer protruding from her skin or visible in anyway.

"Yeah, I'm fine. But this little plant needs a home."

"It looks like you have another admirer," Jonesy joked before carefully picking up the cactus, also noticing the thorns were absent from her hand. "If you would like, I could put it in a pot for you. I'll bring it back tomorrow."

"Thanks. That would be great, Jonesy."

For a moment, the two shared a gaze, before Larkin interrupted. "Hey, Mr. Wylder, would it be okay if I checked out a book?"

"See you tomorrow, Taryn," Jonesy smiled shyly before leaving.

She watched him walk out the door with a wide smile upon her face, as an annoyed Larkin looked on, wondering if she was interested in the runt.

"What book, Larkin?" Gastyn inquired, pulling him from his stare.

"I'm not sure...I was hoping to take a look around if you don't mind."

"I suppose that would be okay. Just please bring it back tomorrow."

"Thanks, Mr. Wylder."

While looking through Gastyn's private library, he watched them disappear into the back room together. Once they were out of sight, he began his search for a book referencing Healers and anomalies within the Gaias history.

ഇരുഗ്രഇരുഗ്ര

Walking into the room, Taryn gasped in awe the moment they stepped through the doorway. Her feet adhered to the floor as she stood, stunned at the unbelievable sight. The ceiling was at least five hundred feet high and the vast room appeared to go on forever as she looked towards the opposing end, not seeing a wall. "How is this even possible?"

"This is my actual teaching classroom. The other one is just for show. There's a lot you will need to learn about our world, Taryn, in order for you to blend in with the other students. But for now, you should take a look around so that the next time you walk in, you don't appear so surprised by this room's existence."

"What exactly do you teach in here? I mean, I can see the variety of stations, but what is it that you teach?"

"That depends on the Gaias and their particular gifts or talents, or what would be beneficial to their pack. But for now, I think we should start with the basic questions. Such as, did you know that when a Gaias is born they haven't any powers?"

"I read that in the book you gave me. It stated that Gaias-born are completely powerless until their sixth birthday when they receive their first and strongest gift. They are supposed to work to master the basics until their twelfth birthday when their second gift is received. The second gift usually reveals whether that particular Gaias will have a latent ability that may not be as strong as their original power. The full strength of our powers are gained on our eighteenth birthday."

"Very good," he acknowledged, leading her back towards the exit.

"Our names contain the letter Y. This letter signifies the two different pathways that we must choose from."

Gastyn studied the tense look in her eyes. "Yes, but with the two pathways, you will find that neither is right and neither is wrong."

With a shrug, she moved the conversation to a new path. "Was Malone always my mother's last name?" she inquired, hoping that he would be able to shed light on a subject her mother refused to discuss.

Realizing that she had questions that went far deeper than just being Gaias, Gastyn shifted the direction of their conversation back to school. "I remember when your mother walked into my classroom for the first time. She was a shy little girl who was so unsure of her powers and what to do with them."

Caught off guard by his disclosure, her mind quickly changed course. "You taught my mother? How is that even possible? You're like the same age, right?"

"I am one hundred and fifty-one years old. And with any luck, I will have a few hundred more years ahead of me." He paused in an attempt to get a read on her, wanting to be certain she wasn't overwhelmed with all of the information she had gained.

Completely stunned, as she had believed him to be in his thirties, her mouth hung open in awe. "So we never grow old and we never die?"

"No, Taryn. The typical lifespan of a Gaias-born is around four to five hundred years, give or take a few decades. Gaias age as a normal human until their eighteenth birthday. Once they inherit their full powers the aging process slows down considerably. Your mother is in her sixties." Watching her face closely, he noticed the lack of change in her expression. There was no sign of emotion or surprise. "What is it, Taryn?"

"Mr. Wylder, if you don't mind...I'd like to go home now." Inside her stomach churned with anger and frustration in the knowledge that her mother had kept such important information from her.

"Of course. I'll call your mother and let her know," he agreed, heading for the exit. "Aren't you coming?"

She stood rooted to her spot as she continued the internal struggle she was currently having. "I'll be there in a minute," she replied, forcing her emotions into their cage. Taking a few deep cleansing breaths, she settled herself and walked out the door back into the regular classroom, stopping short when she found Larkin still there. She gazed at him, feeling something stirring inside, but the second she caught his eye he turned away, making it obvious to her that even when he wasn't in the presence of his friends, he still did not want to talk to her. "Why would I expect anything different," she muttered, shaking her head as she walked out the door. Taking a seat on the concrete steps in front of the school, she waited for her mother.

When the door behind her opened, she glanced back and watched as Larkin and Gastyn exited. They stood behind her, talking about sports and Larkin's jeep.

Several minutes passed before Ilya pulled into the parking lot. Standing, she grabbed her backpack and started to move forward.

"Taryn, if you don't mind...I'd like a word with your mother," Gastyn insisted.

"Sure, go ahead."

"Larkin, please keep Miss Malone company while I speak to Ilya," Gastyn directed, hurrying down the stairs and over to the driver's side of the SUV.

Taryn sighed loudly, annoyed that they were discussing her. Larkin watched as she looked off in the distance, happy to have this chance to study her while she wasn't paying attention. His heart was torn by the lie he was currently stuck in. He hoped he would be able to tell her soon. The secret was killing him but he was too afraid of how she would react once she knew the truth.

ಐಧ಼ಐಧ಼

"Ilya," Gastyn greeted her.

"Is everything okay?" Glancing in Taryn's direction, she could see her daughter's unsettled behavior.

"Yes, but I suspect that she is feeling a little overwhelmed. I explained our life span to her. She seemed fine initially, but then asked to go home. I believe it's the culmination of things from today. Her starting school for the first time, discovering there are so many others like her, and of course the shock that she could potentially live to be five hundred years old. It is a lot to take in, but she did fine."

A sigh of relief escaped her lips as she sent him a weighted smile. "Thank you, Gastyn. I can't even begin to tell you how grateful I am that you are with her, teaching my little girl."

"It's my pleasure. If you ever need anything, I am just a phone call away." He gave her hand a gentle squeeze before nodding to Taryn.

She stepped down from where she stood, heading to the SUV while Larkin looked on longingly. Gastyn walked around and opened the car door for her, shutting it after she slid in. She gave Larkin one final glance before thanking her teacher. For a brief moment their eyes locked, surprising her that he didn't immediately look away. A sense of familiarity washed over her. There was something about him, but she remained unable to put her finger on just what it was that made him seem so familiar. As he disappeared from sight, she leaned back in the seat and closed her eyes, playing back the events of the day in her mind.

⅏⋙⋘⋙⋘

"So how was your first day of school?" Ilya asked, happy to have her daughter back with her safe and sound.

"Fine." She stared out the window, arms crossed in a defensive stance.

"How were your classes?"

"Fine."

~ 126 ~

"It was your first day of school and all you have to say about it is fine?" Ilya tried to joke.

"It was fine." Not wanting to discuss anything with her mother at the present time, she reached over to the radio dial and found a station playing a song she liked. She turned it up, effectively ending the conversation.

Ilya looked towards her daughter. The stony look on her face made it clear that she was in no mood to talk. Not wanting to push her over whatever edge she was teetering on, she decided it was best to back off and wait for her to open up on her own.

The second they arrived at their home, Taryn ran inside and changed from her simple sandals into her hiking boots. After grabbing a bottle of water, she hurried out the French doors at the rear of the house and disappeared quickly into the woods.

Far away from home, in the sanctuary of a cluster of Aspen trees, she sat and fell back gently, allowing the lush vegetation to catch her. She enjoyed the solitude as she laid there, catching her breath and working through the many frustrations she had endured throughout the day. The important information her mother had withheld from her, the boys thinking they needed to come to her rescue in the lunch room, the way Douglas had become aloof after hearing her name. But what had grated on her the most was the way Larkin and Keiryn had responded to her.

Sensing something familiar, she raised her hand and waved to the large black wolf. "I hope your day has gone better than mine."

Knowing that her first day of school had probably been less than ideal, Larkin laid down beside her in an attempt to comfort her. He positioned himself carefully, so that when she turned her head to talk to him, he could see her lovely face and captivating eyes.

"I don't know how old you are but then again, I'm not even sure if I'm really sixteen at this point," she babbled. "Well it doesn't matter. If there's a school for wolves, let me be the first to tell you to run in the opposite direction." She paused to scratch his ears. "Today was quite the disappointment all the way around. First the sacker from the grocery store was really nice, but as soon as he learned my name his attitude completely changed. I mean, I don't think Taryn is a bad name. Certainly not terrible enough to turn someone off like that. What do you think?"

Larkin nuzzled her hand with his snout, making her smile.

"See, that's what I thought. You seem to like it. As if that wasn't bad enough, I find out that my mother conveniently forgot to mention to me that I'm a Gaias, and that we could potentially live for hundreds of years. I'm so mad at her right now, so much so that I'm not positive that I can keep my emotions in check while in her company. So here we are. I headed out here immediately after we got home. I just need a little distance to sort some of this stuff out."

Looking over to the black wolf, she extended her arm to scratch him. He basked in the heavenly sensation of her gentle touch. When she withdrew her arm she went back to staring up through the branches of the trees into the sky.

"Why can't boys be more like you?" she asked with an affectionate glance. "There's this guy I met…more like ran into at the café the other day. It was so weird. He seemed so polite and nice the first time I saw him, but then today he acted like I had upset him somehow."

Larkin released a low growl, annoyed that she was bothered by Keiryn's chilly reception.

"If you think he's bad, just wait until I tell you about the other guy, Larkin Taylor." His ears perked up at the sound of his name but he braced himself for what was surely coming. "The other day he saved me from the lightning and acted concerned, like he was really worried about me. Then today, it was so weird, I kept catching him looking at me, but he didn't say a word and went to great lengths to look away." Looking to the big black wolf, she sighed. "There's something about him…it's more than his stunning good looks, or how his hair parts off to one side as he runs his hand through it," she admitted in a dreamy voice. He warmed on the inside, noticing the smile that had formed on her face as she talked about him. "I know this is going to sound crazy, but if there were a thousand people in a room, I could pick him out instantly. I can feel him. There's something familiar, something that draws me to him."

Her smile turned upside down as she thought back to lunch. "Of course I can't forget about the embarrassing lunch I had. Some jerk was being pushy and apparently both Larkin and Keiryn thought I needed them to step in. Their brutish antics had every eye in the cafeteria pointed in my direction. It was so humiliating."

Taryn shook her head for a moment, pushing out all of the nonsense of the day and moving on to someone she found more interesting. "The day wasn't a total loss. I met a really nice guy who even spoke to me. His name is Jonesy Blake. He might not be as good looking as the two cavemen, but wow, when I sat down next to him during class, I could feel something pulsing off of him. It was really cool to find out that he is like me."

Larkin's snout now rested in the dirt as he snorted, vexed that she had referred to him as a caveman in the same breath that she had inferred that she found Keiryn good looking. The thought that she seemed into Jonesy Blake, of all people, sat most uncomfortably in his stomach.

For the next half hour, the two of them lay quietly beneath the trees. When the sun started to set, Taryn sat up, knowing it was time to return home to face her mother. The wolf followed her as she meandered through the woods, stopping just when her house became visible through the trees.

"Well, Big Guy, thanks for listening. Unfortunately it's time for me to go inside," she yawned, exhausted by her first day of school and all the drama that had come with it.

While Larkin watched her walk inside the safety of her home, Keiryn sat perched high above in the trees, taking in the scene. He began to consider that what he thought he saw that morning wasn't what it had seemed. Maybe he had been too quick to assume that Taryn and Larkin were seeing one another. Deciding it would be best not to make another assumption, he took flight, heading in the direction of home, leaving the black wolf to run through the forest below.

CHAPTER SIX

When Larkin burst through the tree line near his home, he saw his pack sitting on the back deck waiting for him. He released a heavy sigh, knowing exactly why they were there.

"So, all this moodiness was over a girl. Why didn't you just tell us?" Kellan laughed.

"Yeah, after the way you crashed and burned today at school with her...it looks like you could have benefited from some pointers. You know, from some of us who have actually talked to a girl that wasn't one of our sisters," Gerrick teased.

Larkin looked at him and rolled his eyes, willing to accept the badgering if it meant keeping the truth hidden from them in order to protect her secrets.

"When have you ever spoken to a girl, Cuz?" Nalani countered, slapping Gerrick on the back of the head.

Dagney took a seat next to Larkin and leaned into her brother. "Have you talked to her about becoming part of our pack?"

"No."

She studied the distant look in his eyes. "Have you even talked to her?" Shaking his head gently, he answered no. "Why not? It's obvious you like her."

"It's complicated, Dags. Just don't say anything...please."

"My lips are sealed," she replied, kissing him on the cheek.

For the next hour, he spent time with his friends. Once his pack family had left, he headed inside to see his father.

"How was your day?" Maxym asked as he stirred the spaghetti sauce that was simmering on the stove. Larkin filled him in on the events of the day, including the conversation Taryn had with her friend the black wolf.

"Son, you need to tell her what you are."

"I can't just blurt out, hey Taryn, I'm the wolf that you've been hanging out with in the forest. She knows practically nothing about being a Gaias. In fact, she didn't even know she was a Gaias before today," Larkin argued, getting a perplexed look on his face. Taking a moment to think things through, he looked as his father. "Dad, why do you think her mom didn't tell her that she was Gaias?"

Maxym saw the worry and confusion in his son's eyes and wished he had the answers that would help him in handling this unique situation. "I wish I knew, Larkin. Truth is…I haven't any idea why Ilya would keep that girl in the dark. It doesn't make any sense to me. It just makes her far more vulnerable to the darker side of being a Gaias when she doesn't have any knowledge to go by." He glanced over to the photo of his late wife, Lesryn.

"Taryn would never turn to the dark side."

Maxym smiled at his son, knowing he would defend her no matter what. "So while we are on the subject of Taryn and school, what's this thing that happened at lunch today?"

"Gastyn called you, didn't he?"

"Yes, but he wasn't the only one. Teigan Falcon also made a point to call me today."

"Great. What, did Bird Boy run home and tell his daddy?"

"Something about your eyes when you intervened between Taryn and James Riley at lunch today." Maxym studied his son's face, taking note that he was no longer smiling. "I guess I have my answer."

"Yes, but this time was different."

"Different how?"

He was quiet for a moment, trying to find the best way to explain. "I could feel it. I could feel the change coming, and I was able to stop it before that part of me took control."

"Keiryn had a different story. He told his dad that he had to step between you and James and make you take a walk."

"So what? Nothing happened."

"And I'm grateful it didn't, Son. What if Keiryn hadn't been there to intervene? What then?"

Larkin ran his fingers through his hair in frustration. "I don't know, Dad. I just know it was different this time. I can't explain it."

"Alright," Maxym paused. "One good thing did come of this."

Looking at his dad with confusion, Larkin asked "And what would that be?"

"You and Keiryn worked together to keep that girl safe, just like old times," Maxym smiled at the scowl that formed on his son's face. "Like it or not, Larkin, the two of you have always made a good team. Maybe one day, you'll find your way back to each other."

He rolled his eyes. "Don't hold your breath," he stated as he stalked out of the kitchen and up to his room.

ಬಿಛಿಬಿಛಿ

"I called Maxym and spoke with him about your concerns, Keiryn. He was extremely thankful that you diverted what could have ended in disaster," Teigan informed his son.

"So is Mr. Taylor going to tell him to stay away from her?"

"No, Son, he's not," he sighed as he watched his already tense expression tighten. "I know it's not what you want to hear. But he

~ 133 ~

said Larkin is drawn to this girl. He didn't go into a lot of detail, but he said Larkin has very strong feelings for her."

"How can he be okay with this? He knows what he is capable of, what he really is. What about the damage he could do to her if he ever loses control."

"Now calm down, Son. I think you might be overreacting just a bit. He's never hurt anyone outside of the incident between the two of you. What he did to you, it wasn't intentional."

Keiryn laced his fingers together behind his neck. "That's exactly my point! What happens when he loses control and Taryn is standing too close? She doesn't know enough about us to even know she has something to be worried about. Am I just supposed to stand by and wait for it to happen, wait for him to tear her apart?"

"I'm not trying to trivialize what you experienced. But you have to understand, you can't protect everyone all of the time. And if Taryn wants to be friends, or more with Larkin, you're going to have to find a way to accept it, end of story."

His father's words settled deep within him. With annoyed acceptance he decided to let the conversation drop until he had a chance to confirm his suspicion's regarding the status of Taryn and Larkin's relationship.

ೞೞೞೞ

Shortly after eleven p.m. Keiryn flew out his bedroom window and headed towards Taryn's house to take a look around. Perching himself up high and out of sight, he patiently waited, hoping to see if his suspicions were right. Watching her and her mother go to bed, one-by-one, he kept a constant vigil as the lights in the house went dark. Twenty minutes later he saw a familiar face creeping up to the house. With his eyes glued on the scene below, he watched as Larkin shifted into human form and leapt on top of the roof before making himself comfortable on the side of her bedroom window after staring inside for several minutes.

Keiryn woke from his restless slumber, still in hawk form and perched high in the trees. His eyes were immediately drawn to Larkin as he peered inside Taryn's bedroom window again. With the sun starting to break through the dark of night, Larkin jumped off of the roof and rushed into the woods before shifting back into wolf form.

A few minutes later Taryn's bedroom light turned on. Keiryn watched her come to the window and open it, peering out as if in search of something. Her eyes landed on the large black wolf standing in the tree line. A huge grin broke over her face as she waved to him before closing the window and starting her morning routine. Irritation was a sour taste in his mouth when he realized the wolf was exactly who she had been searching for.

His mind started to wrap around a new thought. After mulling it over for several minutes, he smiled internally. It had just become readily apparent that she had no idea Larkin and the wolf were one and the same, or that Larkin had been spending his nights outside her bedroom window. The newfound knowledge caused a flutter of excitement inside his chest. Maybe there was a way to keep the black dog away from her after all. Before he could put his plan into action, he wanted to be certain that he was a hundred percent correct in his new theory.

With a new sense of purpose he took flight, heading for home.

"Are you ready for day two of school?" Ilya inquired, watching Taryn eat her breakfast.

"Sure." She glanced at her mother, flashing a forced smile.

"If you need anything…"

"I know, I know…find Gastyn."

Ilya could feel the bite in her daughter's words. "Do you want to talk about it?"

"I'm sorry, Mom. I should not have snapped at you. If you don't mind, I'd like to get to school a little earlier today."

"Sure, Sweetie, let's get going."

ഇരുള

In the school parking lot, Keiryn and his pack were gathered around the back of his truck. Bentley, Hadley and Bency were perched on the lowered tailgate while Dalen, Eben and Jonesy sat on the sides of the bed. Keiryn leaned against the fender of the blue truck.

"So what do you guys think about the new girl?" Bency inquired.

"She's cute," Dalen yawned, still tired from staying up too late playing video games the night before.

"That's not what I meant. What I'm asking is do you think we should ask her to join our pack," she explained.

"I don't think we should be so quick to invite her," Eben warned. "We don't even know what type of powers she possesses. And the last thing we need is dead weight."

"If we don't court her, then the Larkin and his pack will," Hadley countered.

"Besides, she has an interesting sense of style," Bentley acknowledged.

"Who cares about how she dresses," Dalen mumbled. "Lover boy already has his eyes on her. So I say we do what we can to get her to choose us over them."

Keiryn listened as everyone had their say. Turning to Jonesy he waited to see what his response would be, but instead of joining in on the conversation, Jonesy rolled his eyes in annoyance. "What is it, Jonesy?"

"Nothing."

"If you have something to say, let's hear it," Dalen pushed.

"Why does she have to be part of some macho competition?"

Eben leaned over, placing Jonesy in a head lock, rubbing his knuckles roughly against the top of his head. "I think our little bookworm might be sweet on this girl."

"Shut up, Eben," Jonesy growled, pushing him off. "I'm only saying that she seemed really nice. There's no reason to put her in the middle of our drama."

"The girl is fair game," Dalen snarled. "If we want the strength of numbers to stay with us, then we need her. Otherwise we'll be even with the black dog and his cronies."

Keiryn watched as the white SUV turned into the school parking lot. Catching a glimpse of Taryn was all he needed to focus himself. "Jonesy's right. Be friendly to her but don't pursue her. I have a feeling after I get done, she'll choose us with little to no encouragement."

"What makes you so sure, Lover Boy?" Dalen asked.

"Let's just call it a hunch," he replied, flashing a mischievous smile over his shoulder while watching her enter the school doors.

ജഇജഇ

A few minutes later, Larkin and his pack arrived in a three-car caravan. He parked just a few stalls away from Keiryn and his crew. As they passed, he couldn't help but notice the smirk on the bird boy's face. Being more concerned with Taryn he shrugged it off and headed straight to the office.

Once inside the school he broke away from the pack and went to find the school's guidance counselor, Ms. Cahill. "Good morning. You're looking quite lovely today," Larkin buttered her up.

Looking across her cluttered desk and over her bright red framed glasses, she smiled. "What can I do for you, Mr. Taylor?"

"I was hoping to get into the first hour horticulture class."

~ 137 ~

Looking at his class schedule on the computer, she laughed. "You want to drop weight lifting to transfer to horticulture?"

Arching his brows he flashed her one of his killer smiles, dripping with all of his charm and charisma. "So can you help me out?"

Just outside her door, Keiryn lingered, listening to his request and devising his own plan to be near Taryn. Before Larkin walked out of Ms. Cahill's office, he moved to make it appear that he had been standing at the front desk counter, talking with the secretary.

When Larkin was out of sight, he knocked on the counselor's door and requested a transfer of his own. Much to his disappointment, he received the same answer as the black dog. He made a mental note to check in with her first thing in the morning before school.

೫൬೫൬

Taking her seat next to Jonesy, Taryn settled in comfortably. "Good morning," she smiled.

"Hello." After smiling at her momentarily, he reached for his backpack. "I have something for you." Carefully he removed a small pot with a plant wrapped in a towel. She took the pot from him and looked at him curiously. "It's the cactus from yesterday. I hope you don't mind the color blue. It's the only extra pot I could find in my aunt's shed."

She removed the towel to find the prickly cactus thriving in its new home. "Thanks, Jonesy, that was really thoughtful of you."

Pushing his glasses back onto his face, he gazed at her, glad that someone else in Gastyn's class might actually share his appreciation for gardening.

೫൬೫൬

Once the bell rang, the pair started walking towards their lockers. Larkin lurked in the background while Keiryn took full

~ 138 ~

advantage, surmising that his enemy didn't want to get close to Taryn in fear of her finding out his other identity.

"Hey, Jonesy. Hey, Taryn," he smiled, draping an arm over each one's shoulder. "So how do you like, Williams?"

"Its fine," she replied blankly, shrugging his arm off of her. "I'll see you later, Jonesy." She walked ahead, leaving Keiryn with his jaw hanging open.

"Wow. So, that's what it looks like when Lover Boy gets shot down," Dalen laughed.

"Even the bookworm got more love than you," Eben teased a baffled Keiryn.

Larkin used the momentary distraction to slip past them, trailing after her. Standing at her locker, Taryn noticed him only a few doors away, watching her. She ignored him and went about her business. Carefully she placed the cactus in the locker while trading out books. When she closed the door, she made eye contact with him before he immediately looked away.

Rolling her eyes, she sighed with disappointment, confused at his continuing odd behavior. She walked past him, quite certain that he would follow. Intentionally walking past the door to her second hour English class, she headed out one of the side doors and stepped to the side, waiting for him to follow.

Almost on cue, he exited the door, searching for her.

"Are you looking for someone?" She asked, stepping up behind him.

He swallowed hard, afraid to turn around and look her in the eye. "No, I just needed some fresh air."

"Some fresh air, huh?" she smirked. "I didn't get to thank you properly for saving me the other night. So let me thank you now."

"It was no big deal."

"Now that I've thanked you, I guess you won't have any reason to follow me around anymore," she stated sternly.

"But I wasn't…"

"This might be the first time I've attended a public school, but don't treat me as if I'm stupid. I don't know what's wrong with the guys around here, but I don't have time for your games." Grabbing the door handle, she looked over her shoulder in his direction one last time. "And just so we're clear…that little stunt you and Keiryn pulled yesterday in the cafeteria, it better have been a one-time only performance."

"I was only trying to look out for you."

"I assure you that I can handle myself."

"Of course, that is until there's lightning in the sky," he mumbled once he knew she had gone back inside.

ഇരുഇരു

Lunch time rolled around and everyone sat at their respective tables. Larkin and Keiryn both watched over Taryn, despite her many objections.

"What do you guys see in her?" Adalia grumbled.

"Simple, Ada. She's not you," Bency retorted, unhappy that Ada had decided to ingratiate herself with them again.

Adalia shot her a heated glare. "Shut up, Freak."

"Watch who you're calling a freak, Ada," Keiryn growled. "Bency belongs here, while you're only a guest at our table."

"An unwanted one at that," Dalen clarified.

ഇരുഇരു

On the other side of the room, Larkin's group commented on Taryn. "Look at her sitting there all alone. It makes me feel bad," Dagney exhaled.

"Why don't you go over and talk to the girl, Larkin? It's obvious you are sweet on her," Kellan prompted.

~ 140 ~

Larkin looked at his friend and sighed. "Dagney, Nalani, would you go sit with her?"

"Hell no. I'm not going over there," Nalani sneered.

"Oh come on Nalani. It's your chance to get a better look at the competition," Gerrick whispered.

Frowning at her cousin, she knew he was right. Not only was Larkin consumed by this new girl but so was Keiryn Falcon, the one guy she'd had a crush on since she was eleven. With the division of the group into two packs, it would be unforgivable if she pursued him. But never one to give up a potential advantage, she saw the upside to befriending Taryn.

"Fine. Let's do this," she sighed. "Dagney, you take the lead."

The two girls rose from their seats and casually walked over to her table. "Do you mind?" Dagney asked, lifting her tray.

"Sure," Taryn answered, glancing over to Larkin.

Dagney noticed the look she threw in her brother's direction. "This is Nalani and I'm Dagney."

"Yeah, I caught that yesterday during the class intro."

"Of course you did," Dagney smiled uncomfortably. "So how do you like Williams, Taryn?"

"I haven't seen much of it, but so far it's okay." Glancing between the two girls, she noted their discomfort. "Look, if Larkin sent you over here to keep an eye on me…I can take care of myself."

Nalani laughed at how blunt the new girl was. "Where are you from, Taryn?"

She paused for a moment to study the pretty girl. Her face was simply stunning to look at and her eyes were a brilliant crystal blue. Taryn imagined that they must resemble the waters of the bluest ocean. "Kansas," she finally replied. Nalani scrunched her face in disapproval. "It wasn't that bad," Taryn countered.

Soon the girls were involved in a full fledge conversation, and Larkin's heart warmed, watching as she smiled.

"What are they doing?" Keiryn growled.

"Looks like they're talking," Bency answered sarcastically.

"What are you doing still sitting here? You need to go over and make a play," Dalen insisted.

"No. Just go over and get involved with the conversation. Don't force it," Keiryn instructed Bency and the twins, then nodded for them to get moving.

"Don't you want me to go over?" Adalia asked.

"We're trying to befriend her. Not make her think we hate her," Eben chided.

"Whatever. Like I'd go over there anyways," she hissed.

Paying Ada no mind, Keiryn and his friends watched as the girls approached.

"Do you have room for three more?" Bency asked.

"Sure," Taryn smiled, noting the tension between the first two girls to join her and the last three. "With you guys sitting at the same table, it isn't against pack law or something, is it?"

The girls all looked at one another before bursting into laughter. "No," Dagney giggled. "I've known Bentley and Hadley all of my life."

The guys at both tables watched curiously as the girls laughed, both sides wondering what could be so interesting and funny.

"Okay, so it's like I told them about Larkin. If Keiryn told you to come over, don't feel obligated. I'm fine and I don't need a babysitter," Taryn offered.

"Keiryn might have suggested it, but we were already looking for a way to distance ourselves from evil Ada," Bency confessed, causing more smiles and laughter at their mismatched table.

"What is it with her anyways? Gastyn mentioned something about her not being accepted by either pack. But it seems she's made herself quite comfortable at your table."

"This is only her second year of school with us. From what we understand, her and her father move around a lot trying to find a pack for her to join. But so far there hasn't been any takers," Hadley explained.

"Why does she sit with you guys then?"

"That's easy," Nalani chimed in. "When she arrived last year, she was crushing on Larkin. It didn't take long for him to declare her bid to join our pack as unacceptable. So she can never be part of anything we do."

"Gastyn asked Keiryn to give her a year. If she hasn't become more compatible with our group by then, Mr. Wylder agreed to notify her father that she won't be accepted," Bentley added.

"So how much longer before the year is up?"

"Another five months," Bency sighed heavily. "Summer vacation didn't count towards our time served. She went out of the country to visit family for part of it, and the other part we spent hiding from her."

"I don't envy you there," Nalani admitted.

ဆပ္သဆပ္သ

As Gastyn entered the lunch room he was especially pleased to see the girls from the two groups sitting together with Taryn. With a heavy heart he interrupted the uncommon occurrence.

"Good afternoon, Ladies."

"Good afternoon, Mr. Wylder," they all replied in unison, followed by more laughter.

"It's nice to see you all getting along. But if you wouldn't mind, I need a word with Miss Malone before class today."

"Sure," Dagney agreed. "We'll see you later?"

"Yeah," Taryn smiled. "See you later."

Gastyn led Taryn out the side door, over to a bench under a shade tree. "That was rather impressive, Miss Malone. First you get both Larkin and Keiryn to work together to defend you, and now you have the girls from both packs sitting with you at your table…and there wasn't any bloodshed."

"I wouldn't get too excited, Mr. Wylder. The two Neanderthals told them to sit with me." He studied her closely, making her squirm with self-consciousness. "What is it you wanted to talk to me about?"

"Your mother called me this morning. She said you weren't yourself last night."

"Of course she did."

"Is everything okay?"

"Yesterday was a long day, and it was a lot of new information to take in. I just needed time to myself to process it. That was all," she fibbed.

"If you are better today, then I was thinking you could observe the students practicing in the back room. But I only want you to observe, I don't want you to use any of your own powers…is that understood?"

"You're the teacher."

"And I had better get going if I don't want to be late for my own class," he stated, glancing down at his watch. "I'll see you in class, Taryn."

Larkin watched Taryn from afar, wishing he had met her under different circumstances. Wanting nothing more than to go to her and be by her side, he sighed heavily knowing he had put himself into a corner.

"I thought stalking was illegal," Keiryn chided, walking past Larkin with Dalen, Jonesy and Eben on his way to class.

Larkin growled in response, but then quickly turned his attention back to Taryn, who was now walking towards the doors where he was standing. Pushing the door open, she saw him. He didn't try to hide the fact that he had been watching her, which was a small comfort.

"Larkin," she acknowledged, turning to head to class.

He smiled at the sound of his name falling from her lips and followed her, without hesitation.

ಬಿಛೊಬಿಛ

"Everyone, please take your seats," Gastyn instructed.

Taryn sat between the two groups in a chair that had been added just for her while he took roll. She smiled at Andyn who sat next to Kellan, peering out in her direction from behind his bulky frame.

Once directed, the class trickled into the back room and prepared to receive instructions. "Hi, Andyn," Taryn smiled, taking a seat next to him along the side of the room.

"Hey, Taryn."

"That was really sweet what you did yesterday," she whispered to him while Gastyn directed the other students.

"More like a disaster. I didn't mean to hurt you."

"Jonesy potted the cactus for me. I'm taking it home tonight to put on my dresser," she smiled, taking away the sting of his embarrassment.

"You really liked it?"

"Of course I did. It's the first time I have ever been given a plant. So thank you, Andyn." He smiled sheepishly and moved his chair closer to hers while they began watching the other students.

The guys in Keiryn's group, plus Bency, worked on strength, seeing who could toss a heavy lead ball the farthest. Larkin's pack worked to improve their speed on a trail that circled the entire room.

Taryn watched in awe, never having imagined strength and speed would be part of their gifts. Now she had understood how Larkin had been able to outrun the lightning.

Turning her attention to the corner closest to where she and Andyn were seated, they watched as Bentley and Hadley worked together, creating a cloud overhead. No matter how much they concentrated, it never lasted more than thirty seconds at a time.

Several yards away, Nalani worked on forming a dust devil. The spinning vortex barely reached twenty feet in height and was no more than three feet in width.

Alone in a corner, Adalia concentrated on forming balls of white energy into different sizes, although most were the size of a standard basketball.

Dagney stood over a large tub of water, raising different quantities and manipulating them into various shapes.

Towards the end of class, Keiryn approached her. "You've seen what we can do. So what's your specialty?" he inquired.

"I, I.." she stuttered, unsure of what to say.

Fortunately for her, Larkin bumped into Keiryn, causing a heated shoving match to ensue, with all the pack members jumping in.

Gastyn's voice thundered, filling the air with disapproval. "What's going on here?"

"Larkin knocked into me on purpose," Keiryn seethed.

"Whatever, you stepped in front of me."

"You two, in the other room, now," Gastyn fumed. Turning back to the rest of the class, he dismissed them early and warned them of dire consequences should anyone continue this fight.

Jonesy walked over and took a seat next to Taryn. "I bet you're used to guys fighting over you."

"No, not really," she shrugged. "I don't mean to cause any additional friction between your groups. I hope everyone knows that."

"It's not you, it's them. Something happened between them shortly after Larkin and I turned twelve and Keiryn's never forgiven him.

Puzzled that Larkin and Jonesy had turned twelve around the same time, she posed a question. "You said you were a junior, right?"

"I started kindergarten a year late. I don't remember my parents. They left me with a box of belongings on my aunt's doorstep and she has cared for me ever since. We bounced around from city to city trying to find a place to settle down. Williams happened to be the place where my aunt found peace."

"And what about you? Did you find peace here in Williams?"

"I don't know, and this is going to sound silly, but I feel like I left something behind the first time I moved. I don't know how to explain it, but I know there's something missing from my life," he sadly admitted.

Taryn took his hand, holding it within her own. "It doesn't sound silly. I don't remember my dad either, Jonesy. He left when I was really little. My mom won't tell me anymore about him other than that small bit of information. But I know there's something more. I can feel it in my bones."

The two stayed locked in a gaze, neither looking away. She could feel the warmth radiating from him and realized that what she was feeling was his power seeping out from inside.

"Jonesy," Dalen yelled, sticking his head inside the door.

"I better go."

"I'll see you tomorrow, Jonesy."

"See ya, Taryn."

ଔ୪ଔ୪

Inside Gastyn's small office, he tore into both Larkin and Keiryn. "It's only the second day of school and you're already fighting. Yesterday it was with the football team and today it's with each other," he scolded. "I've told you, this fighting has to stop. It's not good for either of you, and it's certainly not good for your brothers and sisters."

"I started it, Mr. Wylder," Larkin admitted.

Gastyn paced back and forth in the small space. "You're dismissed, Keiryn." Once Keiryn left, he turned his attention to Larkin. "What happened out there? Why would you start a fight with him?"

"Because he put her at risk."

"I see. This was about Taryn. Just because you have dreamt of this girl for the past five years doesn't mean you have a claim to her, Larkin."

"It wasn't like that, Gastyn."

"Then please tell me, Mr. Taylor, what was it like?"

He exhaled heavily, choosing his words carefully before he spoke. "He asked what she was. And I needed a distraction to keep her from answering."

He studied Larkin's facial expression for any hint of what he was holding back. "Why exactly would you need to provide a distraction to keep her from answering?"

"She doesn't know what she is."

"But you do?"

"I think so."

"So that's why you asked to borrow a book. You were trying to figure out what she is. So what this tells me is that she isn't like anyone in either of the two groups here."

"No, she's not. She's special, Gastyn. But because her mother kept her hidden away in Nowheresville, U.S.A. she doesn't know anything about being Gaias," he growled in frustration.

"You're upset with her mother?"

"Yes. She's put her life in danger."

"And you're the one who is going to protect her?" Gastyn inquired, finally seeing the bigger picture.

"I have to. It's my duty. I won't let any harm come to her."

"She means a lot to you, yet you know very little about her."

"I know everything I need to know about her. She's kind, compassionate and absolutely amazing and so special. I can't describe how incredibly special she is, Gastyn. There are just no words that would do her justice."

Observing Larkin's demeanor and listening to the way he talked about her, Gastyn began to realize that what he felt for Taryn went far beyond caring for her or infatuation, teenage crush or the depth of a first love. He was physically, mentally and emotionally bound to her, making him fearful for Larkin's well-being, as well as the well-being of anyone who might pose a threat to her in his eyes.

For the moment, his interest in Taryn's powers waned as he thought about the conversation he would need to have with Maxym Taylor. He did not relish telling him that his worst fears were coming true and that he didn't have any resolution to this unique situation.

"Larkin, I need you to go home for now."

"I can't, Mr. Wylder. Not until she's ready to go."

"Very well, then. I am going to go in with Taryn. Would you like to join me?"

"No."

"I'll see you in about an hour." He gave Larkin one final glance before leaving.

Walking in to find Taryn running down the portion of trail set aside for speed training, Gastyn could see frustration on her face. "What's the matter, Taryn?"

"I can't do it!"

"You can't do what?"

A searing heat pushed through her as her frustration grew, not understanding why. "Why can't I run like them?"

"You obviously don't have the genetics for speed and strength," Gastyn laughed, unintentionally fueling her irritation.

"What do you mean, I don't have the genetics?"

"Please, walk with me, Taryn." He waited for her to join him. "We as Gaias born, we are all assigned specific strengths. Skin-Walkers possess the gift of strength and speed while Elementals possess the ability to control the elements. Ontogenies possess the ability to influence the growth of plants, trees and things of that nature while Animators are able to take any inanimate object and change it into something completely different. Then we have Influentials who possess the ability to influence what others see, feel or believe, and lastly we have Imperiums who can create and control energy."

"So that's what Keiryn meant when he asked about my specialty." Instantly the frustration over the secrets that her mother had kept from her erupted in the form of a fiery burn that scalded its way through her chest.

"Now that you know, what would you say your specialty is, Taryn?"

"I don't have one."

"It seemed to me the other day that you are an Elemental," he noted.

"I'm not an Elemental."

"Then what are you?"

While Gastyn and Taryn were distracted, Larkin stepped into the room and took a seat in the corner on the floor, trying to remain out of sight.

Tears of anger and frustration began streaking down her cheeks. In that same moment, clouds formed near the ceiling and rain began to fall inside of the large room. Tired of hiding what she really was from everyone except for her mother, she inhaled deeply, letting the power course through her veins. With her arms at her sides and hands in her pockets, she exhaled, creating a large vortex that she maneuvered about the large space, using nothing but her will.

Gastyn's eyes widened and a loud gasp escaped his lips. "How are you doing this? Your hands...you're not using them!" He stumbled backwards, trying to make sense of what he had just witnessed.

"No, Mr. Wylder, I'm not."

The look on his face was incredulous, unlike the look of terror her mother would display each time she discovered a new ability. Upon seeing his reaction was more curiosity than fear, she felt it safe to continue her display.

"I'm not just an Elemental. I can do more."

The floor began to shake under their feet and his eyes widened even further. "Focus on the center of the room." As he looked in that direction he stood in awe as he watched the dirt begin to pile upon itself over and over again, until a sapling could be seen. He walked towards the small tree, completely astonished as it continued to grow several feet at a time before him. When it was all over, a seventy foot oak tree stood as the new focal point in the oversized room.

Speechless, Gastyn looked to Taryn, who was standing several feet away, wearing a look of relief. "Taryn, this is unbelievable. You don't have to use your hands," he repeated over and over again. "How?"

"My mom wouldn't be happy that I'm telling you this, but I've never had to use my hands for anything."

"Incredible!"

She smiled, feeling the weight of her secrets lifting off of her small shoulders. "Well, there is something I have to use them for. But I guess it's because I've never tried it without," she confessed, thinking back to when she healed injured animals.

Using his Skin-Walker gene, Larkin listened closely, even from a hundred yards away. Realizing that she was about to share with Gastyn that she was a Healer, his protective instinct flared. This time he could feel his eyes go dark, and in an attempt to keep his curse at bay, he rushed to her side, exposing himself.

"That was freaking unbelievable," he exclaimed, catching both Gastyn and Taryn by surprise.

"What are you doing in here, Larkin?" Gastyn rebuked, noting the dark color of his eyes.

"I needed to talk to you and I thought you might be in here. And you were." Glancing at Taryn, he saw the fear shining brightly in her eyes. "That was impressive. I can't believe you're only sixteen," he carried on obsessively, trying to sell his performance.

"You weren't supposed to see that," Taryn chided.

"I'm not going to tell anyone," he promised, trying to keep their eye contact to a minimum.

"You'd better not."

"I think everyone needs to take a step back and calm down," Gastyn stated, stepping between them. He looked to Larkin and realized he had only interfered in an attempt to protect Taryn, but to protect her from what, he wondered. Turning to her, he could see all of her fears surfacing in her eyes as well as being able to feel it in the air. "Larkin, go have a seat in my office and do not move until I tell you to." Hesitantly Larkin listened and headed for the door. "Taryn, I know you must be worried that he will tell your secrets. But I can assure you, he will never speak to another about the things he has witnessed here today."

"How can you possibly know that?" she sighed, holding back her tears.

"I've known Larkin Taylor for nearly all of his life. He is of sound character, and if you ask him not to share your secrets, he won't, Taryn. He will take them to his grave."

"If my mother finds out what I did here…she's not going to be happy, Gastyn."

"That's why she isn't going to. But I think you need to tell Larkin how important it is to keep this secret. He will honor whatever you ask of him."

"Fine," she sighed. "I'd probably better go home for today."

"Very well." The pair began to walk back to the door of the regular classroom. "Taryn, as you saw today, my other students only have a fraction of the power that you possess. And that is why I can't have you practice with them until we find a way to let you blend in." He placed an arm around her shoulders in an attempt to comfort her. "Your mother wasn't wrong when she said you were special. In all of my life, I've never met anyone like you. We will find a way to let you live a normal life. So please, be patient."

She shrugged in acknowledgement, even though it felt blissful to release her power on such a scale. When they walked through the door, she saw Larkin sitting in one of the chairs in Gastyn's office and shot him a look of warning. She knew that if he shared anything he saw in the back room with anyone, her mother would surely take her back into a life of seclusion. That is the last thing she wanted.

"Please give me a moment to speak with Larkin, then I will call your mother."

Taryn shrugged, watching him stride into his office where he closed the door behind him.

"That stunt you pulled in there, it wasn't one of your better moments," Gastyn scolded him in a whisper.

"I know, but I felt compelled to check on her."

"All I'm trying to do is to help her. You know, if you would just tell her about your secret, it would resolve several issues. If she knew who you were, what you were, you could better help to protect her."

"She's told the wolf things that she's never told another living soul. How can I go to her now and tell her that it has been me the entire time?"

"I'm not sure, but something's got to give here. You can't start a fight every time someone asks her a question that you feel puts in her danger."

"I know, I know, but she's going to be so angry when she finds out," Larkin worried.

"Just think of how angry she's going to be if this continues on much longer. Now, you need to get home. Please tell your father that I will be by later this evening to speak with him."

"He's going to be thrilled. Phone calls yesterday and now a face-to-face visit."

Opening the door, Gastyn saw Taryn waiting not so patiently as she paced back and forth. "If you're ready to go home, Larkin has agreed to drop you off, since it's on his way." A ball of emotion formed in the back of Larkin's throat, terrified of being in such close quarters to her. What if she took a good long look and realized why he was so familiar? She would never be able to forgive him.

She shot a questioning look their way. "You did?"

Gastyn nudged Larkin. "Yeah, I did, only if you're ready."

The teacher walked the pair to the parking lot and watched as Larkin opened the door of his jeep for her, closing it after she was settled in the passenger seat. Once they were out of sight, he rushed back into the school, headed for his private library, looking for information on what would cause Larkin to be bound to this girl. He was also anxious to find out if there was any documentation of another Gaias being born with the ability to use their powers without using their hands.

ೋൽೋൽ

The ride through town was awkward and quiet as neither teenager spoke. Turning to drive south of Williams, Taryn finally addressed the white elephant in the jeep.

"Larkin, I know you don't really know me or owe me anything, but I need for you to not tell anyone what you saw." Pausing, she stopped to brush away the tears that filled her eyes. "I've never been around others like us, and if my mother finds out what I've done today…she'll take me away, and I'd really like to stay."

His heart ached, feeling her pain and fear, knowing that he caused it, even if it was to keep her safe. Taking hold of her hand, he stroked the top of it with his thumb. "I promise you that I won't tell anyone, Taryn. I don't want you to leave either." Still holding her hand, he glanced at her for a split second, pretending he had to keep his eyes on the road.

Emotion overtook her as she felt the pulse of their connection. Her heart warmed with every gentle caress of his thumb against her skin. She'd never had a boy hold her hand before.

~ 155 ~

When they pulled up to her house, Larkin realized her hand was still clasped in his. "Sorry," he stated, slowly withdrawing his grip before flashing an awkward smile.

Shyly, she smiled back. "Thanks for the ride. And please, don't..."

"Your secrets are safe with me, Taryn."

Seeing the sincerity in the brief glimpse that she got of his eyes, she sighed with relief. A feeling of familiarity washed over her once again. "Are you sure we have never met before?"

Immediately, his defenses sprang up and he looked up, down and all around trying to evade her gaze. "Nope, the first time was during the storm and then again at school. I need to get home. See you tomorrow." With that he quickly reached across and pulled the door closed, turning his jeep around and driving away. Only when he pulled into his own driveway did he sigh with relief.

"Hey, Son. How was school?" Maxym greeted him as he walked through the back door.

"Hi, Dad. School sucked and Gastyn's stopping by tonight. I don't have time to talk about it now, but I'll be home in an hour or so."

After grabbing a quick drink, he headed to the tree line and disappeared from sight.

ﾟﾟﾟ

"How was school?" Ilya inquired as Taryn walked through the front door.

"It was fine."

"Hey, slow down a minute. Can't we talk?"

"Mom, I need to go for a walk. We can talk after that," Taryn answered, trying to tuck her emotions away before she came undone.

"Look, Young Lady, I gave you space last night because it was your first day of school. I want to know how it's going."

"School is fine, Mom, but something that's not fine is all of the secrets you've kept from me. Leaving me to feel like a complete donkey, realizing that I knew absolutely nothing about our kind."

"I didn't tell you because I wanted to keep you safe."

"Save it, Mother. That excuse has been worn out for years. You kept me so ignorant about what I am, that when a boy asked me what my specialty was, I had no idea what he was talking about."

"Taryn, you didn't tell him, did you?" Ilya worried.

She cringed with frustration as she pursed her lips together. "How could I have told him something that I didn't even know about?"

"This behavior is unacceptable, Young Lady. And if this is what school does to you…then you're not going back tomorrow."

Stopping where she stood, she glared at her mother. "As if you have the power to stop me."

With her mother's jaw hanging open, she stormed out the French doors and into the woods, taking off in a dead run, yelling and pouring her anger and frustration into the air. Soon the black wolf was running by her side, bringing a smile to her face. After thirty minutes, she stopped and found a tree to rest under.

"It's been a bad day," she sighed, scratching him behind the ears. He leaned heavily against her until she wrapped her arms around him, allowing him to comfort her. "You have no idea how much I needed that. Come on, Big Guy. I think we could both use a walk."

The pair walked for several minutes, coming to a small clearing. Sensing someone like them was near, he released a low growl.

"What is it?" she asked. Looking around she spotted a large hawk perched high above in a nearby tree. "Oh, he isn't hurting anything."

With that, the hawk flew and perched on a lower branch, sending Larkin into a frenzy seeing Keiryn in his preferred form. He snarled and leapt towards the large bird.

"Stop that!" When he didn't listen, she swatted him on the snout. "Bad dog," Taryn scolded him, waving her finger in his face.

Inside his head he could hear Keiryn's laughter. His ears turned downward, angry and humiliated by what had just happened. To make matters worse, a whimper slipped past his lips.

Overjoyed to see Taryn's displeasure with the black dog, Keiryn released a scream in his hawk form. "Stop that," Taryn warned the hawk, now waving her finger at him. "There's plenty of room in this forest for the both of you. Besides, we should all try a little harder to get along, despite our differences." Storming off, she felt her own emotions from the day forcing their way up the back of her throat. "Oh my gosh, my mother. I'm sorry, Big Guy, but I have to get home. I said some pretty horrible things to her that she didn't deserve. I'll see you tomorrow," she called out as she sprinted back home, leaving Larkin and Keiryn alone.

೫೦೮೩೫೦೮೩

Shifting into their human forms, the boys glared at one another. "What are you doing here?" Larkin demanded.

"I'm looking out for that poor girl. She doesn't have a clue who you really are, does she?"

"You don't need to concern yourself with Taryn, Bird Boy."

"You've lost your damned mind if you think I'm going to leave her unprotected with you, Black Dog."

"Taryn isn't your business, Falcon."

"She's just as much my business as she is yours. She goes to our school," Keiryn retorted, emphasizing the word our. "All you do is stalk about and follow her everywhere she goes. That doesn't exactly mean that the two of you are dating, Taylor."

~ 158 ~

"I'm warning you, Falcon, stay away from her."

"I'll stay away from her whenever you decide to stay away."

"I'm her protector."

"Then I'm her protector too," Keiryn declared, finding Larkin's choice of words strange.

With neither boy backing down tempers flared, causing Larkin to shove him. Keiryn responded with a right hook. The boys slugged it out until neither could stand.

"Stay away from her, Keiryn. I've got her."

"You've got her until you phase again, Mutt. What happens when someone's not there to warn you that it's happening again? Does she become your next victim?"

"I would never hurt her."

"Just like you would never hurt your best friend? You'll have to forgive me if I don't take your word for it," Keiryn responded, gesturing to his left shoulder and collarbone.

"Just get out of here."

Keiryn stood, staring at his former best friend. He could see the fear in his eyes. Fear that maybe he could be capable of hurting her, regardless of whether it was intentional or not. That look was proof enough that Larkin could not be trusted with her. Shifting into hawk form, he took to the sky, heading for home, leaving the dog to wallow in his own self-loathing.

ഇരുഇരു

"Mom! Mom!" Taryn shouted, running in the doors.

"What is it?"

Taryn raced to meet her, wrapping her arms tightly around her neck. "I'm sorry, Mom. I didn't mean it."

"I'm sorry too, my sweet baby girl. I should have told you the truth before sending you off to school. I just didn't think about how hard it was going to be for you, or how it might upset you that I hadn't told you."

After mother and daughter hugged for what seemed like an eternity, Ilya brushed Taryn's tear soaked hair away from her face. "Come, sit with me." She led her over to the couch, still holding tightly to her hand. "Do you have any questions?"

Looking towards her mother, a warm smile formed on her face. "Yes, quite a few actually. Though I'm not sure where to start."

"Let's start with the basics. I am sixty-four years old and my main gift is Imperium."

"Gastyn explained the different abilities." She thought back to how Adalia had worked to form white balls of energy. "But I've seen you do other things too. Can all Imperiums do everything that you can do?"

"We all have our specialty that we can perform. But keep in mind, not all equally." Ilya arched her brows while forming one of the balls with her free hand, then easily splitting it into two, then four, then eight different spheres. "Everyone has their sub-strengths, as Gastyn likes to refer to them. They may possess only a few or several different sub-strengths, it just depends on the individual."

"You've known me my entire life. What do you think my strength is?"

"Well, Sweetie, you're the exception to every rule I know. You seem to possess strength in anything you attempt, and that's why it was important to keep you protected from others like us. Most wouldn't be able to come to terms with the abilities you have. You're an anomaly, Taryn, and what we as Gaias don't understand, it scares us."

"If they had the chance to get to know me, do you think they would feel differently?"

Ilya exhaled and looked into her daughter's eyes. "Over a thousand years ago, there existed a special type of Gaias. They were blessed with such a powerful gift that it ended up making them greedy. They used their power of life to evolve into something dark, something so evil that even nature refused to create another like them."

She watched as her mother's eyes took on a vacant expression, recalling everything she had ever been taught about that terrible time in Gaias history. A chill ran up Taryn's spine. "Those must have been scary times. But whatever they were, they must all be gone by now, right?"

"I think that is a conversation meant for another time," Ilya smiled warmly, wanting to spare her the pain of knowing the awful truth of what preyed in the dark. "So have you met anyone interesting at school? Perhaps a boy?"

"I've met a few interesting people."

"Well, don't keep me in suspense!"

"I saw the boy from the grocery store. He was pretty nice…until I told him my name. Then he couldn't get away from me fast enough."

"Don't take it personally. People who aren't like us, they can sense we don't belong in their immediate circle of friends. It's something nature created to help protect our secrets."

"Well, that would have certainly been good to know forty-eight hours ago," Taryn teased, before going on. "Today at lunch, the girls from the two different packs sat with me. It was a little awkward at first but then we all ended up having fun."

"So you're making friends?"

"I'm not sure we are to the point where we would call each other friends. I think initially it was their attempt to get me to consider joining their packs."

"It's a pretty serious thing to commit to a pack. I hope you take your time."

"I'm not sure I want to belong to a pack…is that weird?"

"No, it's not weird. You've lived so long without knowing about packs and such that no one could blame you for taking it slow before making a commitment," Ilya responded, glancing towards the clock. "I didn't realize it was getting so late. You should go take your shower and get ready for bed. We'll have plenty of time to talk over the weekend."

"Okay. But I'm going to grab something to eat first."

Sitting in the living room at the Taylor home, Gastyn discussed his fears regarding Larkin's bond with Maxym. "Gastyn, are you sure about this?"

"There's no doubt in my mind that his affliction, and the dreams he has had of her, are all related somehow. I've never seen anything like it before, and I can't find anything in the history books about it either. The way he talks about needing to protect her, it's unnerving."

"There is something I need to come clean about, Gastyn. He doesn't only go on walks with her throughout the day…he spends every night watching over her from just outside her bedroom window."

"Their bond is far deeper than I had thought. You know that I would never harm the girl, yet he intervened with those darkened eyes when I was working with her. If he sees me as a threat to her well-being, can you imagine how he views everyone else?"

"I won't lose my son, Gastyn. He's all I have in this world."

"He has to expose himself, to show her the truth about his identity."

Both men jumped to their feet at the sound of the back door slamming open.

"Larkin, what happened?" Maxym questioned, taking in the split lip and black eye he was sporting.

"That damned bird won't mind his own business."

"Is Keiryn alright?" Gastyn inquired.

"He looks worse than me, but he's still alive, if that's what you're asking," Larkin answered, before heading upstairs to shower. "He should have stayed away from her," he shouted as he topped the stairway.

Maxym and Gastyn shared a look of concern. "We have to act quickly, before something worse happens," Gastyn admitted.

"What do you have in mind?"

"He's your son, Maxym, and I don't want to isolate him from you. I'll shoulder the responsibility, that way he doesn't think you had anything to do with it. Just be prepared for him to be unhappy by the end of the school day tomorrow."

೮೦೦೪೮೦೦೪

After a quiet dinner with his father, Larkin headed back to Taryn's to watch over her as she slept. He jumped up on the roof and settled in for the night. Thoughts of earlier events consumed him as he looked inside her window.

He considered the consequences of Keiryn knowing his secrets. Even though he hadn't told anyone about the incident five years ago, he was quite certain the same courtesy would not be extended in regards to her, since the bird boy seemed to have a thing for her.

Distracted by his thoughts, he jumped when Keiryn suddenly appeared on the roof next to him.

"What are you doing here?"

"Isn't it obvious? I'm stalking Taryn's stalker."

"You don't belong here."

"I belong here as much as you do, and as long as you are here, I'm not going anywhere," Keiryn retorted loudly, causing her to stir in her sleep. Larkin shot him a frosty glare while holding his fingers to his lips, motioning for him to be quiet. Taking advantage of the situation, Keiryn grinned. "If you don't want to wake our girl, then I suggest you get used to the idea of sharing this perch with me for the foreseeable future."

Larkin glared at him, fighting the fire burning in his belly. Not wanting to cause a scene that would wake up both Taryn and her mother, he conceded. "Fine. You can stay…for now."

Keiryn watched as his former best friend struggled to maintain his composure. As the black rings around his irises started to dissipate, he took a spot on one side of the window while Larkin retained his position directly in front of it. Settling in for a long, uncomfortable night, he closed his eyes.

Only after he was certain Keiryn had fallen asleep, he moved to the opposing side of her window to get some rest of his own.

In the morning as she began to stir, both boys jumped from the roof and ran for cover in the trees. Without speaking, they shifted into animal form. Keiryn perched himself high up in the tree and waited to see her. On cue, she looked out her window and spotted the black wolf standing in the cover of the trees. She shot him a beaming smile, waving before stepping away to ready for school. Seeing how attached she was to the wolf made Keiryn's blood boil. The dog was lying to her, and she had no clue. There had to be a way to expose him for the fraud he was. And if he could succeed, it would be the perfect way to keep her safe. As he watched the mongrel disappear into the forest, he took flight, formulating a plan to expose Larkin's secrets once and for all.

Larkin rushed back home with the taste of contempt in his mouth, realizing how much trouble the bird boy could make for him regarding Taryn. With weighted thoughts, he burst through the back door, startling his father.

"Larkin," Maxym acknowledged, noting his son's troubled demeanor.

"Hey."

"What is it, Son? Did something happen?"

"Yeah, something happened. That damned bird boy showed up, and ended up staying the entire night."

"Did anything happen?"

"He and his big mouth nearly woke her up. He could have gotten us both caught."

Maxym studied his son's demeanor. "You seem really on edge. Maybe you should stay home today?"

"There's no way. I would lose my mind if I couldn't see her for eight whole hours, never knowing if she's safe or not."

Knowing his son was probably right about losing his mind, if his current demeanor was anything to go by, Maxym decided not to press the issue any further. "You know, if you would just come clean with the girl, Keiryn would have nothing to hold over your head."

"That's not true, Dad, and we both know it."

"Keiryn took the Blood Oath. He can't reveal your secret, Larkin."

Shaking his head, Larkin sighed. "He doesn't have to tell her. All he would have to do is show her his scar and she would know that I'm a monster. But I swear Dad, I would never hurt her."

"I know, Son. I know."

℠ℂ℠ℂ

"Where have you been all night?" Teigan asked as Keiryn walked into the kitchen.

"I was with the black dog at Taryn's house."

"You know I'm not crazy about this arrangement. Out of all of the girls Larkin's been around, why are you so worried about this girl in particular?"

"It's not the same. Dagney and Nalani can handle their own. Besides, he's not interested in them the same way he is with her. He follows her everywhere at school and then pretends to be this gentle wolf in the woods behind her house, when he's just using it as a disguise to stalk her freely."

"Have you considered that maybe he has real feelings for her?"

"Yeah, I have. And that's what scares me. She's so gentle and unassuming and he, well, he's a monster. I may not be able to tell her about what he really is but I can stick to her side and make sure she stays safe."

Recognizing the stubborn set in his son's jaw, Teigan knew it was futile to argue with him once his mind was set. "Have you considered that maybe this isn't as much about Larkin as it is about your own feelings for this girl?"

Keiryn rolled his eyes and shrugged. "It doesn't matter. I won't let him hurt her," he declared before standing to walk to his bedroom and ready for school.

ༀༀༀༀ

Keiryn parked his truck in the school parking lot before joining his friends, who were already waiting on the front steps. "Whoa, what happened to your face?" Dalen asked.

"Me and the black dog had a disagreement," Keiryn acknowledged, nodding his head in the direction of the red jeep that was pulling in.

"Tell me you landed a few punches of your own," Eben egged him on. Keiryn arched his brows and nodded again, throwing a smirk in Larkin's direction. "I can see that shiner of his all the way over here!"

"That's only the first step. This afternoon I plan on knocking his feet out from under him for good," Keiryn smiled deviously.

CHAPTER SEVEN

"That's a nice look. I take it you and the bird boy had another run-in," Kellan cackled, cringing at the sight of his brother's bruised face.

"Unfortunately." Larkin's thoughts were heavy with the consequences if Keiryn found a way to out his secrets to Taryn.

"You want me to go and say hello?" Gerrick asked, itching for a fight.

"No, Gerrick. I want everyone to keep their distance from Keiryn and his pack."

Everyone took a step back, noting his normal relaxed posture was now stiff and tense. Even Nalani, who usually had some smart comment, didn't dare breathe a word. The pack stood around quietly until he became distracted by the white SUV pulling in. Once his attention was redirected on Taryn, they broke into quiet conversation.

Larkin watched as she walked up the steps of the school. His heart soared when she didn't give Keiryn a second look, but quickly plummeted when Jonesy followed her into the building, leaving his pack behind.

"Wow, did you see that?" Gerrick grinned. "Bird Boy got passed over for the runt. And the runt broke ranks to follow her," he continued to the laughs and smiles of his own brothers and sisters.

"Let's go," Larkin announced.

As the pack climbed the stairs of the entrance, Larkin and Keiryn shared a look that caused a chill to swirl in the air. No one from either side dared ask what the problem was between them. They all assumed it had something to do with Taryn. It was normal for Keiryn to lock onto a new girl, but it was something else entirely for Larkin to show so much interest. Since his twelfth birthday, he had not so much as looked at a girl with anything more than friendship on his mind.

"I'll catch you guys in a minute," Larkin stated before walking off towards the office to find Ms. Cahill.

A few minutes later, he emerged from her office, beaming that he had received the approval he had been waiting for. He was now officially in Taryn's Horticulture class. As he hurried out of the office, he bumped into Keiryn, who only smirked at him in response, before stepping inside to chat with Ms. Cahill regarding his own class schedule.

Back with his friends, Larkin smiled widely. Kellan caught a glimpse of the pink slip his friend was holding and nudged him. "You've got it bad, My Friend."

"So what if I do."

"It's cool, Larkin. She's a pretty girl. A little mysterious, but she seems alright," Kellan replied, trying to lighten his brother's mood. When he saw a brief smile, he pushed a bit further. "So, do you have time to hang with us this weekend, or do you and Kansas have a date?"

"I'm not sure what my schedule looks like. But I'll let you know before school is out today." With that, Larkin headed to his new first hour class.

As he walked down the hallway towering over most of the student body, he saw Keiryn heading his way, wearing the same smirk from earlier. As the bird boy drew closer, he noticed the pink slip pinched between his fingers. Irritation roiled in his stomach when it dawned on him that Keiryn had switched his first period class as well. Locking eyes, both boys sprinted to the classroom, getting stuck momentarily in the doorway as they tried to shove through.

The teacher stopped them at the front of the room, asking for their transfer slips. While Larkin held his out, Keiryn quickly placed his slip in the teacher's hand and maneuvered around him to the small table where Taryn and Jonesy were seated.

"Hey, Jonesy. Would you be a sport and sit over there?" Keiryn nodded his head to an empty table just across and up one row from them.

Before Jonesy could respond, Larkin arrived. "I wouldn't want to split up your pack. So the two of you should probably sit together."

Jonesy sat quietly, looking down at the table, waiting for her to decide which pack leader she preferred to sit with.

She shot both boys a smile, taking in their bruised and battered faces. "I'm sorry." She placed one hand casually under her chin while reaching with the other under the table to take Jonesy's hand in her own. "Jonesy already promised to be my partner. You'll have to find somewhere else to sit."

He squeezed her hand and a half smile curled on his face, happy that even when she had options, she still chose him.

"Everybody, please take your seats," the teacher announced, looking in Larkin and Keiryn's direction. Both boys glanced around, neither happy once they realized there was only a single table with two chairs available.

"Better take your seats." Taryn grinned a tormenting smile.

They begrudgingly complied, positioning the chairs as far as they could possibly get from each other at the small table. Their stiff postures spoke volumes as she observed them throughout the class. The disdain they so obviously had for each other was evident in the way they refused to speak to or look at one another. It irritated her that they were using her in their macho power match, but she was happy that Jonesy hadn't tucked tail and ran when they had tried their brutish antics on him.

After class, Jonesy walked with her to her locker. It didn't go unnoticed that Larkin and Keiryn followed closely behind, both shooting the other frosty glares.

ᏸᏅᏣᏸᏅᏣ

During lunch, Taryn sat at her normal table and was once again joined by the girls from the two packs. As much as she wanted to ask what the beef was between Larkin and Keiryn, she refrained, knowing it would likely cause a disruption in the peace at their table.

With lunch nearly over, she excused herself to go outside and enjoy the fresh air.

"Hey, Taryn," Larkin stated, standing only a few feet away, admiring her as she sat on the bench.

"Hey," she smiled into his familiar hazel eyes. A warm sensation fluttered in her heart.

Walking over, he took a seat next to her. "You really like being outdoors, don't you?"

"Yeah, it's peaceful out here compared to all of the noise in the cafeteria." She took a closer look at his damaged face. "What happened?" When he only looked at her with a goofy smile on his face, she pointed to her eye and asked again. "Your face…what happened?"

"Oh, it was nothing."

"It looks like more than nothing."

"It was just a dust up with another local."

"Anyone I know?" She already assumed it was with Keiryn, as he sported similar injuries.

"No one important," he smiled back playfully as she arched her brow. They sat quietly for a few more minutes before they heard the warning bell ring.

"I'd better go," Taryn stated, getting up. She stood there for a moment, hoping he would say something but he remained silent.

As she began to walk away, he reached for her hand. "Taryn, would you mind if I walked you to class?"

"Sure," she smiled shyly.

ᏩᏨᏩᏨ

Just outside the double doors, Keiryn watched their entire interaction, displeasure radiating on his face. "Looks like the dog won the girl, Lover Boy," Dalen teased, watching as Larkin and Taryn walked in a different set of doors.

"I wouldn't declare this battle a loss quite yet."

"I don't know what you're planning, but I hope I get a front row seat when it goes down," Eben stated, running his fingers coolly over his jet black hair while checking himself out in the reflection of the glass doors.

"Don't worry, Boys," Keiryn smiled, placing an arm around each of their shoulders. "The show is about to begin."

ᏩᏨᏩᏨ

Taryn and Larkin walked into Gastyn's classroom and received several looks of approval from one side, while the other side rolled their eyes.

"Taryn," Andyn smiled brightly, sitting next to Kellan.

"Hi, Andyn." She took her normal seat in between the two groups.

Gastyn quickly took roll and then released everyone to head into the back room, with the exception of Larkin. "Have you told Taryn the truth?"

"No."

"You owe her the truth, Larkin."

"I know…but not today."

"If not today, then when?" Gastyn inquired, hoping to give him one final opportunity to come clean to Taryn on his own.

"I don't know. Soon though. Can I go now, Mr. Wylder?"

With a heavy heart, he nodded him on to join the rest of the class.

೩೦೦೩೩೦೦೩

Larkin found Taryn observing the other students from the sidelines, with Andyn cozied up beside her. He chuckled to himself, realizing how smitten the little guy was. He could certainly relate since he was currently wishing that he could be the one sitting so close to her, inhaling her sweet fragrance, touching her silken skin. Consumed by his thoughts, he ran straight into Adalia, whose smile quickly faded when she realized he had only accidentally bumped into her because he was distracted by Taryn.

"Watch it, Jerk!"

"Sorry," he apologized, still gazing in Taryn's direction.

"Ugh."

"I can't believe how head over heels he is about this girl," Gerrick laughed.

"What I can't believe is that he touched icky Ada and didn't go ballistic," Thorne snickered.

"I think it's sweet," Dagney smiled.

"Yeah, it works for me," Nalani agreed, halfheartedly.

೩೦೦೩೩೦೦೩

"So what is it you can do, Taryn?" Andyn asked, sweetly.

~ 172 ~

Knowing Gastyn didn't want her to use her gifts in front of the class until she had learned to reign in her powers, she posed the question back to him. "The other day you were trying to transform the pencil into a flower, right?" Still embarrassed, he nodded yes. "Can you show me again?"

"I don't think that's a good idea."

"Andyn, would you try for me?"

"Okay, but I don't think you should hold onto the pencil this time."

"I believe in you," she assured him, taking the pencil from his hand.

Closing his eyes tight, he held his hand only inches from the pencil. "I'm not sure about this, Taryn. What if I hurt you again?"

"Andyn," she placed her hand on his chest. "I feel it inside of you. Don't be afraid to unlock it and let it flow freely."

"What if I can't control it?"

"Do you trust me?"

"Yeah."

"And I trust you. So let's do this." Holding her arm out straight with the pencil on her palm, she instructed him. "Close your eyes. Focus solely on the tingle you feel deep inside." He adjusted in his seat, listening to her calming voice, breathing in deeply then exhaling slowly. "Let it out, Andyn. Let it flow until you can feel that same sensation coursing through every fiber of your being."

After several seconds passed, he smiled cautiously. "I can feel it, Taryn."

Several of the other students stopped what they were doing and began to move closer. Watching curiously as young Andyn took another shot at animating yet another pencil.

"Okay, Andyn, now hold your hand out and open your eyes. Visualize what it is you want to make happen, and when you're ready, let go."

For a split second, his eyes grew wide, immediately followed by a pulse that rocked the pencil in her hand. With power seeping off him, the pencil began to come to life in the form of a spectacular pink and white desert rose. The flower alone was at least ten inches in diameter, with the stem bright green in color, and strong as steel.

Applause erupted from his fellow classmates, while Kellan picked him up, boosting him high in the air. "Well done, Andyn. Well done," Gastyn lauded, winking at Taryn.

"Big deal, so the twerp finally created a flower," Adalia snarled, jealous of the attention he was receiving.

"That's not just a flower, Ada. The kid created a masterpiece," Gerrick smirked.

"Whatever, a flower won't win in a battle, Losers."

Larkin looked in Taryn's direction with admiration. Deep down he knew that it would be nearly impossible for any twelve year old to create such a spectacular and strong flower on their own. She flashed a bashful smile when their eyes met, fueling Keiryn's irritation with the situation even further.

"Thank you, Taryn," Andyn exclaimed, wrapping his arms around her neck.

Placing an arm tightly around him, she reciprocated the hug. "That was all you."

"Nice job, Kiddo," Keiryn acknowledged. "I think it's time to kick it up another level and show Taryn a different type of transformation…Larkin, why don't you go first?" he dared. Taryn looked at him puzzled, having no idea what he was talking about.

"What about it, Taylor...you should show the new girl how you transform. Show her what you are."

Larkin looked at him with utter contempt raging in his eyes. He had been waiting for him to do something...but he had never thought it would be this. "Not now, Bird Boy."

"Oh, I think now is a perfect time."

Both packs watched the exchange, taking in the tense stance of their leaders. Suddenly it became clear to them that Taryn had no idea that Skin-Walkers could transform into any animal they desired. Worse yet, it was obvious that Larkin had been around her in animal form, and that she had no idea of the connection.

"Back off, Falcon," Gerrick warned, stepping to his brother's side.

"What are you going to do?" Dalen taunted.

With tempers flaring dangerously hot, Gastyn intervened. "I think Mr. Falcon has a valid point."

A look of panic washed over Larkin's face. "But, Mr. Wylder..."

Gastyn walked towards him and whispered in his ear. "It's time for her to know the truth, Larkin." He shook his head no, hoping to wake from the terrible nightmare he was currently living in. "Let's have it Mr. Taylor."

With a sick feeling rising up inside of him, he shifted into a red fox.

"You can turn into animals," Taryn gasped, amazed by this new discovery.

"Yes, Taryn. Those who have the Skin-Walker gene can shift into any animal they chose. This gene is typically found in male Gaias, but we have a phenomenon in our midst. Our own Bency Porter also possesses the gene, which is quite rare," Gastyn explained.

"Yep, I'm a freak," Bency smiled proudly.

"That's incredible," Taryn breathed in awe. "But what happened to his clothes?"

"No one really knows," Jonesy piped in. "It's believed that our bodies absorb them temporarily or that our skin transforms over them. Either way, when we transform back to our human form, we are clad as we were before we changed."

She looked at him in utter delight. "You are a Skin Walker, too?"

Jonesy blushed under her rapt attention. "Sure. Most male Gaias are, and some females, though they are rare."

Clearing his throat, Gastyn turned his attention back to Larkin. "Now, Mr. Taylor, please show Miss Malone your preferred form."

Larkin looked deep into Taryn's sparkling green eyes, feeling a large lump forming in the back of his throat, knowing the awe in which she was currently looking at him was sure to fade once she saw the black wolf from the forest. Gastyn shot him an impatient look. Swallowing down the lump, he took one final glance before shifting again.

Her face washed void of emotion as she fought to hold herself together, staring into the familiar eyes of her friend, the black wolf. Just as he had feared, the sparkle in her own began to fade, replaced by a hollow, empty look.

Standing on the sideline, pleased that at least one of Larkin's secrets has been exposed, Keiryn smiled victoriously.

"Now it's your turn, Mr. Falcon," Gastyn asserted, sensing he had been keeping secrets as well.

"Oh, no. I think she's seen enough for one day."

"Now, Mr. Falcon."

Knowing the consequences would be grave if he tried to defy his teacher, he hesitantly complied and shifted into hawk form.

Taryn glanced at his bird form while the anger and hurt raged war inside her. Balling both of her hands into fists, her knuckles turned ghostly white as she fought willfully to retain control over the power that coursed through her.

A loud boom thundered from beyond the walls of the special classroom catching everyone, including Gastyn, by surprise.

"I've never heard anything from outside in here before," Jonesy stated.

Feeling the control slipping away, she tried deep breaths to calm her turbulent emotions. Closing her eyes, she visualized herself packing away every bit of power into a small box, jumping on top of it, and forcing the lid on.

"Are you alright?" Gastyn whispered into her ear.

With her eyes still closed, she took a final deep breath. "I'm fine," she finally answered, shooting an expressionless look in Larkin and Keiryn's direction.

"If you need a moment..." Gastyn touched one of her hands. He could feel the power pulsing off of her. "Perhaps you would like to take a walk with me."

"I said I was fine." She turned her focus back to Andyn, spending the remainder of class praising his beautiful flower and climbing the ridiculous sized tree that still stood in the middle of the large room. Betrayal still burned in her gut, exacerbated every time she felt Larkin's sad eyes gazing on her from afar. Fighting to keep her emotions in check drained her. She wanted to leave, to unleash her fury before it exploded around her. The fact that there were innocent people that could be harmed was the only thing keeping her focused just enough to rein it in.

It didn't matter that she could see regret written clearly in his eyes. He had lied to her, and worse yet, he had seen things that could jeopardize the life she was finally getting the chance to live. She wanted to scream, and then bury her head under her pillow and cry. There had been a real connection between her and the wolf, and now she knew why he had seemed so familiar. Beyond the betrayal and anger, she had a lingering sense of sadness that she had suddenly lost her one and only friend.

₧⎈₧⎈

When school finally let out for the day, Taryn informed Gastyn that she preferred to go home, instead of working one-on-one with him. He readily agreed. The toll the emotional day had taken on her was apparent in the heavy slump in her stance and the dullness in her eyes.

She walked to the parking lot and found her mother already waiting. "Is everything alright?" Ilya asked as she slid into the passenger seat.

"You heard?"

"It doesn't usually thunder like that without a cloud in the sky. I came immediately to make sure you were okay. Besides, I think everyone within a hundred mile radius heard. You know how important it is that you don't lose control, Taryn."

"I didn't lose control. It was only thunder," she growled, rolling her eyes. "Can we please talk about something else?"

₧⎈₧⎈

In the school parking lot, the other students broke off into their two packs and began discussing the events of the afternoon.

"You sly dog. You've been hanging out with the girl in wolf form. That's why you didn't want me going back in the woods the other day," Kellan teased his deflated friend.

"Some smooth-operator you are," Nalani heckled.

"I don't get it," Kellan sighed. "She didn't know that Skin-Walkers could shift. Are we even sure that she is truly Gaias?"

"She's Gaias alright. You can feel it seeping off of her," Dagney offered.

"Maybe she's a half-blood," Thorne theorized. "That could explain why her powers are too weak to sense other Gaias."

"Dude, there hasn't been a half-blood in over two centuries. Besides, if that were the case, Mr. Wylder would have told the Elder Council of her existence and that would have been the end of her and her mother," Gerrick interjected.

Larkin listened as his friends talked, but his heart was broken. He knew she was angry and that he deserved every bit of whatever she would give him.

"She doesn't seem to have any powers to speak of, and she definitely doesn't know anything about what we are. I don't think we should continue to court her," Gerrick stated.

"I don't care what she can do. I like her and I say we court her until she decides where she wants to be," Dagney countered.

Unable to listen to their discussion any longer, Larkin turned. "I'm going home guys. I'll see you later." Without a backward glance he walked to his jeep, head hung low with a heavy heart.

ഇൗരുഇൗരു

"I take it showing her the hawk wasn't part of the plan," Dalen ribbed Keiryn.

"Not now."

"Yeah, that was a real bone-headed move, Lover Boy. Now she probably thinks we're all shady and won't ever agree to join our ranks," Eben frowned.

"Who would want a girl who doesn't even know what it means to be Gaias?" Adalia commented with a sneer, joining them on the stairs.

"Nobody asked you," Bency countered.

"Freak!"

"You're not even a part of our pack, so your opinion doesn't serve a purpose," Jonesy stated.

"Just because you're crushing on her like the rest of them doesn't mean you can talk to me like that, Runt" she snapped, stepping towards him.

"Back off," Keiryn warned her.

"Whatever." With that she walked to the curb and waited for her father.

"Now that Ada the Terrible is gone, why do you think Taryn is so clueless about Gaias?" Dalen asked.

"I don't know, but what she did with the kid today, that was amazing regardless of the strength of her own powers," Keiryn answered.

"It was pretty impressive," Hadley added.

When the group started to go their separate ways, Keiryn noticed his father pulling into the parking lot. "What are you doing here, Dad?"

"I'm here to speak with Gastyn. I want you to go straight home and wait for me. There are a few things we need to talk about, Son."

"Yes, Sir." He couldn't ignore the seriousness in his father's tone.

Before he was able to make it a block away, he passed Maxym Taylor, who appeared to be going to the school as well. "That's just great," he mumbled to himself, realizing his father and Maxym were obviously meeting with Gastyn regarding what happened during class. He certainly wasn't looking forward to the lecture that he would likely be receiving once his dad made it home.

ಬಂ಄ಬಂ಄

The moment Taryn walked into her home, she immediately ran to change into a swimsuit and jumped eagerly into the pool. She

~ 180 ~

swam laps for nearly half an hour before noticing her mother standing poolside.

"I'm surprised you're swimming, Sweetie. I figured that you would want to take a walk when you got home."

"Yeah, I'm not really in the mood for walking through the forest." She swam over to the edge of the pool. "Mom, when Gastyn came over to the house last week…was he trying to see if I could sense what he was?"

"Is that what had you so upset earlier today? Another detail that I failed to mention?"

"Sort of."

"Typically, Gaias can sense one another, but you are anything but typical, Baby Girl."

"So I have gathered. Can you sense a Skin-Walker even when they have shifted into animal form?"

"Of course," Ilya answered.

"Then why can't I?"

Seeing her daughter's eyes filled with such insurmountable frustration, she tried to be as honest as she could with her. "I honestly don't know, Taryn. You are so unique and so special, that even I can't make sense of it all. For years I have struggled to understand why you're so different, but there's nothing that I have found that can explain it. You're the first of whatever you are."

"Perhaps I can answer your question," Gastyn stated, walking around the corner of the porch. "I hope you don't mind. I knew you were home."

"Of course not," Ilya smiled, relieved by his presence. "Your thoughts on the issue would be greatly appreciated."

"Taryn, please come join us," he motioned, waving her to exit the pool and have a seat on the lounge chairs next to them.

Cautiously she did as he asked, fearing he knew all of her secrets just like Larkin, and possibly Keiryn. "Why do you think I can't sense other Gaias?"

"I believe it is because the power that courses through your veins is much stronger than that of those around you. We are nothing more than a tickle against your flesh. Think about exactly what it is that you feel when you are around the other students in my classroom."

She concentrated, attempting to recall moments where she had felt something different from the normal. "I felt Jonesy, but I didn't know what it was at the time," she started, then paused. "Larkin, when he picked me up and saved me from the lightning…it must have been him that I felt, but I thought it was left over static electricity hanging in the air. And Keiryn at the diner, there was a white spark between us when we touched, but I thought it was me. I don't know why I didn't realize it before…"

"Perhaps it was because you weren't open to the idea, Taryn. You didn't know before, and I believe what you sense is far more subtle than the rest of us. The only thing I find strange is that you felt Jonesy's power and could recognize him for what he was. He's the weakest member between both packs."

Her face wrinkled with confusion. "You're wrong. Jonesy has great power living inside of him."

He studied her face and could see that she believed every word that she said. "It was my mistake," he offered, not wanting to stir her emotions any further. "Taryn, would you mind giving me a moment with your mother?"

"Of course not." She headed inside to fix herself a sandwich before running upstairs to shower off the day.

છબછબ

"What happened today at school?" Ilya asked, the second she was out of sight.

"You mean Taryn hasn't told you?"

"No, I heard the thunder and knew it was her. I rushed to the school and waited outside in case she wasn't able to control herself."

"She learned about what it truly means to be a Skin-Walker. She was thrown off a bit at first, but then managed to settle herself down." He thought it best to hold several of the key details back.

"That's strange. She's always loved animals. I thought she would find their particular gift to be incredible."

"She did, but you know teenagers, Ilya...she was simply overwhelmed. I do have a question for you. Have you ever witnessed her projecting her powers onto another being?"

"Projecting?"

"Perhaps a better word would be to share her powers."

Sitting quietly for a moment she considered what it was he was asking. "Not to my knowledge. But I can tell you that if she creates something, she has to be willing to let you undo it...otherwise it becomes permanent. Like with the fog the other day. She allowed me to clear out the area surrounding us near the table. Why do you ask?"

"I've asked that she not use her talents in the classroom with the other students until we can find a way to help her blend in. Today she was sitting with Andyn Mitchell, who is only twelve years of age, observing the other students. She encouraged him to animate a pencil into a flower and he did."

"That sounds like my girl."

"He possesses the animator ability but has struggled terribly with his gift for the past few years, unable to control what he creates, yet he was able to create the most beautiful, oversized desert flower that I have ever seen. The petals were silky soft, yet unable to be damaged, while the stem is green and hard as steel. Do you understand why I might pose such a question?"

She sighed heavily, as a battle began between her head and her heart. Her head was screaming to take her daughter and run, while her heart was telling her that Taryn was finally happy and deserved a chance to try to live a normal life. "Did the other students understand the significance?"

"Yes, but on a much smaller scale than what someone like you or I would take from it. I'm here, Ilya, you don't have to run."

"I know, but that little girl upstairs sitting in her room," she paused, tears building in her eyes. "She's the whole reason for my existence."

He wrapped a comforting arm around her and kissed the top of her head. "You're such a wonderful mother, Ilya. You've done an incredible job raising her, especially considering all that she is." He took her chin between his fingers and turned it to face him, looking deep into her eyes. "I don't want you to be upset by what I'm about to tell you, but I truly believe it will be for the best. There are a few others who I believe should be part of this circle of protection." She started to pull away, fearful of too many people being involved. He reached for her hands, holding onto them firmly, aware that she was fighting against the urge to flee before hearing him out. "It's going to be alright."

"Who?" she asked, still weary at the thought.

"Maxym Taylor and his son, Larkin, whom you've already met, and Teigan Falcon and his boy, Keiryn."

"Why them?"

"Larkin and Keiryn are the unofficial leaders of the two local youth packs. Involving them will insure that no one will do anything to put her in jeopardy on either side."

"But they are only children themselves. How do you know they will protect her secrets?"

Gastyn took a deep breath and exhaled heavily, knowing the answer to this particular question was something that he could not divulge because of the Blood Oath. "Larkin is already extremely protective of her, but I'm afraid that is all I can share with you until you speak with Maxym directly."

"Maxym is already aware of Taryn's power?"

"Not exactly. He suspects there is something more to her only because of the effect she has on his son. But again, you will need to speak with him regarding the specifics before I can say anything further."

"I ran into him earlier today while I was in Williams. He and Larkin are coming over for lunch tomorrow. I suspect we will have a lot to discuss."

"That you will," Gastyn agreed, noting her tense jawline. "Ilya, these are good people. You have nothing to fear from them. After you've had a chance to speak with Maxym, I would like for all of us to get together to discuss strategy before breaking the news to the children. I want everyone on the same page before we speak with Taryn, so I think it would be best if you were to surprise her in regards to your lunch tomorrow."

"Very well," Ilya replied. She walked him to the door and thanked him again. As she watched him drive away she laid her head against the door frame and tried to quell the fear that was causing her heart to race.

ಬಾಣಬಾಣ

Maxym walked into his son's room and took a seat on the edge of the bed. "Larkin, Gastyn told me about what happened during class today."

"Then you know he's ruined everything."

~ 185 ~

"Why would you say that? If she's as amazing as you say, surely she will find a way to forgive you, Son."

"You didn't see her eyes, Dad. One minute she looked at me with awe and the next they were so empty, so hollow."

"She's a young woman, Larkin. A woman at any age doesn't like to be misled or lied to. I'm sure she was only trying to hide how she really felt. The past seven days of her life have been quite different from what she is accustomed to. Give her a little time and it will work its way out," Maxym offered, pausing for a moment. "What happened today, does it change the need you feel for her?"

He sat up in the bed and ran his hands through his hair. "No. If anything it makes me want to protect her even more. I know she's in pain, Dad, pain that I caused her."

"What are you thinking, Son?"

"As much as it rips me apart, I'm going to have to watch over her from afar. It's the right thing to do after what I've done." A smile formed on Maxym's face, catching his son's eyes. "You don't have to be so happy about it."

"It's not that. I was just thinking how hard that's going to be considering her mother invited us over for lunch."

"What?" Larkin shouted jumping from his bed. "Are you crazy, I can't go over there."

"I know it probably seems that way right now, but I promise you, it's better to face these situations head on. Besides, it's been a long time since I've had a woman offer to fix me a meal, and I don't plan on missing the opportunity."

Rolling his eyes, Larkin headed down stairs to the kitchen. He pulled out a container of lunch meat from the refrigerator. Taking a handful he shoved it into his mouth. "Fine, I'll go. But I'm telling you it's not a good idea."

"I suppose you won't be staying in tonight?"

Larkin shook his head no before heading for the door.

"I love you, Son."

"Love you too, Dad."

ଈଔଷଈଔଷ

Standing in the shadow of the trees behind her home, he watched Taryn and her mother as they sat in the living room laughing at the television together. He found momentary delight in seeing the joy on her face, wishing it had been him that had put it there.

A half hour later she kissed her mother goodnight and ascended up the stairs. He waited for the lights in her room to turn on, but instead it remained dark. With growing impatience, he scanned the numerous other windows, unable to catch a glimpse of her.

Suddenly, the lights turned on to reveal her standing at the window, startling him. He could see that she was peering down at him with the same blank look from earlier in the day. It cut him to the very core. As their eyes remained locked on each other, rain began to fall, slowly at first, until it became a torrential downpour.

The light from Taryn's bedroom was barely visible, but he continued to stand rooted, willing to take whatever punishment she deemed appropriate for his betrayal.

After ten minutes the rain stopped abruptly. She reached up, grabbing the curtains, and pulled them closed. A few minutes later her room went dark. Soaking wet and shivering, he stayed to watch over her.

ଈଔଷଈଔଷ

In the morning Taryn woke still tired from a night of restless sleep. She walked to the window and opened the curtains only to discover that Larkin was still standing in the exact spot he had been in before she went to bed. The bitter taste that was still present on her lips from his betrayal caused a flash of irritation in the pit of her stomach.

~ 187 ~

Staring down, her eyes locked with his, stirring a myriad of emotions within her. Even from a distance she could see his body was riddled with exhaustion, but she refused to back down, not wanting to give him any satisfaction or show further sign of weakness.

He finally bowed his head, looking away, glancing back up to her one more time before turning and walking away. She had expected to feel the weight of emotion lifting off her chest with his departure. Instead it felt all the more heavy.

A deep sigh escaped her, confused by the conflicting war between her head and her heart. Sensing the battle was far from over, she headed into the bathroom to take a shower.

℠ಳ℠ಳ

"Where are you going, Keiryn?" Teigan asked as his son tried to creep past him.

"I'm going to check on Taryn. I'll go straight over and come right back."

Teigan motioned for him to take a seat at the kitchen table. "It's like I explained to you last night. You will stay away from her until I tell you otherwise."

"That's not fair," Keiryn hissed, slamming the palm of his hand down on the table top. "I bet Mr. Taylor isn't keeping the monster locked up."

"That's enough! You are going to have to trust me when I tell you that we have a plan...just be patient a little longer."

Although he wasn't happy, Keiryn recognized the seriousness in his father's tone and knew he had no choice but to listen. "I'm going to ask the pack to come over and hang out," he stated, waiting for his father to object.

"Go ahead. I think the distraction will do you good."

℠ಳ℠ಳ

"I need to run to the grocery store. Do you want to come along?" Ilya asked, noticing how distant Taryn appeared to be.

"Yeah, sure."

"Still bothered about the Skin-Walkers?"

"It's not really their ability that bothers me."

"Then what is it?"

After shutting the car door Taryn turned towards her mother. "It's their character, or lack thereof," she confided.

"Like with any gift, it's up to the individual to choose to use it appropriately."

Taryn sat quietly, pondering something she hadn't ever thought of before. "Mom, what if a Gaias misuses their power...what happens to them?"

"If discovered, they would have to face the Elder Council."

"The Elder Council?"

"It's a council made up of some of the oldest living Gaias, as well as members of the most prominent families. Our laws are similar to that of the human world, no killing, stealing and things of that nature."

"Is the council who you've kept me hidden away from?"

"Yes, but they aren't the only ones. Any member of the Gaias community could cause problems if they were to know the full extent of your powers, Taryn. It's a requirement that if you see someone breaking our laws, you have to report them to the council," Ilya warned.

"I don't understand how being what I am could break any laws."

"Where you are concerned, it's not about breaking the written rules. You are unique compared to other Gaias. There is no one else out there like you. You break every law of nature." The sudden darkening of the sky overhead made Ilya realize that the current subject was upsetting Taryn even more. Trying to lighten the mood, she continued, "Did I mention that we are having guests over for lunch?"

"What? No…who's coming over?"

"Oh, I think it would be better if you were surprised."

"I'm not sure that I can handle any more surprises this week," she mumbled under her breath. Assuming it would be Gastyn, she sat back in the seat and tried to enjoy the rest of the ride into town.

In the grocery store, while Ilya picked up a few last minute items, Taryn walked down the chip aisle looking for a bag of honey mustard pretzel sticks. As she was perusing the shelves, Douglas Scott walked by.

"Hi, Douglas."

"Oh hey, Taryn," he replied awkwardly, hesitating before turning to walk quickly away.

"Douglas, please wait."

"Did you need help finding something?"

"No. I wanted to say thanks again for showing me around the other morning."

"Look, I know you're new to Williams and you seem really nice…but you and I being friends…it's not going to work."

"Why?" she asked, grabbing his arm as he turned to walk away.

"Because people in your social group don't associate with people like me, Taryn. It's better if we keep our distance. It makes things less complicated. Now if you don't mind, I have to get to work."

"Okay." She watched him walk away, sad that what could have been a promising friendship had never even had a chance. Forgetting about the pretzels, she went to find her mother.

"Everything alright, Taryn?" Ilya inquired, noticing her slouchy posture.

"Yep, fine. I'm going to head outside."

"Sure, Sweetie. I'll be there in a few minutes."

On the ride home, she sat quietly staring out the window, wondering if every animal they passed was truly an animal or a Skin-Walker in disguise. The anger and embarrassment that she had felt yesterday had settled and taken root in her stomach, slowly eating away at her.

After helping to carry the grocery bags inside, she tried to excuse herself to go back upstairs but her mother insisted that she stay and help prepare lunch.

She cut the green and red bell peppers, cucumber and tomatoes for the salad while her mother layered the homemade lasagna noodles, meat and cheese in a pan. Once the lasagna was in the oven and the table was set both mother and daughter rushed upstairs to freshen up.

Taryn slipped on one of her new dresses and applied light makeup, wanting to make a good impression for her mother, still assuming that Gastyn was one of the guests that had her making such a fuss.

"You look so grown up, Baby Girl," Ilya beamed from just outside her doorway. She smiled widely, never having seen Taryn wear a dress before.

"Wow, you look beautiful, Mom." Carefully she hugged her, trying not to mess up her mother's hair or make-up before joining her to walk down the stairs.

"The lasagna is done. Could you please grab the loaf of garlic bread and put it in the oven?"

"Sure."

The timer on the oven beeped as the doorbell rang. "Taryn, please get the bread out of the oven, and put it in the basket on the table."

Standing with her hand on the doorknob, Ilya realized that once she opened the door, none of their lives would ever be the same. The thought gave her pause, but after taking a few deep breaths she pulled it open and smiled brightly. "Hello, Maxym."

"Ilya, you look lovely," he responded smoothly, handing her a bottle of red wine and a bouquet of flowers. The white sundress she wore was adorned with a bright yellow belt that showcased her trim waist. Her hair flowed in loose curls around her tanned shoulders. It had been a long time since he had appreciated the sight of a beautiful woman.

"They are lovely," she stated of the flowers. "Hello, Larkin."

"Hello, Miss Malone," he smiled awkwardly, thinking about how upset she would be with him if she knew all of his secrets.

"Please call me Ilya."

While walking through the Malone's home, he couldn't help but be amazed as he looked around. It didn't matter that he had peered inside numerous times, or that he had slept on the roof almost as many. The inside was even more spacious than it appeared from the outside.

"Larkin," Taryn gasped as she caught sight of him. Smiling awkwardly, she tried to hide the look of surprise that flashed across her face.

"Hey, Taryn." He ran his fingers through his hair nervously, all the while soaking in how pretty she looked in her light blue halter dress and white strappy sandals.

"It's nice to see you again, Taryn," Maxym interrupted, trying to give his son a moment to compose himself.

"Nice to see you, Mr. Taylor." She was barely able to tear her eyes away from Larkin, stunned to see him standing in her dining room after everything that had happened.

"Shall we sit," Ilya nodded, surprised by her daughter's less than enthusiastic reaction to their guests.

As the four of them took their seats, she pushed her emotions back down, allowing a warm and inviting smile to curl on her face. After batting her long lashes in Larkin's direction, she turned her focus to Maxym. "Did your neighbor ever find her dog, Mr. Taylor?" She smiled as she put a slight emphasis on the word dog.

"What?"

"The dog," she repeated, sensing he was as deceitful as his son.

"Oh, oh, yes. That silly dog finally came home on her own."

"Silly dog," Taryn agreed.

As the foursome began eating, she played the perfect host, causing Larkin to finally relax. Her mother watched in awe as she exuded confidence and charm, making everyone comfortable. Once they had finished with the main course, Taryn cleared the table. With Larkin trailing behind, his hands full of dirty salad plates, she directed him to set them on the counter.

"That was delicious."

"My mother is an exceptional cook," she agreed, rinsing the plates off before placing them into the dishwasher. Once finished, she turned and leaned against the counter, carefully studying his handsome face. "Are you up to going for a walk?"

"Of course."

"Okay, give me a minute to change and then we can go."

"You don't need to change...you look beautiful," he gushed. Taryn's smile began to fade slightly. Fearing he had offended her, he tried to explain. "Not that you don't always look beautiful, because you do." He blushed tens shades of red as her green eyes assessed him coolly.

"Fine," she replied, flashing a brilliant smile. "I'll keep the dress but the shoes have to go."

Running upstairs she changed into her hiking boots. Amazingly, the ruggedness of the boots combined with the softness of the dress meshed together, making her look angelic but edgy. When she walked back down the stairs, he couldn't take his eyes off of her.

"And where are the two of you headed off to?" Maxym asked from the comfort of one of the patio chairs, with Ilya sitting beside him.

"We're going for a walk, Mr. Taylor," Taryn answered.

"Okay, but don't go too far into the forest," Ilya insisted. "We'll have dessert in about an hour."

When Ilya could feel that the children were out of earshot, she turned to Maxym with a serious look. "Gastyn told me that we needed to talk," she started, staring out to the woods, fighting to keep her composure.

"Yes, we do."

"He shared with me that your son feels very strongly about the well-being of my daughter." She paused, hoping he would willingly fill in the blanks for her.

Maxym took a swallow of his wine before running his hand through his hair. "That is correct, Ilya. Larkin feels an overwhelming need to be her protector, to keep her safe from anything or anyone that might cause her harm or bring her pain." It was a struggle for him to keep his voice steady.

"Okay. Do you know why?" She couldn't help but notice his stiffened posture.

"He tells me that she is special, and is absolutely smitten, but it goes far beyond a teenage crush." Pausing to take another drink, he leaned forward, moving closer to her. "The morning after Larkin's twelfth birthday, he woke, telling me about an angel he had dreamt of the night before."

"That's nice, but what does this have to do with my daughter?" Ilya interrupted, growing impatient for answers.

"He described the angel. She had light brown hair, eyes that gleamed like emeralds and a smile that beamed the warmth of a thousand suns. At a time when the other boys his age were starting to appreciate girls, Larkin had no interest. Granted, there were a few other things happening during this same period, but he dreamt only of this girl for the next several months and nothing else."

"Of course, he had a lot going on. Turning twelve is an important time in our lives. It can be very confusing or provide absolute clarity."

"I'm sorry. I'm not explaining this quite right. This girl, the angel who has haunted his dreams, Ilya...it was Taryn." Maxym could tell by the look on her beautiful face that she was finally beginning to understand the scope of his son's attachment to her daughter.

Looking at him, then down to the ground and back to him again, tears began to flow freely. "Does Taryn know?"

"She didn't an hour ago, but I suspect Larkin will tell her while they are out on their walk." He reached for her hand, taking it into his own, trying to comfort her. "I would be lying if I told you that I don't have my own share of concerns about this...but I can assure you that he means her no harm. He would never do anything to jeopardize her safety."

"So you knew about her the night you stopped by...but you didn't say anything. Why not?"

"I'm sorry about that, Ilya, but you have to understand that I didn't know what to think about it either. My son came back from a run distracted by something that he had not seen, something he could only sense. He goes back into the woods and this time when he returned, he tells me that the girl from his dreams is real…living only a few miles away. It was a lot to take in and I had no idea if this was some sort of dark power at work, or worse." Ilya's tears gave way to uncomfortable laughter. "What is it?" he asked, fearing she might be losing it.

"It's kind of funny. I kept Taryn away from this home, away from everything and anyone Gaias, trying to hide her very existence from the world. Yet here, only two miles away from my childhood home, your son was already dreaming of her. It can't be a coincidence, can it?"

"That does seem highly unlikely. There's something else you need to know about, Ilya. Gastyn believes that he is not only protective of her, but that he is bound to her in every possible way," he admitted, happy to get that bit of information off of his chest.

"Bound to her? How exactly do you mean?" She was not fond of the idea of anyone being bound to her sixteen year old daughter.

Sensing that she might not take the news very well, he prepared himself for whatever her response might be. "Larkin feels a special connection with her, emotionally, mentally and physically. If he stays away for too long, he becomes very agitated and consumed with concern. He has to be able to see with his own two eyes that she is safe before he is content."

"Okay, so he comes and checks on her periodically. I suppose I can live with that."

"That's not what I meant," he swallowed hard.

"Then what exactly did you mean?"

"Larkin feels the need to watch over her, all of the time."

"That's absurd. He has to sleep sometime."

"He sleeps. Just not in his bed." He paused as she raised her eyebrows in confusion. "He's been spending the last several nights on your roof, outside her bedroom window."

"What?" She shrieked. "You're telling me that you allow your son to sleep outside of my daughter's bedroom window." Rising to her feet, she paced fitfully about.

"I can't stop him, Ilya, he is bound to her."

"You're a mature Gaias. If you wanted to stop him I'm quite certain you could have!"

He could see the fury building in her eyes. "I know you're upset and I don't blame you, but you have to understand that when I see how much pain the distance causes him, and the desperation and fear in his eyes...he's my son, Ilya. I can't stand to see him in such turmoil."

"That's not an excuse."

"Do you think it was easy letting him go?" Maxym countered. "You have no idea how terrified I was to find out that she was real. Not after seeing what it has done to him. He spends every second of everyday with her on his mind, focusing only on her and her well-being. He barely eats, sleeps, sees his friends or even talks to me anymore, how do you think I feel?"

In an instant the anger left her body, allowing him inside of her heart. "Awful," she whispered, stumbling to find a seat as his words struck a chord deep within her.

"What?" he asked, not hearing her whispered word.

"Awful...helpless...and endlessly terrified...it's exactly how I feel about Taryn." Silent tears flowed down her cheeks once again. "Since the first time I saw her use her gifts, I've had this awful feeling in the pit of my stomach that has eaten away at me every second of the past twelve years. And I've always known, that no matter what choices and sacrifices I've made, that in an instant it could all crumble down around us and they would try to take her away."

He took a seat next to her on the chaise lounge and wrapped her snuggly in his arms, trying to comfort her in some way. Sensing her worries out-weighed even his own, he knew that it did very little to ease the myriad of emotions that she felt.

After several minutes of silence, he cupped her chin with his hand, bringing her eyes to meet his. "Ilya, you don't have to do this alone. You have allies in the fight to protect Taryn and her secrets, but only if you allow us to help."

Searching his face, looking for any sign of deceit, she nodded in agreement when she found only sincerity, knowing this could be their only hope of survival.

CHAPTER EIGHT

A half-mile away, Taryn led Larkin through the woods. "If you like, I could show you the trails that my pack and I run," he offered.

"That's alright." She flashed him a disarming smile as she glanced back.

"Thanks for being so cool about the whole Skin-Walker thing."

"You should probably wait to thank me." Turning to face him, she took pleasure in watching his light, free-spirited expression turn into a look of dismay. "It sucks, doesn't it?"

"What sucks?" he inquired cautiously, fearing she was finally going to unleash her anger on him. He braced himself, knowing he deserved whatever punishment she deemed necessary.

"When someone allows you to believe something that isn't the truth."

"If you would give me a second, I can explain."

"You're opportunity to speak has passed…and now it's my turn." Placing her hands on her hips, she glared at him as flames of anger danced in her jewel colored eyes. "The wolf I met here in the forest…I trusted him, but he turned out to be nothing more than a snake in a fur coat."

"No, you have it all wrong, Taryn."

Shaking her head, she interrupted. "I'm not finished! You lied to me, Larkin. You hid the truth and let me expose myself…for what?" Not giving him more than a second to reply, she tore into him. "Was it because of the packs? The feud between you and Keiryn, or did you just want to have something to hold over my head so I would choose your side?"

"I only wanted to be close to you," he answered, struggling to find the right words to make her understand.

"Lies!" The wind kicked up, gusting forcefully around them. "The second we were safe at your house after the storm, you could have told me, but you didn't. You followed me in the woods, stalked me at school, you made me look ridiculous my first day…and for what?" she thundered, catching more than just Larkin's attention.

ഇരുഇരു

Back at the Malone home, by the pool where Ilya and Maxym were sitting, a strong wind began blowing, tipping the deck chairs with its fury. "I didn't think it was supposed to storm," Maxym yelled, as he tried to hold down the table with the glass-top. The winds began to settle, but things were far from calm.

"It's not a storm, it, it, it's Taryn," Ilya stammered, staring at the pool.

"Don't be sill…" He stopped mid-word as he followed her gaze. His jaw dropped open as the water in the pool began to bubble and churn. "Larkin!" Turning, he ran in the direction the children had gone with Ilya close on his heels.

Running full force, desperate to find his son, Maxym was brought up short by something that knocked him to the ground.

"What happened?" she asked.

Standing, he held his hand out, trying to push forward with no avail. "There's an invisible shield here. We can't get through."

"Let me try." She pushed her hands against the field. After a few moments, she stumbled back, a look of dread in her face. "I can't get through. It doesn't make any sense. Taryn's always permitted me to undo her creations."

"What have I gotten my son into?"

"Don't blame her," she pleaded. "This is my fault. I should never have come back here."

As she fell to her knees, Maxym continued to try to find a way around the shield. Realizing it was no use, he transformed into a hawk, taking flight over the protective dome. Flying high above, he finally caught a glimpse of the teens through the trees. They were standing in the middle of a clearing, both appearing unharmed for the moment.

"They're about twenty yards away," he exclaimed, after landing and shifting back into human form.

"Were they okay?"

"They were both still standing, that's all I could see."

"I don't understand why she would be doing this. It's so out of character." She pounded her fists against the invisible wall.

A guilty look washed over Maxym's face. "I think I do." Ilya looked in his direction, desperate for any explanation that would allow her to make sense of it all. "Larkin's been meeting up with her in the woods ever since you moved in."

"She never mentioned it."

"That's because she didn't know it was him. He was in wolf form when they met, and he was afraid to show her who he really was."

"Gastyn told me she didn't respond well to learning about the Skin-Walker ability, now I know why."

"Listen." He motioned for her to place her ear against the field. "Do you hear that?" She nodded, yes. Faintly, they could hear the voices of their children. Each of them pressed an ear against the field and listened intently, praying for the best possible outcome.

ଛଠଛଠ

"Why?" Taryn thundered. "Why would you do this to me?"

"I never meant to hurt you."

"I don't care what you meant. From this day forward, you and your snake of a father will stay away from my mother and I."

"I can't do that," he shook his head.

Ignoring him, she continued. "There will be no more lurking in the hallways at school, staring at me from across the lunchroom or walks in the woods in any form, human or otherwise."

"That's never going to happen."

"You act as if you have a say in the matter. You will either stay away or I'll…" she paused, conflicted by emotion.

Stepping closer to her, he realized that he was putting his life in her hands, for better or worse. "It doesn't matter what you say or what you do to me, Taryn. I can't…no…I won't stay away from you."

"Then I'll make you," she warned. With her emotions overtaking her, the battle between her heart and her head was becoming more than she could bear. The wind swirled rapidly around them as she started to lose control.

"I've waited all of this time for you to be real and here you are. I'm not letting you go…"

"You have to. I won't give you a choice." Tears streamed down her face as the force of the swirling winds began to pick them up off of the ground.

"I was wrong. I should have been honest from the beginning, and that is on me. So I'll endure whatever punishment you have to give."

"I'll end you, Larkin Taylor."

"No you won't, Taryn Malone." Fighting through the howling winds, he reached out and touched her hand.

"How can you be so sure?"

"Because I know you…"

"You don't know the first thing about me."

"When you were eleven, you wanted a horse, but you got a poster of one instead."

Her eyes widened. *How could he know that?*

Sensing he finally had her attention he continued telling her things that would be impossible for anyone else to know. "You snuck out of your window to sit on top of a rusty old car more nights than I can even count. The blanket on your bed was pink and white and was ripped on one of the corners, but above all of that, I know that you are kind, compassionate and all that is good in this world. And that's how I know you won't hurt me."

Slowly the winds started to calm, gently returning their feet back to the ground. The shield that prevented Maxym and Ilya from reaching them suddenly disappeared. They ran to the children. Maxym was the first to see them. Quickly, he grabbed Ilya and placed his hand over her mouth, pulling her behind a large tree. He motioned for her to watch and not to interrupt the exchange taking place.

"How did you know all of that?" Her voice trembled with emotion.

"On the night of my twelfth birthday, I dreamt of you for the first time. And I've dreamt of you on many occasions since, over the past five years," he answered, pausing a moment to allow it all to sink in. "Do you understand now that I never meant to hurt you?"

Turning, she walked away from him and over to one of the trees to lean against it. The battle between her head and her heart began to wane. "Why didn't you tell me this before?"

"Because, Taryn, I was afraid. Afraid that you might think that I was crazy or that you wouldn't want anything to do with me. And the first time I met you, you seemed so fond of the wolf…I thought it was because of your connection to the forest."

She smiled for the first time since confronting him. "I was very fond of the wolf."

"You know that regardless of what form I take, I'm the same on the inside, right? Talking to me is just like talking to the wolf."

Shaking her head she replied, "No, Larkin, you're wrong. It's not the same."

"Taryn, I…"

She took a few steps toward him as she held his gaze with her own. The turmoil written so clearly on his face tore at her heart strings. With a small smile, she continued, "It's not the same at all, Larkin, it's better."

He searched her eyes for any sign that she was toying with him. As her smile bloomed, he let out a sigh of relief. "Does this mean that we're okay?"

"That depends…is there anything else that I should know about?" She arched her brows, putting him in the hot seat once again.

He sighed while shaking his head. "Yes…but please don't think it's weird."

"Let's hear it."

"I feel an overwhelming need to protect you."

"Is that all?"

"And I may or may not have been sleeping outside your bedroom window at night…"

"Well…did you or didn't you?"

"That depends. If you think it sounds crazy…I definitely wasn't," he blushed.

"It does sound creepy and definitely stalkerish…but it also sounds incredibly sweet." Her smile faded as a new thought invaded her mind.

"What is it?" The distraught look on her face made him wonder if she was already having a change of heart.

"The overwhelming need you feel to protect me…are you sure that it isn't because you feel a need to protect everyone else from me?" Worry and sadness marred the beauty of her eyes.

"No, Taryn. How could you even think such a thing?"

"Until recently, my mother has kept me in hiding, away from the rest of the world. She said it was to protect me, but a small part of me can't help but wonder if she was really trying to protect everyone else from me. She has told me countless times that I am special, that there is no one else like me. If that is true, then how do we know I won't be a danger to everyone else?" She fought desperately to keep her tears at bay. "Look at what I started to do here, all because my feelings were hurt."

From behind the tree, Ilya's heart broke at hearing her daughter's words. Maxym wrapped her in his arms, trying his best to comfort her as their children continued their conversation.

"I'm sure your mother felt the same way that I do now." He brushed a stray hair gently from her face. "I told my father that you were special, but special doesn't even begin to describe you. The things you are able to do are beyond incredible. If any other Gaias had your abilities, I would fear for the earth and anyone and anything that walked upon it. But I'm not afraid, because it's you Taryn. You are everything that is good and pure in this world. Your kindness and compassion for other living things far surpasses anyone else. I saw that every time I walked with you as the wolf. You would never hurt an innocent person. I am to blame for what happened here today, not you. You were angry, and rightfully so, but you reined it in because of that platinum heart. As for your mother, she only wanted to be sure that your secrets were protected. There are others who would see you as a threat to their own power, and even some who would do unspeakable things to have you on their side. That's why your mother made the choices that she did."

"Don't blame yourself for today. When I think about it, deep down inside, I've always known you and the wolf were one in the same. I couldn't quite put my finger on it at the time, but the familiarity, the peace I feel with you, with the wolf, they are identical. I just wasn't able to make sense of it without some help."

"I know." Now that she had forgiven him, he still needed to address the most pressing matter, her safety. "Will it be okay if I continue to watch over you?" He knew, regardless of her answer, he couldn't stay away.

"You only want to protect me?"

"Taryn, everything in my very being tells me that my purpose is to protect you, whether it be from some outside threat or from yourself, at least until you learn everything you need to know about being Gaias." He took her hand in his. "But it's what my heart is telling me that I can't escape."

"And what does it say to you, Larkin?"

Trembling with nerves and emotion that he'd never felt before, he tightened the grip on her hand. "It tells me to grab hold of you and to never let go." His heart was racing in his chest, ready to explode.

For a long moment, they stood sharing a gaze. Their hearts racing in unison as they both experienced this new emotion together for the first time. Cupping her face in his hand and lifting it upward, he leaned down and placed the gentlest of kisses upon her forehead before slowly pulling away.

"I love you, Taryn."

"I know," she whispered, closing her eyes and savoring the words for just a moment. Even though she was enjoying the euphoria that those words had brought, the emotions he invoked in her were new and a little scary. Taking a step back, she let his hand go and walked several feet down the trail. "Are you going to show me those trails or what?" The smile she sent him melted his heart.

Larkin followed after her for several seconds before finally catching up. Picking her up and cradling her in his arms, he spun around before placing her feet back on the ground. "I'm never letting go." Holding onto her hand, he took off at a slow jog down the trail.

Stepping out from behind the tree, Ilya and Maxym breathed a sigh of relief. She wiped the tears away from her cheeks. Hearing just how much Larkin cared for her little girl was frightening, but it also brought joy to her heart. It was commonplace in the Gaias community for love to blossom at a young age. Most of the married couples today had been high school sweethearts. Knowing that Taryn and Larkin could share the rest of their lives together made her smile, but it also broke her heart that she would no longer be the center of her daughter's expanding world.

"I now see what all of the fuss has been about." He grinned while rolling his eyes, happy that things appeared to be working out for his son for once. "They are both safe and sound now, Ilya. I think we should head back to the house and let them have their privacy."

"I can't help but worry."

"She's in good hands with Larkin."

"No, she's in the best hands," she corrected him, flashing a peaceful glance, knowing now that someone else truly understood her little girl.

"You're going to love the view," Larkin assured her.

Stepping up beside him, Taryn looked around. "Everything is so beautiful from here." She gasped as she took in the breathtaking sight. From their vantage point on the peak of the mountain she could see for miles in all directions. The tranquility, combined with the feeling of being the only two people on earth, made her smile. After peering out for several minutes, she turned to look at him. "Do you come up here a lot?"

"Pretty much anytime I need to clear my head."

"It is peaceful up here."

"You should see it at night. If you want, I could bring you back up here sometime."

"I'd like that." She bumped her shoulder into him. Looking down shyly, she leaned into him, resting her head against his chest. Warmth flooded his body as he wrapped an arm around her, nuzzling her hair to place a kiss on top of her head. He wanted to stay here forever, with her standing safely engulfed in his arms, just the two of them, together on top of the world.

ೞೞೞೞ

"I'm glad you called," Gastyn stated, while he and Teigan entered Ilya's home.

"Maxym," Teigan nodded.

"Ilya, this is Teigan Falcon. His son, Keiryn, is the leader of the other pack," Gastyn introduced them.

"Pleasure to meet you," he smiled politely, holding his hand out to her.

Taking it, she smiled back, trying to hide her apprehension. "Mr. Falcon. Please come in."

She led them into the living room and took a seat while Gastyn looked out the French doors. "It appears that you had some excitement around here. Anything we should know about?"

"Let's just say that Taryn and Larkin had a conversation that was long overdue," Maxym acknowledged.

"I take it that everyone is okay?" Teigan asked, more in the dark than the rest of them.

Maxym looked to his friend, knowing exactly what he was asking, and it had nothing to do with Taryn and her abilities. "Yes, they are both fine."

"If everyone is ready, I think it is time for us to get down to business," Gastyn stated, taking the lead.

ᏚᏣᏓᏣᏓ

Two hours later, having devised a plan to protect Taryn and her secrets, Ilya felt more at peace with her decision to return to Williams. She had been fighting this battle alone for far too long. It felt good to know that there were others who wanted to keep her daughter safe as much as she did. "I want you all to know how much I appreciate this. It means a lot, considering two of you barely know me."

"To be completely honest with you, your daughter is the reason this plan is even possible. She's had quite the effect on our boys," Teigan grinned.

"The kids were the best of friends until they turned twelve. They had a sort of misunderstanding and there's been a rift between them ever since," Maxym explained. "Maybe by having to work together, they will find their way back to each other." Teigan nodded in agreement.

"Is that what happened to Larkin's face?" she asked.

"Yeah, but Keiryn's isn't any better," Teigan admitted. "It still amazes me how they managed to spend the night out here together and didn't demolish your home."

"Keiryn's been out there too?" She shook her head, still not crazy about the idea. "I guess it's part of the package."

~ 209 ~

"At least with both of them out there, you know there isn't any funny business happening," Teigan chuckled, soliciting a laugh of agreement from Gastyn and Maxym.

"Okay, I'll talk with Miss Blake about Taryn going over to her place with Jonesy for a few hours tomorrow. After we have a chance to bring Larkin and Keiryn up to speed and get their commitment to the plan, Miss Blake will drop her off and we can share the details with Taryn then," Gastyn reaffirmed, heading towards the front door with Teigan following closely behind.

With the knowledge that tomorrow their lives would be changed forever, Ilya thanked them again and bid them farewell. She and Maxym waved as Teigan turned his vehicle around and headed down the long driveway.

"Everything's going to be okay." He took her hand, giving it a reassuring squeeze. The worry seeped off of her in palpable waves. Wanting to distract her, he guided her back into the living room. "Come on. I'll help you get your deck back in order."

☯ ꧁ ☯ ꧂

"Do you really think this plan can work?" Teigan asked.

"I don't think we have much of a choice. Now that Larkin knows that she is real, he'll never be able to let her go. And Keiryn, the way he feels the need to protect her from him…he's just as committed," Gastyn offered. "At least there will be a balance between the packs this way."

"It sure would have been nice to know about his dreams. Especially since it appears that his affliction may very well be associated with her. The dreams started at the same time, but I guess that's water under the bridge now. What if this girl chooses one side over the other?"

"She won't, Teigan. Taryn isn't like the other children. She has nothing to prove and doesn't seek anyone's approval."

~ 210 ~

"But from the way it sounds, she and Larkin are together. Won't she choose his side?"

"Don't fret, my friend. I think once you have met her, you will understand. Besides, they are young…you never know how things are going to end up."

"I hope you're right," Teigan admitted, trying to let go of all of his worry until he could let his son in on the plan. He wasn't looking forward to telling Keiryn that Larkin and Taryn were possibly together now. Keiryn felt a strong connection to the girl. If they were indeed an item, he wouldn't take the news well.

ഇരു ഇരു

"I wonder when they'll be back," Ilya sighed, wanting nothing more than to wrap her arms snuggly around her daughter.

"Don't worry, Ilya. They needed this time together." Maxym placed the last piece of lawn furniture back in its proper spot.

"I suppose you're right."

A short time later, Taryn returned riding on the back of a beautiful white and caramel colored painted horse. "Look, Mom. I finally got the horse that I've always wanted." Leaning forward, she patted the animal fondly before sliding down from Larkin's back, beaming with happiness.

He shifted back into human-form and stretched briefly. "It's a little different than the wolf, huh?" his dad asked.

"Yeah, but I still pulled it off like the professional Skin-Walker that I am."

"He was going to shift into a mule, but I told him I had already seen him act like an ass," Taryn teased, bumping her hip into him while he was bent over, sending him stumbling. She looked to Maxym and gave him a wink, letting him know all was well between them.

"We were talking and we'd like to have dinner at the Desert Rose Café tonight," Larkin stated.

"I suppose we could all go," his father responded.

"Um, no... I meant me and Taryn would like to go, alone."

"I think that's a wonderful idea," Ilya agreed, surprising everyone.

"Are you sure?" Maxym asked.

"Positive."

"Okay then. We'd better head home so you can get cleaned up if you'd like to take this young lady out for dinner," Maxym suggested.

"Yeah, okay," he agreed, looking at Taryn with nothing but love in his eyes. "See you in a little while."

"See ya." After father and son were out of sight, she rushed inside to shower and change before she began to fret over what outfit she would wear.

₧₨₧₨

"This is your first date. How does it feel?" Ilya smiled.

"Mom, can we please not make this a thing?"

"Oh no, Darling Daughter. Since we've moved here I can see how fast you're growing up and I am going to enjoy every moment that is left of your childhood."

"Whatever," Taryn responded, rolling her eyes. "Do you really approve of Larkin, or is this some of that reverse psychology they always put into the movies?"

Tears filled her eyes when she thought back to earlier and all of the things Larkin had said to her daughter. "Yes, I do. He's a wonderful young man, Taryn. It makes me happy to know that when you are with him, you're in good hands."

"What about his dad?"

"What about him?"

"I don't know. It seemed like there might be a spark between the two of you."

~ 212 ~

"I don't want you to worry about me and Mr. Taylor. Just focus on you and Larkin and enjoy tonight, Baby Girl."

She shrugged in reply, wondering why her mother was so supportive of her and Larkin going out for the evening. Letting worry fall to the wayside, she returned her focus to her hair before fretting over what outfit she should wear.

After trying on only two different shirts, she put on a pair of white shorts with a silver colored camisole and a white bolero jacket. Her mother set out five different pairs of shoes, but she chose a pair of simple silver sandals adorned with decorative flowers.

"You look so grown up," Ilya cried.

"Oh, Mom."

"Well you do!" She swiped at her fresh tears.

The sound of the doorbell saved them both from a mushy scene. Taryn walked to the door, waving her mother out of sight. Taking a deep breath she opened it to find Larkin standing there, looking even more handsome than the last time she saw him. His face had perfect symmetry, showcasing his strong jawline, lush lips and alluring hazel eyes, all things she had noticed before but had been too distracted to truly appreciate. He literally took her breath away. Wanting to hide the effect he had on her, she tried to play it cool.

"Hey," she smiled, with a sparkle in her eyes.

"You look amazing, Taryn."

"Eh-hmm," Maxym cleared his throat. "I'll just get out of your way." He slipped past them with a large brown paper sack in tow, intending to spend the evening with Ilya.

"Ready?" Larkin asked.

"Always."

When they reached his jeep he opened the door for her, shooting her a longing gaze before finally closing it. Running around to the other side, he slid into the driver's seat.

Ilya and Maxym watched the sweet moment from the window. Once Larkin's jeep was no longer visible, they headed into the kitchen to enjoy the smoked meats and wine that he had brought, and wait on pins and needles until their children had returned safe and sound.

ಬುಞಬುಞ

"Are you nervous," Larkin asked as they pulled into town.

"No. You?"

"No." He flashed a charming smile in her direction.

As they pulled up in front of the café, he noticed a few familiar vehicles parked nearby and grinned to himself, knowing that his competition was sitting inside.

The moment Taryn walked into the café, Andyn rushed her. "Hey, Taryn!" He wrapped his arms around her waist.

"Hi, Andyn," she replied, returning his embrace.

"What's up, Larkin?"

"Not much. What about you? You here with your family?" Larkin couldn't help but notice the stink-eyed look the kid shot his way. He knew all too well what that look was about.

"My parents and Andalyn are sitting in the back."

"Andalyn?" Taryn questioned.

"Yeah, she's my kid sister," he sighed, trying to sound grown up. "Would you like to meet her?"

Not wanting to make Larkin feel slighted on what was to be their first date, she looked to him for approval. "Let's go say hello," he nodded, knowing that Andyn was someone she cared about.

"Father, I'd like for you to meet Taryn Malone."

~ 214 ~

"So you're the girl who has my son's attention." Andyn's father gave a nod of acknowledgement to Larkin.

He had the same blonde hair as his son, but his eyes were far less innocent. Even with him seated, she could see that he was tall and bulky and made of solid muscle. "I'm sorry?" Taryn replied, not quite sure how to take him and his empty expression. A slight gasp escaped her as his strong features morphed momentarily into something unfamiliar and strange, leaving her startled, as well as curious. Glancing around, she noticed no one else was reacting to what she had just witnessed, making her start to wonder if the coldness in his eyes had made her see things that weren't really there. Keeping her emotions under control, she showed nothing more than a cautious smile.

"My husband was just teasing you," his wife assured her. "My name is Lilyan, and this is Ardyn Mitchell."

Feeling something tugging at her arm, Taryn looked down to find a pretty little girl. She looked very similar to Andyn. Her hair was long and blonde, with ringlet curls framing her sweet face.

"And I'm Andalyn," the little girl laughed, latching her small arms around Taryn's waist.

Taryn placed an arm around the girl and hugged her back. "Nice to meet all of you," she smiled, keeping a watchful eye on Ardyn, who continued to stare intently at her.

"We'll let you get back to your dinner," Larkin stated, placing his hand softly on Taryn's lower back and guiding her away.

"Nice to meet you as well, Taryn," Lilyan called out.

She flashed a polite smile from over her shoulder and nodded, but not before taking a mental snapshot of their family and saving it to memory.

"Sorry about that," she apologized, sliding into one side of the booth.

"No need to apologize. I saw their car parked outside and knew the kid couldn't stay away from you." He slipped in across from her.

"You're not jealous are you?"

"Nope. However, I can relate to his dilemma." Reaching across the table, he took her hand into his.

The waitress came over to take their order, leaving them to focus solely on one another again. They were lost in their own world, deep in conversation when the door opened and the rest of Larkin's pack filed inside. Kellan stopped abruptly in his tracks when he spotted them.

"Hey, check this out," he whispered, pointing to the booth where they were seated.

"Looks like our boy is finally becoming a man," Gerrick laughed.

"Maybe we should say a quick hello," Thorne suggested.

"Let's," Kellan nodded, leading them over to table. "Hey, Larkin. Hey Kansas," he grinned widely.

"Hi," Taryn replied, sitting back in the booth.

"Hey, Guys," Larkin replied. "What are you doing here?" He gave them a pleading look to go away.

"We were just getting something to go," Dagney stated, cutting Kellan off before he could say another word. "Right guys?" She stabbed her elbow into Thorne's ribs.

"Um yeah, we were just picking up dinner before we head out to Cataract Lake," Thorne added, trying to make Dagney happy.

"Okay, we'll see you later then." Larkin shot a stern look for them to be on their way.

"You should come out to the lake later. We can show Kansas how Arizona parties," Kellan suggested, doing a little dance in the aisle.

"We'll see," he replied, shooting his friend a final look of warning to give them some privacy.

Finally, Kellan walked away, trailing after the rest of the pack who had taken their seats on the barstools by the counter.

"This is probably awkward for you," Taryn stated, studying his face.

"Maybe a little...but not for the reasons that you think. We've done practically everything together since we were around Andalyn's age. When things went south between me and the bird boy, those guys all took my side. They pledged to my pack and have stood beside me, even when I didn't always deserve their loyalty."

"The bird boy...that's Keiryn?" She could only assume they called him that because of his preferred form.

"Yeah." He sat back in the booth as the waitress set their food down on the table.

"What does his pack call you?"

"Black dog," he stated, rolling his eyes.

Taking a bite of her bacon cheeseburger, she pondered about what it was that could have caused such a rift between the friends. Once she swallowed, she inquired. "So the divide between the two groups...what triggered it?"

Larkin finished chewing the mouthful he had and then took a long drink of soda. "It's complicated." Running his hand through his hair, he was afraid to tell her that she very well could have been a contributing factor to the events that took place nearly five years ago.

"You were kids. How complicated could it have been?"

"Keiryn and I were messing around one evening and things got a little out of hand. I ended up on lock down while he ended up with a permanent reminder."

"What do you mean?"

Taking another long drink, Larkin used the time to choose his words carefully. "I left him scarred, Taryn. Every time that he looks in the mirror he can see the four scars that I left him with."

"You didn't mean to hurt him, right?"

"No. The damage was done before I even realized what had happened."

The look on his face told her everything she needed to know in that moment. "You're not a monster, Larkin. Sometimes bad things happen before we can stop them. It slays you to the core that you hurt your best friend. That tells me all I need to know."

"Larkin, Taryn," a deep voice interrupted them.

"Mr. Mitchell," Larkin replied, sitting up straight in his seat.

"I wanted to apologize if I came across as rude earlier, Taryn. My son speaks very highly of you. He told me how you helped him to complete his first successful animation the other day during class."

"All I did was encourage him to use what was already inside of him." She couldn't help but stare as his face flickered once again between his normal persona and the one from earlier.

"Well, whatever you did, we appreciate it. We had our concerns about him, but now it appears that he is well on his way to mastering his gifts." His eyes stayed glued on hers.

"He's a great kid with a huge heart."

"Later, Taryn," Andyn shouted in passing, holding his little sister's hand, distracting her momentarily from the stare she shared with their father.

"Bye, Taryn," the little girl giggled, waving with her free hand.

"Bye," she smiled at them.

"See ya later, Little Dude," Kellan called out, as he and the rest of the pack approached the booth.

"Bye," is all that could be heard before the door closed behind them.

"Have a good evening, Miss Malone," Ardyn stated, holding his hand out to her. After she shook it, he turned on his heel to follow after his family, but not before looking over his shoulder at her one last time.

Once he was gone, there was a collective sigh of relief.

"That is one seriously intense dude," Thorne acknowledged.

"Yeah, he gives me the chills," Nalani admitted, shaking as one ran up her spine.

"You shouldn't look at him like that. He could have taken that little stare down as a challenge. And I'm telling you, that is one dude that you don't want to mess with," Kellan warned her.

"And why exactly is that?" Taryn asked, not fully understanding.

"Ardyn Mitchell is the most powerful Gaias in our territory. Anyone who has challenged him walks away wounded, or worse," Gerrick explained.

"Oh, I see." A sharp pain stabbed inside her stomach. She had a lot to learn about the laws of her people. The last thing she needed was to pick a fight with a powerful member of their community.

Dagney joined the group, carrying two large brown paper sacks. Once the pack bid them farewell and left for the lake, Taryn and Larkin stayed to share a slice of strawberry pie.

"Larkin, what is Ardyn's gift?"

"He's an Imperium, like your mother."

"Are you sure that he's not a Skin-Walker, or something similar?"

"No. Being an Imperium is his main gift, and that's one reason why he is so powerful," he replied, before taking another bite.

"What are the other reasons?"

"For starters he's two hundred, twenty-seven years old, and then there's his bloodline. They're more or less royalty in our kind. It practically guarantees him a seat on the Elder Council. Why are you so interested?"

"His face, did you notice it change?"

"To look like someone else?"

"No. It wasn't a human face. It was something else entirely."

"Uh, no…he would have to be a Skin-Walker to do that. Are you sure that's what you saw?"

"Maybe my mind was playing tricks on me. Forget that I said anything."

He studied her closely for a few moments. There was something more on her mind. Not wanting to ruin their evening, he decided not to press.

As they were finishing dessert, another group of teenagers walked into the café. It was unusual to see Keiryn's pack out and about without him in tow. Each one stared as they passed by the booth where Taryn and Larkin were seated. She smiled and acknowledged them but received only nods in response, with the exception of Jonesy who returned her smile and said hello.

"Is that what I think it is?" Dalen scowled.

"Looks like the black dog is on a date with Keiryn's girl," Eben answered.

"Let's get something to eat and then pay our boy a visit since he's still on lockdown because of the mutt," Dalen declared.

ೋღೋღ

"Hey, Guys," Keiryn sulked as he greeted his pack from the comfort of a lounge chair in his backyard.

"Hey, Keiryn," they replied in near unison. Jonesy hung towards the back of the pack and took a seat on the edge of the deck while everyone else sat in the chairs, surrounding their leader.

"You don't have any idea how much this sucks," Keiryn growled.

"Well it's about to get a lot worse," Dalen admitted, arching his brows and releasing a heavy sigh in his brother's direction.

"What?"

The pack shared a look of worry, knowing that it might not be such a great idea to tell him about Taryn and Larkin.

"What is it?" He was growing impatient with the way they were drawing out his angst.

"Um…" Dalen paused, afraid to break the news.

"Somebody better tell me what's going on."

"We saw Taryn," Eben stated, taking pause.

"Is she okay? She isn't hurt is she?" Worry washed over his face.

"She was perfectly fine," Jonesy answered, drawing looks of surprise from the pack.

"Then what is it?" Keiryn asked, afraid he already knew the answer. There was only one thing that could upset him as much as her being injured.

"It looked like she was on a date with the black dog," Dalen responded, looking away to avoid Keiryn's glare.

He sprang from his seat, sending the chair flying out from beneath him, almost hitting Eben. "You can't be serious. And you left her alone with him?" Stomping about, he grabbed his head between his hands. "This can't be happening."

His friends watched, unsure of how to help him as he continued to spiral downward in a fit of rage. He demolished the stone fire pit with a vicious kick before turning his fury onto the heavy wooden Adirondack chair that he had been sitting in. With a single blow he crushed it into a million splinters.

Teigan pulled into his driveway just in time to witness his son's rage. Barely stopping before placing his truck into park, he rushed to him. "What is it?"

Fire raged behind his blue eyes. "She's with him!"

"I know, but you need to calm down and get a grip, Son."

Once the words fell from his father's lips, a stunned Keiryn stumbled backwards. "What? You knew?"

Teigan looked around at the faces of his son's pack and was none too pleased to know that they must have seen Taryn and Larkin and ran straight over to report the situation. "I think it's time for everyone to go home for the night." His tone made it clear that no arguments would be entertained.

"Yes, Sir," Dalen stated, nodding for everyone else to follow. Without saying a word, they disappeared into their vehicles and took off.

Keiryn opened his mouth, but before he could say a word his father shot him a look of warning. "Let's take this discussion inside."

In the kitchen, Teigan walked over to the fridge and poured himself a drink. Keiryn's insides churned as he watched how calm his father was acting, considering everything he knew about Larkin. For a moment he even considered that his father was choosing Larkin's side, but quickly shook off the absurd thought.

"You're not going to say anything?" He growled, just above a whisper.

Continuing to drink his beverage, Teigan peered at his son from over the rim. Once the glass was empty he set it down on the counter and walked to the living room. Though his father didn't speak a word, Keiryn knew he was expected to follow.

Teigan settled in while nodding for his son to take a seat on the opposing couch. For several minutes he mulled over the words that might give him some peace and comfort. Realizing there was nothing that would bring him either, he gave it to him straight.

"Keiryn." He leaned forward. "I know that you're not happy about this, but the fact is that girl has the right to date whomever she wants...regardless of how the rest of us may feel."

"But, Dad..."

His father held his hand up, cautioning him to listen. "I know you feel strongly about her, but apparently Larkin does as well. And she seems to feel strongly for him. There's a few things you need to know about, but what I'm about to tell you is covered by the Blood Oath we all took. Do you understand?"

Keiryn nodded in acknowledgement. The Blood Oath was all-binding. When a Gaias pledged a Blood Oath it was impossible for them to divulge the secrets they swore to protect. The Oath would literally take the air from their lungs if they tried to speak it. If they tried to write it, it would break the bones in their hands. If they tried to out someone in front of others, the repercussions were much more serious. The Oath would make you share in the secrets or afflictions you had sworn to protect, as was the case with Larkin. Wanting to share no part in his suffering, Keiryn gladly kept the secrets of his enemy.

Teigan shared the new revelation regarding how Larkin had dreamt of Taryn since his twelfth birthday. The consensus was that the dreams might somehow be directly related to his affliction. He listened, even though it didn't change his view on the situation. Larkin was still a monster in his eyes, and that monster could be a danger to Taryn, regardless of how everyone else felt.

In telling him about the dreams, Teigan felt it best to give his son a heads up regarding the events that would take place the next day. Since Keiryn was essentially going to be the third wheel, and would have to accept the heartache that came with an impossible love, he tried to lessen the blow.

By the time his father had explained the plan, he had a new sense of purpose as well as a few plans of his own. To him there were two possibilities, the first being that he would be able to see that she was safe from the black dog and the second provided hope that she wasn't lost to him.

After showering, he crawled into bed and drifted off blissfully to sleep.

ℬↃ☙ℬↃ☙

At Cataract Lake, Larkin and Taryn snuck off to one of the docks, leaving the pack behind. The moonlight reflected off of the water's calm surface as they dipped their toes in.

"I've really enjoyed today." She smiled, looking up at him fondly.

"Me too." Lifting one of his hands, he ran his fingers down her cheek. "You're even more beautiful than in my dreams." Tilting her chin up, he moved closer. His pulse quickened, wanting nothing more than to kiss her rosy pink lips, but nerves got the better of him.

Never having kissed a girl before, and knowing that she was just as innocent, he started to turn away the moment he felt her warm breath caressing his lips, but she caught his cheek gently in her hand.

"Does it still hurt?"

Lost in her eyes, he didn't quite know what it was that she was asking. "Uh, what?"

"Your eye and lip…does it still hurt?"

"My lip still stings a bit when I smile too widely."

Pulling one leg up, she turned to face him. "Do you trust me?"

"Yes," he answered softly.

Closing her eyes, she moved her hand to his cheek and ran her thumb across his bottom lip. He watched her, his eyes full of the trust and love.

He felt her power as an incredible sensation danced across his lower lip. The sting from the cut that had kept re-opening every time he smiled or ate was gone. "Did you just heal my lip?"

She nodded her head yes, displaying the warmest of smiles. "Now for your eye."

Distracted by the lingering sensation on his lip, he grabbed her hand just before it touched him. "You, you, you can't," he stammered, stopping her before it was too late.

"Sure I can. It won't take but a second." She attempted to move her hand back to his face.

"No!" Taking both of her hands into his own, he pulled them to her lap.

"Did I do something wrong?"

He took a brief moment to formulate an answer, looking to the sky, hoping to find the right words to tell her. Finally looking back down, he saw the worry written plainly on her face. "Taryn, you know that you can do things that no Gaias should be able to do, right?"

"Yeah."

"Okay, so what you just did…you can't do that ever again."

"But why?"

"Because, Taryn, people would think that you are dark, maybe even demonic. It's not a power that is looked on favorably in our kind."

Freeing her hands from his, she placed one directly over his heart. "Can you feel that?"

"Yes." Her power was coursing through him.

"Does that feel dark or demonic to you?"

Feeling nothing but the beauty and peace that she was pushing out from her hand, he struggled to answer. After several seconds, his protective instinct took over. He wanted to lie to her, keep her in the dark, but in order to keep her safe, she had to know. "You are all that is good in this world, but it doesn't matter what I feel, Taryn." He placed his hands over hers. "To heal someone, or to be considered as a Healer, is an offense punishable by death. The Elder Council wouldn't stop at only destroying you. They would come after anyone who had knowledge of your gifts...me, your mother, Gastyn, my dad, possibly both packs and even Andyn," he explained, hoping to make her see the dire consequences if that particular gift were to become public knowledge.

"I don't understand. How can such a beautiful gift, the gift of life, be such a hated thing?"

Larkin leaned in and placed a kiss on her forehead. "I know you don't. There is so much that you have to learn about the history of our kind. For the most part, we are a peaceful people. There were others, long ago, that shared your gift for Healing. It was a coveted trait for many centuries. They were looked up to and often referred to as the supreme beings, but having such an extraordinary power made them greedy. Much like you pull life from the earth to heal, they found a way to pull life from a person to prolong their own."

Taryn looked at him with a horrified expression. She was beginning to understand why her mother had kept her under lock and key for so long. A single tear slipped down her cheek.

He brushed it away with his finger. "Healers all but dropped out of existence as their powers began to be used for darkness. It was declared by the Elder Council that any Gaias-born that possessed the gift to heal would be destroyed before their power could be used to take another's life. You aren't like the others,

Taryn. Your heart is pure and true, I see it. I feel it. But we can't risk them finding out about you."

She sat quietly for several minutes, turning her focus back to the water in the lake. It tore him to pieces to see how upset she was. He wanted nothing more than to take her in his arms and never let her go, but he knew she needed a moment to process everything he had just told her before he did anything else to comfort her.

"So this is what you meant earlier...you know...about protecting me from myself?" she asked, fighting to hold back the tears that wanted so desperately to flow.

"Yes. I'm aware of just how little you know about what we are, how we live and the rules that we must follow. But it's not your fault...your mother could have told you about a lot of things."

"Does it upset you that she didn't?"

"When you first moved here and I began to discover that she had kept you in the dark, I was furious with her. After having time to think about it, I realized she had her reasons." Lying back on the wooden planks, he took her with him in his arms. "Let's say that she told you everything there was to know about being Gaias...living in Galatia, Kansas you had no one to bounce the information off of, no one other than her to turn to with your questions. At the same time, if she would have moved any sooner it would have been much harder to explain any number of things that you were able to do, and inevitably someone would have been bound to report you to the Elder Council."

"I suppose you're right," she sighed, snuggling against him.

"How did you know about the Elder Council?"

"My mom and I discussed them briefly this morning. But like with everything else, she held back...Larkin?" She pressed up on his chest to look at him directly.

"Yes?"

"Thanks for being honest with me," she smiled, kissing him on the cheek before snuggling back into the warmth of his arms.

ഇരുജ്ഞെരുജ്ഞ

On the short ride home from the Malone's, Maxym asked how the date had gone. "It was amazing, Dad. She's so incredible and so, so, so..."

"Pretty?"

"Yeah, she is definitely pretty."

"I'm glad you enjoyed yourself," he acknowledged, knowing tomorrow's events might serve to damper his son's spirits.

Once back at their home, Larkin showered. Pausing for a moment, he wiped the fog from the mirror and ran his finger over his freshly healed lip. A euphoric shiver crept up his spine. He could still feel her lingering inside of him. Realizing what she had given him, he was envious of the bobcat she had healed in the forest, knowing she had projected far more of herself onto the gravely injured animal than what she had done for his split lip.

Soon he ventured out their backdoor and into the woods, intent on taking his normal place outside her window. When he arrived, he found her already peacefully sleeping. No sooner than he had settled in, someone called his name from below, startling him.

"Larkin, come down," Ilya called quietly.

Apprehension riddled his body as he cursed himself for being so absent-minded not to check if her mother was asleep before he had leapt onto his perch. "Miss Malone."

"You shouldn't be sleeping up there..."

"I know, Miss Malone. I'll go home." He did not know how he would get through the night, not being able to be near her.

"You misunderstood me, Larkin."

He paused, staring at her with a bewildered expression. "Excuse me?"

"I know you care about my daughter very much, and you're only trying to look after her." She surprised even herself by what she was about to suggest. "Why don't you come inside? You can sleep in one of the spare rooms."

"What?"

"Taryn needs someone like you who can see her for what she is. Someone who understands what she needs in those critical moments, Larkin. She also needs someone who understands how important it is to protect her, and all of her secrets. So I'm opening my home up to you. You're welcome to stay anytime you would like, just not in her bedroom. Understood?"

"Yes, Ma'am."

"Good, then let's get some rest," she nodded to the door. "Nice lip. Though I'm glad to see you still have the shiner," she remarked, thankful that he hadn't allowed her daughter to heal his eye.

After showing him to a room down the hall from Taryn's, she headed into her own and wisely left the door open.

———

In the morning, Ilya rose early, wanting Larkin to return to his own home before Taryn woke so that she could have a few hours alone with her before everyone's involvement became official. When she walked out the bedroom door, she was startled to find him lying on the floor just outside her daughter's room. She stepped quietly towards him. His head rested on a pillow and was positioned perfectly to have a view of Taryn while she slept.

Conflicting tears of happiness and sadness built in the wells of her eyes. She was filled with elation that her daughter had someone to, quite literally, watch over her, but she couldn't help but imagine the pain that Maxym must feel every time that his son walked out the door, knowing he was bound to a girl he barely even knew.

"Miss Malone."

"Good morning, Larkin. Please, call me Ilya." She wiped away a few loose tears.

"I'm sorry…I couldn't sleep in that room, not being able to see her." He was embarrassed by his explanation and the way it must have sounded. The last thing he needed was for her to think he had been trying to sneak into Taryn's room.

"It's alright…I understand."

Rising, he straightened himself up and grabbed the pillow to take back into the other room.

"I know this has to be weird for you, but I do appreciate you letting me stay. It was much more comfortable and warm than compared to your shingles."

"Of course, Larkin, but I think it's time for you to head home. I'd like a few hours alone with her, and I'm sure your father would like to see you."

Glancing at Taryn's face, peaceful in sleep, one last time, he nodded. "I'll see myself out."

ဆဟဆဟ

After spending a quiet morning together, Ilya informed Taryn that she would be going over to help Jonesy and his aunt Jayma with their garden. Other than being surprised to learn that her mother knew Jonesy's aunt, she was thrilled to be assisting them.

She dressed in a worn out pair of blue jeans, an old gray t-shirt and tennis shoes. During the short fifteen minute drive to the Blake's home, she and her mother talked about everything imaginable. As she parked in Jonesy's driveway in front of their quaint bungalow, Ilya hugged her daughter tightly, almost afraid to let go.

"Okay, Mom. They can see us."

"I'm sorry, Sweetie. Go have some fun and I'll see you later." Standing there, she watched as Taryn hugged Jonesy and his aunt before disappearing around the side of their home.

On the car ride back to her home, she wept to the point of exhaustion. Once there, she pulled herself together, finding the strength that had brought them to this point, and prepared for the arrival of her allies.

ഇൽഗ്രഇൽഗ്ര

Taryn, Jonesy and his aunt Jayma worked at repotting several of the plants, preparing for the fall and winter season.

"Thanks for helping," Jonesy smiled shyly.

"It's my pleasure. I've always wanted to get out and get my hands dirty." She held them up as evidence.

"We do have gloves," Jayma insisted.

"Oh, I'm good, Miss Blake. I love the feel of the earth between my fingers." She smiled at the older woman, wondering just how old she really was. Her blonde hair was straight and cut in a chic bob that framed her heart-shaped face. She had deep blue eyes that sparkled with kindness. She didn't look a day over forty.

"Then you've come to the right place. How about we take a quick break?" Jayma suggested, looking to Jonesy, who was by far the cleanest.

"Sounds great," Taryn agreed.

"Jonesy, would you mind picking up a few sandwiches from the Desert Rose while Miss Taryn and I get cleaned up?"

"Sure, Aunt Jayma." He flashed his aunt an endearing smile before heading towards the outside water spigot, stopping near Taryn. "You okay with being here alone with her?"

"Of course, your aunt is the best," she retorted, chasing after him the rest of the way to the spigot with the threat of wiping her dirty hands all over him.

Once he was headed off to the café, Jayma suggested they go inside and clean up before he returned. Walking inside their small home, Taryn took in every minute detail. It reminded her of the house she had shared with her mother back in Galatia. Hardly an inch to move in if you were a normal kid, let alone if you had all of this power trapped inside of you trying to get out. Luckily for Jonesy, he had a huge back yard to run and play in that was surrounded by the protection of a thick tree line.

"The bathroom is down the hall, second door on your right, Taryn."

"Thanks."

Walking down the narrow hallway, she was about to push open the bathroom door with her elbow when something caught her eye in the room across the hall. Stepping inside, she could instantly tell that it was Jonesy's bedroom. She smiled at the periodic table of elements that hung just above the bed and the twenty plus plants that adorned nearly every available surface in the room, but it was something much smaller that had caught her eye. Moving towards the large bowl, she could see the small outline swimming about in the water.

"I see you've met the other member of our family," Jayma stated from the doorway. "Ugly little thing, isn't he?" She pointed to the goldfish.

"He's not that bad," Taryn replied, studying him curiously. "How long have you had him?"

"Oh, that fish has been here as long as Jonesy has. The day he was dropped off at my doorstep, all he had was the clothes on his back and that darned fish."

"How long has that been?"

After appearing to have been calculating in her head, she finally answered, "About thirteen years."

"Wow, that's a long time for a gold fish to live, isn't it?"

"I suppose so. Around here, we call him Ralph, the Indestructible. It doesn't matter if we feed him or not, that little fish keeps on plugging away."

"Good for him." Taryn smiled, peering back at the fish.

"I suppose we should get you cleaned up before he returns with the food," Jayma nodded to the door across the hall.

When Taryn emerged from the bathroom, she found Jonesy waiting for her. "You want to eat outside?"

"Sure." Grabbing two bottles of soda, she followed him out the backdoor and to a picnic table under a large tree.

"Thanks again for coming over. We don't get a lot of visitors."

"You know what they say…it's not about the number of guests you have as much as it is about the quality."

Jonesy arched his brows and smiled from ear-to-ear. "You're really something, Taryn Malone."

"You're pretty awesome yourself, Jonesy Blake." She took a monster bite of her turkey sandwich.

After they finished their meal, they both laid down on the seats of the table, enjoying the gentle breeze. "Taryn, can I ask you something?"

"Anything, Jonesy. Ask away."

"You know how you worked with the kid…could you maybe help me?"

"I didn't really do anything, but I'd be happy to help you in any way that I can. So what exactly is your gift?"

"That's the thing…I don't really know. I have the Skin-Walker gene, but it's a pretty weak trait. Then again, everything I attempt is pretty weak," he blushed, causing her to sit up suddenly.

"Jonesy Blake, I don't ever want to hear you say that. You have something incredible inside of you and it's just waiting to be released."

"Have you seen what I can do?"

"I've watched you with the plants and that's pretty awesome."

"They're plants. I can make them grow, just like Mother Nature if given time. Forget that I ever asked."

Studying him closely, she could see that his ego was battered and deflated. "I won't forget it. You asked for my help and I want to in any way that I can."

"Really?"

"We're friends, right?"

"Yeah."

"Then let's see what we can do."

The pair walked over to an open section of the yard near the freshly fertilized garden. She walked him through the same steps that she had done with Andyn, but even with the extra focus, he did not experience the same success.

"Thanks for the help, but it's useless. I'm always going to be the runt of the pack, and that's just the way it is," he sighed, disappointed.

"Well I'm not giving up on you. I know what I feel, and you have great power within you. It's just a matter of finding the right trigger to release it."

"I guess that I'll just have to take your word for it, because honestly...I've got nothing."

"Jonesy Blake," she growled, growing frustrated with his constant self-doubt. Looking up, her eyes widened. "Jonesy!" A look of horror passed over her face.

"What?" he asked, lifting his arms trying to find whatever it was that was causing her to freak out.

"Stop, drop and roll!" She tackled him to the ground, rolling back and forth.

"What the hell are you doing?" he snapped, trying to push her off.

Sitting on the ground, she looked at him in utter confusion. "You were on fire...how, how are you not burnt?"

"No, I wasn't. I was just standing there until you tackled me like some kind of crazy person."

"No, I'm not crazy. I saw you, and you were engulfed in flames from head to toe."

"Look at me, Taryn. Do I look like someone who was on fire?"

Examining him, she couldn't find any sign of the flames she had seen only moments ago. "I'm sorry. I could have sworn it was real."

"The flames weren't real, but the stench from the manure certainly is," Jayma chuckled as she approached. "You alright, Jonesy?"

"Yeah, but I can't find the other half of my glasses."

"Here, let me help you look," Taryn insisted, stepping back into the garden. After only a few seconds she found the missing piece. Holding them up, she gave Jonesy and his aunt a sorrowful look.

"It's alright, Taryn. I break them at least once a week," he stated, taking the half from her and handing both pieces to his aunt.

In a matter of seconds she had repaired the broken frames using her secondary gift of Imperium to fuse them back together. "There you go," she chuckled, handing him the glasses before taking a few steps back, pinching her nose. "Please don't be offended, Dear Ones, but you both stink something terrible."

Taryn and Jonesy shared a look and immediately burst into hysterical laughter. They were really quite the sight, smattered with dirt and manure.

After rinsing off with the hose outside, she changed clothes in the garage, putting on a pair of Jonesy's shorts and one of his t-shirts. She placed her smelly clothes into a heavy duty trash bag, but it did very little to ease the stench of the manure. Maybe she really was losing her mind. Wasn't seeing things that weren't real one of the signs of craziness? First with Andyn's father and his changing faces, and then with Jonesy and the flames. Deciding it was best to ponder it all when she was alone, she joined Jonesy and Aunt Jayma in the back yard.

ဿလဿလ

"What's he doing here?" Larkin growled from one of the barstools as Keiryn walked in.

"Son, it's like I told you earlier. We have a plan, but it's going to take all of us to protect not only her, but everyone living near Williams," Maxym explained, knowing his son was still upset with Keiryn about outing him in front of Taryn.

He made his way into the living room. "Fine. Let's hear this brilliant plan of yours."

The two boys sat on opposite sides of the couch, shooting one another frosty glares until Gastyn walked in. "Are we good here?" he asked, looking from one to the other.

"Yes, Mr. Wylder," Larkin acknowledged.

"Yes, Sir," Keiryn replied.

"Very good. Let's begin."

Larkin listened intently as his trusted teacher explained in great detail, what was needed and the parts each would play in keeping the balance between the packs as well as protecting Taryn.

"He has no business being here. He has nothing to do with Taryn or protecting her," Larkin fumed.

"Just take a step back and think about it, Larkin," Gastyn started. "Ilya, would you mind giving us a minute?" he asked, thinking of the consequences of the Blood Oath.

"Sure. I'll be out by the pool." She figured it would be best to let the men handle the testosterone-fueled issues between the boys.

When she was out of ear shot, he continued. "Larkin, while I understand your deep attachment, you have to understand that you aren't the only one who feels strongly about her. I believe it serves everyone better to have both of you involved. While I don't believe you would ever intentionally harm her, I never thought that you would harm Keiryn either, so his concerns merit our attention and this is the best compromise."

"You two are going to have to figure out a way to put your differences aside and work together, otherwise you put everyone in jeopardy," Maxym stated.

"He's right. You boys need to make this work," Teigan agreed, his tone absolute.

"She's early," Larkin startled, jumping to his feet.

Keiryn shot him a withered look, "What are you talking about? She's not even close."

"Shut up, Falcon. She's going to be furious when she realizes we've been making plans behind her back."

"You're wrong. She isn't…"

"You were saying?" Larkin jeered.

"How did you know that?" Keiryn asked, not understanding why it took him longer to sense her.

"Because he is bound to her, Keiryn, and I don't want you to do anything to mess with that. You will follow Larkin's lead…end of discussion," Teigan reiterated, reminding him of the conversation where he had laid out the plan to him the night before.

"I'll let Ilya know." Maxym headed to the door. She met him as he opened it, already sensing her daughter's early return.

"I'm trusting every one of you to do your part to protect my little girl. Please don't let me down."

CHAPTER NINE

As the trio made their way up her drive way, Taryn noticed several vehicles parked out front. "Looks like you're having a party," Jonesy observed.

"That's odd...no one told me about it." She recognized all but one of the trucks. "Do you know who that red truck belongs to?"

"Yeah, that's Teigan Falcon's truck."

"Keiryn's dad?"

"Yep, and the other one is Maxym Taylor's. I don't envy you having to walk into that battle field. If Keiryn and Larkin are both there, I'm shocked the place it still standing."

Ilya emerged from the front door and walked to the car. "Hello," she greeted them with a smile that quickly faded. "What's that smell?"

"There was an incident next to the garden and we had just fertilized it for next year," Jayma offered.

"An incident?"

"It was nothing, Dear."

"We did discover that Taryn should probably go out for the football team next year. She could definitely play a tackle position," Jonesy teased.

"Well thanks for having her over," Ilya smiled.

"It was our pleasure. I do hope we can do it again sometime," Jayma grinned as she began to back the car up.

Mother and daughter waved as they drove out of sight. "So what happened?" Ilya asked.

"It's not that big of a deal. I thought Jonesy was on fire and I tackled him. We fell into their freshly fertilized garden."

"You thought he was on fire?"

"Yes, Mother," she growled in irritation, knowing that she was only playing twenty questions because her mother thought that she had something to do with Jonesy being on fire. "Look, Aunt Jayma said it was probably the sun reflecting off of all of her glass globes, sun catchers and other yard ornaments...it's not a big deal. So it's your turn. You want to tell me what the Taylor's, Gastyn and the Falcons are doing here?"

"Aunt Jayma?"

"Yes, Aunt Jayma. Now don't try to change the subject...what's going on here?"

"Don't be upset, Taryn. We needed to speak with the boys before talking with you."

"You know how much I hate surprises. So whatever you've been plotting and planning without me...count me out."

"We can't leave you out, Taryn. This isn't just about you anymore. We've moved into this community and we have to do whatever necessary, to not only protect you, but to protect everyone else who lives here."

"Whatever..." she mumbled.

"I know this isn't ideal, but I think that you will be pleased with the solution we've come up with."

"Before you drop the bomb on me, can I please take a shower?"

"Oh, Baby Girl...I must insist that you do."

Leaving her sack of stinky clothes next to the front door, she inhaled deeply, making sure her emotions were in check before stepping inside. As she walked in, she took in everyone's face. Gastyn appeared calm on the surface, but she could sense his apprehension. Maxym smiled warmly at her, but did nothing to hide the worry in his eyes. Keiryn sat on the couch looking at her strangely, in a way she couldn't get a read on. She could only assume the man standing next to the couch was his father. His face was full of worry, confusion, apprehension and a myriad of other troublesome emotions, but even in his turmoil, he flashed her a brief smile. Last but not least, she looked at Larkin. He smiled at her, his eyes lighting with excitement at seeing her face, but it didn't cover the concern lurking beneath the surface.

"Hello," she greeted everyone.

"What happened to you?" Larkin asked, motioning to her clothes and messy hair.

"Jonesy and I took a tumble into their garden." Her stench had yet to permeate their senses.

"Did he hurt you?"

"Don't be silly. Jonesy's a sweetheart…we just took a tumble." She made her way between them as she walked to the French doors.

"What's that smell?" Keiryn asked, wrinkling his face as she breezed by.

The smell soon caught up to all them, causing scrunched faces and pinched noses. "Why don't you guys go out by the pool, and after I shower, you can fill me in on what I've missed."

"That sounds more than reasonable," Gastyn agreed, trying to hold his breath.

Teigan let out a chuckle, watching her. "Well one thing is for certain…she isn't afraid to get her hands dirty."

Her sweet fragrance, paired with his desire to be near her, left Larkin unaffected by the stench of the manure. He followed her up the stairs. "Hey, are you alright? I mean…this isn't too much, is it?"

"I'm not exactly crazy about being the last one to know, but I'll manage. Having you here definitely lessens the sting of it."

He looked down at her fondly. "I'm glad to hear you say that."

"Give me twenty and I'll be down, okay?"

"I'll be waiting…"

₧⃣*₧⃣*

A half hour later Taryn walked out the French doors and onto the deck to find everyone waiting patiently for her. Immediately Larkin joined her, walking by her side until she took a seat. He hovered beside her, watching over her intently.

She didn't bother making herself comfortable, afraid to become too complacent when she had no idea what they had been planning. "Lay it on me."

Gastyn stood and moved closer. "Taryn, as you are well aware, you are not like other Gaias. Your gifts easily surpass that of someone five, or even ten times, your age. With that said, your very existence poses a threat to the well-being of not only you, but those around you."

"You told them about me?" she admonished, nodding to indicate Keiryn and Teigan.

"Yes, but with good cause. We need to make a circle of protection around you. And with there being two packs in the same age group, we need cooperation on both sides. Since you already have a bond with Larkin, who is the leader of one of the packs, it only makes sense that we include Keiryn, as he leads the other."

Glancing to Keiryn, she noticed a smirk on his face when he looked at Larkin. "Do you find this funny?"

Sitting up straight in his chair, he stammered about. "Um, yes, I mean no."

"Then I suggest you stop trying to rile him, otherwise I see no point in discussing a plan that is obviously going to fail." Noticing a smile curling on Larkin's face, she addressed him as well. "Don't think you have some sort of get out of jail free card...the same rules apply to you."

Teigan leaned forward in his chair, amazed at how direct she was in calling them both out on their childish behavior. What amazed him more was how quickly they submitted to her request, even if it was only for the moment.

"Please do continue, Gastyn," Ilya insisted.

"Very well, then. Both Mr. Taylor and Mr. Falcon, along with their sons, have agreed to assist your mother and I in protecting your secrets. Larkin and Keiryn will be by your side, virtually everywhere you go, to see that you don't inadvertently expose yourself to the rest of our community as well as the ordinary humans."

"Wow, lucky me. Sixteen years old and I get assigned glorified babysitters." Her tone was full of sarcasm. "So this is about me potentially exposing myself and bringing the wrath of the Elder Council down on the local Gaias community...is that what I'm hearing?"

"Yes, but it's not only the Elder Council," Maxym responded. "There are those who would stop at nothing to take possession of someone as gifted as yourself, Taryn..."

"Who would want to use me?"

Silence fell heavy in the air. No one answered as they looked to Maxym and Larkin. Even Keiryn displayed a distraught look.

"I think that is a discussion for another day, Sweetheart," Ilya finally responded, taking a seat next to her and grabbing hold of her hand. "You will need to just trust that we know what we're doing for now."

She wanted to scream. Hadn't there been enough secrets? Instead, she shrugged in agreement, sensing this wasn't the time to press for answers. "Okay. If this is what I have to do to keep those I care about safe, I'll do it."

"Thank you, Taryn," Gastyn nodded. After he went through a short list of rules for her to follow in regards to the use of her powers, he turned to address the rest of the group. "Unless there are any questions or objections, I think we should move on to the Blood Oath to seal the circle of protection."

"What's a Blood Oath?" she inquired.

Gastyn smiled, knowing that it must sound terrifying to someone who had never heard of it. "I know it sounds ominous, but the reality is that it is an act binding us to our word. The Oath will prevent any of us from accidentally exposing your secrets. There's no need to be concerned, our kind has used the Blood Oath for centuries."

"There is one thing," Teigan announced. "It seems that everyone else knows what you can do, but all my son and I know is what we've been told. While I am certainly intrigued, I must admit that it seems a little farfetched. So would you be willing to indulge a concerned father and show us something before we bind ourselves, and I give my son over to protecting you?"

"I'd prefer that we do the Oath first," Ilya injected, wanting to protect her daughter.

Placing her hand on her mother's shoulder, she nodded. "No, it's okay. They're being more than generous by helping out two complete strangers. If I am as big of an anomaly as you say, then I think it's only fair that they fully understand what it is they are committing to."

"Thank you, Taryn," Teigan nodded. She smiled at him and placed her hands gingerly in her lap. He watched her closely as he waited for her to show him her gift. "Did you want to do this later?" he asked after a few minutes had passed.

"I'm already doing it." She nodded in the direction of the chair next to him.

Looking over he found an exact water replica of himself sitting in the chair, mimicking his movements. "You're not using your hands," he panicked, jumping to his feet, knocking over the chair.

"I know."

Keiryn sat silently in his chair as his mouth curled upward forming a wide smile. His father looked toward him, "What do you think?"

"Freaking amazing!"

"That's some sort of control you have there," Teigan noted, studying the details of his water buddy.

"I think that's enough show and tell until the Blood Oath is completed," Larkin declared, becoming uneasy with her display and the fact that her secrets were now out in the open, and in the hands of the bird boy.

"Thank you," Ilya agreed, wanting everyone bound as soon as possible.

"I trust the Falcon's, but if it makes you both feel better, then I say okay," Taryn complied.

While Gastyn and Ilya went inside to grab a few items, Larkin sat next to her, trying to put her at ease when a look of apprehension washed over her face.

"Are you sure you're okay with all of this?" He took her hand in his own.

"If it will help keep you and everyone else safe, how could I possibly refuse?"

"I don't care about everyone else…I care about you and your well-being. If this is going to be too much for you, we'll stop it right now."

"With you by my side, I know I'll be fine." She leaned her head onto his shoulder.

From a few yards away, Keiryn watched their exchange as his blood began to boil. Disgusted and annoyed, he forced a smile and grabbed a chair, pulling it up on the other side of her. "Hey."

"Hello," she nodded.

"That thing you did with the water…that was pretty cool."

"Thanks," she replied, sensing his unrest. "Thanks for helping us out. You and your dad can still back out if you want."

"That's not going to happen."

Gastyn and Ilya returned a few minutes later with a small white ceramic bowl with strange markings on the side and a knife. "Everyone, gather round please," he directed, placing the bowl on the table in front of him.

Once everyone was in place the males removed their shirts, exposing their sculpted, bared chests. Taryn couldn't help but notice how Keiryn kept his hand near the left side of his chest, trying to hide the scars that ran across his collar bone. A chill shot through her, thinking of what could have possibly happened between he and Larkin to result in such a gruesome reminder. She fought the urge to reach out and touch them, recalling Larkin's warning, knowing nothing good could come of it. No matter how accepting they had been of her other talents, she was certain that was the one that would push them over the edge.

Next Ilya removed her shirt, exposing the low cut tank top she wore beneath it. Taryn flashed her mother a look of uncertainty.

"It's all right, it's part of taking the Oath," she assured her.

Relieved that she was already wearing a tank top, she looked around the table. With Larkin to her right and Keiryn to the left, she began to blush, surrounded by so much exposed flesh. "It'll be over shortly," Keiryn smiled, sensing her innocence.

"Larkin, I think you should start," Gastyn insisted, considering the possibility of how he might react if someone else were to draw the necessary blood from her.

Hesitantly Larkin took the knife from Gastyn and slid the bowl over to Taryn. He looked at her with a pained expression. Knowing he had to physically hurt her in order to protect her tormented his very soul. "I'm sorry, Taryn."

"It's alright, Larkin."

He trembled as he took her delicate hand into his own and locked his eyes with hers. Holding the blade against the palm of her hand, he held his breath. Finally, he pressed it into her flesh, exhaling as the knife cut through her like warm butter.

Quickly she moved her hand over the bowl and let her blood drip into the bottom. Afterwards, she wrapped her wound in Larkin's t-shirt to hide the fact that it was rapidly healing.

Taking the knife from Larkin, Taryn cleaned it as directed then proceeded to cut Keiryn's hand in the same fashion. The steps were repeated, with each person taking their turn slicing the next person's hand, until everyone's blood was added. Gastyn picked up the bowl and swirled the contents around in order to be certain that it was thoroughly mixed before moving on to the next step of the ritual.

Stepping to Taryn, he dipped two fingers into the blood before removing them to draw an 'X' over her heart. One by one he repeated the same on each member of the circle, leaving Larkin for last. The instant the blood touched his skin, it began to smolder, causing shocked gasps throughout the group.

"What's happening to me?" He fought to hold back the screams of agony building inside of him as the blood seared into his flesh.

"Larkin!" Taryn reached for him.

"No, we have to finish it." He gritted his teeth, knowing that if they stopped now the Oath would not be fulfilled, leaving her vulnerable and unprotected.

Terrified, everyone kept their eyes on Larkin as he fought against the pain that was threatening to consume him. Gastyn placed the X over his own heart, then directed everyone to hold hands.

"Repeat after me. By the blood of my brothers and my sisters, I solemnly swear that no other shall learn the secrets that I know. Through my actions and through my words, I will protect them always, and they will die with me at my grave. This is my declaration that is true and sound, and by my blood that I am bound."

As the last words of the Oath were spoken in unison, a silver circle of light encompassed the group.

"It is done," Gastyn stated.

Once the light dissipated, Larkin released his hold and sprinted towards the pool. Not bothering to take his pants and shoes off, he jumped in as fast as he could and began scrubbing at the blood on his chest.

Confused as to what was happening everyone, including Keiryn, ran to the pool to try to help him. "Larkin," his father shouted before jumping in. His body went limp as he gave in to the excruciating pain.

Maxym grabbed hold of his son and pulled him to the side of the pool, where Gastyn and Teigan helped remove him from the water. The smell of burning flesh permeated the air. Though the water had removed the blood, an angry red welt in the shape of an X still burned over his heart.

"What's happening to him?" Teigan asked, looking at Gastyn.

"I have no idea. I've never seen anything like it before." He held his hands over Larkin's chest.

"There has to be something that we can do to stop it," Maxym yelled, his voice laden with fear.

Gastyn's forehead wrinkled in concentration as he drew from the Influential power living within him to try and stop the burn. He could feel Larkin's body rebelling against him as it began to contort from the pain. When Taryn recognized that even Gastyn could not help, she rushed forward, intending to use her own powers to heal him.

"No," Ilya yelled, grabbing hold of her.

"Let me go!" A deafening rumble of thunder sounded overhead. "Mom, I can help him. Let me help him."

Ilya held onto her with all of her strength, locking her fingers together with her powers of Imperium. As Taryn continued to fight her hold, Ilya pushed her power outward, encircling them both within a protective cocoon. The sky overhead began to darken as Taryn struggled against her.

"He wouldn't want you to do this."

"I can't let him suffer." Tears streaked down her cheeks. The skies opened up, blanketing them all in a torrential rainfall.

Maxym, Teigan and Gastyn carried an unconscious Larkin inside, placing him on the couch. "Ilya, Gastyn needs your strength too," Teigan yelled.

Looking to her daughter, who still struggled beneath the weight of her powers, she pleaded to her. "Give us a chance to help him, Taryn." With a hollow expression in her eyes, she nodded in agreement. "Keiryn, please stay her with her."

"Gastyn is brilliant and very powerful. He'll find a way to stop it," Keiryn offered, placing a comforting arm around her.

She fell to her knees, sobs wracking her body as she opened herself up to feel Larkin's pain. The burn was excruciating as it tore through him. Despite whatever the adults were trying, it continued to intensify. As Taryn's body began to shake from the tremendous pain, cloud-to-cloud lightening danced overhead.

Terrified to see her in such a state, Keiryn sank to his knees and drew her into his arms. Though they were both being pelted by large drops of cold rain, her body was almost hot to the touch. The two watched from outside as the four adults held their hands above Larkin. Maintaining her link with him, she knew that their efforts to save him were failing. The pain only surged higher. Feeling her trembling next to him, Keiryn pulled her in even closer.

Sensing that her love was beginning to slip away, she forced her hands to her sides, hovering just above the ground below. As Keiryn continued to hold onto her with all of his might, she drew life from the earth and pushed it with every ounce of strength she had into Larkin's limp body several yards away. Only when the burn inside of her began to wane, did she stop drawing from the earth. Continuing to focus her power solely on Larkin, she pushed, giving one final burst of energy, knocking the four adults to the floor.

Exhausted, her body fell limp as the rain tapered off to a light drizzle. Her head fell forward, allowing her to see the remnants of the decimated earth beneath her. As Keiryn began to pull away from her, lightning filled the sky, causing him to look up.

A bolt crashed into the earth a few feet away, sending both teens flying through the air. Still holding onto her with one hand, Keiryn landed on his feet. Scooping her into his arms, he ran towards the open doors, lightning crashing behind them every step of the way. Though her strength was depleted, she opened her eyes just before they made it in the house. There, near a large tree not far from where they had been, she saw a blurry image of what looked like a man staring at her through the rain. She tried to lift her hand in acknowledgement, but darkness closed in, surrounding her as she went limp in Keiryn's arms.

ༀ◌ཨༀ◌ཨ

Still dazed, Taryn sat up to find her mom sitting on the edge of her bed, looking over her with worried eyes. "Mom?"

"Here, take a drink." She held a glass up to her lips. After taking a few small sips, Taryn fell back onto her pillow. "How do you feel?"

"Tired, but okay. What happened?" Suddenly she sat up, her face alight with panic. "Larkin!"

"Calm down, Sweetie. He's outside with the others."

"I need to see him," she insisted, pushing her way out from underneath the covers and stumbling to the window. Peering down she saw Jonesy and his aunt, Teigan, Keiryn, Larkin and Maxym all working on the backyard. Her shoulders slumped with relief when she spied him working circles around them all. "The earth," she mumbled, recalling the events that had taken place.

"It seems he has some new found energy," Ilya sighed, pausing for a moment. "That was pretty clever, covering your tracks with lightning."

A strange feeling pooled in the pit of her stomach. "I didn't." She looked back at her mother.

Ilya's jaw drew up tightly. "Another freak storm."

"Yeah, a freak storm." *A freak storm and a strange man in the woods*, she thought to herself.

"Ah, I see our patient is feeling better," Gastyn smiled from the doorway.

"I am, thank you."

~ 250 ~

"May I look you over?"

"Sure."

Taryn sat down on the edge of the bed while Gastyn looked for any lingering side effects from the previous events. "Do you know what day it is?"

"Sunday," she answered. He shared a look with Ilya. "What is it?"

He continued looking her over. "It's Thursday, Taryn."

"What? That's not possible. How could I have missed four days?"

"Gastyn believes that the bond between you and Larkin allowed you to share in his pain, thus causing you to weaken from it," Ilya offered, hoping she would pick up on the hidden meaning behind her words.

"Did you feel his pain?" he asked.

"I definitely felt something."

"That's incredible. I've never heard of such a thing...but it doesn't surprise me that it's happening between the two of you."

Walking back over to the window, she peered down again. "If you don't mind, I'd really like to go see him."

"Of course, I'll leave you to get cleaned up."

"Why don't you take a quick shower, and I'll let everyone know that you're awake."

"Yeah, I'm sure I look frightful."

"You have seen better days," Ilya joked. "Taryn, you should know that he hasn't left your side until about an hour ago. I had to remind him of how much it would pain you to see the earth damaged, so he wanted to pitch in to help restore it before you woke."

"Thanks, Mom."

"I love you, Baby Girl."

"Love you, too."

When Taryn came down the stairs, she was delighted to see Larkin waiting for her. "Hey." He scooped her up into his arms, spinning her around.

"Hey," she replied back, oblivious to everyone else in the room.

"Uh, hem." Maxym cleared his throat.

"Everyone thinks that you were struck by lightning," Larkin whispered in her ear as he placed her feet back on the ground.

"It's great to see you have recovered," Maxym smiled, surprising her as he hugged her tightly.

While everyone else took their turn giving her hugs and expressing their jubilation that she was well, Keiryn stood cautiously to the side, only nodding a half-smile in her direction.

"What's that about?" Taryn whispered to Larkin.

"I don't know. He's been quiet and even more standoffish than usual." He guided her towards the open French doors.

Something sitting on the dining room table caught her eye, causing her to stop in her tracks. "What's this?" She nodded to the large bouquet of flowers with several balloons hovering above it.

"Those are from the Mitchell's."

Regardless of who they were from, she couldn't help but be excited. She had never received flowers or balloons before. "But why?"

"Apparently Andyn was quite worried about you when he heard about the accident. So his father brought over a get well bouquet and checked in on your progress," Maxym answered.

"Larkin was adamant that you wouldn't want them in your room, and he wasn't in any mood to be argued with about it either. So we left them downstairs," Ilya smiled, loving how protective and caring the boy was in regards to her daughter, even when it came to vegetation from strangers.

Continuing to make their way outside, Jonesy and his aunt explained the work that had been completed to restore the yard. Jayma even noted how the lightning had zapped the earth, draining it of all of its energy.

Taryn sighed with relief, thankful that no one, outside of her mother, had realized what it was that she had done.

Gastyn and Teigan grilled up a feast for everyone as they sat outside around the pool. It didn't go unnoticed that Taryn kept positioning her chair to keep herself faced toward the sun. The warm rays felt good against her skin and gave her a much needed surge of strength.

"It feels good, doesn't it," Teigan stated.

"Yes it does."

"That's because it's replenishing what the lightning took from you," Aunt Jayma commented, completely buying in to the lightning theory.

"Yeah, I find that to be strange how the sun recharges us while lightning can drain us of all our powers," Jonesy added.

"And that's exactly why lightning is a dangerous element for even mature Gaias to play around with," Keiryn stated, looking directly at Taryn.

"However, it does make an excellent offense if one should ever need," Gastyn offered, sounding very much like the teacher that he was.

As the adults began to talk about the merits of a strong offense or a good defense, Larkin and Taryn slipped away into the woods, stealing a few moments alone.

Holding her hand gently, he led her through the trees. "Did they ever figure out what went wrong with the Oath?"

"Gastyn thinks that it has something to do with me already being bound to you."

Pulling her hand free of his, she walked over and leaned against a tree near a small clearing. "So my blood was toxic to you?"

He moved to stand behind her. "No one really knows. He was just speculating…that's all." Sliding one arm around her waist, he pulled her in close. "Besides, I know what you did for me."

"I didn't do anything except almost kill you."

"You can't lie to me, Taryn. I can still feel you lingering inside of me." He moved around to look her in the eye as he tried to describe what he felt. With her back against the tree, she listened intently as his eyes burned into hers. "The sensation you left behind the other night when you healed my lip was amazing. But what I feel now…it's extraordinary. I mean, I feel like I could run around the world ten times and still have energy left to do it ten more."

"You were slipping away from me and I couldn't let you go."

Taking her cheeks between his hands, he peered deep into her emerald eyes. "Even though everyone else, with the exception of your mother, thinks it was because of something they did, I know it was you who saved me," he paused, sadness washing over him. "While I am eternally grateful for what you did, you have to promise me that you'll never do it again. Living my life without you…it would be worse than death." He fought to hold back his tears.

"I can't promise you that, Larkin. You know that wherever my heart goes, I must follow."

"I know." Leaning down, he kissed her forehead gently. "I suppose I should get you back before your mother sends out a search party."

As they approached her backyard, Taryn looked over to the spot where she recalled seeing a man standing just before she lost consciousness.

"Hey, Larkin..."

"Yes?"

"Did anyone mention seeing a man out here?"

"No. Why do you ask?"

"No reason. It's probably my mind playing tricks on me. It's been doing that a lot lately."

As they approached the others, they could see more visitors had arrived. "Taryn," Andyn yelled, running to her and wrapping his arms around her so tightly that he almost knocked her over.

"Hi, Andyn. What are you doing here?" she asked as his sister, Andalyn, latched on to her from the other side.

"Here, step back and give her some room to breathe," Lilyan insisted, tugging at both of her children. "I hope you don't mind. Andyn wasn't going to be content until he was able to see for himself that you were okay."

"Oh, I don't mind at all. It's great to see my friends," she replied, tousling the hair atop his head.

"We're glad to see you are feeling better. It's not every day that someone in our community survives a direct hit by lightning," Ardyn offered, staring down at her strangely.

Larkin stepped between them, shielding her from Ardyn's gaze.

"Larkin," his father admonished, fearing that his son's behavior could be viewed as a challenge to the very dangerous and powerful member of their community.

"It's alright, Maxym. I remember being young and in love. I would have killed anyone who looked at her twice." He locked eyes with Larkin, his tone anything but light.

Much to everyone's chagrin, Larkin stood rooted to the spot, keeping Ardyn as far away from her as possible. "Keiryn, Jonesy, Taryn needs to rest. Could you escort her back inside?" he asked, as surprise filtered throughout their group.

"We'll see you later," Ardyn grinned, reaching past Jonesy and taking hold of Taryn's hand to shake it, causing Larkin to release a low growl.

Pulling her hand away from his, she smiled politely. "Good-bye, Mr. Mitchell."

Quickly, Keiryn and Jonesy carted her into the house and out of sight.

"Larkin," Ardyn nodded. "It's nice to see that she has someone like you looking out for her. You know my son is rather fond of her as well." He smirked in the teen's direction one last time before gathering his family to leave.

Once certain that the Mitchell's were gone, Maxym tore into his son. "Have you lost your mind? You know better than that. You know what he's capable of. Why would you go and provoke him?"

"I don't trust that man and I won't have him around her."

"Larkin." Maxym was shocked that his usually polite son kept walking.

"I'll go talk to him," Gastyn insisted, heading towards the house.

"Wow," Aunt Jayma sighed. "Who knew that sweet little girl could cause so much trouble?"

☙℞☙℞

"Wait," Taryn uttered, overcome by nausea as her knees buckled beneath her.

Keiryn caught her before she hit the floor. Quickly, he carried her into her room and placed her down gently onto the bed.

"What the hell just happened?" Keiryn posed, looking to Jonesy.

"I don't know." Looking around for clues, he pointed. "Your shirt, there's blood on it."

Keiryn looked down and saw several spatters of blood on his gray t-shirt. "She's bleeding, but where?"

They began looking her over and discovered that the fingers on her right hand had several places where blood continued to pool.

"Get her mother and Gastyn," Keiryn ordered as the blood dripped down onto the floor.

Jonesy ran out of the bedroom door, intent on bringing help.

Sitting on the bed, Keiryn took in her pretty face. Even amidst all of the chaos, she still somehow managed to look peaceful, pulling at his heart strings. "How can I feel this way about you, knowing what you are?" He gently caressed the hair away from her face. "My head tells me one thing, but my heart says another. Please tell me what I'm supposed to do, Taryn." Pulling her uninjured hand to his lips, he kissed the top of it softly.

“❬“❬

On his way down the staircase, Jonesy could see Gastyn and Larkin locked in a heated discussion. "Hey!" Neither paid him any mind. "Hey!" he shouted, this time gaining their attention.

"Not right now, Mr. Blake. Mr. Taylor and I have a few things to discuss," Gastyn responded, turning his attention back to Larkin.

Used to being unseen by most, anger began to rise in him. Rushing the rest of the way down the staircase, he pushed in between them. "Taryn needs your help. Now!"

"Taryn," Larkin responded, rushing up the stairs in less than a second to find her lying there, unconscious once again. "What happened?" he demanded as Keiryn rose to his feet.

"I don't know. We brought her inside and she just collapsed, then we saw the blood."

Larkin released a shrieking howl that brought everyone else running to her side. Ilya pushed through and gazed down at her daughter. Seeing the blood, tears filled her eyes. She had never seen Taryn bleed that much. Even the knife wound on her hand from the Blood Oath had healed in only a matter of minutes.

"What's happening to my little girl?" she sobbed, looking to Gastyn for answers.

"I don't know, but we need to get her into the sunlight before it disappears for the day. It might be the only thing that can save her."

Larkin quickly ripped off his shirt and wrapped it around her hand to keep the blood from touching him. Scooping her into his arms, he informed them he was taking her to his house and rushed out the door, leaving barely a blur visible in his wake.

Racing through the woods in human form with her in tow, he used the power that she had forced inside of him to push himself faster than even his wolf form could carry him. A few minutes later, Keiryn burst through the tree line, finding Larkin sitting on the ground, cradling her in his arms as the sun's final rays bore down upon them.

"My dad's calling the Love's to ask them to keep the sun from setting for as long as they can."

"You hear that, Taryn? You need to hold on," he said, his voice cracking with emotion. Stroking her cheek, he rocked her back and forth. She grew colder with each second that passed. "No, I won't let you go."

Keiryn watched in horror as his enemy spiraled downward, and the girl he loved faded away from them both.

"No," Larkin thundered, causing the earth to move beneath them.

"Return what she has given," a man's voice whispered in Keiryn's ear.

"What?" He looked around trying to see who else was there. Seeing no one besides Larkin and Taryn, he called out. "Who's there?"

"You must give it back," the voice whispered again.

"Give what back?" Keiryn stood, staring wildly around, trying to find the source.

Larkin watched as he began walking about, pulling at his hair and raging at some unseen being, going insane.

"Return that which she has given so freely..." the voice whispered before disappearing into the air as the winds picked up around them.

Ready to scream his frustration, Keiryn raised his fists as comprehension dawned. Rushing to Taryn's side, he slid to the ground. "You have to give it back to her."

"What?" Larkin asked, not understanding, lost in his grief.

"You have to give back her power." Stunned, Larkin looked at him. "I know what she is, Larkin. You have to give it back, otherwise she'll be lost forever."

"How?"

"I don't know, but you have to try."

Placing his hand over her heart, he tried to will the power she had given him back into her. Nothing happened. Not ready to give up, he tried holding her left hand over his heart, but it was useless.

"How?"

"I don't understand," Keiryn thundered at the winds. "You said to give it back to her. Tell me how." For a moment the winds stood still and he heard the sound of his own breath as he exhaled. "Breathing!" Even though the thought of Larkin's lips touching hers made his stomach churn, he had to save her. "Breathe for her."

Laying her down, Larkin looked at her beautiful face, growing paler by the second as the life seeped out of her. Leaning down, he placed his lips over hers and exhaled sharply, repeating the gesture several times. His hope grew as a touch of color started to return to her cheeks. Her glassy eyes fluttered open and tried to focus on his face, but the blurry image of a man standing over the three of them caught her attention. Desperately, she tried to reach a weak arm out to touch him.

"All of it," the whisper returned, as her arm fell back to the ground and the color began to leave her cheeks once again.

"No!" Larkin shouted.

"I have to give back the power she gave to me," Keiryn confessed.

"What are you talking about?"

"She didn't only heal you that night...she healed me too," Keiryn divulged, taking his shirt off as proof.

Larkin stared incredulously. The scars that Keiryn had carried on his collar bone for the last five years were no longer there. "How?" Shaking his head, he focused back on Taryn. "Do it." The thought of Keiryn's lips on hers caused him immense pain, mixed with disgust. If it could save her, he would find a way to live with it.

Keiryn kneeled over her. Leaning down, he pinched her nose closed as if he were going to perform C.P.R. "I don't want any of it to escape," he explained, placing his lips on hers as he exhaled deeply, filling her lungs. He continued at a steady pace until her face was alive with color and the beating of her heart could be heard, strong and steady over the wind.

Not wanting Keiryn's lips to be the last thing that had touched her, Larkin leaned down and gave her a simple kiss. As his lips pressed against hers, he too could feel the warmth of life within her. "That's right. You're going to be alright." He pulled her into his arms.

"What happened?" she squeaked out, still extremely weak.

"It doesn't matter. You're going to be okay." Looking to Keiryn, he nodded, showing his gratitude for helping to save her life.

As Maxym's truck pulled into the driveway, Ilya jumped out before it even stopped and ran to her daughter.

"Taryn!" She fell to her knees, taking her daughter's hand into her own, holding it against her cheek. Tears of joy filled her eyes. "Baby Girl, you had me so worried."

With everyone now gathered round staring down upon them, both boys felt lumps forming in the back of their throats. They knew there were questions that would need to be answered, but for now they kept the focus on the fact that Taryn was improving.

"Was it the sun?" Gastyn asked.

"I think so," Keiryn answered.

"I want to take her home," Ilya said, looking to Maxym.

"Son, let me take her," he stated, kneeling down in front of them.

"No. Keiryn and I will carry her back through the forest. It's the best thing for her," he explained, hiding the fact that she could usurp some much needed energy off of the lush vegetation in the woods during their hike.

Maxym shared a look with Ilya before she finally nodded, giving her approval. "Okay. We will see you back at the house shortly."

৪৩৪৩

Taryn slept in Larkin's arms as the two boys walked at a steady pace to ensure that nothing would be decimated as she drew energy from the earth, just as he had suspected she would.

"Does your father know?" Keiryn asked.

"No, and I have no intentions of telling him. I'm afraid it might be too much for him to accept."

"And it's not for you?"

"If it was the first thing I learned about her, then maybe, but it wasn't. I know how good she is on the inside. Her heart is pure platinum. She loves the earth as she does every living thing upon it."

"Does she know about your mother?"

"No, and I'm not quite sure how to tell her. She knows so little about us. I don't think she will be able to wrap her head around it. You should have seen how devastated she was the other night when I told her that Healer's misused their powers to prolong their own lives. You've probably figured out that she's guided by emotion. For her, it's a delicate balance to stay in control." Glancing over towards Keiryn, he noticed him rubbing his scars. "I'm sorry about that."

"Oh, I guess it wasn't meant to be. We saved her life. She is worth more than some old scars. Besides, it's not as though I could have taken my shirt off ever again without giving away her secrets. It felt kind of weird not having them there after all of this time. Though, it does make me wonder how you are still standing if you returned the powers that saved your life."

"I don't know. Maybe it has something to do with the fact that I'm bound to her. Whatever the reason, I'm grateful."

Keiryn shrugged at the explanation. It could make sense, though he wasn't one hundred percent sold on the idea of them being bound just yet.

"Keiryn, what exactly happened back there? I mean, how did you figure out the whole breathing thing?"

"You're going to think that I'm nuts…"

"Dude, I already do…you should have seen yourself."

"I heard some guy whispering in my ear. Sounds crazy, right?"

"It does seem pretty farfetched, but considering everything that I've learned over the past week, it's definitely plausible. You want to know something even crazier?"

"Sure," Keiryn nodded.

"Taryn asked me earlier if we had seen a man in the woods the other night. Maybe she really did see someone, and just maybe he was the one whispering to you."

೫ೞೞೞೞ

A worried Jonesy met them at the door as they approached. "Is she going to be alright?"

"Yes, but she's going to need to rest for a while," Larkin answered.

Ilya stood waiting at the top of the stairs. She followed him as he laid her down on the clean sheets and tucked her in.

"I don't know what exactly happened out there, but what I do know is that I owe you both a debt of gratitude. I could sense that she was practically gone and yet the two of you found a way to bring her back," she sobbed, wrapping an arm around each of them and squeezing tightly. "If you wouldn't mind…I'd like a little time alone with my daughter."

"Of course." Larkin leaned down to kiss her forehead one final time before leaving.

At the top of the stairs, a nervous Jonesy stood waiting. "Can I talk to you guys for a minute?"

"Sure, Jonesy…what's up?" Keiryn asked, patting him on the back.

"Not in here."

The boys followed him outside and into the woods, far away from prying ears. "What's going on, Jonesy?" Larkin asked, sensing something was off.

"I really shouldn't say anything, but if I don't and there's something to it..."

"What is it, Jonesy?" Both boys inquired in unison.

"The other day at school...When the kid tried to make her a flower, but instead formed a prickly cactus..."

"Come on, out with it already," Larkin advised, growing impatient.

"When Gastyn went to remove the thorns, they disappeared."

"What do you mean disappeared?" Keiryn asked.

"One second they were there and the next they weren't. Larkin, you were there...didn't you see?"

"I saw Gastyn take her hand, but that was all. What does this have to do with today?"

"When Ardyn grabbed her hand earlier I...I...I could have sworn that I saw the thorns leave Taryn's hand and go into his. I think that's what caused the bleeding."

"Are you sure about what you saw?"

"Yes, no...maybe. I mean, it all happened so fast, but I think so."

Larkin released an agonizing growl as anger surged through him. "I knew something was off with him the other night at the Desert Rose, and then again when he stopped by earlier this week."

"Jonesy, we appreciate you sharing this information with us...but you can't tell anyone else. Do you understand?" Keiryn asked, motioning for Larkin to chill until they were alone.

"I care for her too. I'll keep quiet," he agreed, before quickly heading back towards the house.

"What are we going to do? It's not as if any of us could take him on. We wouldn't stand a chance. Gastyn's the most powerful Gaias in our territory, next to Ardyn, and even he wouldn't go there," Keiryn grumbled.

"If what Jonesy said is true, then we may very well have a practicing Mortari living in our midst."

"I have a hard time buying that he's Mortari. I mean, he's being considered as a possible candidate for the Elder Council. There's no way he could fool them, not with all the mutts they have protecting them, it's just not possible."

Larkin looked at Keiryn with disdain, taking offense to his mutt reference.

"Sorry, Man. I wasn't thinking. Speaking of...if he was, wouldn't you be able to sense it too?"

"You would think..." he admitted with a heavy sigh, letting Keiryn's faux pas slide. "If he's not Mortari, then what is he?"

"I don't know. Maybe he's like Taryn, a little bit of everything."

"We've all seen him in battle and heard the stories. His gift is being an Imperium, but it doesn't matter what he is, one thing is for certain, we can't let him get near her again."

೮೦೦೪೮೦೦೪

Over the next few days, the boys stayed close by Taryn's side, helping to take her into the sunlight the moment it peaked through the morning sky and keeping her in its reach until it set in the evening. Gastyn, Maxym and Teigan watched in awe as the shared responsibility of caring for the girl seemed to heal old wounds between the two childhood friends.

By Sunday morning, she was back up and moving around on her own, and by afternoon she was feeling more like herself. She enjoyed spending time with the boys. They both made her laugh, each in their own way, and brought much happiness into her life, which was the safest emotion for her to experience, especially considering all that had happened.

On Monday morning Taryn bounded out of bed, stepping first on Larkin before stumbling across Keiryn, who was sleeping on her bedroom floor. They all shared a laugh, waking the rest of the house.

"Good morning you three," Ilya smiled from the doorway.

"Good morning, Mom." She gave her a healthy hug before bounding off to take a shower.

Larkin and Keiryn smiled and nodded as they walked past her and Maxym.

"It is very understanding of you to allow them to stay in there with her," Maxym remarked.

"What would you have me do? Make them sleep in the hallway when we all know that neither would be content until they could see her. Besides, they love my daughter so very much."

When Taryn made it down the stairs, she was dressed and ready for school. Teigan had prepared breakfast for everyone and the boys were busy scarfing down heaping piles of steaming scrambled eggs and crispy bacon.

She took her seat in between them and began to eat.

"Are you sure that you're up to going to school today?" Ilya worried.

"For the hundredth time, yes, yes, and triple yes. I'm feeling almost as good as new."

"Larkin and I will be looking out for her the whole time," Keiryn assured her.

"And don't forget, Gastyn," Teigan reminded them, taking a sip of his coffee.

"Gastyn too," his son mocked.

After they ate, Ilya, Maxym and Teigan watched as the three teens headed out to Keiryn's truck and slid into the front cab, waving them good-bye as they drove out of sight.

❦❧❦❧

When the trio pulled into the parking lot at the school, several heads turned in their direction. Looks of disbelief passed between students as they started to notice that Larkin and Keiryn were riding in the same vehicle. Several shocked gasps could be heard, especially from members of each pack.

"Holy hell, I wouldn't believe it if I wasn't seeing it with my own two eyes," Dalen smirked, less than happy.

"I told you they've been hanging out, so pay up," Jonesy stated, holding his hand out to collect on the bet he and Dalen had made.

"No way, this has to be some sort of trick."

"She's a pretty girl, but I have a hard time believing that a pretty face is all that it took to fix their drama," Eben insisted.

"Whatever, the three of them look so cute together," the twin's exclaimed.

"Yeah, I guess so," Bency smiled slightly, still irritated that they had not heard a word from their fearless leader in over a week.

"Don't be mad at him," Jonesy insisted, sensing her discord. "You have no idea how bad things got with Taryn before she finally started to come around."

"I know, I know...It's just that we should come first...we are his family after all."

"So which one is she with again?" Eben asked, noticing how Taryn stayed in near constant contact with both boys as they approached.

❦❧❦❧

On the other side of the parking lot, the conversation was not nearly as pleasant.

"Look at him," Gerrick grunted. "It makes me sick the way they're acting like everything is fine between them."

"Gerrick, can you try to be happy for him? He's crazy about this girl, and if she can bring the two of them back together again, I say good for her," Dagney disagreed with her brother.

"I'm with Gerrick," Nalani snarled, unhappy to see Keiryn smiling and laughing with Taryn.

"Don't be jealous," Thorne snapped, noticing her green-eyed monster rearing its ugly head.

"Yeah, just try to be happy for him," Kellan sulked, afraid he had just lost his best friend of the past five years.

ὅ☧ὅ☧

"Hey, let me go get the pack and I'll be right back," Larkin smiled, kissing her on the cheek before running over to greet them. "What's up, guys?"

"So you got the girl and automatically forgot how to pick up a phone?" Kellan asked, shooting him a dirty look.

"It's not like that, she needed me. Gastyn told you about what happened."

"Yeah, and we needed you too," Gerrick growled, rolling his eyes. "You're supposed to be our leader, yet the first time you see a pretty face you get all gaga over her."

"I guess I deserve that," Larkin replied. "I know you are mad, but it isn't like that. You know she's cool."

"So cool," Nalani glared, growing more irritated by the second that Keiryn was fussing over her.

"Look, Keiryn and I made some progress over the past week. Maybe we can all try to get along." His words were met with mixed looks of disbelief and resentment from his pack.

"Or not," Gerrick growled, walking towards the school doors.

"Come on Ger, give it a chance." He followed after him.

Stopping in his tracks he turned to look at his friend. It was as if a weight had been lifted off of Larkin's shoulders. The week before last his eyes had been clouded with worry and his demeanor tense and on-edge. But now he appeared to be perfectly relaxed and carefree. "Fine, but the first time one of those donkeys say anything, they're one and done...understood?"

"I'm sure it won't come to that," he smiled, patting him on the back. When Kellan came into reach he wrapped his arm around his neck and walked with him to the steps.

"What's up, Guys?" Keiryn greeted them.

"Not a lot," Gerrick retorted dryly.

"How are you feeling?" Dagney asked Taryn, who was now standing between the pack leaders.

"Much better, thank you."

The packs began to mingle, with the exclusion of Nalani, who saw nothing but red at the way both boys fussed over her. "Why does she get them both?" she muttered to herself.

"Boy troubles?" Adalia smirked, walking up the steps behind her.

"Go away, Ada."

"I wouldn't be so quick to dismiss me. After all, I've been here about a minute and already see there's one more standing in line for the bird's affection. It looks like she took the number one spot."

"Whatever." Nalani walked inside, not wanting anyone else to see how upset she was.

Soon everyone else followed suit and entered the school to begin their day. In their first hour class, Larkin accepted that Taryn and Jonesy were going to stay partners. He knew, without a doubt, that she held a special place in her heart for the weakest member of either pack. It was just one more thing he loved about her.

When lunch time rolled around the members from the two packs sat at their usual tables, minus their leaders. With Larkin and Keiryn by her side, Taryn chose to sit at her normal table. Larkin sat to her left while Keiryn sat on her right. Without any warning, Jonesy jumped up from his seat and rushed over to join the trio.

"What a suck-up," Dalen whined, nodding in his direction.

"One's thing is for sure, that girl has the voodoo," Eben smirked, referring to how she had worked some sort of magic on Keiryn and Larkin.

"I don't care what you losers say. I think he has the right idea," Bency shrugged, picking up her tray to join Taryn's table with the twins trailing behind her, leaving Dalen and Eben all alone with Adalia.

Across the lunchroom, Larkin's pack was having a very similar conversation.

"Look at them," Kellan growled. "You can't even tell which one she's supposed to be dating."

"Maybe she's dating both," Thorne joked.

Dagney jabbed him in the ribs. "Don't be ridiculous. She's definitely into Larkin." Looking at Nalani, she could see how bothered her best friend was by all of the attention Keiryn was paying Taryn. "Hey, you heard Gastyn tell everyone that Keiryn was there when she was struck by lightning. I bet he's just staying close, trying to make her feel safe. I mean seriously, can you imagine…she could have died."

"I know, I know," Nalani sighed. "It just sucks that the second it looks like there's hope for me, he has eyes for someone else."

"I know, Lani, but it'll fade. Give it a few days and I'm sure everything will work its way out."

Nalani leaned in, bumping her shoulder playfully and sighed, "I suppose we should go say hello."

With that, the girls grabbed their trays. With two seats open across from Taryn and Keiryn, Dagney pushed her friend to sit directly across from him. As they sat down they were greeted with wide smiles from everyone.

"Hey, Nalani," Keiryn grinned, gazing at her momentarily, taking in her gorgeous crystal blue eyes against the caramel color of her skin that contrasted nicely with her silky dark hair. He had never failed to notice how stunning she was. She played up her exotic looks well. It was something he had always appreciated about her.

"Hey," she nodded, trying to play it cool.

Her attempt to pretend uninterested didn't go unnoticed. Watching with a casual demeanor, Taryn took in their interaction while chatting with Dagney. Despite Nalani's tough exterior, she could see that there was a soft, girly-girl underneath who sought his affections.

Soon everyone, with the exception of Adalia, joined them. Even though Taryn knew she had an ugly side, she felt empathy for the girl. Standing, she excused herself momentarily and walked over to where she was seated.

"What do you want?" Adalia chided, glancing at her with disdain before taking a bite of her sandwich.

"Adalia." She chose to ignore her hateful attitude. "There's room for one more at our table if you're interested."

"I don't know what kind of game you're playing, Princess, but I'm not drinking your punch."

"Suit yourself, Adalia. Enjoy your lunch."

As Taryn walked away, Adalia mumbled to herself. "She thinks she's so perfect. I haven't a clue what it is they see in her, but one thing is for certain…I'll find her weakness and expose her for the fraud that she is."

"What were you doing over there?" Dalen asked.

"I told her we had room for one more."

"Why would you go and do something so daft?" Kellan hissed, thinking about what would have happened had Ada the Menace decided to accept.

"Kellan," Larkin admonished.

"Larkin, it's okay," Taryn assured him. "He's entitled to have his own opinion on the subject..." Kellan grinned, pleased to hear her acknowledgment. "However, it doesn't mean that he's right," she winked, razzing him and lightening the atmosphere.

"I think we should go outside and sit in the sun for a few minutes before the bell rings," Keiryn suggested, reaching to take Taryn's tray as Larkin nodded in agreement.

⁎C⁎C

Taryn leaned back, resting her head comfortably against Larkin's chest as they sat on the grass at the rear of the school. Members of both packs settled in around them while Keiryn sat to the left.

"So, Kansas, what was it like...you know, getting struck by lightning?" Thorne asked.

"Surprisingly draining." Larkin wrapped her snuggly in his arms while she spoke.

"And you were both there?" Eben asked Larkin and Keiryn.

"Yeah, it was the scariest thing that I've ever seen," Keiryn answered, recalling the actual events of that day in his head.

"It's a miracle that you survived. When I was just a kid, my great uncle was struck by lightning at a family get together. He wasn't as lucky as you," Bency shared, a brief flicker of sadness in her eyes.

"I'm sorry to hear that," Taryn replied sincerely, wishing she could do something to lessen her pain, but knowing that she would give her secrets away if she did.

"It happened a long time ago," she shrugged, still seemingly haunted by the memory.

Soon the bell rang and the group headed to Gastyn's classroom. Taryn laced her fingers with Larkin's, holding his hand the entire way.

Keiryn walked behind them, battling the resentment that was trying to surface. He had promised Larkin and his own father that he wouldn't interfere with their relationship, but it was a constant struggle to keep his feelings for her at bay.

In class, Taryn took her seat at the front of the middle row while the rest divided into two packs, seating themselves on either side.

When Andyn walked into the classroom, he immediately ran to her. Wrapping his arms tightly around her neck, a few silent tears escaped his weighted green eyes.

"What's this about?"

"I was so scared."

His heart was so heavy that she could feel his pain. "I'm fine, Andyn...see?" She smiled warmly, although she sensed that something far greater was troubling him. Taking a quick glance at her face, he once again wrapped his arms around her neck. She patted him gently on the back, trying to reassure him that she was truly fine.

When he finally released his hold on her, he surprised everyone in the room by what he did next. Instead of taking his normal seat next to Kellan on Larkin's side, he moved to the desk directly behind her.

"Taryn, can I join you?" he asked, his voice trembling.

Standing, she placed her hands on each of his shoulders and looked him deep in the eye. "Of course, Andyn. I'd be honored."

Gastyn carefully watched the exchange from the doorway of his office. Once everyone had settled in, he took role and then dismissed the class to go into the back room and begin practicing.

Andyn stayed by her side, leaving only to race Kellan down the trail a few times. She smiled as she watched, thankful that Kellan cared enough to let him win each race.

ೞೞೞೞ

For the next few days, the routine remained the same. The two packs continued to grow more tolerant of one another, even seeming to enjoy the renewed camaraderie.

When Friday rolled around, Adalia had just about all that she could tolerate of the new peace between the two sides. As they laughed and chatted during Gastyn's class, her jealousy and hatred finally boiled over.

"What would you do?" Hadley asked Taryn after she and Bentley had failed yet another attempt at creating rain clouds.

"I think that you two are focusing too hard on the wrong element."

"Then what should we do?" Bentley asked.

Before Taryn could speak, Adalia unleashed her snide sarcasm. "Oh yes, we should all bow down to the all-knowing Perfect Little Princess."

"You'd better watch out, Ada…your jealousy is showing," Nalani smirked, drawing laughter from the others.

"You make me sick. The way you fall all over yourselves when she's around. I mean, haven't any of you noticed that she doesn't seem to have any talents of her own? Why would you think that she would have the first clue how to be an Elemental?"

"No one cares what you think, Ada," Andyn replied protectively.

"Andyn, don't pay her any mind. Some people like misery and there isn't anything the rest of us can do to help them," Taryn

~ 274 ~

sighed, wishing Adalia would allow herself to be likable. She placed a comforting arm around his shoulders, walking him to where Jonesy was working on growing plants.

Furious that the little twerp would dare speak to her that way, and even more so that Taryn always walked away smelling like a bouquet of roses, Adalia held her hands out towards her. Using her gift of being an Influential, she forced out her powers to make Taryn believe she was a duck. When Jonesy saw her intentions he jumped in the way, catching the full force of it. Instantly, he squatted down, tucking his arms to his sides and began quacking loudly.

Taryn turned to Adalia. "Why would you do this?" she frowned, not understanding why anyone would use their powers against another member of their community in such a humiliating way. Larkin and Keiryn moved to her side, both trying to calm her.

"Darn, I missed my target, but at least I nailed the runt," she grinned, realizing the best way to get under the princess' skin was through those she cared for the most.

Taryn knelt down next to Jonesy. Placing a hand on his shoulder, she absorbed Adalia's Influence from him, allowing him to return to his normal self. "I'm sorry about that." She felt badly that he had taken the brunt of something that was intended for her.

Shaking his head, Jonesy forced a half-smile. "At least it didn't last as long as it normally does."

Gerrick held his hand out, offering it to Jonesy. After helping him to his feet, the duo stood, backed by members of both packs.

Taking a deep breath, Taryn tried to quiet the disdain she now felt for Adalia. All of the empathy that she had previously held for her was now washed away. "If Jonesy is alright, then I believe we should return to our practice." She hoped that ignoring Adalia would send a message to the mean girl.

"You need to back off," Keiryn warned Adalia, shooting her a frosty glare.

Larkin placed an arm around Taryn's shoulders, trying to distract her, fearful that Adalia's torment might cause her to come undone in front of everyone.

"What's going on here?" Gastyn asked, walking into the room and seeing the two packs clearly standing together as one, with Adalia facing them.

"Nothing," Keiryn replied, continuing to glare in her direction.

Adalia stood for several minutes, stewing as she watched how unified they appeared to be without her. Knowing that her powers would have very little impact on Larkin, due to his unusual speed and strength, she targeted the next best thing. Without so much as a word, she created an energy orb the size of a basketball and hurled it directly at an unsuspecting Andyn.

It happened so fast that no one had time to react. Just as the orb came within inches of his small head, Taryn's hand flew up and stopped it.

Everyone stood stunned. Taryn could feel the anger tearing through her. Knowing that Adalia had intended to seriously harm Andyn made her blood boil. With her hand still in the air, she held the orb in place, turning to face her. Locking her eyes on the surprised girl, she tilted her head to the side and studied her with an ominous gleam.

"Taryn, don't," Larkin pleaded, reaching for her hand.

She ignored him, while remaining focused solely on the now trembling girl. "You wanted my attention, Adalia...and now you have it." Her voice was full of calm while she looked at her blankly, fighting through the myriad of dark emotions that surged through her.

"Uh, um, I, I, I…" Adalia stammered, shocked at the ease that she seemed to control the orb, and fearful of what she might do with it.

"If you ever try to hurt someone that I care about again…" She crushed the orb into dust by simply balling her hand into a fist. With her heart racing inside her chest, she fought to suppress the rage that churned inside.

Adalia's face turned ghostly white as gasps could be heard from the other students. Not one of them had ever witnessed a power orb being crushed like that before. Not even by a mature Gaias.

"Adalia, go to my office, now," Gastyn ordered, fearing what might happen if she stayed within Taryn's view another moment. Without hesitation, she ran for the door and quickly disappeared on the other side. He glanced to Larkin and Keiryn, and they nodded, letting him know that they would look after Taryn.

"Taryn, look at me," Larkin stated calmly, taking her hands into his. "Thanks to you, Andyn's fine. But I need for you to look at me. I need to know that you are alright."

Closing her eyes, she envisioned a box inside of her and pushed all of her emotions into it. After a few minutes, she opened her eyes to find his beautiful face inches from hers. Looking deep into his eyes, she sighed, "You're so beautiful."

"Beautiful?"

"I guess you *are* just another pretty face," Keiryn teased, standing next to them, trying to help lighten the atmosphere. "You have an audience." He nodded his head just over his shoulder to where everyone was standing.

"Are you okay?" Larkin asked before stepping aside.

"As long as you are by my side."

"Looks like somebody's been holding out on us," Dalen howled excitedly.

"Yeah, Kansas…it looks like you are a certifiable badass," Nalani declared.

Rushing over to her, Kellan picked her up and spun her around several times. "That was so freaking amazing."

"So why didn't you ever tell us that you were an Imperium?" Bency asked.

Feeling overwhelmed by all of the attention, she walked over to Andyn and wrapped him tightly in her arms. "I'm so sorry, Andyn. If she hadn't been so angry with me she would never have targeted you."

"It's alright. I know that you'll always protect me, Taryn," he replied, hugging her long and hard.

ಬಿಂಬಿಂ

At the end of the school day, Taryn and the rest of the students filed out from the back room. They quieted down and made a speedy exit to the hallway when they saw that Gastyn had company in his office.

Outside, each of them sighed with relief. "I bet Adalia's wishing she hadn't messed with the kid now," Kellan laughed, referring to that fact that not only her father, but Ardyn Mitchell was also standing in their teacher's office.

"Well I'm glad that Gastyn called Ardyn. It's not as though her own father would do anything to punish her for such a vile act," Dagney stated.

"Sorry that we can't stay and hang today…I promised my dad that I would help him out around the house with a few things," Larkin lied, wanting to get Taryn away from the school as soon as possible, fearing that at any minute Ardyn could walk out the door.

"Yeah, we've got to go," Keiryn echoed, receiving several groans.

Understanding their disappointment and wanting to make amends for what she could only imagine must have felt like betrayal from their leaders, Taryn turned to them. "Why don't you guys come over tomorrow around noonish, we can grill out and swim."

"Um, is that okay?" Eben asked, looking to Larkin for approval.

"Of course." He granted his permission for them to come into what had been his pack's territory for nearly five years.

"We hope to see you all there," she smiled, before turning to walk away with her two protectors following closely at her side.

CHAPTER TEN

"You did what?" Ilya gasped.

"Look, it's only fair. If you expect them to protect me, we need to find a way to allow them time with their packs."

"But the entire point of all of this is so they *can* protect you. Having all of those kids over, gives you more opportunities to expose yourself."

"Bottom line…before they took the Blood Oath to protect my secrets, they pledged an Oath to their brothers and sisters. I won't be the reason they neglect their responsibilities," Taryn declared, taking a seat on one of the barstools, while shooting her mother a disapproving look for having such little faith in her. She reached for a pen and the notepad already sitting on the countertop. "Now…shall we discuss what we need from the store?"

"Fine," Ilya sighed, knowing that she wasn't going to accept no for an answer.

After writing out a rather lengthy grocery list, she grabbed her purse. "Do you want to come with me?"

"I hope you don't mind. Maxym let me in," Gastyn interrupted, walking into the kitchen. "I would like to speak with Taryn for a moment if you don't mind."

"Did something happen?"

"There was an incident, but you would be proud of the way she handled herself."

She studied Gastyn for a moment before deciding that it could wait until later. "Very well then," she sighed. "But when I return I want all of the details...understood?"

"Of course," Taryn shrugged, knowing her mother was going to make a fuss about it even though nothing bad had happened.

"While you all stay here, I'll go with Ilya and help buy the groceries," Maxym announced, trailing after her.

Once they left, Gastyn directed her to go into the living room. She sat down on the couch as a heavy sigh passed her lips.

"You're not in trouble," he assured her as Larkin and Keiryn joined them. Settling into the chair, he crossed his legs and looked at her. "Adalia upset you today." She nodded in agreement. "You remained in control of your emotions. Would you please explain to me how you managed to do that?"

"I was so mad about what she did to Jonesy. I mean really, to try and humiliate someone like that...I can't understand it. But then what she tried to do to Andyn...I felt ugly."

"Ugly?"

"I wanted to do something vile to that awful girl."

"But you didn't..."

She exhaled as turmoil washed over her. "Only because I was afraid."

"Why would you be afraid?" Gastyn asked, knowing that she could have easily hurt Adalia.

"I'd rather not say." She stood, walking to the doorway.

"I'm only trying to understand you, in order to help."

Larkin went to her, placing his hands on her shoulders. "It's okay. You're amongst family."

Reaching up, she placed her hand over his. "Before today, I've never felt the desire to hurt another being. With all of that emotion, that terrible anger, I was so afraid that if I started…I wouldn't be able to find a way stop myself." She hung her head low in shame.

"Feelings like those are natural, Taryn. Most would not have found the strength within themselves to prevent taking action," Gastyn offered.

"He's right. We all wanted to kick her butt for what she did," Keiryn admitted. "But when you crushed her orb instead of thrusting it back, it was you who kept us grounded."

"Thrusting that orb at her was the last thing on my mind."

"I think you have enough information, Gastyn," Larkin asserted, sensing she was growing weary.

Gastyn nodded, knowing the boy's bond with her made him feel the need to protect her from everyone, including those amongst their circle. "Very well. Get some rest, Taryn. You've had a very long day."

ᏒᎾᏣᏒᎾᏣ

Later that evening, Taryn, Larkin and Keiryn climbed up the mountain and sat watching as the sun began to set across the valley.

"I'd forgotten how great the view was from here," Keiryn sighed.

"It is pretty amazing," Larkin responded, though his eyes were focused solely on Taryn as she took in the peaceful sight.

Keiryn glanced over and couldn't help the feeling of torment that he held inside while watching them. Even though his own eyes were telling him that they were destined for each other, he just couldn't let go of his desire to protect her from the monster lurking inside his old friend. And he certainly couldn't get past the fact that he loved her too.

Once the sun had disappeared over the horizon, the trio headed back to the house and watched a movie. Ilya, Maxym and Teigan observed from the dining room, comforted by how close their children had become, sensing that their bond was growing more impenetrable by the minute.

"Hurry, Mom," Taryn shouted, as their guests began to arrive.

"I'm coming, I'm coming." She rushed down the stairs.

Hava and Beldyn Love accompanied their twin daughters to the party. "Hello, Mr. and Mrs. Love," Taryn beamed, flashing a brilliant smile.

"It's a pleasure to meet you, and to find you in such good health," Hava replied, gripping her husband's hand tightly.

Taryn smiled at her. She had straight blonde hair like her daughters, and kind gray eyes. Their father was tall and robust, with darker blonde hair. "I owe you both thanks for what you did the other day to save me," Taryn acknowledged, even though she knew their efforts had very little to do with her current state of well-being.

"Please, do come in," Ilya greeted them while the three girls hurried to the backyard.

"I hope we're not intruding," Hava smiled.

"Not at all." She escorted them inside to the living room. "I can't thank you enough for what you did for my little girl."

"It was our pleasure," Beldyn nodded, looking out to the backyard where he could see Larkin and Keiryn watching over the grill with their fathers nearby. "I never thought that I would see that again."

"The twins told us that they had finally worked through their differences. It really is great to see," Hava agreed.

Soon the sound of the doorbell filled the air as one guest after another arrived. Parents stayed, barely able to grasp that the two packs were being amicable, while others lingered just to get a look at the girl who had survived a direct lightning strike.

As soon as the final guests arrived, everyone jumped in line and began filling their plates with all of the delicious food. There were grilled hot dogs, hamburgers, chicken breasts, potato and pasta salads, coleslaw, deviled eggs, fresh garden salad, and much more.

They ate and laughed, as though the past five years of turmoil had never happened.

"This is incredible," Hava exclaimed as she watched the teens. "Who would have ever thought things would turn around in such a profound way?" The other parents nodded in agreement.

"I believe this change comes from the presence of your daughter, Ilya," Lucan Skye, Gerrick's father, posed.

"I like to believe that she is special," Ilya blushed.

"He's right. She seems to bring them together in a way that the rest of us could not," Gideon Skye, Lucan's brother stated. "Nalani couldn't quit going on about how she struck fear into Adalia Moore."

"I have to say, it was great to hear that she was finally put in her place after all of the misery she has brought since her arrival. Gerrick said she couldn't get away from Taryn fast enough after she crushed Adalia's orb as if it were nothing. Is that even possible?" Lucan questioned.

Ilya shrugged, unsure of how to answer. Lucan was a carbon copy of his son. The only difference was that his hair was a shade lighter and his nose slightly longer than Gerrick's.

"Taryn has something that the rest of the children haven't yet mastered," Teigan offered.

"And what exactly is that?" Gideon asked.

"She has such intensity when it comes to her own control," Maxym interjected. "I know Gaias that are decades old who haven't yet mastered that feat. Ilya has done a phenomenal job with her."

Ilya sat quietly, feeling their eyes bearing down on her. Maxym stood and moved to her side, placing a comforting hand on her shoulder.

"Nalani told me how she helped young Andyn complete his first successful animation," Gideon said.

"She's very insightful for only being sixteen," Gastyn offered. "I contribute this to Ilya's alternative choices in raising her. While the other children were out playing, young Taryn worked on her focus through meditation," he fibbed, hoping to satisfy their curiosity.

୨୦୦୫୨୦୦୫

Walking inside, followed by a line of girls, Taryn stopped in the living room. "We're going to go change into our swimsuits."

"That sounds great, Sweetie." Ilya was happy to see her daughter acting like a normal teenager, and thankful for a break in the conversation with the other adults.

After a few hours in the water, the guys grew restless. "Why don't you go for a run," Taryn suggested, intending to push them together as a singular pack, just like old times. "I can see that you are itching to."

"What do you think, Keiryn? Should we take these boys for a run?" Larkin mused.

"I don't know…" he replied, looking members from both packs over curiously.

"You boys aren't going anywhere without this freak," Bency asserted, taking a place between them, while gaining whistles and cheers from the girls.

"You tell 'em girl," Nalani cheered.

"What about it, you losers afraid that you can't hang with me?"

In under a minute, all of the Skin-Walkers had shifted, running into the woods. While they ran, the rest of the girls lounged about on the chairs. They talked about everything from clothes, hair, make-up to boys, human and Gaias alike.

"So, Taryn, you and Larkin seem pretty serious," Dagney stated, hoping to get her to disclose something that would put Nalani at ease. Much to her disappointment, she only smiled.

"It's strange seeing him fussing over you all of the time. He hasn't so much as looked at a girl with even a hint of interest until you showed up," Bentley acknowledged.

"Nope, not once," Hadley echoed.

"Has he invited you to the Annual Williams Festival?" Nalani inquired.

"The Williams Festival?"

"It's a pretty big deal around here. There's a parade to kick it off, then they have carnival games, a Bar-B-Que contest, food and craft vendors, all followed by a street dance. It's actually pretty cool," Dagney explained.

"Since you didn't know about it, I take it he hasn't asked," Nalani surmised, with a disappointed look.

"Larkin and I will be fine," Taryn smiled confidently. "So who are you guys going with?"

"Thorne asked me to go with him last Wednesday," Dagney beamed.

"Bency asked Jonesy yesterday after school," Hadley and Bentley giggled in unison.

"She didn't?" Nalani gasped.

"Why not? She runs with the boys, and she likes him regardless of where he ranks in the pack," Bentley shrugged.

"It just seems strange to ask a guy out," Nalani frowned.

"I never knew you were so old-fashioned," Bentley stated with a look of surprise.

"I think you should go with Keiryn," Taryn smiled at Nalani.

"He's been a little too preoccupied to notice me lately."

"I disagree." She shook her head. "I see how he steals glances of you when he thinks no one else is looking. And I also see how you try to play it cool, but there's something between the two of you."

Nalani gasped in horror, not realizing she had been so obvious in her feelings for Keiryn. In Taryn's short time around them she had been able to pick up on just how much she liked him. Even though she was petrified at the thought, she was also elated that she believed Keiryn was interested in her too.

"Talking about a love-connection…it looks like your mom and Mr. Taylor might be hitting it off," Dagney smiled, hoping that she wouldn't take offense to her observation.

Taryn grinned, not surprised that others could see what she had so plainly seen the first night her mother and Maxym had met.

A short time later, Larkin burst through the trees in mid-phase. Quickly he rushed to her and scooped her up in his arms, holding onto to her tightly.

"I've missed you." He nuzzled his nose against her neck.

"I missed you, too." It was so easy to forget that anyone else in the world existed in that moment while she was wrapped securely in his embrace.

"Ah, how romantic," the twins gushed in unison as they watched the exchange.

Placing her feet back on the ground, he looked at her with great love radiating in his eyes. Twirling her hair between his fingers, he smiled brightly at her. "Taryn, would you allow me the pleasure of being your escort to the Williams Festival?"

"As if you even had to ask."

Soon everyone else returned, surprisingly refreshed by their long run. With plenty of food left over, many prepared themselves another plate and sat next to the fire pit that Jonesy had insisted on building the previous weekend.

While Larkin and Taryn snuggled against one another as the evening air turned chilly, several of the parents joined the teens around the fire, telling stories of their great history. Normally one to soak up any bit of information that she could, Taryn found her thoughts drifting elsewhere. It didn't matter that Larkin was literally at her fingertips, he consumed her mind in such a way that she could no longer ignore.

Noticing her distraction, he stood, holding his hand out to her. Looking up at him, her heart ached in a pleasant sort of way and she immediately took his hand, allowing him to lead her into the woods to steal their first private moment of the day.

"Is everything alright?" he asked.

"Couldn't be better."

"I love you, Taryn."

"I know."

Cupping her cheeks carefully in his hands, he leaned down, bringing his lips closer to hers. "I love you, Taryn."

"And I lo…" She stopped abruptly as Keiryn joined them.

"Your mother's looking for you, Taryn."

"I'll be there in a sec."

"I wouldn't keep her waiting."

Nalani walked up behind him. "Oh, I think her mother wouldn't mind if we gave them a few more minutes."

"That's okay, it's seems rather crowded out here," Larkin moaned, taking Taryn's hand in his and walking back towards the house, passing them along the way.

Once they were out of sight, Nalani called Keiryn out. "Why did you do that?"

"Do what?"

"You know exactly what." She turned on her heel to head back to join the others.

"Hold on," he shouted, chasing after her. "Whatever you're thinking, I can assure you that you're wrong."

"Oh, am I? To me it looked like you were jealous that they snuck away without you. And it seemed that you were even more bothered by the fact that she was about to tell him that she loved him too."

He leaned heavily against a tree. "You don't understand."

"I think it's pretty obvious, but I can promise you that she will never look at you the same way that she looks at him."

"I know," he shook his head in frustration. "I don't want to come between them…but I just can't seem to let go of what I feel for her."

Stepping to him, she smoothed back the hair that was hanging down in front of his eyes. "I know first-hand how much it sucks to love someone who doesn't love you back, Keiryn."

For a moment their eyes caught in a gaze. He moved his face closer to hers. Just as their lips were about to touch, she pulled away.

"I don't want to be your second choice," she whispered sadly, before walking away.

When Nalani returned, she watched Taryn and Larkin as he protectively swaddled her and acted as though no one else was around. Battling the jealousy she felt for what they had, she no longer harbored ill-will towards the new girl. It was quite obvious to everyone that she only had eyes for Larkin.

Soon Lucan and Gideon began to share stories of their time spent with the Necro-Chaser Alliance. Ilya immediately sent Larkin a pleading look. Understanding what she was trying to convey, he scooped Taryn up into his arms, rushing inside.

"Why did you do that?"

"I don't think that you need to hear what they're about to say in the company of others. Would you like to go to my house for a while?"

"Sure," she smiled, trusting him completely with her well-being.

"Let me tell my dad and we'll drive over."

ᛞᚲᚷᛞᚲᚷ

Walking in the back door of his home, Taryn thought back to that fateful evening the storm had chased her into his arms. Chills crept through her when she thought about how close they had both come to being struck that day.

"Here's the kitchen and there's the living room."

"I remember. Where's your bedroom?" she asked, curious as to what it might look like.

"Come on, I'll show you." He took her hand and led her up the narrow stairway.

When she first entered she studied the room carefully, making mental notes of every detail. His bed had a dark blue comforter with three oversized pillows on top. There was an oval mirror that hung on the wall, while a small three-tiered shelf held a large glass jar that overflowed with various types of change, and a magic eight-ball sat next to it. As she continued, she noticed a light oak-colored acoustic guitar resting in one corner, surrounded by several different colored picks scattered haphazardly about on the floor. Sitting down on the bed, she pondered for a moment. It was painfully obvious that their home lacked a woman's touch.

When Larkin noticed the sad smile that had formed upon her face, he sat beside her. "What is it?"

"I just realized how different my life might have been if I would have known my father."

"Did he die before you were born?"

"I'm not exactly sure…"

"Your mother didn't tell you?"

"Are you really surprised, knowing everything else that she has kept from me?"

"I guess not. Did you live in Kansas all of your life?"

"For as long as I can remember," she answered, swiping away a few stray tears. "You know, you watch television and everything seems so easy…even when it's hard. But watching everyone with both of their parents by their side tonight, really had an effect on me."

"I know exactly what you mean. I still remember my first parent's day without my mother being there. Keiryn and I were the only two there with only our fathers, but poor Jonesy didn't have either parent, just his aunt."

"What happened to her…your mother?" Taryn asked, feeling the ache from inside his chest.

He sat quietly for a few moments before finding the strength and courage to tell her about the awful truth regarding their kind. "When I was eight, my mother and I often took walks in the woods behind our house. I still remember holding onto her hand as we waved to my dad while he headed into town to pick up some lumber. Once we reached the tree line I ran ahead of her. Every so often she would call out for me to come back…it was our little thing. The last time I ran ahead, I waited for what seemed like an eternity for her to call out to me…but she never did. I ran back in the direction that I had come from and that's when I saw them." His voice cracked with emotion.

"Who did you see, Larkin?"

"The Mortari," he exhaled, looking at her with glassy eyes. "I watched as they robbed her body of every ounce of energy. I ran to her as fast as I could, but it was too late. She was already gone. They stood there, watching me as I cried out for her. One of them even leaned down and patted me on my head. I stood up, intending to face them, but with a wink from one and a nod from the other, they disappeared into the air."

"I'm so sorry, Larkin…I had no idea."

"It happened a long time ago," he replied, fighting to flash her a smile through the fresh pain brought on by the memory of that day. He reached for her, but she shrugged, avoiding his grasp. Looking at her face, all he could see was an empty expression.

"The Mortari…I'm like them," she gasped, placing her hands over her mouth.

"No, Taryn. Don't ever say that…you're nothing like them." He wrapped his arms around her as she struggled against him.

"Yes, I am," she sobbed.

"I know you and I know your heart. You would never do the vile things that the Mortari have done."

"You don't know the first thing about what's in my heart. If you did you would run away from me as fast as you can and never look back," she shouted, forcing him away with a pulse of her Imperium power before running down the stairs and out the back door into the darkness.

Once he managed to get to his feet, he ran after her. "Taryn, stop!"

"Stay away from me."

Tackling her to the ground, he pinned her down, hoping that she would listen. "I know that you're afraid, afraid of being like them. But you're not."

"I am, I wanted Adalia to suffer for what she tried to do. She wanted to hurt me, so she went after Andyn. All I could think about as the rage consumed me was draining every ounce of her power." In the light of the moon, she could see the look of surprise upon his face. "I told you to run away."

"No, Taryn. You don't understand," he replied, realizing that she had misread. "I've felt what it's like to have even a small amount of your power coursing through my veins, and it's incredibly overwhelming to say the least. Yet somehow you found the strength to put your emotions in check and let her walk away with only a warning. You're so much stronger than the rest of us."

"But I wanted to drain her powers."

"The Mortari…they call what they do progress and say it's a sacrifice for the greater good, when all they really care about is stealing the powers of others in hopes of obtaining immortality. You wanted to drain her powers because she tried to use them to harm others. Your intentions were not malicious. You are nothing like them!"

"But I'm a Healer."

"Yes, but you're so much more. Will you walk with me and let me explain their history to you?" he asked, his voice now calm.

Once she agreed, he rolled off of her and stood, holding out a hand to pull her to her feet.

"I've already told you how Healers were once considered to be the supreme beings of our kind. For centuries we lived in peace. Everyone had their own role to play. About one thousand years ago, a healer named Coyan became jealous of the gifts that other Gaias possessed. Apparently his ability to heal the sick and wounded was not enough. Not when others could call on the elements to bring much needed rain, or create pure energy out of thin air. His jealousy quickly turned into desire, and then to greed. He began to ponder that if it was possible to pull life from the earth to heal, would it not also be possible to pull powers from another Gaias? With the help of his two brothers, Chrystian and Clad, they began to experiment and eventually found a way to steal the powers that they so desperately coveted. What they didn't foresee was that they wouldn't be able to use the stolen powers in the same way as the original possessor, but instead discovered that it prolonged their lives and provided them with additional physical strength and speed. This sparked a new longing to find a way to become immortal."

"They're a thousand years old?"

"Yes, these brothers are the oldest living Gaias in our history."

"So that's why they are called Mortari…because they sought immortality?"

"Yes, but that's only the beginning. They were never able to find that one source of energy that would allow them to live forever, so they had to continue stealing power, killing even more Gaias. When the Elder Council discovered their atrocities, they sought a way to stop them. While the Council searched for a solution, the brothers began recruiting other Healers to join them, teaching them their ways. As the Mortari grew in numbers it became virtually impossible for anyone to fight them…they would steal the powers of those they battled, absorbing whatever was cast out against them, decimating everyone and everything in their wake. The Council declared it a crime to be born a Healer, and ordered the execution of anyone who possessed the gift. However, Mother Nature intervened and decided to stop it in her own way. Soon there were no longer any Healers being born. As the

Mortari's numbers stopped multiplying their attacks became even more vicious and targeted. No one was safe..." he paused momentarily.

"How is it that anyone survived if they were so dangerous?"

"A new affliction began to occur in certain Gaias who possessed the Skin-Walker gene. Those that suffered from the unheard of affliction found themselves taking on a new form that proved to be deadly to the Mortari."

"What were they?"

Taking a deep breath then exhaling sharply, Larkin focused. "Werewolves. They would transform anytime a Mortari was around. The scratch or bite of a werewolf is toxic to the Mortari. As the number of Skin-Walkers with the werewolf gene grew, the Mortari went into hiding, trying to preserve their numbers while finding a way to increase their ranks."

"So they were able to survive without stealing power?"

"Not exactly, they would find the occasional Gaias who broke away from the pack, away from the protection of the Werewolves. Our history books state that stealing the power and soul of just a single Gaias would give them enough energy for several decades before they had to steal from another. Fear consumed our community, even though the death toll had dropped considerably. Still the Elder Council wasn't content. Some of its members thought it was too risky to allow the Werewolves to exist on their own. A very powerful Oracle gave them the answer they were looking for and the Council soon found a way to force all those afflicted with the gene to answer to the Council."

"Is that so bad?"

"You don't understand. Werewolves are bound to the Council, having to follow whatever course of action they deem appropriate. It completely took away their free-will and made them slaves.

Right or wrong, they must do as they are told. Although the Werewolves provide a great service to our community, they are thought of as lesser beings because they cannot act on their own accord."

"That's awful! To not be appreciated for the gift they provide, it's just horrible." She hated the idea of someone not having free-will. It made her think about the bond between she and Larkin, and if his free-will had been taken from him. Deciding that it wasn't an appropriate time to discuss it, she allowed him to continue.

"It is, but it gets worse."

She wrinkled her forehead. "How is that even possible?"

"The action the Council took in binding the Werewolves to them inspired the Mortari to reconsider their own path. With Healers no longer being born, they found a way for other Gaias to steal power and become like them. There were several who chose to join the Mortari freely, as the actions of the Council seemed to be more about benefitting themselves, and less about the well-being of our community as a whole. What the original Mortari didn't realize was that most non-healers don't possess the ability to control their desire for power on any level. Claiming one life every few decades wasn't enough for them, so they turned to the humans. Stealing power from a regular human was nothing like stealing from another Gaias. They had to kill hundreds to even start feeling a charge from them. One day a new member of the Mortari, Dagrin, decided to try something different with the humans, and he consumed their blood while their heart still beat."

"Like a vampire?" Taryn asked, turning pale.

"Sort of, but once they tasted human blood their thirst grew and grew until Mother Nature intervened yet again. For years they were able to walk in the sunlight without concern, however that soon changed. Just as the sun recharges us, it began to drain them, forcing them to hide in the dark and to only feed at night. Unfortunately that wasn't the only thing that changed. The humans they drank from…if they left even an ounce of blood within them, they became soulless beings who continued to walk the earth and feed off of blood and human flesh in order to survive. We call these beings Necro-Walkers because they are on the brink of death, but yet they still walk. The Mortari use the power of Influence over them to compel them to do their bidding. Most often they're used to bring other humans back for consumption."

"What does a Necro-Walker look like?" she asked curiously, although she wasn't entirely sure she wanted to know the answer. Maybe there really was something to the dreaded zombie apocalypse.

"They still look human, except their skin is cold and pale while the whites of their eyes are blood-red in color. They're not as fast or as strong as the Mortari, but they are far superior in strength and speed compared to the average human."

"Are the Mortari faster than you?" She sensed there was much more to their abilities than she could possibly learn in one conversation.

"Yes, they are so fast that not even the Werewolves can catch them."

"The humans who survive, so to speak…are they able to produce more Necro-Walkers?"

"No, only the lesser Mortari who have become corrupt from human blood can create them. It is possible that a human could survive an attack by a Necro-Walker, but it's very unlikely as they don't possess the control it takes to stop themselves, and the Mortari find the brutality of their attacks entertaining."

"Wow, I get why my mother chose not to share this with me before."

"It's a lot to take in, even when you have grown up in the community all of your life."

"The werewolf affliction…at what age does a Skin-Walker know if they have it or not?"

"If they have it they will transform at the stroke of midnight on their twenty-first birthday."

"That has to suck not knowing."

"Most of us don't really give it much thought until after our eighteenth birthday…then it becomes real. The Elder Council watches us closely to make sure no one escapes their control."

Taryn took a seat on the edge of his back porch. All of the information only caused her to have more questions than answers. "The current Elder Council…is it corrupt?"

"Probably more now than ever. But they are the supreme beings of our community, and we have to follow their laws or suffer the consequences."

"Surely someone has challenged them before."

"There are a few groups who have managed to break away from their rule. But they have paid a hefty price for their choices," Larkin explained.

"Something you said earlier…it got me to thinking about you and me."

"What about us?" He smiled fondly.

"You said the Werewolves were bound to the council and enslaved to them…is that how you feel about being bound to me?"

"Absolutely not." Taking her hands, he raised them, placing them on his chest directly over his heart. "My heart is yours, always and forever, Taryn. With every beat my love for you grows stronger…and that has nothing to do with being bound to you. It is my free-will to love you as I so chose, and my choice will always be to love you."

"And you're not worried that I'll become like them someday?"

"I worry about a lot of things where you're concerned, but I can honestly say that isn't one of them," he smiled, brushing a few loose strands of hair back behind her ear. "You are a beautiful soul, Taryn. The world is better with you in it."

"Everything good here?" Keiryn asked, walking up from the tree line.

"Taryn?" Larkin asked, looking to her.

"Perfect."

"It's a good thing that you left when you did. The Mitchell's showed up a few minutes later and I got the feeling that it had very little to do with the kid wanting to see you."

"Were they still there when you left?" Larkin asked.

"Yeah, but they were getting ready to leave. I suspect he might stop by here looking for you."

"Then we should probably get going in case they do." Taking her by the hand he led her towards the truck. Noticing headlights coming down the road, he turned and pulled her running for the tree line.

"Wait," she insisted.

"We don't have time," Keiryn argued.

"It will only take a second." Concentrating, she stared at the porch. While they could tell that she was doing something, neither boy had any idea what it was.

As the headlights started up the driveway, Larkin's protective instinct kicked in. "We have to go, now." He scooped her into his arms, sprinting with all of his speed into the tree line.

They crouched down, watching as Ardyn's massive figure passed the headlights. "Taryn, Larkin," he called out, approaching the porch. For a moment he paused, appearing to sniff the air. He walked to the door and let himself inside the house, emerging a few minutes later to linger on the porch. Stepping off, he looked out to the tree line then curiously back to the deck. He focused on it, even trying to look beneath it. When he couldn't see anything, he ripped two of the boards off and threw them aside.

Keiryn and Larkin watched in horror as he began to rant, demolishing even more of the deck as he flew into a fit of rage.

"Why is he doing that?" Keiryn asked.

Taryn motioned for the boys to follow after her. Instead of their usual path, she led them another way. Once they were a half mile away, they all breathed a little easier.

"I don't understand. What was he looking for under the deck?" Keiryn asked again.

"He was looking for Taryn," Larkin answered, as she smiled at him. "I didn't realize at first what you had done, but once he started tearing apart the porch, I knew."

"What did you do?" Keiryn asked, still not understanding.

"I left some of my power beneath the porch to throw him off our trail."

"Not only is she beautiful, this girl is extremely clever," Keiryn lauded.

"That she is," Larkin agreed.

ဗာ၏ဗာ၏

When the trio arrived back at Taryn's home, they found that most of their guests had already left for the night.

"There you are," Ilya sighed, the tension and worry leaving her body as she finally laid eyes on her little girl. "Why didn't you ride back in Larkin's jeep?"

"Ardyn Mitchell showed up and I wasn't about to let him get near her again," Larkin answered.

"They seem like such a nice family. Why are you so against them seeing Taryn?" she asked.

~ 300 ~

"The kid and his sister are fine, but I don't trust him or his wife. There's something about him, and I think it'll be better for everyone if he stays away from her."

"If you think so." She knew there was nothing she could do or say to change his mind. "If you guys wouldn't mind, we could use some help with the clean-up."

"Sure thing, Ilya," Keiryn agreed, quickly taking the bag from her hand. Larkin followed after him, picking up trash and shooting baskets into the bag as he held it open.

"Thanks for today, Mom. It was really a lot of fun having everyone over."

"It was a nice change." She wrapped her arm around her daughter's shoulder. "Did you and Larkin have a good talk?"

"Yes actually."

"Did he explain to you…"

"About the Mortari, the Elder Council, the Werewolves and the Necro-Walkers…yes he did. I understand why you never told me about them before. I'm not sure that I would have been able to comprehend it all without falling apart before now."

"All I've ever wanted is to protect you and to keep you safe." Tears welled in her eyes.

"I know, Mom. But now you have others who are helping."

"And I'm so grateful for them all," she nodded, looking at the two boys still making picking up trash seem like an amusing game.

ഇൽ

The next few weeks flew by quickly. Taryn, Larkin and Keiryn spent time with the packs regularly. They went on runs together and even went to other member's homes for dinner. Each pack member showed Taryn their favorite thing about living in the area. She was delighted to discover a few more lakes, another mountain and the Wild Life Preserve just west of Williams.

Taking in so much nature and new experiences really helped to grow Taryn's knowledge of not only being a Gaias, but also being a normal teenager with several friends.

Her time spent with Gastyn after school had started to pay off. The control she had over her emotions was greatly improving, and it gave her a much needed release for her pent up powers.

Ada kept her distance from both packs, but especially Taryn. She sat alone during every lunch period and stayed to herself in the corner of Gastyn's back room.

ಬಂಐ೮ಬಂ

As the morning of the annual Williams Festival arrived, Taryn could barely contain her excitement. It would be the first event of its kind for her, and she couldn't be happier that Larkin was her escort. She and her mother had made a special trip to the Flagstaff Mall to pick out a new outfit just for the occasion.

"Good morning," she beamed, hopping onto one of the barstools around the kitchen island.

"Good morning, Taryn," Maxym smiled, wrapping an arm around her, giving her a quick hug.

"Hello, Taryn," Teigan nodded, holding up two large plates, one stacked with homemade waffles and the other pancakes.

"Waffles, please." Her mouth watered as she watched him plate two of the waffles, covering them with whipped cream and fresh strawberries.

"There you go, My Lady," he grinned, using his best attempt at a British accent.

"Thank you, Kind Sir." As she smiled up at him, her jaw dropped open in astonishment as he stood before her in a gleaming suit of armor.

"Is something wrong?"

Shaking her head, she looked at him again and saw that he was now normally dressed in jeans and a t-shirt. "Um, no. I just spaced out for a minute."

"Were the boys up?" Teigan asked, while working his magic on a veggie omelet for Ilya.

"No. They were still sleeping when I stepped over them. I've been thinking…we should bring the mattresses from their beds and put them in my room."

"Oh, no, Darling Daughter, I'm still holding out hope that they will one day sleep in their own beds, and leave you in yours," Ilya retorted, walking into the kitchen.

"Oh, Mom, they've been sleeping on that hardwood floor for more than a month now. I'd really feel better knowing that they were comfortable while they slept. I mean the only reason they're in there is to watch over me."

"And so that I don't break an ankle tripping over them in the mornings," Maxym added, with an ornery smile.

"We'll talk about it later, but right now young lady, you need to get ready for a day of pampering. We have appointments in town at the salon to get our hair and make-up done, as well as manicures and pedicures. And that's not all…but you'll have to wait to find out the rest until we get there."

"Let me finish these amazing waffles and then I'll be ready to go." She swirled her finger around in the whipped cream.

"Good morning, Boys," Ilya smiled in Larkin and Keiryn's direction as they sauntered into the kitchen.

"Morning," Keiryn yawned.

"Morning," Larkin nodded, before stopping to give Taryn a bear sized hug. "Good morning," he whispered in her ear.

"Good morning, Wolfy."

"What would you boys like this morning...pancakes or waffles?" Teigan asked, tousling his son's hair.

"Pancakes, Dad."

"Larkin?" Teigan asked.

"Waffles please."

As the boys scarfed down their breakfast, Taryn finished hers and went upstairs to change for the salon. Before leaving, she folded their blankets and stacked them along with their pillows against the wall.

"We'll see you boys later," Ilya called out.

"Where are you going?" Larkin asked, wrapping Taryn in his arms, pretending as though he wasn't going to let her leave.

"Mom planned a spa day," she beamed.

"I suppose that'll be alright," he teased, kissing her on top of the head as he walked her out the door. "Remember to steer clear of Ardyn and Lilyan Mitchell if you should happen to see them. Okay?"

"Yeah. I'll see you later."

"That boy is absolutely crazy about you," Ilya smiled as they headed down the driveway. "Can I ask you a personal question?"

"You're always welcome to ask...but it doesn't mean that I'm obligated to answer."

"Touché, Darling Daughter, touché. I'm trying to be serious now...have you and Larkin...well have you and Larkin..."

"Have me and Larkin what?"

"You know, taken your relationship to the next level?" Ilya finally asked.

"Mother!" Taryn shrieked, completely mortified. "How can you ask me that? You're my mother."

"If not me, then who? Would you rather talk to Teigan or Maxym about this?"

"Absolutely not! I just don't understand what would possess you to ask me something like that."

"Well, Sweetie, you and Larkin spend nearly all of your time together."

"So? Keiryn is there too."

"Yes, but not all of the time. What about when you went to Larkin's house, or when you've taken walks together alone?"

"When we were at his house he told me about his mother and how she died at the hands of the Mortari. Then he explained a rather large part of our history to me…there was no time for any funny business," Taryn rolled her eyes.

"I was once young like you. A handsome young man like Larkin would have made my head spin."

"That was you, this is me. We haven't even had our first kiss yet," Taryn confided.

"What?" Ilya tapped the breaks of the SUV.

Looking out the window and feeling even more awkward than before, she sighed. "We haven't ever kissed…on the lips."

"You're not joking, are you?"

"Well, yeah. It's not exactly something a person would kid about."

"Is there a reason why you haven't kissed?" Ilya pressed, considering Keiryn might have something to do with it.

"It just hasn't been the right time. I mean, we almost did a few times, but it always seems like one of us turns away at the last second or Keiryn shows up."

"You're serious?" She was trying to decide if she should secretly thank Keiryn for being their third wheel.

"Yes, Mother."

"I'm sorry, Sweetie. The two of you have such an intense connection. I just assumed that you were already past this point."

"Well we're not, and if you don't mind, I'd really like to talk about something else."

"So what would you like to talk about?"

Taryn paused, pretending to be thinking hard regarding an appropriate topic. "So exactly where are you and Maxym at with your relationship?"

"Taryn Delaney Malone!"

"Exactly what I thought." She laughed while poking her mother in the ribs. "Not exactly a good time sitting in the hot seat, now is it?"

"I guess not, but it doesn't mean I don't worry."

"Fair enough, but I need you to do me a favor."

"Anything, Baby Girl."

"Please tell Mr. Taylor that he doesn't need to worry. I don't want him sitting around wondering if he's going to be a grandpa anytime in the near future."

"Taryn…"

"I'm just saying that if you're worrying about it, you shouldn't."

Sensing there was something deeper bothering her daughter, Ilya pulled off to the side of the road. "Ok, spill it. I can tell when something is bothering you."

"I'd rather not say. It's silly anyway."

"You've been doing so well. I don't want to see you regress because you're holding something in."

"I hold things in every day, Mom, so this isn't any different."

"Look, Taryn, I share you with Larkin, Keiryn, Maxym, Teigan, Gastyn and all of the other kids from your class. That doesn't mean that I can't tell when something's bothering you. I am your mother. I can hear it in your voice."

"Fine, but it's just one more thing for you to be worried about," she responded gloomily. "Have you ever considered how Maxym is going to react when he finds out that I'm a Healer?"

"It does cross my mind from time to time."

"Well I think about it every day. It seems cruel that fate has brought us to their doorstep, knowing what I am. Letting Larkin and I fall in love, making him obligated to watch over me when it was someone with powers like mine that killed his mother."

"That's ridiculous, Taryn. Larkin knows that you would never use your powers like that."

"If it's so ridiculous then why don't you tell Maxym?" she countered, frustration showing on her face.

"You know exactly why, Taryn. Besides, when did you become so cynical?"

She fought to hold back the tears that had swelled in her eyes. "What if I break, Mom? What happens then? Who survives the fall out when the Elder Council discovers me? Everyone I care about is at constant risk because of what I am. Damned those three brothers for what they did."

Ilya sat quietly, stunned by her daughter's disclosure. She had never realized exactly how much responsibility fell on her young shoulders. "I'm sorry, Taryn." She reached for her hand, wanting to provide comfort to her.

"Please don't." Taryn pulled away. "This is something I have to figure out for myself. I have to find a way to come to terms with the consequences that exist should I ever slip up." More silence filled the air around them.

After a few minutes, she looked to her mother. "Can we go now?"

Recognizing that she was in a delicate place, Ilya pulled back onto the road. For the remainder of the drive they sat quietly, listening to the radio.

ᏕᎧᏣᎳᏕᎧᏣᎳ

As they exited the SUV, she asked, "Are you excited about your first spa day?"

"Of course. So what's this surprise you have in store for me?"

"You'll see," Ilya taunted, pretending that their earlier conversation hadn't taken place and that Taryn's disclosure had not rocked her to her very core. In reality she was in awe, seeing how someone so young could carry the weight of their secret world so gracefully on her tiny shoulders. But as awestruck as she was, she couldn't help but think about the numerous things that could go wrong in their new life. If even one of them happened, everything would come crashing down on them all, causing an unbearable toll on her daughter.

Walking towards the salon, Taryn stopped abruptly in her tracks. "They're all here!" The fact that all of the girls from both packs were waiting inside put a smile on her face. She was pleased that she could sense every one of them based on the power she could feel within them.

"So much for trying to surprise you."

"It's a wonderful surprise, Mom." She laced her arm through her mother's, pulling her in closer. "Don't worry. I'll pretend to be surprised. How does that sound?"

"I'm sure the girls would appreciate it. After all, this was their idea."

As they entered the salon, she gasped, pretending to be surprised to see all of her friends there as they squealed with excitement. They were sitting haphazardly around the open shop. Nalani and Bency were perched on a bench, with their heads together, looking at one of the hairstyle magazines while the twins were already ten minutes into their pedicures. Dagney was currently in a styling chair getting her hair cut.

"Hi, Taryn," she waved, not able to look up at her.

"Hi Dags."

"Grab a chair, Kansas, and get ready for some serious pampering," Nalani called out to her, smiling brightly.

After giving her a goodbye hug, Ilya left the salon and went to join the other mothers across the street for coffee.

In typical teenage girl fashion, she and her friends gossiped about boys, clothes and hair while snacking on cucumber sandwiches, sliced cheeses and fresh fruit that the Love's had provided, in between getting their nails, hair and make-up done.

Letting go of all her worries, if only for the moment, Taryn thoroughly enjoyed the pampering time with her friends. It really was just like they portrayed it in the movies. She felt like a celebrity getting the royal treatment, something she had never dreamt possible before. After an entire lifetime of seclusion, she was certain that this very special moment would be one she would never forget.

Perusing the numerous nail polish bottles displayed on shelves attached to one of the salon walls, she startled when someone came up beside her.

Nalani tapped one of her perfectly manicured nails against her bottom lip. "Hmmm…I think you should go with this one," she stated, selecting a bright candy-pink polish. "It will make your toes really pop!"

Taryn grinned and looked down as she wiggled her toes. This was another day of firsts, as she had never had fingernail polish on her toenails before. Throwing her arms around her friend, she gave her a hard squeeze, "Thanks, Lani."

"Well, you looked a little lost so I thought I should take pity on you. Trust me, you are going to love it."

Taking the bottle, she could feel the joy in her heart multiply tenfold. Finally, after sixteen lonely years, she could honestly say she had friends. As a single tear slipped down her cheek, she dashed it away and looped her arm through Nalani's as they walked over to take their seats in the pedicure chairs.

After two hours of blissful relaxation and pure pampering, she hugged everyone goodbye before meeting her mother at the car.

"So...how was it?" Ilya asked, dying to hear her daughter's thoughts.

"It was wonderful! You know, I never understood the desire when I saw people on TV at salons, but I totally get it now. I am so relaxed." She stretched languidly in her seat.

"I'm glad you enjoyed it. Now you can sit back and enjoy the ride home before you have to deal with the stress of your first dance." Ilya started laughing as the look of panic flashed across her darling girl's face. "Don't worry, Baby. Just let Larkin take the lead and everything will be fine."

ৰ০৫৪৪০৫৪

As Taryn walked in the door of her home, she was overcome by an immense sadness. "Where's Larkin?"

"Maxym took him home so you could finish getting ready for tonight. I reminded him of how you girls like to do your big reveals and all," Teigan answered, giving her a hug. Seeing the disappointment in her eyes he feared that he might have done something wrong in convincing the Taylor's to leave.

"But it doesn't begin for another three hours," she groaned, voicing her displeasure at not being able to see him the minute she had walked in the door. She had grown used to him being a constant presence in her life. It was disconcerting not being able to sense him at all.

"Wow, why don't you go ahead and drive a stake into my heart?" Keiryn teased. Though he joked with her, inside his heart was breaking knowing that she did not have the same reaction whenever he and his father left for a few hours. It didn't matter that she always told them to hurry back, she never wore that anxious, forlorn look when she told him goodbye.

"I guess you'll have to do." She smiled, wrapping an arm around his waist.

"You look great."

"Thanks," she smiled up at him before stepping away and wiggling her bright pink toes. "So what do you think?"

He pretended to study her pretty toenails for several moments before shrugging his shoulders. "They are ok, if you're a girl."

"Well, Mr. Falcon, it just so happens that I AM a girl…and I like them very much!"

Bending over at the waist with uncontrollable laughter, he chuckled until he was breathless.

Tapping her pink toes on the polished wood floor, Taryn stood with her arms crossed and waited for him to finish. "I fail to see what is so funny."

Replacing his grin with a sober look, he reached out to her and pulled her into a hug. "I'm sorry. The look on your face was pretty funny. But I shouldn't have laughed. It's just…guys don't really understand the whole painting your toes thing, you know. They do look great. Very festive."

"Festive?"

"Cute?"

"Better than festive."

He rolled his eyes in exasperation before it finally hit him. "Hot!" he exclaimed, wiggling his eyebrows at her.

She flashed him a brilliant smile while Teigan shook his head incredulously from behind her. "Now that's more like it," she beamed. Leaning up to plant a kiss on his cheek, she turned and made her way up to her room to start the arduous process of getting dressed and picking out the perfect shoes to accent her outfit and pretty pink toes.

With Taryn upstairs, Ilya found her way inside of the garage and collapsed to her knees as tears flowed uncontrollably down her cheeks. All of the worry and concern she had been suppressing finally found its way to the surface. As she let the sobs consume her, she was startled by the light touch on her shoulder.

"Ilya?" Teigan asked, seeing the pain written so plainly on her face.

Unable to respond, she simply leaned against his strong frame as he knelt beside her while the violent sobs continued to wrack her body. After crying herself to the point of exhaustion she dabbed at the tears in her eyes before looking at him.

"I'm sorry you had to witness that."

"No need to apologize." He swiped away a few rogue tears from her face. "I know first-hand that it's not easy being a single parent. If I were to be completely honest...I haven't a clue how you have managed for so long by yourself without the help of a community."

"Taryn can be a handful, but she's always been such an amazing person...even when she was just a little girl. Her heart is so big and full of love and generosity. The weight of our world rests solely upon her shoulders, Teigan."

"You've raised a wonderful young lady. It's that big heart of hers that will always see her through. She's special, but not just because of her ability. It's because of the person that she chooses to be and how she chooses to use her gifts."

She gave him a watery smile. "Thank you." He understood her daughter far more than she had previously thought. Patting her eyes, she rose to her feet. "If we could keep this little melt down to ourselves, I would really appreciate it."

"Of course."

₧♋₧♋

Keiryn sat on Taryn's bed admiring her as she walked back and forth between her bathroom and closet, reconsidering her outfit for the night. "Can I ask you something, Taryn?"

"You just did." She rolled her eyes playfully at him from the closet door. "What's up, Keiryn?"

"You and Larkin…it's the real deal?"

"What do you mean?"

"Do you really love him? Or is it the bond you two share that makes you think you do?"

She took a seat on the bed next to him and studied his expression. "Yes, I love Larkin very much." She ran her fingers lightly through his hair as the sadness came into his eyes. "But I love you too, Keiryn."

He sat quietly for several minutes before standing to walk to the bedroom window. "But you love him more," he sighed, looking out over the backyard.

"It's not about who I love more. You know that I love you both very much and I would do anything for either of you."

"Then why didn't you choose me?"

She hesitated, trying to find the right words to explain without hurting him further. "It wasn't a choice, Keiryn. Larkin and I…it is simply what is meant to be."

"So it's because you're bound to one another?"

"No," she shook her head, growing frustrated that she wasn't conveying her feelings correctly. "I'm with Larkin because it's where I want to be."

"But there's something real between us too…I know there is."

"Yes, there is definitely something special between us. You're like a piece of my heart and without you near, it would be broken."

"Wow! Even after saying something like that…you still can't see us being together, ever?"

Taryn placed her hand on his shoulder, offering him comfort. "You and Larkin are best of friends. I won't come between the two of you. I would suggest that you focus on what can be."

"And what exactly does that mean?" Looking down at her he couldn't help but notice how completely angelic she looked while delivering the heartbreaking news.

"Nalani is crazy about you, and I know that you like her too, even if you won't admit it. You need to give the two of you a chance before it's too late. Someone that stunning won't stay single forever."

He stood silent thinking about what she said, remembering the promise he had made to not only Larkin, but also his father. "Taryn."

"Yes?"

He rubbed the back of his neck with his hand and sighed heavily. "I've really enjoyed being friends with him again. It feels like old times between us and, well…"

"I know. Like I told you, I won't do anything to come between the two of you and mess that up." She looked into his eyes and saw the torment that she was causing him. On the one hand, it deeply saddened her to know how much she was hurting him, but on the other she could totally relate. The feelings she had for him went far beyond that of a friend. She refused to imagine her life without him. If he made the choice to be part of her life from afar, she was not sure she could live with it. He was just as important to her as Larkin, but in a different way, one she could not easily explain.

She knew exactly what she felt for Larkin, but with Keiryn her head and her heart were in a constant war. Though she knew that she was destined to be with Larkin, she needed Keiryn near her just as much. Hopefully, one day, she would be able to look back and understand the pull that he had on her, but for now it didn't matter. It was simply there, and she could not ignore it.

ঙেওিওেওি

Taryn surveyed her image in the mirror. The pale green dress she had chosen was youthful and fun, perfect for a girl her age. The two-tone bodice had a bright pink floral design with a pale green fabric beneath, a sweetheart neckline and spaghetti straps. The skirt of the dress had long glittery tulle layers and stopped a few inches above her knee. To showcase her bright toenails, she chose a pair of plain white sandals paired with simple white and silver jewelry to accent the look. As she secured the back of her earring, her heart fluttered with excitement. Larkin was close. She could feel him with every fiber of her being.

Catching a glance of her as he entered the room, Keiryn could hardly speak. "Larkin's here…"

"Thanks, Keiryn, I'll be right down."

Still unable to tear his eyes away from her, his feet stayed rooted. "Wow, you look really great, Taryn."

"You think so?"

"Definitely. You probably shouldn't keep him waiting. It's been a long afternoon for the both of you," he acknowledged, after just witnessing first-hand how the distance had worn on Larkin.

"Yes it has. Let me grab my jean jacket and then I'll be ready."

"Okay. I'll see you downstairs in a minute." He walked to the door placing his hand on the frame and released a heavy sigh, fighting to suppress the emotions that bubbled up in his throat at seeing how beautiful she looked. His love, along with his desire to

~ 315 ~

protect her, burned inside of him. Taking a deep breath, he headed towards the downstairs to join the others.

As Taryn came into sight, Larkin's heart resumed a steady rhythm. All of the worry and concern of the day washed away as he drank in the sight of his sweet Taryn, walking towards him with a relieved smile on her face. Unable to wait even a second longer to have her in his arms he rushed up the stairs, meeting her more than halfway.

"You look beautiful."

"Thank you," she blushed as her heartbeat synced with his.

Taking a step closer, she wrapped her arms around him and closed her eyes, inhaling his scent. He enveloped her in his arms, lifting her feet from the stairs and held her tightly as they became oblivious to everyone else who stood waiting at the bottom watching the sweet exchange.

Keiryn looked away and moved to the open French doors. He was happy that his best friend had, quite literally, found the girl of his dreams. And was glad that Taryn was happy, yet something ate away at his insides, watching them. Jealousy, perhaps, but it felt like more, an as yet undefined feeling that he could not explain.

"Don't mind us," Maxym called out from the bottom of the staircase while rolling his eyes to Ilya and Teigan. He felt awkward as he watched their intensely private moment.

"Shush," Ilya insisted. Her heart warmed as she saw how oblivious the two teens were to everything and everyone else. She hoped that in moments like this, Taryn would be able to find peace from the weight that rested solely on her young shoulders. If Larkin could provide her with such a distraction she would do everything she could not to interfere. "Let's go outside."

When they reached the doorway Teigan noticed his son standing strangely in the middle of the backyard.

"Keiryn."

He stopped abruptly causing Ilya and Maxym to bump into him, pointing his finger in response to their unspoken question. Looking around they stood in awe of the incredible scene unfolding around them. The once grassy lawn sprang to life with a large variety of flowering plants, trees and vines. Everywhere they looked another incredible and beautiful flower formed, filling the air with an intoxicating aroma.

"I guess we know that she's happy," Teigan chuckled, receiving a smile from Ilya.

"That she is."

Maxym stepped to her, placing a hand on her shoulder. She reached up, covering it with her own and sighed happily as they continued to watch in amazement, much like they were watching fireworks on the Fourth of July. Even Keiryn was able to find comfort in knowing that she was truly happy and carefree for the moment.

ಬಂಗಳಬಂಗಳ

"I love you, Taryn," Larkin exhaled, finally easing his hold on her.

Looking into his eyes, she smiled sweetly. "I know."

For a moment longer they gazed lovingly at one another. It did not bother him in the least that she had not told him that she loved him too. The look in her eyes told him everything he needed to know.

"We should probably go join the others."

"I suppose we should."

Larkin placed his arm around her waist and escorted her outside as he planted delicate kisses on her temple.

"Whoa," he exclaimed, seeing the living bouquet for the first time. The entire backyard was abloom with fragrant flowers and trailing vines.

"It's beautiful, Taryn," her mother stated, leaning over to smell a grouping of lilies.

"Sorry," she blushed with embarrassment, realizing she had let her emotions get away from her. She looked at Keiryn and instantly saw the struggle to keep his composure. She also knew that he was trying to do right by Larkin. Not wanting him to have an in-your-face reminder whenever he walked outside, she exhaled and began retracting the flowers, trees and bushes.

"Why are you taking it back?" Larkin asked, saddened by her decision to undo it all.

"What if someone comes over? How are we going to explain it?" The expression on his face was so heartbreaking, she gave a small smile and turned back to the yard. A few feet from the house, she left a single coral-colored rose bush intact. Placing her arm around his waist, she squeezed him. "See that bush over there?"

"Yeah."

"That's ours."

He pulled her in tightly and gently kissed the top of her head. "It's perfect."

ဆာလ္ဆာလ္

The three teens drove separately from their parents in Larkin's jeep as they headed into Williams. Taryn was brimming with excitement knowing she was about to attend her first real town festival.

While trying to find a parking space, they passed a few of the parade floats that were already lined up on a side street waiting for the events to begin. She beamed from ear-to-ear as she looked over each colorful one.

"This is so cool."

Reaching over, Larkin laced his fingers with hers, caressing the top of her hand with his thumb. It made him happy to see the joy she found in so many things, things that he normally took for granted. Her enthusiasm was so infectious that he found himself beginning to appreciate all of the little things as well.

Keiryn slapped his palm to his forehead. "I forgot...this is your first parade. There's so many things that we've got to show you tonight." As soon as the words left his lips he realized how they must have sounded to Larkin. "I'm sorry about that, man. I wasn't thinking."

"What are you talking about?"

"She's your date tonight. I figured that you would want to show her around, you know...just the two of you."

"I think it's best if we stay close together," Larkin replied while placing the jeep into park. Turning around in his seat, he looked at Keiryn. "The Mitchell's will be here tonight. We need as many eyes keeping lookout as possible to make sure Ardyn keeps his distance."

"You're right."

He turned back to Taryn. "We won't let anything happen to you."

"I know." She looked into his hazel eyes. The sincerity that she found in them melted her to the core. Those eyes were the very gateway to his soul. It was the beauty that she saw inside of him that she loved, far more than his gorgeous exterior.

While sitting in the jeep, Larkin and Taryn startled when Kellan and Gerrick slapped the hood.

"Come on out, Kansas," Kellan smiled, opening her door. "It's time to show you how we party here in Arizona," he howled, drawing looks from those nearby.

"Hey, guys," Keiryn nodded.

"What's up?"

"Where's Nalani?" Taryn asked Gerrick, hoping to give Keiryn a little push in her direction.

"She's with the twins. They are saving everyone a spot near the Desert Rose."

Taryn gave Keiryn a wink, reminding him of their earlier conversation in hopes that he would at least give the idea of him and Nalani a chance.

She and Larkin walked hand-in-hand through the already crowded streets, following behind the others as they made their way to the Café. Once they arrived, they found everyone else already there waiting.

The girls squealed with delight, hugging one another while gushing about the outfits each was wearing. The guys greeted one another with their special handshakes and half hugs. They laughed and chatted while waiting for the parade to begin.

Taryn caught Keiryn looking at her and nodded her head subtly in Nalani's direction, flashing a cheesy smile. He rolled his eyes in response, knowing that she wasn't going to let go of her ludicrous idea of them being together. Pursing her lips together, she gave him a look, telling him to hurry up and make a move. Finally, he walked to where Nalani was standing and struck up a conversation with her, receiving a look of approval from Taryn, along with an enthusiastic two thumbs up.

The sound of sirens filled the air as the parade began. A young serviceman who was home on leave carried the American flag proudly as he was followed by a handful of retired veterans in formation. As they approached, she watched intensely as the men removed their hats and everyone placed their hands over their hearts, just like she had seen in the movies. But unlike in the movies, the real emotion the simple act stirred could be felt in the air. Pride and gratitude swelled inside the chests of the majority of the spectators as the flag passed by. Closing her eyes, she soaked in the good vibes.

The floats came next, advertising every business in town. Some were absolutely amazing, while others lacked imagination. But for Taryn, it didn't matter, she loved them all. Her favorite float was created by the William's Animal Clinic and Shelter. Shelter employees and volunteers rode on the flatbed trailer adorned with trees made of chicken wire and tissue paper. At one end of the float a park bench was placed with a bright yellow fire hydrant next to it. Each person held an animal available for adoption carefully in their hands or on leashes. It wasn't the fanciest float, but it was the one that represented what she held near and dear to her heart.

Antique muscle cars followed the floats. There were about twenty-six in all. Towards the middle of the pack, one of the cars, a shiny black 1965 Mustang, swerved towards their group.

"Losers," James Riley called out from the driver's side of the car while one of his football buddies taunted them from the passenger side.

"I'll kick your ass for less," Gerrick shouted, lunging at the car while Kellan and Larkin grabbed hold of him.

"What was that about?" Jonesy asked, pushing towards the front of the group.

"I don't know. The guy has always been an ass, but I've never seen him be so ballsy before," Eben replied.

"Adalia," Dagney seethed, catching a glimpse of the top of her pale blonde hair in the back window.

"She wouldn't," Bency gasped.

"Of course she would. That girl is so nasty, and it's not like she hasn't done something like this before. Remember last year in chemistry?" Nalani growled, glaring daggers in the car's direction.

As they stood fuming, the car stalled and white smoke could be seen coming from underneath it. Dalen laughed as he and Thorne high-fived Gerrick, knowing that he must have used his sub-power of being an Elemental to draw the coolant from the car's radiator.

"That's enough," Taryn insisted, her tone as serious as the look on her face.

"Why? You saw what he did," Gerrick whined.

"That's enough!" Her eyes locked on his until he finally looked down to the ground. "James may be a jerk, but he wasn't acting of his own freewill. There will be no more retaliation against him for something that was out of his control."

"So we're just supposed to sit back and take whatever he dishes out tonight?" Nalani questioned.

"It's been handled." Taryn nodded down the street as James and his friends pushed the stalled car into the Desert Rose parking lot before making their way towards the two packs.

"Hey, about earlier, I'm sorry...I'm not sure what came over me," he apologized, with a baffled look on his face.

"It's cool," Larkin nodded, holding back from showing his general disdain for the guy and his followers, although the same could not be said for the rest of his pack.

"You might not, but we do," Thorne snickered, drawing a look of disapproval from Taryn.

James shrugged and walked away, leaving everyone in Taryn's group at a loss, with the exception of Larkin and Keiryn.

ೞಚೞಚ

The parade came to an end and the large group of teens made their way to the food booths. Everyone one of them had a pulled pork sandwich, potato salad and coleslaw. The only difference on each plate was the choice of bar-b-que sauce.

Distracted by all of the people and the many things she was seeing for the first time, Taryn picked at her food.

"Not hungry?" Larkin asked, nudging her gently.

She shook her head no, while pushing the plate aside. "What was it like growing up, knowing you were going to get to do this every year?"

"It was alright." He twirled a few strands of her hair around his finger. "I have to admit…this year blows every other one out of the water, thanks to having you here with me." He kissed her sweetly on the cheek causing her to blush when she realized everyone was watching them.

Kellan and Eben made kissy faces at one another, while batting their eyes dramatically. On the opposing bench, Gerrick and Dalen gave an elaborate show of gagging, pretending to put their fingers down their throats.

"It's official…if we go see a movie the love birds can't pick it out," Thorne teased. "We've had enough chick flicks to last a lifetime without you two sappy sweethearts adding to it."

"I think it's sweet," Bentley argued.

"And it's so romantic, the way he is with her," Hadley sighed, wishing she could find someone special of her own.

"Taryn," Andyn shouted, running towards her.

"Hey, Andyn." She wrapped her arms tightly around him.

"Don't forget me," Andalyn called out, running ahead of her parents.

Taryn held one of her arms out and scooped up the young girl, who looked so much like her older brother, hugging her tightly. "How are you, My Little Pink Princess?" Taryn asked, referring to the pink dress and tiara she wore.

"I don't feel very good."

"Are you sick?" The little girl shook her head no, and forced a smile as her parents approached.

"What did I tell you about running so far ahead?" Lilyan scolded her.

Larkin and Keiryn both moved to stand directly in front of Taryn, keeping Ardyn and Lilyan at a distance.

"Don't be so hard on the girl, Lilyan. After all, she's been cooped up in the house from being ill. Now that she feels better, she only wanted to say hello to her friend," Ardyn smiled, peering between the boys at Taryn. "You look like you're feeling better."

"I feel amazing."

Standing, she placed a hand on Larkin's shoulder. Trying to move forward, she pushed gently against him, but he refused to budge even an inch.

Looking down at her, his eyes widened, displaying his concern for her well-being. "No," he mouthed to her.

"You look really pretty, Taryn," Andyn stated, pulling her back towards the picnic table and away from his father.

"Come here, Andyn," Ardyn growled, keeping his eyes locked desperately on Taryn, longing and a great desire readily apparent.

The boy hesitated, but eventually stepped between Larkin and Keiryn to stand by his father's side. He gave Taryn a pleading look before his mouth curled upward strangely into a brilliant smile. He now looked happy and content, as did his little sister.

Lilyan wrangled Andalyn back as well and the Mitchell's stood staring, all eyes focused on her.

"We'll be seeing you around, Taryn," Ardyn smiled lustfully at her.

"That you will," she replied. Her face was serious and unphased by the darkness in his tone.

Larkin held his position firm, even though he knew if Ardyn wanted to get to Taryn badly enough, there would be very little he or Keiryn could do to fight him off. He hoped that their presence would be enough to discourage him from making a scene in front of the humans. "Good night, Mr. Mitchell," Larkin stated pointedly, letting him know that it would be the last time he spoke to them this evening.

Ardyn smirked as he looked the tall teen up and down before walking away with his family in tow. He glanced over his shoulder one final time at Taryn before they disappeared into the crowd.

"What the hell was that about?" Kellan asked, feeling sick by what he had just witnessed. "I mean, he's always been scary but the way he looked at you, Taryn…that was something entirely new, even for him."

"Yeah, I feel like I need to shower now," Nalani shivered, receiving several nods of agreement from the others.

"Are you okay?" Larkin asked, looking her over from head to toe, afraid that Ardyn may have done something even from a distance.

She pursed her lips together, pulling her mouth up to one side. "I'm fine."

Keiryn placed his hand gently on her shoulder while Larkin continued to scour over every visible inch of her skin. "You're worried about the kid and his sister aren't you?"

"There was something strange about the way they were acting." She tried to shake the cold, stabbing feeling that Ardyn stirred within her.

Larkin paused in checking her over. "They'll be fine, Taryn. He wouldn't do anything to his own kids, it'd be too obvious. Besides, he isn't that stupid."

"I suppose you're right."

"Did you notice anything off with Ardyn?" Keiryn inquired of Larkin, arching his brows, hoping that he understood exactly what it was he was asking.

"No, not a thing." Shaking his head, he placed a protective arm around her. He could see how desperately she needed a distraction.

Knowing there were still so many firsts for her to have that night, he made a suggestion. "What do you say we go find you a snow cone and some cotton candy?"

"Okay." She forced a smile.

ಐರ೮೩ಐರ೮೩

Taryn enjoyed a grape snow cone while they walked about, taking in all of the sights. As her mood lightened, she began having fun once more, enjoying the festival. With renewed excitement she found herself longing to ride the Ferris wheel. Taking her cotton candy in one hand and Larkin's hand in the other, she pulled him over to the line. He made a show of pretending to not want to ride it, even though he knew that he would follow her anywhere and do anything that he could to bring a smile to her face.

While waiting in line, she fed him a piece of cotton candy. He nibbled playfully on her fingers, causing her to blush. Her cheeks flushed, turning rosy pink as she looked shyly to the ground, biting her bottom lip. It was a subtle reminder of how truly innocent she was.

His heart fluttered as a warm sensation crept its way through every inch of his body. She was everything and more than he had ever imagined possible. Her face was where he found peace, while her eyes showed him love, and her embrace was the place he considered his home. A place he never wanted to leave.

Cupping her chin in his hand, he gently lifted her eyes to his. He stroked her cheek tenderly as they gazed at one another, alone in their own private world. Lost in the moment, they hadn't realized that most of their friends were now standing close to them.

"Earth to Larkin and Kansas," Kellan laughed, wrapping an arm around each of their necks, snapping them instantly from their gaze. "The street dance starts in twenty. You two do plan on joining the rest of us, don't you?" Reaching over, he stole a bite of the cotton candy.

"You don't want to miss out on seeing me and my awesome moves," Thorne grinned, shaking his hips humorously.

"Dork," Nalani snickered, bumping into him.

"Next," the Ferris wheel attendant called out.

"That's us. See you guys in a bit," Larkin stated, turning all of his focus back to Taryn. He held her hand as he escorted her to their seat. As the attendant secured the bar across them, her eyes widened with anticipation. "You'd better hold on, it usually gives a jerk before moving forward."

During the ten minute ride, she looked around in awe. She loved how different everything looked from atop the giant wheel. With every go around, she would try to focus on a different area below. Larkin sat with his arm around her, finding his own joy in seeing hers. When the ride was over, she hugged him fiercely, thrilled to share the moment with him.

"Okay, Whirly Girl, it's time to go find our friends."

As they made their way through the large crowd, they could see Kellan, Thorne and Dalen already dancing as the band played. They appeared to be having a great time, even if the rest of the group stood around mocking them.

"Dance with us, Kansas," Dalen shouted over the music, while he and Kellan grabbed her hands, pulling her over towards them.

Larkin held onto her tightly, not wanting her first dance to be with one of them. "I've got dibs."

"Thanks," she whispered, glad for the save. She had danced numerous times in her bedroom while listening to music, but she had never danced in front of anyone else.

Soon the entire gang, with the exception of Nalani and Keiryn, danced in the sea of people on the street. Taryn watched her friend, aware of how desperately she wanted Keiryn to ask her to dance.

"I love this song," Nalani squealed as the tempo changed.

"If you're not going to ask this beautiful girl to dance, then I guess I'll have to," Taryn rolled her eyes at Keiryn. "Miss Skye, would you care to accompany me for a go-round on the dance floor?"

Nalani's eyes perked up as she realized what Taryn was trying to do. "But of course, Miss Malone."

She grabbed Taryn's hand and maneuvered through the crowd. Once they found a suitable place, Nalani released her hold and the two began dancing. They sang along with the music, as it was one they both recognized and loved. It wasn't long before the two boys joined them.

Soon they were surrounded by all of their friends. For the next few hours, they danced, laughed and lived totally carefree in the moment, all of them appearing to be ordinary, everyday teenagers, when they were anything but.

Ilya, Maxym and Teigan joined Gastyn and the other parents that had gathered nearby. Like their children, they too enjoyed the evening and the normalcy it provided from their daily lives. On occasion, the parents would dance over by the teens, receiving varied responses. The twins rolled their eyes and their cheeks turned a bright shade of pink when their parents danced too close to the group. By the way they boogied about, it was obvious that they had loved the seventies.

As the final band of the night took the stage and started playing slow songs, Larkin smiled at Taryn, holding his hand out to her. She accepted it shyly and immediately found herself pulled into his strong embrace.

"Tonight has been incredible," she breathed, resting her head comfortably against his chest.

"I'm glad to hear that, since the night is far from over."

"There's more?"

"There's a huge fireworks display that starts around eleven." He paused for a moment. "Have you ever seen fireworks before?"

"Only on T.V. The farmers back in Galatia didn't really like the idea of lighting things on fire next to their fields."

"Can't say I blame them." He brushed a strand of her hair behind her ear. "Good news is the displays here get bigger and better every year. So tonight we're going to start making up for lost time."

"You're so good to me, Larkin Taylor. I love you." She traced along his jawline with her fingertips.

"I know," he smiled as he leaned down, moving his lips to hers. Just before they connected, Keiryn, who had been taking in their exchange, decided to interrupt before they cemented their relationship with their first real kiss. He wrapped his arms around their necks, much to Nalani's discord.

"What are you two kids doing over here?"

Nalani stood behind him, arms crossed, with a full pout on her face. She knew the real reason for his intrusion, and it crushed her.

"Trying to have a moment," Larkin grumbled, rolling his eyes.

"I'm getting thirsty. Would you ladies like something to drink?" Keiryn asked.

"I'll take a soda," Nalani sighed, her irritation present.

"Taryn?" Larkin asked, sensing their moment had past.

"I'll have a soda too."

Once the girls were alone, they began chatting. "I'm sorry," Nalani offered.

"You have nothing to apologize for, Lani, but I am sorry that he hurt you. He's protective of me, even when it comes to Larkin."

"There's that…and the fact that he loves you. I'm not mad at you. I know that you love Larkin. But I can't compete with you."

"I know it probably seems that way, but if you hang in there and fight for what you want, you'll find what you're looking for in the end."

Nalani wrapped her arms around her, squeezing tightly. "Thank you." She prayed her new friend was right.

ഇൗഃഇൗഃ

Once the final song ended, the townspeople began to head back toward their vehicles to get a better view of the fireworks, leaving Taryn and Nalani waiting for the boys to return with their sodas. Larkin used his keen senses to locate them in the sea of people.

"This way," he called out to Keiryn, pointing in their direction. Rushing to her side, he handed her the cold soda and hugged her gently with one arm. "Let's go find you some fireworks."

They found a perfect spot atop his jeep. A few parking spots down, the rest of their friends sat in the back of Gerrick's truck bed and watched the display. She lounged between Larkin's legs, resting against his chest. He wrapped her snuggly in his arms when she shivered in the cool night air.

Her face lit in awe as the night sky erupted with the dazzling colors and crackling displays of booming fireworks. Everything she had ever seen on television could not begin to do justice to the beauty she was seeing first hand. With each new bang her eyes grew wider as the colors danced about in the air like millions of little fireflies. Larkin found himself watching the expressions on her beautiful face, enjoying them far more than the show above.

As the grand finale approached, the fireworks intensified in a rapid-fire cessation, filling the sky with a rainbow of colors. She held her breath, her visual senses overwhelmed as each explosion sounded in the air. After five full minutes of nonstop action, the crowd erupted in applause as the last burning embers went out.

Wrapped up in the excitement of it all, Taryn turned to Larkin, throwing her arms tightly around his neck. "That was incredible! This whole night has been amazing."

"You're incredible."

He moved his lips to hers, intent on finally having their first kiss, but was foiled once again as Kellan jumped on the hood of the jeep, causing it to rock beneath them. Larkin's eyes widened as his nostrils flared. This was the second time in one night that they had been interrupted.

Seeing his frustration, Taryn pulled him in and gave him a quick peck on the cheek. "It will happen."

"We're going to the reservoir. You guys coming, or what?" Kellan asked, referring to the Dogtown Reservoir that was just a few miles east of Taryn's home.

"You want to go?" Larkin asked.

"Sure. But if you don't mind, I'd like to change my clothes first."

"Yeah, we'll be there," Larkin nodded.

"Great. We'll meet in about an hour," Gerrick laughed, placing Kellan in a playful headlock. "All the girls have to change." Rolling his eyes, he dragged Kellan away.

"You can borrow some of my clothes if you don't want to go home and change," Taryn offered to Nalani.

"That'd be awesome. I'll just call my parents and let them know."

❧❧

At the reservoir everyone gathered around the bonfire that Gerrick and Kellan had built. Thorne and Dagney were snuggled up to one another, while Bency and Jonesy sat with their heads together, deep in conversation. Nalani stayed close to Keiryn as he divided his attention between her and Taryn. She tried her best not to let it get her down.

On the other side of the fire, the twins were carrying on an animated conversation with Kellan, Gerrick, Dalen and Eben. They talked about a myriad of subjects, and as much as they loved to talk hair and clothes, they were just as knowledgeable about cars and boxing.

Larkin stood from the bench where he and Taryn were seated, taking her by the hand and leading her away from the group.

Keiryn started to follow them, but Nalani grabbed his arm and shook her head no. "You're just going to have to accept it. They're together, and every time you do something to interfere, it's only prolonging the inevitable."

He took his seat again and sighed in resignation, knowing her take on the situation was spot on.

"I know that I'm not her, but maybe you'd like to at least pretend to be having fun with me tonight," she said, unable to hide her growing frustration.

"I am having fun, Lani. You're awesome. You deserve better than what I can give you."

"Don't you get it?"

"I don't want to lead you on or hurt you."

"Then don't. Accept that she isn't going to be with you and move on." Tears filled her eyes.

Keiryn studied her with a sad look on his face. He didn't want to hurt her, but he couldn't get his mind off of Taryn alone in the woods with Larkin. Trying his best to fight the urge to run after them, he leaned over and placed a kiss on her forehead. "You're beautiful," he replied, swiping away her tears.

Laying her head against his shoulder, she closed her eyes. It wasn't exactly an invitation to the prom, but at least it was something. Maybe, given enough time, he could move on, and she would be there waiting when he was ready to take that step.

Larkin led Taryn to a clearing a few hundred yards away from the others. He was happy to have her all to himself for a little while. The sky was free of clouds and the moon reflected clearly against the calm surface of the water.

"It's so beautiful out here," she breathed, settling into his arms.

"Not nearly as beautiful as you."

She turned to face him, gazing deep into his hazel colored eyes as she stepped closer. Cupping her cheek with his hand, he leaned in for a kiss as the breeze picked up.

"Do you feel that?" she asked, her eyes widening, while her cheeks went pale.

"Feel what?"

"In the air, it's coming!" She could sense the electricity as the hair on her arms stood on end. "We've got to get to the jeep." She turned to run away.

He reached out and grabbed her wrist with one hand, pulling her back flush against him. "I'm not going to let anything hurt you, Taryn," he promised, before crushing his mouth against hers.

As their lips met, lightning lit the sky before striking the ground repetitively, circling around them. Completely lost in the moment, she forgot to be afraid, and instead melted into his loving and protective embrace. Wrapping her arms around his neck, she kissed him back, marveling at how her racing heart perfectly matched his own.

When their lips finally parted the freak lightning disappeared as quickly as it had come, leaving the earth smoldering around them. Taryn stood, completely unaffected by the strange electrical storm, as her eyes stayed locked on his.

"I promised that I would keep you safe," he grinned as the smell of burnt earth permeated the air.

"And you did."

He leaned in and stole another kiss, lifting her up by the waist and hugging her tightly.

"Are you guys alright?" Dalen shouted as he and the rest of their friends rushed to them.

Neither replied as they continued kissing, locked in a loving embrace.

"Looks like they are more than fine," Gerrick laughed.

Everyone, with the exception of Keiryn and Nalani, turned around to go back to the bonfire. "I'm sorry. I know this has to suck," she sighed, patting him on the shoulder.

"I only want her to be safe." His voice cracked with emotion.

"I don't think she can get much safer than that," she chuckled, grabbing him by the arm and leading him back to join the others.

CHAPTER ELEVEN

Over the next several weeks, Taryn marveled at how well everything seemed to be going for herself and her friends. Since that night at the reservoir where she and Larkin had shared their first kiss, they had become even more inseparable. Though neither was ready to take their relationship to the next level of intimacy, they stole kisses every chance they got.

Nalani spent a greater amount of time at the Malone home as she and Keiryn continued growing closer, despite his ongoing feelings for Taryn. Dagney and Thorne had made their relationship official, holding hands and sharing kisses regularly. The only person Taryn worried about was young Andyn. He had become quiet and almost introverted since the night of the festival, trying to keep his distance from everyone, especially her.

"Andyn, don't you want to practice with the others?" she asked, as they watched everyone working on various tasks in Gastyn's class.

"No, I think that I should just stay over here," he replied, sadness dripping from his words.

She studied his face again, as she had done every day over the last three weeks, looking for clues to his drastic change. "Whatever's going on, I would like to help." She took a seat next to him.

"You can't."

"Is it Andalyn? Is she still sick?"

"It's a lot of things," he answered vaguely, looking down the length of the room.

She reached out, taking his hand, caressing the top of it gently with her fingertips, trying to soothe the pain she could sense inside of him. "I care about you and your sister. You both mean a lot, not just to me, but to all of us. I know it would make Kellan's day if you went over and challenged him to a race."

"I know you want to help. But you can't...no one can." He pulled his hand back. "You need to stay away from me. It's the only way." Standing, he walked away.

Larkin and Kellan walked over to where she was still sitting, staring at the floor.

"How's the kid doing?" Kellan asked, truly concerned.

"Not good. He won't let me in and I'm really worried."

"We're all worried about him," Larkin stated, holding his hand out to her. "If anyone can get through to him, it's you."

She took his hand and stood, leaning into his chest seeking comfort.

Andyn was absent from class for the next two days. On Friday he returned and seemed to be his old self again. When he saw Taryn, he ran to her, wrapping his arms tightly around her neck. While she was happy to have him back, she couldn't quite put to rest the unsettled feeling inside her chest.

He stood beside her as she talked the twins through creating a pair of small tornados. Everyone watched in awe as Bentley and Hadley displayed extraordinary control over their identical twisters.

"Wonderful," Ardyn lauded as he entered the room, clapping his hands.

Immediately, Larkin and Keiryn moved protectively to Taryn's side in hopes of keeping him at a distance.

"Ardyn," Gastyn greeted him. "I didn't realize that you were stopping by today." He shook his hand and welcomed him into the classroom.

"I was hoping to observe your students for a little while to see their progression."

"But of course."

Larkin threw him a look of contempt, unhappy with the decision. "How could he agree to this?"

"I'll be fine," Taryn assured him, carefully studying their guest.

"Alright then, let's see what everyone can do," Ardyn stated, pulling up a chair from the side.

He watched eagerly as each student showcased their abilities for him. When it was Adalia's turn, he offered Andyn to her as a pawn to demonstrate her ability as an Influential, much to Taryn's dismay. Larkin held her firmly in his arms to keep her from stepping forward. He could feel the power pulsing from her as she fought to hold it back, not wanting to react in front of Ardyn and show him her hand.

Jonesy displayed his gift to grow plants and earned a degrading chuckle from the man. Next Nalani demonstrated her ability to form clouds and rain, receiving an approving nod.

Ardyn locked his eyes on Larkin and grinned. "Taryn, I believe you're next." He was secretly hoping to trigger a reaction from her protector.

"I'm sorry, Ardyn, I haven't prepared anything for show and tell today." She knew that she had irked him as his face briefly flashed between his human form and some type of monster that she always caught a glimpse of when he was around.

"Not in the mood today," he queried, his tone heavy with a seduction.

Her face wrinkled with disgust as his attempt to prod her failed miserably. "My mood has nothing to do with it. I have nothing to prove to you, or to anyone else, so I opt to pass, thank you," she retorted, her casual tone more stern this time around.

"I'm still working with her privately to develop her powers," Gastyn interrupted, feeling the downward turn in the atmosphere.

"I've heard through reliable sources that she is more than capable of demonstrating her abilities. I want to see something," Ardyn demanded. His tone made it clear that he was not asking and his patience was growing thin.

"She said no," Larkin growled, staring fiercely at him.

"You should remember your place, Boy." A large orb of pure energy formed at the tip of his fingers. With a flick of his wrist he sent it straight at Larkin's head.

Reacting quickly, Taryn reached her hand out and stopped the orb only millimeters from striking Larkin. It was so close that he could feel the heat pulsing from it, burning his skin. Her hand trembled from the amount of effort it was taking to hold it in place.

"Well now...that's more like it," Ardyn lauded. "Let's see what you can do with it now that you've stopped it."

Wanting nothing more than to lob the sphere back at him with all of her might, she focused, desperately trying to control her anger. A second later she inhaled sharply, obliterating the orb into dust. "You're vile."

"Why my dear girl, it was your boyfriend who challenged me. I responded much kinder and gentler than I would normally. I gave him the exception, as I know young love can cause one to act impulsively." The lust was burning hot in his eyes. "Now about what you just did with my orb...I've never seen such a thing. I must admit that it was rather impressive."

"I think everyone needs to take a step back," Gastyn asserted, fearing that Larkin would indeed challenge him in order to protect her and her secrets. "I'm sure Larkin meant no disrespect, Ardyn. He's just very protective when it comes to Taryn."

"Yes, I can see that for myself. Can't say I blame the boy for being so possessive of her. I certainly would be."

"That's it!" Taryn shouted. "I'm done, Mr. Wylder. I can't tolerate another minute with these Neanderthals," she fumed, stomping towards the door.

"Taryn, wait," Larkin pleaded, chasing after her.

She forced him to follow her all the way to the parking lot, continuing to make a scene. "I don't need you rising to my defense every time someone talks to me!"

"I only want to protect you."

"Just take me home," she growled, pretending not to notice that Ardyn and Gastyn had followed them and were standing only about ten yards away, witnessing the whole scene. The look of amusement on Ardyn's face made her sick. The man was deeply disturbed.

"I'm sorry," Larkin submitted.

"I don't care about how sorry you are, Larkin. I just want to go home." She jumped in the front seat of his jeep and slammed the door closed.

He shook his head in frustration as he glanced up at Gastyn. "See you tomorrow, Mr. Wylder."

"That little girl is quite the handful, isn't she?" Ardyn laughed.

"I do think of her as being rather special," Gastyn replied, noting something strange in the way Ardyn spoke of her. "Being part of a community is still very new for Taryn. And as you might have already surmised, she isn't big on showing off her gifts. Control like hers is very uncommon for someone her age, and any acknowledgement of it causes her embarrassment." He tried to present Ardyn with a reasonable explanation that might appease him.

Ardyn continued to stare in the direction that Taryn had went, though the Jeep was no longer in sight. The girl was something special, indeed. He could feel the power and the life that oozed off of her, even after she was long gone. Turning back to Gastyn, he clapped him on the shoulder.

"You are a fine teacher, Gastyn. I can't wait to see how she progresses under your watchful eye."

ഇൽൽൽ

"I'm sorry, Taryn," Larkin sighed, turning southbound to take her home.

She reached for his hand and laced her fingers with his. "I'm not angry. I just needed to do something to diffuse the situation back there before things got any more out of hand."

"So all of that was for show?"

"Yes, but you can't let him lure you into a fight, because I can't stay out of it."

"I have to protect you."

"Then next time, protect me by walking away. He hasn't done anything improper that can be proven. If he attacks you he can easily justify his behavior when you challenge him like that."

"I just hate the thought of him being near you or seeing the way he looks at you. It makes me sick. I know he's up to no good, and I still think he's responsible for what happened to you that second time."

"I know," she sighed, leaning back in the seat. "When he offered Andyn to be Ada's puppet, I wanted to unleash everything I had on him, but I knew that I couldn't without jeopardizing everyone's safety. I had to force myself to see that she wasn't physically harming him, and accept it for what it was."

Larkin placed the jeep in park and sat with his hands on the steering wheel as he thought back to of all of the things that he had done wrong in his attempt to protect her. He had chosen not to follow instinct, and instead let his emotions guide him. His error could have cost them all dearly.

"I'm sorry, Taryn. I let my emotions control my response...it won't happen again."

She smiled at him lovingly, understanding his frustration where emotions came into play. It was not as if she did not struggle nearly every second of the day to keep her own in check. Happiness, sadness, anger or any other emotion she let slip past her delicate control could bring the wrath of the Elder Council down on everyone she loved and cared about.

They exited the jeep and headed down the sidewalk to the front door. The house was unusually quiet as they entered. Walking into the living room, they found their parents and Teigan sitting there solemnly.

"What's happened?" Taryn asked, sensing something was terribly wrong.

"It's Andalyn...she's been taken to the children's hospital in Flagstaff," Ilya answered, dabbing at her tears as Maxym rubbed his hands up and down her arms.

"When?" Larkin asked, seeing that Taryn was too stunned by the news to speak.

"She collapsed at their family home about thirty minutes ago. Lilyan was home alone with her and she called the paramedics," Teigan explained.

"Is she alive?" Larkin pressed, wanting to know every detail.

"They were able to get her heart beating again."

"Andyn," a soft voice whispered in Taryn's ear. She gasped and her eyes widened. Turning, she headed for the door with her heart set on going to him.

"Taryn," Larkin shouted, running to her and wrapping her in his arms from behind.

"Andyn needs me."

"We don't have all of the facts, Taryn." Teigan brushed the hair off of her face as she continued to struggle against Larkin's powerful hold. "Sweet Girl, he's going to be fine. He's with his father right now, heading to see her."

Taryn's legs gave out beneath her as she heard the soft voice whisper again. "Andyn." Larkin gently guided her to the floor, but never loosened his grip.

Kneeling down to her level, Ilya watched as her daughter sobbed uncontrollably. "Taryn, I know you're worried, we all are. Andyn needs to be with his family right now. He knows that you are thinking about him and his sister."

"I can help."

"You know why you can't do that," Ilya countered, keeping her voice low in hopes that Teigan and Maxym wouldn't read the meaning behind Taryn's words.

"But I can."

"Think about it, Taryn. The consequences would be great if you were to be discovered. And not just for you," her mother whispered, her heart breaking as she used her daughter's greatest fears against her.

The phone rang, drawing everyone's attention.

"Hello?" Maxym answered.

He stayed on the phone for several minutes, leaving the others waiting anxiously for news. Taryn's tears dried for the moment while she observed his body movement as he listened intently to the person on the other end of the line.

"Thanks for calling, Gastyn. I'll let them all know."

"What is it?" Teigan asked.

"Andalyn regained consciousness. But they decided it would be best to sedate her while they run tests and try to figure out what's causing her symptoms."

"It sounds like things are already starting to turn around for the girl and her family," Teigan stated optimistically.

"See, Baby Girl, she's doing better," Ilya insisted.

She leaned heavy against Larkin, her thoughts consuming her as a battle waged between her heart and mind. Something in the pit of her stomach told her that things were far from turning around for little Andalyn.

"Taryn," Larkin stated, easing his grip on her.

"Yes?"

"Are you alright?"

She shook her head yes, even though she was anything but. "How can a regular doctor treat someone like us? Won't they notice something is different?"

"Sometimes what we need is regular medicines and treatments. Just like regular humans, we are susceptible to viruses and bacteria, especially when you are as young as Andalyn. Fortunately, somewhere in our late twenties our bodies become immune to the common diseases of this world," Ilya explained.

Taryn shook her head and pursed her lips together, fighting to hold back the mountain of emotion that surged through her. "I need to get some air." She headed for the open French doors before anyone could say another word.

Ilya looked to Larkin, her eyes pleading for him to look after her. He nodded, understanding her wishes as they mirrored his own. Outside he ran, headed down her favorite path, knowing that was where he would find her.

"Ilya, what did she mean when she said she could help?" Maxym asked.

"She wanted to comfort Andyn with the power of being an Influential," she stated, glad Taryn's pleas were vague enough that she could easily cover with the men.

"Gastyn and Keiryn just arrived," Teigan stated, sensing his son and the teacher as they pulled into the driveway.

"Where's Taryn?" Keiryn demanded, rushing into the living room.

"She and Larkin went for a walk."

"Was she alright?"

"She was upset, but we all are," Ilya answered.

"No, was she still mad at Larkin?"

"She didn't appear upset until we told her the news about Andalyn," Teigan stated, walking over to his son. "Something else happened today. What was it?"

"Keiryn, you should go find them. I'll fill them in on the rest of the day's events," Gastyn assured him, waving him on.

"What happened, Gastyn?" Ilya asked the moment Keiryn was out of sight.

"Ardyn showed up today and wanted to observe, putting both boys on edge with his presence. When he asked Taryn to demonstrate her skills, she refused. Ardyn was insistent and that's when Larkin intervened. Ardyn took it as a challenge and lobbed an energy sphere at him."

Maxym jumped to his feet, his blood boiling with anger.

"Don't worry Maxym, it was a struggle, but Taryn stopped it just before impact. I was afraid she was going to try to retaliate, but luckily she crushed it and then began yelling angrily at Larkin and Ardyn."

"She didn't appear upset with him when they arrived home," Ilya stated.

"Truthfully, I don't think she was upset with him at all. I think it was all a ruse to diffuse the situation. To put distance between Larkin and Ardyn before things got out of control. She put on a good show in the parking lot before they left."

"She's a clever girl," Teigan grinned.

"Thank God one of them showed common sense," Maxym growled, unhappy with his son and angrier still at Ardyn.

"I believe I was able to appease Ardyn with the excuse that Taryn is embarrassed to share her powers since she's new to living in a Gaias community. I also think I convinced him that Larkin's so smitten with her that he forgets his place sometimes. We'll need to work with him on evaluating the situation and controlling his responses where her safety is involved. Today could have ended disastrously."

"The orb that he lobbed…was it a warning or was he trying to injure my boy?" Anger still resonated in Maxym's tone.

"You're angry, Maxym, and I understand that. But I think we need to consider ourselves lucky that things turned out the way they did today."

Maxym's jaw pulled up tight and his face flushed. "He wanted to harm my son." His hands balled into fists.

Standing in the doorway, Larkin saw the look on his father's face and knew that Gastyn had told him about what happened at the school with Ardyn.

"I'm sorry, Dad."

"He could have killed you."

"It wasn't his fault," Keiryn interjected, trying to defend his best friend.

"It doesn't matter what he did, Keiryn. That man is dangerous and he is most certainly more powerful than any of us," Teigan scolded.

"You're both right. What I did today was both stupid and immature. He wasn't posing any threat to her safety and in the end it was my actions that were the real issue."

Maxym threw his arms around his son and hugged him tightly while tears welled in his eyes. "I'm so glad to hear you say that, Son. I don't know what I'd do if something happened to you."

"Where's Taryn?" Ilya asked, noticing her absence.

"She's sitting on the edge of the pool with her feet in the water," Keiryn offered.

"Ilya, she needs a little time to herself. Everything that happened today, along with finding out about Andalyn…she's struggling to keep it together," Larkin nodded.

Glancing out the window she saw Taryn sitting on the edge of the pool, a lost and forlorn look on her face. As much as she wanted to run out and wrap her in her arms, Larkin was right. She needed space and time to process whatever emotions she was currently battling. "Thank you, Larkin. You seem to always know exactly what it is she needs."

ಏಂಔಓಏಂಔಓ

"It's been nearly two hours," Ilya stated, pacing back and forth in the kitchen.

"I believe she's using the water as a way to self-soothe and work through her emotions," Gastyn observed.

"Well it's pretty amazing," Maxym added, watching in awe from the window as Taryn manipulated the water into spectacular shapes and incredible fountains.

"If you don't mind, Ilya, I'd like to try to talk with her," Teigan offered.

"Please do." She feared that her own state of mind might derail whatever progress her daughter might have made.

He walked out the doors and joined Taryn at the edge of the pool, watching in silence as she continued manipulating the water, ignoring his presence. After a few minutes, he finally spoke. "What you're doing with the water…it's pretty cool."

Taryn glanced briefly in his direction.

"Gastyn told us about what happened today during school with Ardyn. I know Maxym is grateful for what you did."

The water that was in the air splashed back into the pool while she looked at him and shrugged, barely flashing even a hint of a smile. "I think he did something to Andalyn, and I'm afraid that Andyn's next."

"He couldn't have. He was at the school when he received word that she was in route to the hospital."

"It's still possible."

"Ardyn Mitchell is a great number of things, but a child abuser isn't one of them."

She turned to face him. "What makes you so sure about that?"

"Beldyn and Hava stopped by the hospital to see her with their own eyes. The doctors came in and told them that she has a bacterial infection in her lungs and that it appears to be affecting her heart as well. That's why her heart stopped, Taryn."

She sat quietly for a moment, pondering his words. "What is Lilyan's gift?"

"She's an Animator."

"Are you sure?" Taryn mused, kicking her foot gingerly in the water.

"I've known her for years. She is a very gifted Animator. I hear that Andyn is following in her footsteps, much to his father's chagrin. Why do you ask?"

"No reason."

"Are you sure?"

"Just good ole-fashioned curiosity." She turned back to the water, creating two frogs that leapt over one another back and forth across the length of the pool.

"What was it like?"

"What was what like?"

"Stopping the orb that Ardyn hurled." He leaned back casually on his elbows.

The frogs disappeared into the water as the question drew her full attention. "Strenuous."

"That's it? You stop the orb of a two hundred-fifty year old Gaias whose very name strikes fear into those who exceed your years by decades, and all you have to say is it was strenuous."

"Would you prefer me to say how amazing it felt stopping that pompous jerk's energy in its tracks?"

Her normally sweet face was void of expression. "I didn't mean to offend you, Taryn."

"I know," she replied, raising all of the water in a solid rectangle from the pool. Without so much as batting an eye, the water appeared to separate into individual sheets, sliding back into place, refilling the pool. "He was on a fishing expedition today, curious as to what I am capable of."

"From the way Gastyn tells the story, it doesn't sound like you gave anything away."

"I responded, giving him exactly what he wanted. So no, I found no pleasure, except in the fact that Larkin wasn't hurt."

"You should be proud of yourself. You kept your cool, and as a result no one was injured, or worse."

The water in the pool began to bubble and churn as steam rose off of it.

"Did I say something wrong?"

"No," she sighed, allowing the water to calm again. Turning, she faced him, scooting closer. "I want to tell you something, but you can't tell my mother."

Sensing she needed to get something off her chest, he nodded. "It will be our little secret."

"I wanted to hurt him."

"Ardyn?" Teigan asked for clarification.

"Yes. I wanted him to suffer for the things he has done." Anger flared behind the brilliant green color of her eyes. Almost instantly the flames were doused by shame. "Does that make me a monster?" She looked distantly into the woods.

He could see her torment, and now fully understood her struggles. "Ardyn can be a savage when he battles an opponent, and he can be heartless in his daily life. Wanting to give him a dose of his own medicine doesn't make you a monster, Taryn." He cupped her chin in his hand and lifted her eyes to his. "In fact, I am quite certain that if you ask almost anyone in our community, they would tell you that they feel the same way. I know that I do."

She looked at him, studying the details of his face, smiling when it briefly morphed into that of a knight in shining armor. "You're a good man, Teigan Falcon." Leaning over, she kissed him on the cheek, much to his surprise. "I hope that my father was half the man that you are."

"It would be a blessing for any man to call you his daughter," he replied, his heart overwhelmed with emotion. Tears welled in his eyes as he looked down at her. "You really know how to get to a man."

"Can I ask a favor?"

"Anything," he replied.

"Can I have a hug?"

"Come here." He opened his arms, pulling her in close. "You're an amazing young woman, Taryn." He squeezed her tightly for several seconds before letting her go.

"Thank you."

Exhaling to settle his own emotions, he looked to her. "Are you hungry?"

"Famished," she replied, jumping up from the edge of the pool and rushing inside. Realizing that her mother must have been worried, she immediately found her and wrapped her arms around her tightly. "I love you, Mom."

"I love you, too, Taryn."

Walking into the kitchen, Teigan looked at mother and daughter and felt a peacefulness come over him. "Our little water sprite is hungry."

"How does a B.L.T.A. sound?" she asked, referring to Taryn's favorite sandwich of bacon, lettuce, tomato and avocado.

"Perfect," she grinned, as if nothing bad had happened.

"You alright?" Larkin asked, taking a seat next to her on one of the barstools.

"Yeah." She reached over and squeezed his hand.

"Son, do you think you could give us a moment?" Maxym inquired.

"Sure, Dad," he nodded, before kissing Taryn sweetly on the temple.

Sitting down in the chair his son had just vacated, Maxym settled in. "I hear that I owe you a debt of gratitude for saving my son today, Taryn, so thank you." He looked at her with wonder in his eyes, trying to comprehend how someone so young and small managed to possess such great power and finesse.

"Then I guess I owe you a debt of gratitude as well, Maxym."

"How do you figure?"

"For having such a wonderful son for me to save."

"You shouldn't be so modest, Taryn. You saved my son, not only from that monster, but from himself."

"So you believe that Ardyn is a monster, too?" she inquired, happy that he could see what she had seen in him numerous times.

"Anyone that would try to harm a youth in any community is a monster."

She smiled politely as disappointment settled into her gut, realizing that she had misunderstood what he had meant by his statement.

"I'll let you get back to your sandwich," he nodded. Before walking away, he leaned over, kissing her on top of the head. "Thank you." His whispered words cracked with emotion.

∞CB∞CB

Taryn laid in bed, unable to sleep. Giving way to her unrest, she crept quietly from beneath the covers to her window. Taking a seat on the sill, she looked to the night sky and sighed.

"Can't sleep?" Larkin asked, creeping up behind her.

"No."

"You're thinking about the kid and his sister, aren't you?"

"I can't imagine how scared he must be."

He caressed her cheek with his fingers as she leaned into his gentle touch, desperate for the calm that only he could provide.

"I'd like to show you something," he whispered, taking her hand.

They snuck out of her room, downstairs and out the French doors.

"Do you trust me?"

"Of course I do."

"Better hold on then," he laughed, sweeping her into his arms and leaping to the roof. "I've got you."

They nestled together near the pitch of the roof. Larkin held her hand while they laid back and looked up at the clear night sky. For the next two hours, they stayed up there, gazing at the stars while he pointed out the various constellations. She closed her eyes and made a wish with every shooting star they saw.

She fell asleep in his arms. Not wanting to wake her, he gently picked her up and leapt to the ground, landing lightly. He carried her to her room and placed her in bed. After pulling up the covers, he laid down on top of them beside her, watching as she slept peacefully. She looked like an angel, captivating him until his body gave way and he drifted to sleep.

ഇരുഇരു

Keiryn woke to find himself on the floor alone. As he stood and saw Larkin lying on the bed with Taryn in his arms, his temper flared. Taking a deep cleansing breath, he pushed his emotions down and decided it would be best to wake him and tell him to hit the floor before Ilya found him on the bed with her.

She barely stirred as Larkin slipped his arm out from beneath her head before moving to the floor. Soon, he was fast asleep.

Knowing there was no way he would be able to go back to sleep with the irritation and jealousy currently battling in his head, Keiryn decided to go for a run to release his pent up frustrations. As he ran, mental images of Taryn sleeping in Larkin's arms popped into his head. It was disgusting the way her head rested on his arm while she snuggled against his chest. Thoughts of punching him square in the jaw brought a smile to his face. He was utterly appalled that the black dog would be on her bed with her, even if they were just sleeping. A ferocious growl passed from his

~ 352 ~

lips as he shifted into his wolf form. He ran for miles before deciding he was calm enough to return and face them.

"Good morning, Keiryn," Ilya smiled as he entered the living room.

"Morning, Ilya." He headed into the kitchen to get a glass of water.

"It's strange seeing you up so early. Is everything alright?"

"Yeah, just peachy," he fibbed, forcing the image of Taryn in Larkin's arms from his mind. Filling the glass full of water, he quickly drank it down.

"Will Nalani be coming over today?"

"I suppose."

"She's a beautiful girl, rather opinionated too."

"She is definitely opinionated," Keiryn grinned, knowing that Ilya was referring to her fiery, never the type to back down personality.

Opening the refrigerator door, she took out a carton of eggs. "The two of you seem to be getting close."

"Yeah, she's a cool girl."

"Good morning," Maxym greeted them, walking into the kitchen.

"Good morning," they both greeted him in unison.

"I'll make breakfast today," he insisted, taking the carton of eggs from her. For a moment they shared a tender gaze, causing Keiryn to look away awkwardly. When she noticed his discomfort, she quickly excused herself and headed upstairs to take a shower.

"So, you and Ilya?" Keiryn chuckled.

Choosing to ignore his comment, Maxym asked, "How do you want your eggs?"

"Scrambled I guess."

"What are you grinning at?" Maxym inquired, tossing a tea towel at him.

"What's going on in here?" Teigan asked, rubbing the sleep from his eyes.

"Morning, Teigan," Maxym nodded, while putting on a pot of coffee.

"That'd better not be decaf."

"Fully loaded with one hundred percent of your daily caffeine requirement."

"Where are the love birds at?"

"Still sleeping," Keiryn answered, a hint of bitterness in his tone.

"Will we be seeing Nalani today?"

"What's with everyone asking about her?" Taking his glass of water, he slammed it on the counter in irritation.

"It was a simple question, Son. There's no need to get upset about it."

"Sorry. This thing with the Mitchell's and Andalyn...I guess it has me on edge."

"Is there any news?" Taryn asked as she walked into the room with Larkin trailing behind her.

"No, Sweetheart. But we're expecting an update in the next hour or so," Maxym answered. "You up for breakfast?"

"Sure."

After eating their fill of eggs, bacon and toast, the three teens went back upstairs to Taryn's room.

"What's the plan for today?" Keiryn asked, taking a seat on the window sill.

"We could go to Havasu Falls," Larkin suggested, wanting to do something to keep her mind off of Andyn and his sister.

"Good call. The tourists will be gone and you'll love it there, Taryn," Keiryn assured her.

"Sure, but only on two conditions. First, Nalani and the rest of your packs have to go with."

"Done," Larkin answered without looking to Keiryn for agreement.

"Second, we do what I want tomorrow. Just the three of us, and no questions asked."

"Done," Keiryn agreed without consideration, miffed that Larkin had answered for him only moments ago.

"I want you to both promise me."

"I promise," Keiryn quickly reiterated.

Larkin shook his head, sensing he was about to make a mistake. "I promise, Taryn."

Keiryn shrugged casually before stepping away to call his other brothers and sisters to invite them to the falls.

CHAPTER TWELVE

After a lengthy ride, the caravan of four cars parked outside of Supai and began their hike to the falls. They had walked only a half mile when grumbles started to be heard.

"Are you guys seriously going to make us walk all the way there?" Hadley growled, her current discomfort on full display. She and her sister were not exactly fond of hiking in the great outdoors. Their specialty was more the mall and any number of shopping centers where there was a food court and cute boys.

"I think we should be good now," Larkin nodded.

One-by-one each of the girls, with the exception of Bency, climbed on the back of one of the boys. Dagney held on tightly to Thorne, while Nalani paired up with Keiryn. Hadley climbed on Gerrick's back and Bentley on Eben's. Taryn placed her hands on Larkin's shoulders and pulled herself up onto him. He turned his head and flashed a beautiful smile, melting her heart at its core. In return, she kissed him sweetly on the cheek.

Using the strength, speed and agility that being a Skin-Walker afforded them, they headed off. They ran the trail to the falls with lightning speed and grace as they maneuvered effortlessly through the canyon. Larkin and Taryn arrived several minutes before everyone else.

"Oh my goodness." She took in the extraordinary sight as they stood at the top. The falls, which were close to one hundred feet in height, poured down in spectacular fashion. The roar of the water did nothing to detract from the gorgeous showcasing of the blue-green pool below. "This has to be one of the most beautiful places in the world." Wrapping her arms around Larkin's waist, she snuggled against him.

He held her in his arms, squeezing her tight as the rest of their group showed up. Kellan and Dalen, who were not carrying anyone on their backs immediately removed their shoes and leapt over the falls into the pool waiting below. Their carefree howls of laughter could be heard on their way down until they were swallowed by the water.

Not one to shy away from adventure, Nalani refused to be left standing above. "What about it, Kansas? You ready to take the plunge and show these Skin-Walkers that we don't require their special gene?"

Taryn's lips curled into a fierce smile. "Bring it on." She peeled off her hiking boots and socks, tossing them to the side.

Wearing shorts and t-shirts, they stood near the edge, peeking over.

"Are you scared?" Nalani asked.

"Not at all," Taryn answered as adrenaline coursed through her veins from excitement.

The two girls took a few steps back before nodding at one another. Sprinting forward, they bounded over the falls and plunged into the water below.

Larkin looked on with a pleased expression.

Keiryn placed his hand on his shoulder. "You did it again. Like always, you knew exactly what it was she needed," he admitted, though it felt like a stake had been plunged into his chest.

"Thanks, Brother. You and I make a great team. You ready to do this thing?" he grinned, nodding to the waterfall.

"Hell yeah. Besides, we can't keep the ladies waiting."

ഇരുനും

For the next few hours, the friends enjoyed their time in what felt like their own private paradise. They made the trek back to the top numerous times, in several different groups and individually, to take the plunge once again. Each time the boys jumped, they would get more creative, doing backflips, front flips and cannon balls.

As Taryn, Larkin, Keiryn and Nalani stood at the top preparing to jump, Taryn noticed a distinct change in the air.

"What is it," Larkin asked, grabbing her hands, sensing something was off. The second he touched her skin, he could feel the electricity pulsing through her.

Panic filled her eyes. "Run!" she shouted. Nalani and Keiryn stood, feet planted, staring at her, not grasping the severity of what was coming. "Run!"

When they still didn't move, she held her hand out, pulsing out her Imperium power and sending them over the falls just as the first bolt of lightning struck the ground beside her. It sent her body flying through the air, but Larkin caught her as the lightning struck again and again in a path headed straight for her. She climbed onto his back and held on with all of her strength as he sped back in the direction of their vehicles.

Lightning crashed all around them as he successfully ducked and dodged bolt after bolt. When the cars came into sight he realized that his keys were still back at the falls inside his shoes. Knowing there was no place for them to hide, he slid along the dirt and rock, taking both Taryn and himself to the ground. Before another bolt struck, he used his body to cover her.

The lightning continued to strike all around them in rapid-fire cessation. He shielded her with his body, trying desperately to protect her, his heart racing with adrenaline as each bolt struck the ground.

"Run away," she yelled, tears streaming down her face at the thought of losing him.

"Never!" He held onto her with all of his strength, never once considering his own safety. His need to protect her outweighed everything else.

The strikes were so numerous and loud, they had no idea that the rest of their friends stood less than a quarter mile away, watching helplessly.

While the lightning continued its incessant deluge only inches from them, Taryn opened her eyes and caught a brief glimpse of someone standing just a few feet away. She could see a pair of shiny black men's dress shoes and the bottom part of the legs of his black trousers. Desperately, she tried to turn her head to get a look at the stranger's face, but Larkin pulled her tighter, effectively barring her head from further movement.

"What do you want?" she thundered, wanting the stranger to answer. The sound of lightning striking the ground was the only response. She closed her eyes in frustration before opening them again to find the shoes were gone.

After nearly twenty minutes of continuous crashes, the lightning finally ceased. Within mere seconds their friends rushed in to check on them.

"Taryn? Larkin?" Keiryn called out cautiously as he ran towards them, fearing what he might find after the dust settled.

When there was no answer, he knelt down and touched Larkin's back. Fear lumped in his throat until he felt his muscles twitch.

"Help me!"

Larkin rolled off of her and fell to the side, his chest heaving as adrenaline pumped furiously through his veins. "Taryn?"

"I'm here, Larkin." She sat up, placing her hand on his chest. "You saved me." The ache in her chest grew stronger. Though Larkin's actions had been noble and valiant, they could have been his undoing. She thought of exactly how close the lightning had struck, almost as if was trying to scare him into moving away from her, but he had refused to let her go. He had remained firmly rooted, lying on top of her, protecting her just as he had promised so many times before.

"What was that?" Keiryn asked, kneeling down to wipe some of the dirt from her face.

"A storm. You all saw it," Larkin lied as he moved to his feet.

"That wasn't like any storm I've ever seen," Kellan frowned, realizing that his friend was trying to hide something from them.

"From where I stood, it looked like the lightning was chasing after you guys," Dalen added.

"Actually, it looked more like it was chasing after her," Gerrick stated seriously, nodding in Taryn's direction.

"Drop it!" Larkin growled, looking over his shoulder at them.

"It's alright, Larkin," she insisted as she stood. "I owe you all an explanation and an apology."

"For what, exactly?" Nalani inquired. She was just beginning to think of Taryn as her best friend. The idea that she had been keeping secrets from her, from all of them, made her wary of the new girl once again.

"Ever since I can remember these freak storms of lightning have chased after me." She looked around at each of their faces, trying to gauge their reactions. "Coming out here today, I put you all at risk, and for that I am truly sorry." Everyone stood silent, looking at her with apprehension in their eyes. "I understand if you want to keep your distance."

Gerrick and Kellan glanced at one another, sharing a look. After a few seconds, they nodded to the rest of the group.

"Kansas, you're not going to get rid of us that easy," Kellan grinned.

"Definitely, not," Gerrick agreed, resting his arm around Kellan's neck.

Taryn blushed, looking shyly at them as she became overwhelmed with emotion. She had never imagined what it would feel like to have a friend, let alone several, that would support her. The feeling was strangely euphoric. "Thanks. That means a lot." She glanced at Nalani, recognizing the unsure look on her beautiful face.

Nalani studied her for several seconds before flashing her a smile and grabbing her into a fierce hug. "I'm glad you are okay, Kansas." Taryn hugged her back, grateful that their new friendship had withstood this first test. In the back of her mind Nalani tried to squelch the nagging little voice that was saying those secrets were just the tip of the iceberg.

"You alright?" Larkin whispered, happy to see how easily everyone had accepted her disclosure.

"This whole thing of belonging to a community…it really is something special." She placed her arms around his torso, hugging him tightly. He kissed her softly, thankful that she was safe.

ಬಂೞಬಂೞ

Shortly before midnight Taryn, Larkin and Keiryn arrived home to find their parents waiting up for them. When they walked in the front door, Ilya rushed to her, wrapping her arms tightly around her neck.

"I was getting so worried."

"What, don't you trust us?" She hugged her mother as she flashed both men an ornery grin.

Ilya pulled away and saw the devilish look upon her daughter's usually angelic face, and smiled with relief. "If you guys are hungry, there's smoked brisket, grilled chicken legs, baked beans and coleslaw in the fridge."

Immediately, they dropped the backpacks they were carrying and hurried into the kitchen. Keiryn pulled open the refrigerator door and began slinging containers to Larkin, who placed them onto the counter.

"Taryn, do you want a plate?" Keiryn called out as she walked up to the island counter.

"Sure."

"One or two?" Larkin inquired, holding up a cold chicken leg before biting into it and letting it hang from his mouth.

"Seriously, Caveman?"

"What? I'm starving," he mumbled with the piece of chicken still firmly in his mouth.

"One," she replied, shaking her head. "I'm going to go shower. Be back down in a sec."

⁗⁕⁗⁕

When Taryn returned, she found that all of the adults had gone to bed, leaving Larkin and Keiryn sitting alone in the kitchen at the island. She took her normal seat between them and began eating.

As she took a bite of coleslaw her face broke out in a huge grin, recalling the rush she had felt the first time she had jumped off the top of the falls.

"What are you thinking about?" Larkin asked, noticing the glow on her face.

"Today."

~ 362 ~

"The first time you jumped, right?" Keiryn inquired, taking a drink. "I still remember the rush I felt the first time I took the plunge."

"The only difference between you and Taryn, Brother, was the fact that she was fearless and you stood at the top of the falls for nearly twenty minutes before mustering the courage to jump."

"Cut me some slack! I was only ten years old and you know that jumping wasn't my thing back then." He blushed with embarrassment.

"Dude, even Jonesy jumped before you."

While the boys bantered back and forth, Taryn's mind began wondering elsewhere. She could still remember the taste of fear that had filled her mouth when she felt the electricity of the freak storm in the air. The way that it had caused the hair on her body to stand straight on end, and the sensation of dread that had overwhelmed her knowing it had been so close to her friends.

Slapping her hands on the countertop, she grabbed their attention. "I need to be fast like you."

"What do you mean?" Larkin asked, giving her his full attention.

"I need to learn to run fast like you."

"You can't, Taryn," Keiryn laughed. "To run fast like us, you'd have to be a Skin-Walker or a..." he paused, noticing Larkin's unhappy expression. Realizing the slip of the tongue he was about to make, he continued in a new direction. "And no offense, you might be a lot of things, but I haven't seen a hint of that gene."

"Larkin?"

He gazed into her beautiful green eyes and knew he couldn't refuse her. "If you want to try, I'll help. But I don't want you to get your hopes up...okay? It's not realistic for you to have that type of ability."

"All I'm asking for is the chance to learn." She leaned into him, kissing his lips softly.

"Get a room already," Keiryn scoffed, tossing a tea towel over their head. Larkin immediately grabbed it and tossed it back at him, rolling his eyes in mock annoyance.

Her lack of interaction drew their attention once again.

"Something wrong?" Larkin asked.

She looked at them both, her eyes full of uncertainty. "I want to ask you both a question, but I don't want you to think that I'm crazy."

"What's up?" Keiryn questioned.

"During the storm today…you guys didn't see anyone else around did you?"

"Anyone else? No, but then again, I couldn't see anything but dirt being kicked up from the strikes," Larkin answered.

"I didn't see anyone else, with the exception of our packs."

"What is it?" Larkin could sense she was holding something back.

"Forget that I said anything." She kissed them each on the cheek before heading upstairs to crawl into bed.

ഇരുഇരു

The next morning Taryn woke before everyone else and made her way to the back yard. She stood at one end taking a deep breath before sprinting as fast as she could to the pool. Over and over she tried to find a way to make her feet move faster than they were willing to do on their own. As her frustration built, a boom of thunder filled the air, rattling the windows on the house.

"What are you doing out here?" Teigan asked, walking through the French doors in a pair of long black cotton pajama bottoms and a grey colored tank, his wavy hair still messy from the nights' sleep.

"I want to learn to run fast like a Skin-Walker."

He walked over and took her hand. "Please, come sit with me." They made their way over to the patio table sitting next to the pool. He rubbed his fingers through his messy hair and sighed. "Why exactly do you want to run like us when you have so many other gifts?"

"Because I want to."

"When I was about fourteen years old, I wanted to be an Elemental more than anything else in the world. Day after day I'd spend hours trying to create a simple rain cloud."

"So did you ever do it? Did you ever make a rain cloud?"

"Nope, not a single one," he shrugged, sitting back in his chair casually.

"Was this your idea of a pep-talk?" She furrowed her brows at him, pursing her lips.

Teigan chuckled. "No, Taryn. I just wanted to let you know that sometimes we end up disappointed no matter how much effort and time we put into something. We weren't meant to do it all."

"Speak for yourself. Anything is possible, providing you find a way to unlock it."

He studied her and the serious look she now wore on her face. "You do realize how special you are, right?"

"That's what I've been told," she shrugged, tiring of hearing the word special being used to describe her.

"I've only seen a small amount of what you can do and I must say that I'm already thoroughly impressed. But you need to accept that while you are able to do extraordinary things that most Gaias can only dream about, you may not be able to do it all. Just try to find the satisfaction in the gifts that you already possess."

"What I am…it isn't enough if I can't protect the people that I care about."

"You incredibly sweet, sweet girl. So learning to run fast…it's about protecting someone else?" She shrugged her shoulders and looked away, biting her bottom lip to hide the fear that resided within her. "It's not your responsibility to protect everyone, Taryn."

She stood, rolling her eyes in frustration. "It is if I am the one who brought the danger to their doorstep."

Teigan studied her carefully, wondering what exactly she meant by that. She was a mystery to them all, and it pained him to see her struggling with such torment. He couldn't help but wonder exactly how far her gifts and powers could reach. Realizing she did not understand how others might interpret her desire to run like the Skin-Walkers, he decided it best to be direct with her. "Taryn, I need to tell you something and it's important that you listen."

"Okay?"

"Please, stay," he insisted, motioning for her to sit back down. She followed his wishes with a hint of hesitance. Once she sat back in her chair, he scooted in closer. "What you are trying to do…well there's not a delicate way to put this so I am just going to say it. People might think that you are trying to align yourself with the Mortari."

Instantly, her face wrinkled with disdain. "I'm nothing like the Mortari."

"I know you're not," he quickly replied, grabbing her hand, trying to take away the burn of his words. "You want to protect everyone, I see that. But you need to consider how others will view what you are doing. Don't forget to take into account their feelings as well. Surely you know about Larkin's mother."

"Is there anything those selfish brothers didn't ruin for the rest of us?"

"What?"

"I know about his mother." Flames still smoldered as she cast a glance in the distance. Her thoughts turned ugly as she considered what she would do if she ever met them face-to-face. After only a few seconds, she pushed her dark thoughts down and packed them away in a special box that could contain such vile things. "I suppose that I've never considered how this would make them feel."

Just as Teigan was about to say something, Larkin and Keiryn emerged from the house. Knowing that he had done all he could for her, he excused himself to go make breakfast.

"Good morning," Larkin greeted her with a kiss on the forehead as he took a seat beside her.

Still sleepy, Keiryn nodded, crossing his arms and flashing a weak smile.

"I'm glad you're both awake."

"Yeah, yeah, real awake," Keiryn mocked, sliding down into the chair and resting his neck on the back of it.

"You're up to something. What is it?" Larkin asked, leaning in closer.

"Actually, we're up to something."

"What the hell did we get ourselves into, Brother?" Keiryn questioned, leaning forward, placing his head between his hands.

"I did what you wanted yesterday, now it's your turn to return the favor."

Both boys shared a look and exhaled heavily, fearing what she had planned for them. "Let's hear it," Larkin sighed.

"I want to go to Flagstaff and check on Andalyn." Her voice was barely above a whisper.

"Don't be ridiculous, Taryn. That hospital is the last place you need to be."

Pulling her jaw up tight, she reminded him of their agreement. "You promised. No questions asked."

"Yeah, that was before he knew you were certifiable," Keiryn interrupted, his tone laced with disapproval.

Larkin looked at her, his eyes pleading desperately for her to drop her heinous idea, but he could easily see that she was bound and determined to go check on Andalyn by herself if needed. "What did you have in mind?"

"I thought we could go there and have a word with her doctors."

"Okay, I know you're new to this regular world living and everything...but haven't you ever heard of the little word 'confidentiality'?" Keiryn reminded her.

"I know they aren't going to tell me anything." She rolled her eyes at the limits of his imagination. "But they would tell her father anything he want to know," she smirked, using the power of being an Influential to make Keiryn see what she wanted him to see.

"What the hell," he stammered, raising up in his chair and stumbling over it, startled to see Ardyn Mitchell sitting opposite of him.

"If I can make you see Ardyn when you look at Larkin, the humans won't have a clue."

"I don't like this, Taryn," Larkin stated, caught off guard by Ardyn's deep voice coming from within him.

"I know you don't, that's why I had you promise." She pulled back her Influence over them.

"That was creepy," Keiryn shivered, fighting the chill that ran down his spine.

"Are you guys in or not?"

Larkin looked to her, then to Keiryn, shaking his head. "If you're in, then I'm in."

"Looks like I'm in, too," Keiryn answered half-heartedly.

"Good. We'll tell them we're going to the wildlife refuge for the afternoon. That should give us plenty of time to find out what we need to know." She ignored the sour expression that both boys wore.

ಬೂಡಬೂಡ

Larkin turned the key in the ignition and pulled it half-way out. "Are you sure about this?"

"Positive."

"Keiryn, could you give us a moment?"

"Sure, but just for the record, I think this is a terrible idea," he remarked while stepping out of the car.

Taryn glanced at Larkin and then out the window in an attempt to avoid his gaze.

"He's right you know. Have you thought about what will happen if this all backfires?"

"Do you have a better idea?" When he sat quietly, she knew his answer. "That's what I thought. Besides, if we get caught, we'll chalk it up to my connection with Andyn. Everyone in our community knows how I feel about the kid and his sister."

"Getting caught isn't what worries me. It's how you'll respond to all of the other children and their families, Taryn. I know you and I know that you'll want to heal them all."

Taking his hand in her own, she began to trace over the lines on his palm. "You're right, I do want to save them all, but I know that I can't."

"But you're planning to heal her right, for the kid?"

"Yes."

"I don't want to lose you, Taryn." Trembling, he recalled the day that she had nearly died.

~ 369 ~

"You won't. It's different this time. I promise." She pulled his hand to her chest and placed it over her heart. "You are my always and forever, Larkin…always."

He gazed into the depths of her jewel colored eyes and could easily see that she meant every word. His only concern was how she was so certain that it would be different from the last time. "Let's go before I change my mind," he conceded.

ᎯᏣᏣᎯᏣᏣ

"Ready?" she exhaled as the doors to the elevator closed, taking them to the seventh floor of the hospital. "All we need to do is walk past her room and see if they are inside or not."

"Why do I have to be the child?" Keiryn whined, referring to his present state of looking and sounding like a ten year old girl. "Why did she have to be wearing a bright pink dress with white polka dots and glittery black shoes?"

To conceal their presence, Taryn had picked out a family of three from the parking lot that appeared to be leaving and cast her Influence so that she and the two boys resembled them.

"I think it's a good look for you, Brother," Larkin teased, easing some of their tension until the doors opened up, revealing their floor.

She swallowed hard, knowing she had to keep in absolute control of her emotions, a task that had seemed much easier before inhaling the lingering scent of sickness.

"Are you alright?" Larkin asked, sensing her struggle.

"I'll be fine."

The threesome walked the hallway, giving the appearance that they somehow belonged. She searched for any hint of the Mitchell's being on the floor. A stabbing sensation tore at her gut when she found none. She changed their appearance and walked to the nurse's station, casting out her Influence on everyone except themselves in case the real Mitchell's were to show.

"I'm sorry, it's been such a stressful time for me and my family. Could you remind me of what room my daughter, Andalyn Mitchell, is staying in?" Larkin asked.

The older woman who sat behind the desk wore a pleasant, comforting smile. "Room seven forty-three," she replied, pointing them in the right direction.

"Thank you," Taryn nodded in appreciation, before turning and heading to find her sweet little princess.

Every step they took closer to Andalyn's room, the stabbing sensation in her gut sharpened, nearly knocking the air from her lungs.

"You good?" Larkin asked, sliding his arm around her waist.

"We can still turn around," Keiryn whispered.

Taking a deep breath, she found her resolve. "No. We don't back out when it comes to helping family." They were now standing just a few feet from the little girl's doorway. "Stay close," she whispered to Larkin.

"Nothing and no one could ever keep me away." He gripped her hand in his own.

She stepped forward, pushing the door open. They made their way inside, around the short corner to where Andalyn's bed sat. Taryn gasped at the sight of the small child lying in the twin sized bed hooked up to a variety of monitors and machines. She released Larkin's hand and moved closer. Andalyn's normally rosy cheeks now held a grayish pallor. Her lips were dry and cracked around the tube jutting from her mouth.

"I thought they said it was an infection," Keiryn whispered.

"Andalyn." She placed her hand just above her tiny frame.

After a few minutes her expression turned solemn, alerting Larkin and Keiryn that something was terribly wrong. Both boys moved nearer to her.

"What is it?" Keiryn asked, fearing he already knew the answer by the look on her face.

"She's gone." Her voice was barely audible as a tear slipped down her cheek.

"What do you mean, gone?" Larkin asked.

"Her energy, it's gone. There's nothing here."

"Good afternoon, Mitchell's," a man who appeared to be a doctor greeted them as he entered the room with his nurse following closely behind.

"Hello," Larkin nodded, pulling Taryn gently away.

"How's our little lady doing this afternoon?"

Feeling Taryn's tremors beneath his fingertips as his hands rested on top of her shoulders, Larkin took a deep breath and pulled her flush against him. "We were hoping you could tell us."

"We'll take a look and see how she's progressing," the doctor replied, flashing a business-like smile at them. For a few minutes he checked her over before turning to glance at the chart his nurse had been holding. "A few more rounds of antibiotics and she should be good as new in a couple of days," he announced, washing his hands in the sink. "I'll be back in to check on her later this evening." Turning on his heel, he and his nurse headed out the door

"That's good, right?" Keiryn asked, confused by Taryn's demeanor in contrast to the strangely upbeat attitude of the doctor.

She stood silently, her body shaking as she tried to make sense of modern medicine and how an educated doctor could make such a grievous error. "She's gone," she whispered again, never glancing away from the child's lifeless body.

"I think it's time for us to go." Larkin tried to ease her to the doorway.

She shrugged him off and took a seat on the bed beside her. Using her fingers, she combed through Andalyn's hair. "Sleep well, my little princess. May you find peace and happiness in your ever-after." She leaned down and kissed her on the cheek.

"Taryn," Larkin said woefully, holding his hand out to her, fearing she was on the edge of an emotional meltdown. "You have your answers. Now it's time to go."

Hesitantly she nodded before standing to step towards him. He wrapped his arm around her shoulder, giving it a gentle squeeze before guiding her to the door. Just before they were out of sight, she glanced back over her shoulder and took one final look at the little girl's face, saving it to memory.

As they walked the long hallway, Taryn's body began to jerk. Her attempt to hold back the emotions that were fighting to escape from inside of her began to wane.

"Breathe, Taryn," Larkin encouraged. "I need you to keep it together until we make it outside." When she didn't respond, he shot a look of worry to Keiryn, who immediately placed his arm around her waist in an attempt to blanket her with their comfort and love.

Emotions churned rapidly inside of her making her oblivious to their very presence. Suddenly, a loud clap of thunder boomed, causing vibrations to be felt throughout the entire building. It was quickly followed by a barrage of thunder that continued to shake the building, startling its occupants.

Realizing she was responsible for the sudden change of weather outside, both boys pulled her tighter. "We've got to get her out of here, now," Keiryn panicked, fearing the building would be leveled if she continued.

"And exactly how do you propose that we do that without being seen?" Larkin countered, nodding his head to the multiple cameras that were visible at every angle.

While the boys tried to figure out an acceptable exit plan, Taryn, who was still lost in her downward spiral, somehow managed to notice a man standing a few feet from the elevators. He was around six feet tall with a strong build. His hair was light blonde and he had the most intense, piercing blue eyes that she had ever seen. Her eyes locked with his and instantly a strange calm washed over her. It momentarily silenced the heartbreak she felt over Andalyn's passing and the guilt she harbored for not having done more when she had the chance.

The claps of thunder ceased, catching Larkin's attention. "Do you hear that?"

"It stopped," Keiryn replied. The boys glanced down at Taryn, who stood secured between them, and noticed a peaceful look on her face. "What's happening?" Keiryn mouthed to Larkin, surprised by her sudden emotional change.

Larkin replied with a slight shoulder shrug and a shake of his head. He had no idea what had come over her, causing this new sense of calm, but whatever it was, he was eternally thankful.

When the elevator doors opened they stepped inside the carriage, guiding Taryn along with them. "Aren't you coming?" she inquired to the stranger who stood just outside the doors looking in at her. The man with the piercing blue eyes did not speak as he continued watching her until the doors finally closed.

ဆဃဆဃ

Driving west on Interstate Forty Larkin adjusted the timing on his windshield wipers as the rain picked up. He glanced at Taryn who sat quietly, staring out the passenger side window with her hands in her lap. As much as he wanted to reach over and take her hand in his own, he thought better of it. This day had been another

~ 374 ~

first for her. Andalyn was the only person that she had known to have passed. She would blame herself for not doing more to help the young girl, regardless of the consequences that would have followed.

Keiryn leaned up between the seats, glancing over to her before turning back to Larkin. "My dad's blowing up my phone back here."

"I know. Mine has been calling too. I think it's probably for the best if we wait to deal with them when we get home."

Keiryn shook his head in agreement before glancing over at Taryn again. A chill ran through his spine, seeing how still she sat.

When they pulled into the driveway, they found all three of their parents waiting outside. Larkin opened his door and immediately felt the weight of his father's eyes bearing down on him. He walked around and opened Taryn's door. Without so much as an acknowledgement, she slid from the seat and headed to the house.

Ilya's fury instantly dissolved, seeing the intense look of distress on her daughter's face. "What happened?" she demanded, looking to the boys for answers.

"Don't blame them," Taryn sighed, walking to the window and peering into the woods, silencing the grumbles she heard from Teigan and Maxym. "I made them take me to Flagstaff so that I could check on Andalyn."

"You did what?" Ilya snapped, surprised by her daughter's disclosure.

"By the time we made it there, she was already gone…she was already gone." Her tone painted the grim picture for them.

"That's impossible," Maxym insisted. "Gastyn called shortly after you guys left and said that she was improving." Maxym looked to his son for some sort of sign that she was mistaken.

"Ardyn and Lilyan must be devastated," Ilya trembled.

"They don't know," Taryn stated, looking over her shoulder.

"Then what makes you so certain?" Maxym asked.

"Because when I touched her, I felt a cold, dark nothingness." She walked to the bottom of the staircase and looked at them shamefully. "I'm going to my room." With that she ascended to the top and disappeared down the hallway.

Ilya placed her face in her hands and stumbled backwards to the couch, taking a seat. It was obvious to her that Taryn had went to the hospital with the intentions of healing the little girl. Sobbing, she shook her head, imagining the guilt that now weighed heavily on her daughter's shoulders.

"Son, are you sure?" Maxym asked, taking a seat next to Ilya on the couch.

"Yes."

Maxym wrapped Ilya in his arms as she mourned for the little girl and secretly grieved for the lost innocence of her daughter.

"I'm going upstairs to check on her," Larkin nodded to Keiryn.

"Sure," he sighed, trying to contain his own sadness.

Once Larkin was headed up the stairs, Teigan pulled Keiryn into the kitchen and poured him a glass of water. "Do you need to talk about it?"

He sat back in the chair and looked at his father. "It's not fair. And none of it makes any sense. I mean, you say they told you that she had improved…"

"That's what they said."

"The doctor that came in was a buffoon. He looked her over and said that she only needed a few more rounds of antibiotics. It just doesn't make any sense," he shouted, throwing the glass against the wall, shattering it into a hundred little pieces.

"It's alright, Son. Let it out." Walking around the corner, he pulled him into a tight hug.

ಬಂ೮೮ಜ೮೮ಜ

"Taryn," Larkin called out from the doorway as she sat on the window sill. When she didn't give any response, he walked over and stood beside her. "Taryn," he said again, softly this time, swiping the hair away from her face.

Choosing not to speak, she took his hand and pressed it against her cheek, hoping to find some sense of calm from the emotional storm she was trapped in.

It was nearly midnight when her body gave way to exhaustion, and the rain that had fallen steadily since her grim discovery finally began to taper off. He scooped her up into his arms, careful not to wake her. Ilya, who had stood in the doorway for the past several hours, rushed over and turned down the covers on her bed.

"Thank you," she whispered to him.

When he tried to lay her down, she grabbed hold of his neck and held on tightly. Seeing how much her daughter still needed him to be near, she nodded her consent. He slid into the full-size bed and tried to get her settled. Ilya pulled up the covers over both of them. Still apprehensive about allowing him to share a bed with Taryn, she brought in a bean bag and prepared to sleep in the room with them.

ಬಂ೮೮ಜ೮೮ಜ

In the morning the sun began to rise, breaking through the darkness of the night. Ilya woke to find Maxym sleeping next to her, his head resting on the bean bag. Keiryn and Teigan slept haphazardly on the floor near the doorway, and her precious Taryn was still asleep, wrapped in Larkin's caring embrace. She stood and walked over, appreciating how at peace her daughter appeared to be in the moment, and how he continued to hold onto her protectively even in his sleep.

Knowing that this moment of bliss would only last as long as she remained asleep, she quietly stepped over Teigan and Keiryn, heading into her own bedroom to ready for the day, fearing it would be much longer than most.

ಬಂಬ

It was nearly ten in the morning before Taryn began to stir. Larkin caressed her cheek, intent on easing her into the day. "Hello," he whispered, kissing her long on the temple.

"Hi." Sadness still marred her eyes. Burying her head into his chest, she inhaled deeply, hoping to savor one last moment before she faced the reality that she had exposed.

"We could stay in here all day if you want."

"That sounds great, except there's one problem."

"What's that?"

"It doesn't change what is," she exhaled, attempting to lock down her emotions. "Andalyn's gone. If I would have tried to heal her at the festival when she told me that she didn't feel good…maybe she'd still be with us."

Larkin placed his hand against her cheek and brought her eyes to meet his. "Taryn, don't ever say that again. You had no way of knowing this was going to happen, or just how sick she was."

"I have the ability to Heal. I should be able to sense when someone is sick or in distress. After all, I felt you slipping away after we took the Blood Oath. So tell me how it is that I didn't have a clue about her."

"I don't know. Nothing about this makes sense to me."

Pushing back to rest on her knees, a nauseous feeling washed over her. "How am I ever going to be able to face Andyn? He doesn't even know that she's gone."

"He's going to need you more now than ever, Taryn. All you can do is be there for him when he does find out the truth." He

~ 378 ~

reached up, tracing the side of her cheek with the back of his knuckles.

"Eh-hem," Keiryn cleared his throat in an attempt to gain their attention.

"Hey," Larkin greeted him, waving him into the room.

Turning to look at him, she flashed a forced smile, putting on a brave face. She could still see his lingering sadness over Andalyn's passing as he walked to the bed. His shoulders were rounded and his footsteps were heavy.

"Your mom and our dad's discussed it and thought it would be best if we stayed home from school today and tomorrow. I guess they wanted to make sure that we were all okay before letting us go back."

"You mean they wanted to make sure that I didn't have another melt down," Taryn frowned.

"There's that too," he grinned, trying to lighten the mood as he took a seat on the bed next to them. "Gastyn's going to stop by tonight. He's bringing homework from our regular classes, and he wants to talk with us."

"That sounds like fun," Larkin grumbled.

"Yeah, my dad called him yesterday evening and told him about what happened. He wanted to come right over. Fortunately, Dad explained that we needed some time to process everything before discussing it further."

"Joy, joy," Taryn rolled her eyes.

"If you don't want to talk about it, Taryn, you don't have to," Larkin assured her.

"It'll be fine." She nuzzled between them, locking her arms through theirs.

They sat quietly, drawing comfort from one another.

ಬಂದ ಬಂದ

"Taryn, you didn't eat breakfast or lunch. I insist that you eat your supper," Ilya asserted.

"I'll eat when I'm hungry, Mom."

"You need to keep your strength up, Sweetie."

Maxym noticed her growing frustration with her mother's non-stop hovering over the past two hours. Paired with her already tense mood, he decided it would be best to intervene before Ilya suffered from a misdirected meltdown. "Ilya, let's give her some space. When she's hungry, she'll let you know. Isn't that right, Taryn?"

"Yep. You'll be the first to know, Mom." Leaving the kitchen, Taryn headed into the living room and took a seat between Larkin and Keiryn on the couch. "What's on the television?"

"There isn't much to choose from," Keiryn moaned, as he continued to steadily flip through the channels.

"No need to worry. Gastyn just pulled up, and he's bringing homework," Teigan kidded, even though he was serious.

The three teens sat on the couch quietly and shared anxiety-laden glances. Not one of them wanted to rehash the details of the previous afternoon, but they knew they didn't really have a choice.

After a few minutes of pleasantries, Gastyn took a seat in the chair near the sofa and moved straight to the reason he was there. "Taryn, I'd like to start with you. Would you please tell me exactly what happened yesterday?"

She obliged, providing the events in great detail. Everyone in the room could see the toll it was taking on her. After she finished, he asked Keiryn and Larkin to do the same. Each boy provided their own perspective on the events that had taken place.

Gastyn exhaled, leaning back in the chair while he continued studying the teens. "Taryn, what purpose was to be served by you seeing the little girl for yourself?"

Ilya immediately stiffened with fear, knowing exactly why Taryn had went to the hospital. She said a silent prayer that her answer would be plausible.

"You know how much I care about Andyn and his sister."

"Yes, I do, Taryn. But what I don't know is why you created such an elaborate plan to be deceitful, when all you needed to do was ask one of us."

Larkin shot him a look of warning.

"Larkin," his father admonished, seeing his son's strong reaction.

"It's alright, Maxym. I would expect nothing less of him where she is concerned."

"My gut told me something was off, so I listened to it. As far as being deceitful, I knew that my concerns wouldn't be taken seriously based on the constant reports of her improving."

"So based on the fact that you felt emptiness within her, you think that she has passed?"

"No, Gastyn. I don't think she is gone...I know she is. Her body was warm to the touch only because the machines have kept her heart pumping. But her energy, her spirit, they are gone, leaving her cold and hollow on the inside."

"Would you please give us a moment?" Gastyn asked, motioning for the teens to leave the room.

Taryn rolled her eyes, displaying her discord before leading Larkin and Keiryn into the kitchen. She paced back and forth angrily. It was easy enough to see that he did not believe her.

"He shouldn't talk to you like that," Larkin stated, releasing a low growl.

"What's up with that? He might as well have just called you a liar," Keiryn agreed.

"Shush," Taryn directed them, trying to eavesdrop while he spoke with their parents.

"Ilya, I know you want to believe her. But I'm telling you that she's wrong about Andalyn. Besides, it's not the first time she's been mistaken about what she feels residing within a member of our community."

Taryn's nostrils flared with anger as she stormed into the living room. "I know that you're referring to Jonesy Blake, but I'm not wrong. One day you and the rest of our community will see him for what he truly is. And where Andalyn is concerned, you have no idea how much I wish I was wrong. But she is gone, of that I am certain."

"Taryn," Ilya snapped.

"No, Mother…if he's going to call me a liar, he should at least have the decency to do it to my face." Tears of anger filled her eyes.

"Taryn, you misunderstand. I don't think that you're a liar. I can see that you believe this to be the truth, but it simply can't be."

"And why is that?" Larkin growled, wrapping his arms around her trembling body.

"Because I was at the hospital yesterday evening with the Mitchell's, in Andalyn's room. When the doctor was checking her over I saw her wiggle the fingers on her right hand with my own two eyes."

She took a deep breath and pushed her Influence out to Gastyn and the other adults.

"Hava…Beldyn, what are you doing here?" Gastyn greeted the Love's in confusion.

Taryn allowed them to have a brief conversation before she exhaled, taking it all away. The adults looked around, momentarily confused, uncertain of what had just happened.

"Where did the Love's go?" Gastyn asked.

"They were never here," Taryn smirked with a satisfied look on her face.

"Are you suggesting that I was Influenced to see Andalyn's fingers move?" he frowned, taking insult to the idea of such a thing.

"It's possible, isn't it?"

"Taryn, I can see that you are upset, but you shouldn't use your powers against us," Ilya scolded.

"All I did was point out another possible cause for what he saw."

"There's only one issue with your theory, Taryn. Neither Ardyn nor Lilyan are Influentials. He is an Imperium and she is an Animator."

"A Gaias can have more than one gift."

"Yes, Child, they can. With the normal Gaias, the secondary gifts are usually much weaker. And to pull off what you are suggesting, that would have to be their primary…and as I have already stated, neither are an Influentials," Gastyn's voice was suddenly stern.

Teigan glanced outside and saw steam rising from the water as it churned rapidly inside the pool. "Keiryn, Larkin, I think you guys should take a walk with Taryn."

"Please grab a jacket," Ilya insisted, knowing the evening air was much cooler now.

"You grab a jacket," she hissed, dropping the temperature inside the house to a chilly thirty-two degrees in under a second. Without batting a lash, she moved to the French doors and headed straight into the woods.

CHAPTER THIRTEEN

Ilya quickly moved to light the gas fireplace to warm them. "I'm sorry, Gastyn. I've never seen her act this way. It's so out of character."

"You do not need to apologize, Ilya. It's abundantly clear that she believes what she is saying to be the truth. Right now she's angry and grieving based on that belief." Watching as Maxym attempted a third time to raise the temperature with his second gift, after no luck he moved closer to the fire for warmth. "She is certainly strong willed."

"That she is," Teigan stated, with a hint of jealousy in his smile. In his own childhood, he would have loved to do what Taryn did, and with such flare. Though he was a gifted Skin-Walker, it wasn't even a comparison to what he thought it would feel like to have control over the elements.

"Is it possible that she's confused because the child's life force is weakened from the illness? It's apparent how strong she is on the inside...maybe her own power drowned out her ability to feel Andalyn's," Maxym considered, rubbing his hands up and down Ilya's arms, trying to warm her.

"That is definitely plausible," Gastyn nodded. "It's probably best that I take my leave. I cannot imagine that she will be happy to see me here when she returns. I'll check in on her tomorrow and see if she is in a better place."

"Thank you, Gastyn." Ilya escorted him to the front door.

"I only wish that I could have helped her to realize the error in trusting her abilities so blindly. But she is young yet. That is something that comes with age." He kissed her on the cheek before heading to his vehicle.

After closing the door, she walked back into the living room to join Maxym and Teigan while they waited for their children to return.

ೞೞೞ

"Wow, so this is you angry?" Keiryn chuckled nervously.

Larkin sent his elbow plunging into Keiryn's rib cage and gave him a serious look of warning. He could see that she was teetering dangerously on the edge, and the last thing he wanted to do was to send her over. The threesome walked haphazardly for nearly an hour before anyone dared to speak.

"Hey, my house is nearby. You want to go there and hang for a few?" Larkin asked, hoping that Taryn would agree.

"Whatever."

"It's an adult-free zone," he offered, trying to sweeten the deal.

ೞೞೞ

Inside, Keiryn rummaged through the Taylor's cabinets and fridge only to find disappointment. Since they had all been staying at the Malone's for some time, there was no reason to stock groceries.

"Hey, Taryn and I are going upstairs for a bit," Larkin announced, tossing Keiryn the remote to the television in hopes that it would keep his friend occupied while he tried a different approach to calm her.

They walked up the narrow staircase and entered his room. She laid down on the bed and stared blankly at the ceiling. Deciding the best way to engage her was indirectly, he picked up his guitar that rested against the wall and a bright red pick that was lying on the floor and began strumming a tune as he sang softly. By the time he hit the chorus, he could see her body had already started to relax, and the cold blank look had been replaced by hurt and sadness.

"Better?" he asked, still strumming.

"Yeah." Watching his long fingers caress the strings as his low voice sang the beautiful melody put her at ease. "You are my angel, Larkin Taylor." Seeing the grin curling on his face, she asked "What?"

"Funny, I was thinking the same thing about you, Taryn Malone." He leaned down to steal a kiss.

Not even a second after their lips met, Keiryn busted in. "Ugh, why do chicks always fall for the guy with the guitar?"

Larkin reached over her, grabbing one of the pillows and tossed it at his friend, striking him in the head. Keiryn caught it before it hit the floor and brought it over, taking a seat on the bed.

"Are we good?" he asked, arching his brows at Taryn.

"Yeah. I'm sorry for dragging you two into my mess."

"Please…if you haven't noticed, me and this guy would follow you anywhere." He wrapped an arm around Larkin's neck and gave him a noogie.

Sitting up on the bed, she thought for a moment. "Thanks for that."

"We love you, Taryn. Me a bit more than him, but you get the idea," Larkin grinned.

"Yeah," Keiryn awkwardly agreed, thinking to himself how wrong his friend was.

"I was thinking about yesterday. Do you two remember seeing the guy standing outside the elevator when we were leaving?" she asked.

"No," Keiryn answered.

"How did you not see him? He was standing right in front of the doors as they closed. I even asked him if he wanted a ride."

Larkin set the guitar to the side and turned to face her. "Taryn, there wasn't anyone there. And you didn't speak after leaving her room until we were back at your house."

"But there was. He had blonde hair and the most intense blue eyes," she argued.

"He's right, Taryn. There wasn't anyone else there," Keiryn agreed.

"Does this have something to do with the freak storm and the person you thought that you'd seen out there?" Larkin questioned.

"You don't believe me?" She scooted away from him.

"Taryn, I didn't say that."

"You didn't have to. I can see it in your eyes." The hurt and disappointment were clearly written on her face. She stood and skirted around him, making her way to the door. Shaking her head, she glanced at him and rushed down the stairs, out the back door into the darkness.

"Dammit," Larkin growled.

"You really stuck your foot in it this time," Keiryn shook his head, standing to look in Larkin's closet.

"What are you doing?"

"If history serves, I'd like to have some warm clothes on before she decides we need to chill out."

"Whatever, Man. I'm going after her."

೮�೮ಅ

"Wait," Larkin shouted, chasing through the woods after Taryn, Keiryn trailing right behind him.

"Leave me alone."

"You didn't see what you thought," he shouted again, this time grabbing hold of her arm and spinning her around to face him. "This is new to the rest of us...we can't all do, see or sense the

~ 387 ~

things that you can, Taryn. And when you say something, we have to put our trust in you and take you at your word."

"I'm sorry for the imposition that knowing me puts you in."

"It's not like that. I love you."

"Loving me doesn't mean that you don't share Gastyn's concern, Larkin. Just admit it."

"I did for like a second. But it's only because my brain is trying to rationalize everything. It doesn't make sense. You don't make sense, Taryn," he confessed. "Every little thing about you is impossible...don't you see. Every Gaias that has ever been born has to use their hands to project their powers, but not you. You breathe and make things happen. You should be just starting to get a good grip of your primary gift, yet you do things that only mature Gaias can do, and even some things they can't. Instead of one primary, you can do it all. But let's not forget the fact that I've dreamt of you since I was twelve years old, and you suddenly appear one day...and you're real. Two out of the three times my world has been turned upside down, it's had something to do with you. So please, forgive me if it takes me a second or two to wrap my head around it all."

Silence fell between them. Shocked and embarrassed by his own disclosure, he suddenly found himself at a loss for words, though it was too little, too late.

She stood staring at him while she processed what he had just said. When the reality hit her, it took her breath away, cutting her to the very core. "Wow. I didn't realize that you had put dreaming of me in the same category as the death of your mother, Larkin. Now if you'll release my arm, I would like to return home." Her tone was void of all emotion.

꙰ꙮ꙰ꙮ

"Taryn," Ilya breathed in relief as her daughter entered the house, the two boys following quietly behind. She stood as Maxym and Teigan remained seated next to the fireplace.

"I'm sorry, Mom, I shouldn't have spoken to you like that," she conceded, while returning the temperature inside the house to a comfortable seventy-three degrees.

"Are you alright?"

"Yes, but I believe I should be grounded for my behavior. I'll go to my room and accept my punishment. No talking to friends or listening to my radio." She turned and headed toward the stairs.

"Taryn."

"Yes, Mother?"

"I'm sorry." *If only she would have kept them in Galatia, Kansas, none of this would be happening,* she thought to herself.

"Me too." She disappeared up the stairs to her bedroom.

Ilya turned to the boys and gave them a questioning look. "I suppose neither of you want to tell me what that was about?"

"I think that I've said enough for one day," Larkin mumbled, heading to the stairs.

"Don't look at me," Keiryn insisted. "I'm not the one that put my foot in my mouth."

ঙে৩৪৩৪

Larkin knocked repeatedly on Taryn's door, but she never answered. Her heart broke as she sat on the other side. With her knees pulled to her chest and her head resting against the door, she tried fathoming the possibility that she was mistaken. Maybe she was crazy. After all, she saw Ardyn as a monster, Teigan dressed as a knight, and now she was apparently seeing well-dressed gentlemen that were invisible to everyone else in the midst of a lightning storm or at hospital elevators. Even with all of that, she still knew deep inside that Andalyn was gone and something terrible was happening within their community. She was not wrong. She could feel it in her very being. Where once the vibrant spirit of a beautiful little girl had shined through, now there was absolute nothingness. She did not have any answers as to why she seemed to be the only one who could sense it. If she did, maybe she would not be sitting against her bedroom door listening to the pleading of the boy she loved. As much as she wanted to open that door and let him in so that she could feel his comforting arms around her, she couldn't get past the comparison of his dreams of her to the death of his mother.

Standing, she turned and leaned her head against the door, imagining him doing the same. She could feel him on the other side. His emotional turmoil was almost as great as her own. Grabbing her ear buds off the dresser, she turned on her I-Pod and raised the volume. Crawling into bed, she curled herself into a tight ball, and drifted into a fitful sleep.

In the morning, Taryn opened her bedroom door to find Larkin sleeping on the floor on the other side. Stepping over him gingerly, she made her way quietly down the hallway to the stairs. After grabbing a sandwich and a glass of milk, she snuck back into her room and locked the door behind her, knowing that was where she would spend her day, trying to lock down her emotions before she lost control and did the unthinkable.

He tried turning the door handle several times throughout the day, but she wouldn't allow him, or anyone else in. She could sense that he stayed just on the other side. Wanting comfort, she longed for his sweet and tender touch, but letting him in wasn't an option when he was plagued by the doubts he had about her. She wasn't sure she could handle another avalanche of perspective on her already fatigued shoulders.

When Gastyn arrived, a strange feeling washed over her that she could not explain. She was angry, but it was more than just that. She felt an intense pain at the core of her stomach, and numerous times it brought her literally to her knees causing Larkin to pound at the door furiously, sensing that something was happening to her. Continuing to ignore the pleas from everyone who came to her door, she lost herself in the music and the memories.

ঙ৫৩ঙ৫৩

When Taryn walked into the kitchen the quiet chatter paused. She went about her business, pouring herself a glass of orange juice and making a slice of cinnamon and sugar toast. Quietly she took her seat between the boys on the barstool and ate her breakfast before grabbing her backpack and heading out to Larkin's jeep. She sat patiently in the passenger seat waiting for them to join her.

"She's shut down," Ilya whispered to Maxym.

"Larkin and Keiryn will look after her. If anything happens they, along with Gastyn, will be there to help."

"Boys," Ilya stopped them on their way out the front door. "Please look after my little girl."

Larkin nodded in agreement, as did Keiryn.

The drive to school was silent. No one even sighed aloud. When they exited the vehicle she walked ahead of them, giving neither any acknowledgement.

"Hey, Kansas," Kellan greeted her, noting her strange demeanor.

She walked up to him and pulled him in close, whispering in his ear so quietly that no one else was able to hear, regardless of their abilities. Both Larkin and Keiryn watched as the bitter taste of jealousy rose up in the back of their throats, wondering what it was she was saying to him.

"I can't believe she's doing this," Larkin growled, glaring in Kellan's direction.

"Looks like you two boys are in the bird-dog house with the little lady," Thorne grinned, noticing the distance between the normally inseparable trio.

"Shut it, Thorne," Keiryn warned.

All day long Kellan stayed close to her. They continued sharing secrets, and once they entered Gastyn's classroom, they both guarded Andyn, paying him extra special attention.

It became readily apparent to Larkin what she was up to. She had aligned herself with Kellan since he was so close to Andyn. They were trying to cushion and protect the young boy before he learned the truth about his sister. He could not deny how incredibly happy Andyn seemed at garnering their full attention for a brief time. But he grew more worried when Ardyn arrived to pick his son up and Taryn stared at him intensely. However it was Ardyn's reaction to her that concerned him the most. The much older man looked at her with grand desire in his eyes, making no attempt to disguise it.

"Sick, isn't it?" Keiryn stated, standing near Larkin as he witnessed the creepy look on Ardyn's face.

"Very," he agreed, watching over her protectively, ready to react if need be.

೫೦೧೮೫೦೧೮

For the next two days everything remained exactly the same. Taryn only kissed her mother on the cheek, grabbed a bite to eat and then locked herself in her bedroom.

Early Friday morning, Larkin waited for her to open the door to her room, then pushed his way in. "Taryn, please talk to me."

Without saying a word, she leaned into him and wrapped her arms around his waist. Holding onto him tightly, she inhaled his scent and found momentary comfort in the warmth of his embrace. After only a few minutes, she released him and proceeded down the hallway, hoping that he would understand what it was that she wasn't presently able to say to him.

"I love you, too," he whispered, holding onto the lingering sensation that she had left behind.

Their day continued with the little things. She acknowledged his presence more and more. At lunch she did not hold his hand, but did rub the back of hers against the outside of his thigh.

Sitting at their desks in Gastyn's classroom waiting for him to take roll, a sharp pain stabbed in her stomach knocking her from the chair.

"Taryn," Larkin shouted, reaching out to catch her. He helped her back into her chair, brushing the hair from her face. "Are you sick?"

"No," she shook her head, looking to the door.

A few minutes later, Gastyn walked through wearing a look of great sadness. "Class." He cleared the lump in his throat while glancing at Taryn. "I have sad news. Andalyn Mitchell passed away this morning at the Children's Hospital."

"I thought she was getting better?" Bentley questioned.

"Unfortunately she suffered a setback in the middle of the night and she was unable to recover. Her heart gave way to the infection at eleven a.m."

Having already spent time mourning for the little girl, Taryn's thoughts turned solely to Andyn and his well-being. "Where's Andyn?" she asked, while tears filled the eyes of everyone else in the classroom, with the exception of the cold-hearted and selfish Adalia Moore.

"He's with his parents, mourning the natural passing of his sister," Gastyn stated, making it abundantly clear that he still believed that she had been mistaken regarding Andalyn.

She gave him a blank stare, knowing there was nothing she could do or say to convince him otherwise.

🖣🍋🖣🍋

Monday, the day of Andalyn's funeral came, and it was yet another first for Taryn. She wore the traditional color of mourning, a demure black dress and flats. When she walked past the tiny open casket, she paused, absorbing how peaceful and still her little princess looked. When she first saw Andyn, his eyes were glassed over and distant. But the moment she wrapped her arms around him, he broke down and sobbed uncontrollably.

"Taryn," he whimpered.

"I'm here for you, Andyn, whatever you need."

"You're my family now," he whispered, ever so quietly in her ear as he trembled uncontrollably.

"Family," she answered back, using her Influence to calm him.

"Andyn, join us," Ardyn smirked, looking at Taryn with hungry eyes. "Your friend is welcomed to come along as well."

She swiped away the tears that marred her young friend's cheeks and nodded. Holding his hand, she walked with him to stand near his mother and father. Larkin gave a disapproving look but she paid him no mind. Her focus was on the boy.

Andyn acknowledged the numerous people who passed by, offering their condolences, never once letting go of her hand. The grip he kept on her was crushing, yet she only felt his pain and infinite sadness. The desire to wash it all away was there, but she knew he had to grieve for his sister.

🖣🍋🖣🍋

After leaving the cemetery and stopping by their own houses to change, everyone headed over to the Mitchell's for a celebration of life dinner in the young girl's honor. There were a large variety of casseroles, smoked meats, sides, breads and desserts laid out for everyone to enjoy. Taryn walked Andyn through the line, helping him with his plate. He chose only the foods that he knew his sister would have eaten. It was his little way of honoring her.

Kellan sat with them at one of the tables set up in the backyard, while Larkin and Keiryn continued to watch from a distance. She was still hesitant to allow them back in fully as she continued to battle her emotions, and she was still uncertain of how to handle their doubt.

Pushing a noodle from her pasta salad around on her plate, she looked up, catching a glimpse of a familiar face in the crowd near the patio. The blonde hair and piecing blue eyes were unmistakable. It was the same man that she had seen at the hospital by the elevator.

"Andyn, stay here with Kellan," she said, brushing his hair from his forehead, much like a mother would do.

As she passed Larkin and Keiryn, she noticed that neither appeared to look at her, something that she found strange considering Larkin almost never took his eyes off of her. Shrugging it off, she continued to make her way toward the man, who had slipped inside the house. She walked through several rooms before finding him standing alone in the family's great room.

"Hello," she stated, walking up to him.

"Hello, Taryn." His voice was silky smooth.

The fact that he knew her name did not concern her at the moment. "You were at the hospital the other day."

Tilting his head to one side, he studied her. "I was."

"Are you a friend of the Mitchell's?" His crystal blue irises seemed to swirl around like the waves of the ocean.

"I do not have friends." It was a simple statement, without inflection.

"Then why are you here?"

"We needed to speak with you, Taryn."

She peered deeper into his eyes, looking for some clue as to who he was and why he would want to speak with her. "Who are you, exactly?"

"I have many names, but I want you to know me as Farren."

"Farren?"

Looking past her to the backyard through the large window, he smiled briefly. "He needs you, Taryn."

"Yes, I'm aware of that." Her tone reflected a hint of warning to the stranger at the mention of Andyn. He smiled at how protective she was over the boy. "Before, you said that 'we' needed to talk to you. Who else were you referring to?"

"Patience, my dear child, patience," he soothed in his silky tone.

"I don't have time for games, Farren. So if you will excuse me, I need to get back to Andyn." She headed back to the hallway, but paused, looking over her shoulder at him when he spoke again.

"He needs someone strong like you looking out for him if he's going to survive."

Flames rose behind her eyes. "What's that supposed to mean?"

"You know exactly what I mean, Taryn. The answer has been churning in your stomach for more than a week now." He walked towards her.

The stabbing pain that she had experienced numerous times during the past week ripped through her. This was the worst one yet, sending her crashing into the decorative display table against the wall. As she fell, she knocked several picture frames to the floor.

Farren knelt down, offering her his hand. "Get away from me," she hissed, continuing to hold her stomach as the pain lingered deeper and longer than ever before.

"Listen to it, Taryn."

"Shut up." The pain stabbed into her again, causing her to cry out. "Larkin," she whimpered, wondering why he was not rushing to her side when she needed him.

"He can't help you, Child, no one can," Farren stated, appearing to read her mind. "Now open yourself up to the pain."

Fearing there was no other way to make it stop, she did as he directed. The pain turned sharper and became more intense until it suddenly disappeared. Still on her knees, she looked around the room and found herself completely alone. Shaking her head, she considered that she might be losing her mind. Nothing else made sense. Preparing to stand, she reached out, taking one of the fallen frames in her hand. While she was still looking down, a tiny hand reached out for it.

"I have it..." she broke off, speechless when she saw the child's face.

"Hi, Taryn," Andalyn smiled sweetly.

She closed her eyes tightly and tried to focus on her breathing. She was now quite certain that she had, in fact, lost her mind. Tears began to roll silently down her cheeks.

"Don't cry, Taryn."

"This isn't real. You're not here. You can't be here," she said aloud, trying to rationalize and wake herself from the cruel dream she was suffering through. Instead of waking, she felt the gentle touch of the small hand against her cheek.

"Andalyn," she whispered, cupping the hand with her own. She could feel the child's spirit in her touch.

The little girl giggled.

"How?"

"Him," she beamed, nodding to Farren, who seemed to appear out of nowhere again.

Taryn rose to her feet, placing herself between the man and Andalyn. "But she's dead."

"Yes," he replied.

"How is this possible?"

"Earlier, I told you that I have several names. You're a smart girl, Taryn."

She looked thoughtful for a moment before her eyes widened in surprise. "You are Death," she gasped. She looked back to the child and found that she was gone. When she turned her focus back to Death, Andalyn was standing at his side, holding his hand. "How is it that can I see you?"

"Your gifts afford you the ability to sense and see things that most cannot."

Taryn studied them both for several moments. While she was happy to see the precious little girl, she could not help but wonder if anyone who saw her thought she was talking to herself. Before she could pose the question, Farren answered her thoughts and more.

"No one can see you talking with us, Taryn. An hour in my realm is the equivalent a second in their reality. To them, you are still outside sitting beside the boy."

"Andyn," Andalyn sighed at the mention of her brother. Her eyes held a hint of fear as she said the name.

"What is it?" Taryn asked, moving nearer to her.

Andalyn looked to Farren. He nodded as if to give her his approval. "Taryn, you have to save him." Her eyes widened and her lower lip trembled.

"Save him? From what?"

"You already know the answer to your questions," Farren replied.

"I don't understand, and I'm getting really tired of all the cryptic stuff. Why don't you just come out and say it?"

Again, the little girl looked to him for approval, and again he nodded his consent. She motioned for Taryn to kneel down. Once she did, the girl placed her hands over Taryn's eyes and unveiled the dark secrets that her family had harbored for the past three years.

For Taryn, it was as if she was seeing the events through the child's eyes in real time and experiencing all of the emotion and hurt. First she was in a dark room, swaddled in her mother's arms. Suddenly Ardyn stormed into the nursery, ripping her from her from the embrace and dropping her to the floor. Taryn was unable to see Lilyan's face, but she knew it was her mother based on the fierce love and sadness she felt in the moment. Ardyn wrapped his hands around his wife's neck and strangled her until her body went limp.

Next it flashed to what Taryn could only assume was their basement. There was a large wooden table in the center of the room with shackles on both ends. She could hear the screams of her brother before Ardyn dragged him into view. He slammed the boy on the table and bound him to it. Andyn struggled against the restraints, but he was far too weak. After all, he was only a little boy and his primary powers had not set in yet.

"No," the tiny voice begged of his father.

Ardyn's face curled up into an evil grin. He placed his hand over the boy's chest and closed his eyes, attempting to draw out the power inside of him. Andyn's screams from the intense pain grew louder as a woman's horrid laughter broke through. Immediately recognizing that laugh, Taryn saw that it was Lilyan who found delight in her child's suffering. Her face wrinkled in confusion. The love she had felt when Lilyan had swaddled Andalyn in the nursery was now gone.

Before she had time to consider how a mother or father could be so heartless and cruel to their own child, Andalyn showed her more. This time the children cried as they were forced to take part in a Blood Oath ceremony. Ardyn and Lilyan had insured protection for themselves by binding their children to hide their secrets and the horrible things that were being done to them.

Next Andalyn showed her a cessation of short memories of both her and Andyn being strapped to that same wooden table as their father stood above them slowly draining their life force a little at a time. With each new vision she could see them being taken to the brink of death repeatedly before the torture would end.

The final memory began to form, showing Andalyn's death. Taryn could feel every ounce of pain that the sweet little girl had endured. Her body shook as she experienced what it was like to have the power and spirit drained from within. As tears spilled down her face, the memory continued. She could feel Andalyn weaken, and knew within seconds, that she would witness her death as if it was happening this very moment.

As she started to close her eyes to shut out the horrific memory, she caught a glimpse of a necklace that swung free from under Ardyn's shirt as he leaned over Andalyn's dead body with a look of satisfaction on his face. As she focused on it, she realized it was a vial that contained several spikey thorns just like the ones he had absorbed from her body the day he shook her hand.

Trying to make sense of it all, she gasped as Ardyn disappeared. She watched as Farren came to claim Andalyn's soul. Though he looked slightly different in appearance, she knew that it was him. He was calm and comforting, taking away the pain and fear that she felt as she left her body behind. Kneeling down beside the small child, he brushed a stray hair off her forehead and whispered something to her. Taryn could not hear what was said but the child's laughter sounded like music to her ears. Andalyn smiled up at Death as she took his hand.

Slowly the little girl pulled her hands away from Taryn's eyes, relieving her of the suffering that she and her brother had went through.

"I'm, so, so, sorry, Andalyn. I didn't realize that was happening to you." Angry tears tracked down Taryn's face.

"I'm alright now, Taryn," she replied in her tiny voice. Placing her small hand on her cheek, she whispered, "Save my brother," before fading away.

Farren gave her a moment to process all that she had seen before speaking. "Do you understand why he has chosen to spare the boy thus far?" With tears still filling her eyes, she shook her head, no. "It's because of you. You aren't even aware that you leave traces of yourself, of your powers, in those you align yourself with. It's part of the reason other Gaias' gifts appear to be greater when you are around. It's as if your very essence attaches to that person when they take root in your heart. Surely you have noticed how the boy's powers have improved dramatically since the two of you have become close. His father has certainly noticed, and he has become incessantly greedy since he realized that it wasn't just his son's essence he was draining. Ardyn Mitchell covets you, and intends for you to be his ultimate prize. But he also fears you because he can sense that the power within you is stronger than anything he has ever seen. So for now, he takes what he can from the boy. Soon, it won't be enough and the child's fate will be the same as his sister."

"Is there a way to stop it? Now that I know, maybe I can control whether part of my essence attaches to another. If I could, would Andyn be safe?"

"Even I do not hold all the answers, Child. What you are and what you can do is unique to your kind. You are an enigma. You may learn to control it, but it won't change what Ardyn is. He drained every last ounce of life from his daughter because of his greed. And while her death should have made her father wail in grief, instead it only served to make him more lustful. You pull life from the earth and push it inside what is hurt to heal the sick and the dying, much like you did with Larkin that day. Ardyn Mitchell takes life into himself seeking to prolong his own."

"It was you that I saw near the tree," she exhaled, realizing how close she had been to losing her love.

"I am everywhere that death lingers, Taryn. I should have taken Larkin Taylor that day, but you stopped me. It has been a very long time since I have been beaten. I must say, I find you rather fascinating."

"And you...Death, you are lingering here now because of Andyn?"

"Yes, my dear. As I said, you give freely. Your energy adheres to those you surround yourself with. The boy is covered heavily in your scent and his father grows even hungrier for a taste of you. To him, you are much like the most addicting of drugs. He will not be able to control himself the next time he begins taking it from the boy."

Fire flared dangerously hot behind her eyes. "His father is a monster...that I can see. But their mother...how could a mother allow this to happen to her own children? Mine would kill to protect me."

"You're holding the answer in your hands." He nodded to the picture frame that she still held.

With shaking hands, she slowly turned it over exposing the family portrait captured inside the frame. A searing heat tore through her body as she studied the picture intently. Closing her eyes, she exhaled. When she opened them, she found herself sitting next to Andyn underneath the tree, just as she had been before she spotted Farren.

Knowing that she could not ask Andyn to confirm what she already knew because of the Blood Oath that he had taken with his family, she turned to Kellan. "What color is Lilyan's hair?"

"Light brown."

"What about her eyes?"

"Green, like the kid's."

A gust of wind howled through the backyard catching everyone, except her, by surprise. Larkin knew instantly that she had caused the sudden shift in weather. He rushed to her side with Keiryn following closely behind.

"Andyn." She grabbed hold of his hands. He turned, looking up at her with his green eyes. Now that she knew how Andalyn had died, she could see the truth mirrored in them. She hugged him to her, her heart breaking for his sweet sister and all that they had endured. "I know everything." His eyes grew wide as relief flooded into them. "I'm not going to let them hurt you ever again," she promised as she stood. The relief she had seen quickly turned to worry. "I don't want you to witness this, Andyn. I need for you to go with Kellan right now." She motioned to Kellan, who moved in closer. "Take him to my home and wait for me there."

He nodded, understanding this was the moment that she had told him would come to pass. Without hesitation, he scooped the boy into his arms.

"What are you guys doing?" Larkin asked, inadvertently bringing attention to them.

"Stop," Ardyn thundered, silencing everyone. She placed herself between the hulking man and the boys. "What exactly do you think you're doing with my son?"

"He's leaving." Her face was stone-cold and unwavering.

"Nobody is taking my son anywhere," Lilyan warned, flipping her wrist discreetly in their direction and pushing her powers out against them.

"I think we both know that he isn't your son."

An audible gasp could be heard throughout their guests. Everyone who had been in the house was now standing outside, watching as the events unfolded. Ardyn and the woman known as Lilyan shared a confused look, before she held her hand out, aiming solely at the teenage girl.

"Taryn, don't," her mother shouted, running towards her, fearing for her life.

"Everything's going to be fine, Mother." Taryn threw a smirk at the imposter who was trying to Influence her.

"Andyn, come here," Ardyn thundered. The boy clung to her arm and shook his head defiantly. "I said come here!"

His would-be mother held her hand out to him, trying to force him to comply. "It's over. I know the truth, all of it. Your power of being an Influential is useless here," Taryn warned.

"Stop this nonsense, Taryn," Gastyn insisted, pushing through the crowd that circled them. "I know you're devastated by Andalyn's passing, we all are. But you can't give in to foolish notions."

Standing face-to-face with her teacher, she winked "Take a good look at her now and tell me if I'm being foolish," she directed as gasps and shrieks were heard throughout the guests.

"That's not Lilyan," Hava cried out.

Gastyn turned to the woman. Instead of the light brown hair and green eyes of Lilyan Mitchell, her hair was now black as night and her eyes a dark brown. His face frowned upon seeing the truth behind the lie. "Karvyn, you demon." He raised his hands to her offensively, along with the other members of their community.

"Impossible! That girl...she is the demon," the woman barked. "I am Lilyan Mitchell."

"No, you're not," Gastyn warned, his voice thunderous, knowing exactly how corrupt and vile she was.

Realizing that Karvyn's Influence over their community had waned, Ardyn gasped, trying to pretend to be as shocked as the rest of them. "What have you done with my Lilyan?"

Rage filled Taryn's heart as she watched him trying to play the innocent victim. "Liar!" She stepped to him as dark clouds formed overhead and thunder boomed angrily in the background.

"Taryn, stop this please," Larkin begged, knowing just how powerful Ardyn was.

Ignoring him, she continued to stare the large man down. "She was your child and you stole every ounce of who she was. She's dead because of you."

"I don't know what you're talking about, Foolish Girl."

"Lies!" she shouted. "Kellan, go now."

"My son isn't going anywhere," Ardyn growled.

Maxym, Teigan and Beldyn moved between the giant and the teen. Taryn sensed the rage that Maxym had been harboring since the exchange at school between Ardyn and his son. She knew that there was only one way to keep everyone else safe while she dealt with the monster.

"Leave," she ordered Kellan. Andyn jumped on his back and they disappeared into the woods, with Gerrick chasing after them, refusing to leave his brother without backup. Turning, she pushed her way through the men. "I challenge you, Ardyn."

"No," Ilya and Larkin screamed in unison.

Teigan wrapped his arms around her, trying to pull her back. "Let me go," she demanded, her tone absolute. He kissed the top of her head and released her, knowing she was using her Influence against him to force him to comply.

Ardyn's demeanor changed as he began to laugh. "You foolish girl. Did you really just challenge me?"

"Do you accept?"

Taking off his suit jacket, he smirked with delight. "I think it's time that someone teaches you a lesson about respecting your elders, Little Girl."

"It won't be you," Maxym growled.

With a gleam in his eyes, Ardyn smiled widely as he lobbed a large power orb at him.

Taryn raised her hands, stopping it before it made contact and crushing it to dust without as much as a blink of the eye. "Fight me, Coward."

"You can't do this, Taryn. He'll destroy you," Larkin begged, trying to pull her away.

"I love you, Larkin. But I have to do this. You don't know the vile things that he's done. I won't let him hurt my family."

Everyone had pushed back from her and Ardyn, with the exception of Larkin and Ilya. "Baby Girl, please don't do this."

"Mom, you're going to have to trust me. If I don't do this, Andyn's as good as dead."

"Run along, Mommy. Your daughter and I have some unfinished business," Ardyn taunted, rolling up his sleeves.

Larkin looked at her long and hard, sensing the danger lingering about in the air. Much to his dismay, his affliction refused to rise to the surface to allow him to protect her. "I'll fight beside you."

"You know how this works. I made the challenge and only I can battle him. It's the Gaias' way. You have to go. I don't want either of you getting hurt."

Knowing that she spoke the truth, both reluctantly stepped aside.

"I'm going to enjoy ending you," Ardyn grinned.

Not sure what to expect, she stood there waiting for him to make a move. It was not long before he hurled three enormous orbs at her. With her hands shaking, she managed to stop them all before they made contact. Though it was a struggle, she held them steady long enough to turn them to dust.

Never having faced an opponent who could do what she had done, Ardyn stood thoughtful for a moment, devising a plan to throw her off balance in hopes of breaking through her defenses. He sent six orbs in the direction of the bystanders. When she reached out to stop them, he hurled a monster of an orb at her, giving him his first direct hit.

Flying through the air, she smashed against a tree before falling to the ground. As she struggled to her feet, he hit her again. This time it pushed her against the surface of the dirt for about ten yards. While she was momentarily dazed, he created another orb but quickly bent it to the shape of a whip. Cracking it, he wrapped the end around her neck.

She could feel the constriction of his power as he pulled her closer to him while she clawed at the ground trying to get away. Finally he had her in his grasp. Placing his hands around her throat where the whip had been, he lifted her off the ground and began strangling the life out of her.

"No," Larkin roared, stepping forward to try to help her. He was stopped short by an invisible shield separating the battling duo from the rest of the onlookers.

"It's Taryn. She's keeping us out for our own protection," Ilya stated, remembering how she had created the same type of shield the day that she and Larkin had gone into the forest when she had been angry with him.

"I'm going to take my time with you," Ardyn proclaimed.

Taryn could feel herself slipping into a state of unconsciousness. "Listen to your pain," Farren whispered in her ear over and over again until he was certain that she heard him. Her eyes opened, showing the flames within. Drawing strength from her anger at everything Andalyn had shown her, she began to fight back.

She reached to touch his face, but it was no use. His arms were stretched out to the full length, making it impossible to make contact with him. With her feet dangling in the air, she tried to kick at his torso but he was too strong and powerful to be hurt by her weakened attempts. In desperation she grabbed at his hands, pulsing the power of Imperium through him.

"Give it to me, Baby," he howled in ecstasy, absorbing each new pulse of her attack deep inside.

Sickened at the realization of what he had just done, she pulled back and rapidly considered her options. When the only thought that came to mind was draining his powers from him, she shuddered with disgust. She was not a monster. There had to be another way. Closing her eyes, she tried listening to the pain like Farren had told her. Though it was faint, a little voice inside her head told her there was a better way.

"Kiss me," she gasped, using his obvious desire for her to her advantage, catching him completely by surprise.

"What did you say?" he smirked, loosening the grip he had around her neck ever so slightly to allow her to speak.

"I want to know what it's like to kiss someone so powerful before I die. Kiss me." She ignored Larkin's anguished cries.

A satisfied grin formed across his face. "Is that your final request?"

"Yes," she replied, appearing to have resigned herself to the fact that she was going to die at his hands.

"Then how could I deny you." He pulled her in closer while her feet still dangled in the air.

The moment she was close enough, she reached out with both hands and placed them on his chest. Immediately, she began pushing her own power into his body. Once she felt it had reached his core, she held it there to serve as a marker of sorts. Wrapping it around his, she began forcing his power back inside of him.

"No," he shouted, realizing her request was nothing more than a ruse. But for him it was too late. As she continued to force his own essence deep within him, it moved further and further away from his grasp.

Conscious of the fact that everyone's eyes were still focused on them, Taryn continued to hold her hands to his chest until she was certain that all of his power was back inside. Ardyn moaned as her gifts took hold and overwhelmed him. She was far more powerful than even he had known. Much like she did with her own emotions, she bound his powers into an imaginary box and forced the lid closed, effectively locking them away where he would be able to feel them, but not access them. As she began to withdraw her own from him, she felt another presence that didn't belong to him. Latching onto it, she took it with her.

"What have you done to me?" he shrieked, releasing his hold on her and dropping her to the ground. Taryn said nothing as she stood. In a desperate attempt to strike back, he held his hands out to her, trying to form an energy orb. He screamed in agony as his hands remained empty.

The entire community, including her own mother, gasped at what they saw. It appeared that she had stolen his power while somehow managing to leave him alive. It was the only thing that made any sense, and the only explanation possible in their eyes.

Unable to fathom why her daughter would expose herself in this way, Ilya could feel the shock setting in. Maxym pulled her against him, holding her tightly as she trembled.

"She can't be one of them," he prayed, fighting the tears that were building in his eyes. The girl that his son loved could not be the very thing that had killed his mother. How could that be possible?

The members of both packs watched in awe, even though it was more than apparent that their parents all felt very differently about the current situation.

Fear and worry blossomed through much of the crowd as their eyes remained focused on Ardyn. However, Agustin and Adalia Moore watched with rapt attention as the battle continued.

"Why you little..." Ardyn paused, noticing the smirk on Taryn's face.

"Careful there, Ardyn. You no longer have your powers to back up your bullish personality."

Full of rage, he ran screaming straight for her with the intentions of physically beating her to death if he could not use his powers to get the job done.

Arching her eyebrow while raising her hand for show, she watched as he ran into the invisible wall she had cast between herself and him, knocking himself unconscious.

Larkin, Keiryn and their packs howled with relief and pride. The mighty Ardyn had fallen, and Taryn had survived her battle with one of the most feared and powerful Gaias in the region.

The second she let the shield drop, Larkin ran to her, grabbing her up in his arms tightly and spinning her around numerous times. When he placed her feet back down on the ground, he looked deep into her eyes. Though flames still burned within them, he could see that she was in control of her emotions.

"Taryn Malone, don't ever do that again." He pulled her lips to his. It was their first kiss in nearly a week. Though it was brief, it brought them both a moment of joy in the midst of the chaos, renewing their connection to one another.

"Taryn," Gastyn called out, standing over Ardyn's limp body.

She walked to him and looked him in the eye. "Gastyn?"

"You need to go with Keiryn. Let him take you home, now." His tone was serious.

"What about her?" She glanced to the woman now known as Karvyn, concerned about what would happen once she left.

"Her power has been contained with rondoring rope," he answered, referring to the thin gold colored rope that was being used to bind her wrists. "It stops the flow of power to the hands of the Gaias that is bound by it, rendering their powers useless."

She would have preferred to lock the evil woman's powers away as well. That way she would know for certain that she could never use her power of Influence again in such a monstrous manner.

"Go now," he motioned to her.

"I'll take her," Larkin insisted.

"No," Gastyn argued. "We need you to stay here."

Taryn looked to Larkin and flashed him a half-smile trying to ease his concern, though she could not make sense of Gastyn's strange demeanor.

Larkin hesitantly tossed Keiryn the keys to his jeep and stepped aside, allowing her to pass by. "I'll be home as soon as I can."

She nodded to him in acknowledgement. Turning to walk with Keiryn, she paused, running back to Ardyn's body and grabbing the chain from around his neck. She pulled the clear vial that held her thorns out from beneath his shirt and jerked it off, placing it in her pants pocket.

"See you soon," she whispered, running her hand down Larkin's arm as she passed him once more. He extended it out as far as he could, trying to make their contact linger for as long as possible. Glancing over at her mother, who was ensconced in Maxym's arms, she saw the blank look on Ilya's face. Desperate to get her away as quickly as possible, Keiryn placed his arm around her shoulders and escorted her to the jeep.

CHAPTER FOURTEEN

The ride to the Malone home was mostly quiet as Keiryn struggled to find the right words to say. He could see the stress that had worn on her for more than a week had finally lifted. "Taryn?"

"Yeah?"

"I'm sorry that I ever doubted you," he stated, sorrow heavy in his tone.

She turned to look at him. "Don't worry about it. This was a learning experience for all of us," she shrugged, realizing her own shortcomings in what had happened. She knew that if it had not been for Farren allowing Andalyn to show her what she and Andyn had endured, things would have turned out much differently, especially for her young friend.

༄ႚ୧ඏႚ୧ඏ

Taryn called out to Andyn as she burst through the doors. He ran straight into her arms and held onto her for what seemed like an eternity. Tears of joy streamed down his face when he saw that she was safe.

"You're going to be okay. They can never hurt you again." She ran her fingers through his hair as he continued to hold onto her.

"What happened after we left?" Gerrick asked, surprised to see her unharmed.

"Taryn battled Ardyn," Keiryn answered proudly.

She pulled Andyn aside while Keiryn, Gerrick and Kellan discussed the events that had taken place, not wanting him to hear the details.

"Is he dead?" Andyn asked of her.

"No."

"Then how do you know that I'm safe?"

"I locked his powers deep inside. He can feel their presence in his very heart...but he can't touch them or use them." Seeing the sadness that continued to resonate in his eyes, she held her hand over his heart. "I want you to close your eyes." Trusting in her completely, he did what she asked. "I want you to think of Andalyn and the happy times that you shared." While she spoke, she pulsed the reclaimed energy of Andalyn's that she had taken from Ardyn into the boy. A smile formed on his face as it took hold inside of him. "No matter where you are or what you're doing, part of her will always live within you." She kissed him gently on the cheek.

When he opened his eyes, part of the sadness had disappeared and had been replaced by the twinkle that used to shine in his sister's. "You saw her didn't you?"

"Yes," she answered, sensing that he had spoken with his sister in his dreams.

"She said that you were going to be my family now. Was she right?"

"You are the little brother that I've always wanted," she smiled, embracing him in another hug.

Their quiet and peaceful moment was interrupted by the panicked shouts of Larkin. "Taryn!"

Sensing something terrible had happened, she rushed to him. "What is it?" she questioned, fearing that Karvyn had somehow broke free from her restraints. He grabbed her arms and began frantically pulling her to the front door. "What's happened?" she demanded, struggling against him.

The four other boys looked on in fear. In all the time that they had known him, they had never seen Larkin as desperate as he was now. "They're coming for you, Taryn. We have to get out of here."

Before she had a chance to say another word, Keiryn spoke. "Who's coming for her?" he asked, fearing that he already knew by the darkness in Larkin's eyes.

"The wolves."

"She's not Mortari, so why are they sending the wolves?" Kellan asked.

"There's no time to explain. Kellan and Gerrick will look after Andyn. But we have to go...now." His eyes darkened even more. The two boys nodded, accepting the responsibility that he had bestowed upon them. "Satisfied?" He looked to Taryn.

Seeing his fear and the strange color of his normally hazel eyes, she knew that whatever was coming terrified him far more than the thought of her battling Ardyn. "Yes."

Without another word, he took her hand and led her quickly to the jeep. Keiryn followed behind them, jumping into the backseat. "This isn't your fight," Larkin warned him.

"We took a Blood Oath. If they are coming for her, it's as much my fight as it is yours. And let's not forget one small detail, Brother," Keiryn stated, referring to how much of a threat Larkin would be to her.

"Fine." He threw the jeep into drive and spun the tires as he sped down the driveway.

The second they hit the paved road, Taryn turned to the boys looking for answers. "I don't understand what's happening. Who's coming and what does the Mortari have to do with it?"

"Ada's father sent word to the Elder Council that you stole Ardyn's powers during your battle. They've released the wolves to destroy you." His anger for the Moore family had never been greater, and if they survived what was coming, he intended to deal with them once and for all.

"The werewolves," she gasped. "Who told you that?"

"No one had to tell me, Taryn. I heard it when they put out the call."

"What do you mean, you heard the call?"

"It doesn't matter. They've been sent to kill you, Taryn," he replied, his voice trembling, hardly able to speak the last part.

"How's running away going to stop them?"

"I don't know, but we can't sit around and wait for them to knock on your door. They'll rip you to pieces before you have a chance to prove your innocence. I won't let that happen. We need time to figure a way out of this mess."

The sun was starting to set as they headed north out of Williams. Larkin drove with the windows down, concentrating on every distinct scent in the air, searching for any hint that the wolves were near.

Keiryn rummaged through the contents behind his seat, looking for anything that could be useful. "Here, put this on," he said, handing Taryn one of Larkin's hoodies to help stave off the chilly air.

"Thanks." She pulled it on over her head with great sadness in her eyes.

"What is it?" Keiryn asked.

She shook her head and inhaled deeply, trying to settle her emotions. "They're coming after me."

"We know."

She fought to hold back her tears. "Maybe you should just let them have me."

"No," Larkin admonished, turning his focus completely to her now.

"There's no reason for either of you to die because of me."

"I'll never let them take you, Taryn," he swore, as if his very existence depended upon it.

"Watch out," Keiryn shouted.

Larkin jerked his focus back to the road, but it was too late. The jeep plowed into the massive figure that stood in the middle of the roadway, causing the vehicle to roll over five times before it came to a rest on its top. When the dust settled, Taryn found herself alone with Keiryn still inside. Unbuckling the restraints, she dropped from the seat. As quickly as she could, she crawled to her unconscious friend. Placing one hand on his chest and the other on the ground, she healed the injuries he had sustained in the crash.

"Hey." She smiled as his eyes fluttered open.

"It was a wolf," he replied quietly, as he took a deep breath, surprised that he felt as good as new.

"We need to find Larkin and get out of here," she insisted, motioning for him to follow her out of the driver's side door that looked as if it had been ripped off while they rolled. Once outside, they crouched down beside the broken jeep and looked around for any sign of Larkin.

"He's close," she whispered, sensing his energy.

They had crept not even ten feet from the vehicle when they heard a low growl coming from nearby. Scanning the terrain that was lit only by the light of the moon, they caught a glimpse of a large shadowy figure less than fifteen yards away.

"Run," she shouted.

When he tried to scoop her into his arms, she pushed away. "I'm not going without you!"

Placing her hands on his shoulders, she pulsed her Imperium power against him, sending him sailing high into the night sky, hoping he would shift into his preferred form. With Keiryn now out of harm's way, she turned, planting her feet to stand her ground. She was prepared to let the beast have her if it meant saving both Keiryn and Larkin. As the large figure stalked towards her, she could see that it stood at least eight foot in height on its hind legs, and had to weigh close to four hundred pounds. It had light brown hair and black eyes. As those dark eyes bored into her, it continued to move closer, stopping a few feet away.

The creature bared its teeth in a menacing snarl. Just as he raised his arm to take a swipe at her, he was knocked off his feet by something even larger. The air filled with the sounds of growls, snarls and yelps as the two beasts battled ruthlessly.

In the midst of the chaos Keiryn made his way back to her, angry with himself for letting her force him away. He stood with his arms protectively around her as the two animals clashed. After only a few minutes, a final shriek pierced the air and was followed by a lingering silence.

She pushed away from him and walked quietly over to where she had last seen the creatures fighting. In the moonlight, she could see one of them lying motionless on the ground, with no sign of the other. As she crept closer to the body, she studied its strange features. The snout was elongated, much like a wolf. Fierce looking canines stuck out on either side of the creature's jaw. The hands and feet had razor sharp claws that were shiny in the moonlight. He wasn't dead. She knew that. Though he was injured and unconscious, he would recover soon, still intent on her destruction.

Keiryn snuck up behind her and placed a hand on her shoulder. "We need to go, Taryn."

"Not without Larkin." Jerking away from him, she looked around in search of her love. "Larkin," she called out, no longer worried about who heard. "Larkin!" She could sense that he was near, but there was something different, something she couldn't quite put her finger on.

Opening her mouth to call out to him again, she froze when a hulk-sized beast appeared before her from the shadows. It was much taller than the last. Standing at nearly ten feet high and weighing more than five hundred pounds, it was covered in jet black fur and had the most intense black-colored irises.

"Get away," Keiryn shouted, jumping between them.

"It's alright." She maneuvered around him to get closer to the beast. There was something strangely familiar in its eyes that called out to her. She studied the creature for a moment, searching those fathomless eyes as they bored into hers. "Larkin?" Reaching her hand out, she touched his fur-covered face as he bent down to her.

While she stroked her fingers curiously over its cheek, the beast shifted back into human form, revealing his true identity. "Larkin," she exhaled forcefully, wrapping her arms so tightly around him that it left him struggling for air.

"You didn't run."

"I won't run if it means saving either of you," she insisted.

"Would you run if it was the only way to protect us?"

"Of course I would."

"Good. Then you should know that when they arrived at your house and discovered that we were on the run with you…they extended the order to include killing us too. We are just as wanted as you now."

"How do you know that?" she asked, completely unaffected by the fact that he was a werewolf.

"It's part of being what I am. When the council makes a request, it sort of echoes through my head. Fortunately for us, they don't know that I exist, since the affliction set in at an early age for me.

"Can you communicate with them?"

"No. It's all one-sided," he shrugged in relief. He could only imagine what the council would have done to him if they had discovered that a twelve year old werewolf had existed.

Keiryn listened closely as Larkin shared the details of his affliction with them. It pained him to realize that he had spent so much time being angry with his best friend for something that had been out of his control. He could not fathom how difficult it must have been hearing the numerous orders being sent out, directing him to kill someone at such a young age. While his heart went out to him, he knew the danger was far from over. "We should probably get moving before he regains consciousness, or his friends show."

With the jeep totaled, they continued northbound on foot. Larkin carried Taryn on his back, running lightning-fast, while Keiryn took to the sky in the form of an owl, scouting for any sign of danger. They had no idea where they were going, but they knew it had to be as far away from friends and family as possible in hopes of keeping them safe.

Soon they neared the Grand Canyon's North Rim. The terrain quickly became treacherous as Larkin strayed from the regular trails. After nearly half an hour, Taryn convinced him to let her walk.

While they hiked, she thought about her mother and how she must be going out of her mind with worry and regret with everything that had happened since moving to Williams. The blank look on Ilya's face as she had walked past her earlier at the Mitchell's haunted her. Would her mom be alright? She would never forgive herself if something happened to her. Quickly, she pushed the memory aside knowing that she needed to be in control of her emotions, rather than a puppet to them.

Suddenly, Keiryn flew in, shifting into human form mid-flight. Larkin reached out his arm to help steady his friend. "There's about a dozen closing in four miles back. What are we going to do?"

"If we could get to the other side it would buy us some time," Larkin thought aloud.

"You both could fly across." Her suggestion was met with furrowed brows and frowns from her two companions.

"Maybe Keiryn could fly across, but I definitely can't," Larkin stated.

"Why not?"

"It part of the package of being sired, if you will, to the Elder Council. When they send out a call to our werewolf side, it halts our abilities to shift into another form until our mission has been fulfilled, or they withdraw the command that was set forth."

Taryn studied him thoughtfully. "Maybe the others can't shift...but you can, can't you?"

"I told you it's an Elder Council thing," he evaded.

"Then why aren't you trying to kill me like the rest of them?" she retorted. He paused, shooting her a contemptuous glance. "That's what I thought. You're not bound to the rules like everyone else. They didn't know about you, which makes their control over you much weaker than the others. If you wanted to, you could shift into any form you choose and fly away to safety with Keiryn."

"Taryn, I won't leave you. I can't…don't you get that?"

"I won't let the two of you die for me," she answered back heatedly.

Just then, a familiar voice whispered in her ear. "Go to the top of the highest plateau. The answers you seek are waiting there."

Knowing that his presence could only mean one thing, she had no reason to doubt him. She was not ready to lose either of these two precious boys to Death. "We have to get someplace high and that flattens out a bit."

"But that'll expose us and make us vulnerable," Keiryn argued.

"I need you both to trust me. It's the only way."

The boys shared a brief glance before nodding in agreement. "We're with you." Larkin motioned for her to hop onto his back again.

She did as he wanted, and soon they were ascending to one of the highest parts of the canyon. The distant howls of the werewolves echoed behind them.

"Hurry," Larkin shouted back to Keiryn as they climbed nearer to the plateau.

When they reached the top, breathless and exhausted, Keiryn exhaled, "Now what?"

"I'm not sure. Give me a minute," she replied, desperately listening for any sign of Farren, or the answers he had said would be waiting there.

Hearing the howls growing louder, Larkin knew it was only a matter of minutes before they were outnumbered with nowhere to run. "Taryn, Baby, no pressure …but they're almost here." His voice cracked with nerves as his eyes began to darken. In his heart he knew that he would fight to protect her until he took his final breath, but it wouldn't be enough. He loved her with every fiber of his being, and the few months that they had shared were far too short a time to have with her.

She ran to the edge and looked out over the massive canyon. Realizing she had led them to their doom, she sighed with a heavy heart, ready to sacrifice herself to the mercy of the beasts if it meant she could save them. Suddenly, a distinct pain stabbed inside of her stomach, causing her to double over and nearly fall off the edge. "Farren," she cried out, knowing that this was his way of showing her the answers she needed. As she rose to her feet, a strong gust of wind blew through, lifting her several inches off the ground, allowing her to hover in the air briefly.

With wide eyes and a smile on her face, she turned to face the boys. "I've got it."

"Great. You want to clue us in?" Keiryn stated, a hint of sarcasm present as the first werewolf came into view at the edge of the plateau, staring them down. The massive figure appeared all the more threatening in the light of the moon.

Larkin rushed over protectively, ready to defend her. "Well?" he asked, waiting for her to share the epiphany.

Taking him by the hand, she ran forward to where Keiryn stood, and grabbed hold of his hand as well. Still feeling the wind circling around them, she shivered with excitement as adrenaline coursed through her veins for a myriad of reasons. The army of beasts and their impending deaths should have been enough to send her heart rate through the roof, but instead she was giddily focused on the task before them.

By now, three more werewolves stood less than twenty yards away, joining the first.

"Well," Larkin prodded, seeing five more joining the ranks across from them.

"On the count of three, we need to turn and run straight for the edge and jump. Whatever you do, don't let go of my hands, either of you."

"What?" Keiryn shook his head in utter disbelief.

"Trust me, I know we can do this."

He looked to Larkin, who could only shrug in agreement, knowing this was their only chance of escaping imminent doom.

The werewolves formed a line as the rest of the members filled in, blocking what they saw as their prey's only chance of escaping. Snarling and chomping at the bit, they looked on, waiting patiently to take out the great threat to their kind.

Taryn released their hands and turned, studying the thirty or so feet that lay between them and the ledge of the canyon. "One," she said, settling her excitement for the moment. "Two," she continued, taking each of the boys by the hand again. "Three!"

As the trio began to run hand-in-hand, the werewolves made their move, chasing after them.

To Taryn, everything began to play in slow motion. While they ran, she looked over, glancing briefly at both boys. Feeling the heat of the werewolves breathing down their neck, there was not a moment's hesitation as they approached the edge. Taking a complete leap of faith, the trio jumped, both boys holding tightly onto her hand.

The moment their feet left the edge of the rock, she forced an invisible shield up to protect the werewolves from leaping to certain death. She knew they had no control over their actions. Letting them fall to the canyon floor below was unfathomable. Turning her head slightly, she watched as the beasts slammed into the barrier before stumbling around dazed and bruised, but unharmed.

Not even mid-way across the canyon, Keiryn looked down and immediately began shrieking, sounding much like a four year old girl would. Larkin looked around in awe. He could feel her controlling the winds swirling around them, carrying them across the wide expanse of canyon below. Reaching up with his free hand, he felt as if he could touch the moon.

"Whoa," he shouted with delight, glancing over at Taryn, whose face radiated with excitement. For a brief moment, they shared a look while Keiryn continued his high-pitched shriek.

As the other side of the ridge came into sight, Taryn found herself unsure of how to stop their momentum. Larkin quickly picked up on the change of mood as he saw the uncertainty wash over her face. She screamed, "hold on," at the top of her lungs.

In an instant, all three teens shrieked in near unison, sounding as though they were some part of a pre-school choir. When their feet hit the surface of the ridge, they let go of one another, flipping and rolling haphazardly until their bodies came to a rest.

Battered and sore, they lay on the ground with their chests heaving. Keiryn stared distantly into the night sky, sending up a silent prayer of gratitude for their survival.

Knowing everyone was safe, Larkin rolled over to where Taryn was a few feet away. He looked her in the eye with astonishment. "Exactly how many times have you jumped a canyon?"

"It was my first." Almost immediately after divulging this fact, she and Larkin broke into uncontrollable laughter.

"You're freaking insane, Taryn Malone," Keiryn scolded, still reeling from the nearly five mile jump they had just made.

Turning her head in his direction, she smiled an ornery smile. "How is it possible that you, The Bird Man, if I may, is so afraid of heights?"

"Ugh!" Finding her to be his most favorite pain in the ass ever, he reached over and placed his hand on the top of her head, rubbing it about. "Birds have feathers, duh."

"What a rush," she exhaled, taking one final look at the amazing night sky above them.

"What about the guys we left across the canyon?" Keiryn asked.

"I suspect they are just now finding their way off that plateau."

"Why didn't you let them jump behind us? It would have been problem solved, at least for a while."

"Keiryn, they didn't have a choice but to come after us. I can hold them no more responsible for their actions than I can Gastyn, and the rest of the adults for believing Karvyn's influence."

"Wow, I forgot how sensitive you were to all of that stuff."

Taryn rose to her feet and looked around, trying to settle her irritation with Keiryn's mentality. Sensing her struggle, Larkin suggested a plan. "I think we need to head north then cut across until we meet up with the Colorado River and follow it into Utah. Once we're there, then we can decide exactly where we want to go."

"The faster the better," Keiryn sighed, wondering how much progress the wolves that pursued them had made.

"Sounds good to me," Taryn agreed.

She looked so beautiful standing on the edge of the cliff with the moonlight shining down upon her. Deciding to take advantage of the moment, Larkin grabbed her and kissed her passionately, not knowing if it would be the last chance he would have to kiss her soft lips. When he pulled away, he found peace in the calm he had restored within her brilliant eyes. "We should really get moving."

ഇന്ദ്രഇന്ദ്ര

Over the next hour, Larkin and Keiryn took turns carrying Taryn on their backs as they sped across the ever-changing terrain.

Once they were several miles north of Glen Canyon Dam, she asked them to stop for a moment. She could see that both boys were beginning to grow weary, even though neither would admit it. Listening to the wind as it blew past, relief flooded her body when the voice that often accompanied it remained silent. For now, at least, they were safe.

"Are you alright?" Larkin asked.

"Yeah," she nodded, while stretching. "Larkin, if you were chasing after us, how would you go about tracking us?"

"I'd look for your scent. Why?"

"Is it our physical scent or the trace scent that our powers leave behind?"

"We track Gaias and Mortari by the lingering of their powers. If we couldn't find it, I guess we would start working off of physical scent."

"I see the wheels spinning, Malone," Keiryn stated, thinking how incredibly brave and fearless she'd been so far, making his heart ache for her even more.

"I have an idea." She hesitated. "I think I can scatter our scents in a different direction, to throw them off track. But there's just one thing."

"We're listening." Larkin ran his fingers through the length of her hair, offering his reassurance.

"I'll need to absorb some of your powers to do it." She waited to see their disgust. Much to her surprise, both boys shared a glance and shrugged without hesitation.

"Sure, whatever you need."

"Ditto," Keiryn echoed, noticing the relieved look upon her face. He could see just how much it scared her to even broach the subject. Not wanting her to pull away, he addressed the issue head on. "You do know that neither of us believes that you stole Ardyn's powers...right?"

She shrugged uncomfortably and bit her bottom lip.

"Of course we don't," Larkin reiterated, seeing the apprehension in her eyes.

Taryn walked to the edge of the small cliff where they rested, looking out over the water. "I think my mother did."

He came up behind her, slipping his arms beneath hers and walking his fingers gently across her stomach underneath the bulky hoodie that she wore. "What you did...it surprised a lot of people."

"What did Gastyn and the others say?"

"Look, it doesn't matter what they said or what they believed, Taryn. Keiryn and I, and our packs thought you acted heroically."

"But the adults think I'm like the Mortari?"

Having listened to their exchange, Keiryn's blood began to boil. "They are all fools. You shouldn't give a damn what they think, Taryn. I saw the look on the kid's face when you told him that they couldn't hurt him anymore. Relief like that only comes from leaving, what I can only imagine, felt like his own personal hell. When everyone else doubted you, you never backed down and never gave in. Because of that, he's still alive, and Ardyn and that imposter were exposed for what they truly are. I'm not going to stand here and watch you beat yourself up for our short-sightedness."

Just as she started to reply, a breeze kicked up and she heard Farren's faint voice. "Taryn," he whispered then disappeared, leaving her with a chill.

"We have to hurry," she cautioned, urgency showing on her face.

"What do we need to do?" Larkin asked.

Sensing their time was running out, she turned around and placed her hand on his chest, pushing her own power into him and wrapping it around his. She withdrew her own essence along with the part of his she had claimed, before moving quickly to Keiryn to do the same. Each boy felt a slight pinch of pain when she did this, but neither dared to show any sign of discomfort, afraid of the guilt that she would feel over it.

"Keiryn, I need for you to find a few sticks, size doesn't matter just as long as it is fibrous," she directed, moving to stand on a large rock.

Positioning herself on its peak, she inhaled deeply. She focused on amplifying the powers she had taken from each of them, and saturated it with her own. Exhaling, she carefully forced out a trail heavily laden with their scents, eastward.

Larkin held out his hand to help her down after she had finished. Almost as soon as he had, he chuckled.

"What is it?"

"You literally just jumped over the Grand Canyon, and here I am, offering you my hand to help you down off this little rock."

"Just because I'm capable of doing something for myself doesn't mean I can't appreciate that you care enough to offer anyways." She leapt into his arms.

As Keiryn approached, he saw the sweet moment between them and tried to suppress the irritation that rose in the back of his throat. "Here." He held out his hand, displaying the sticks that she had requested.

She slipped from Larkin's arms and reached out, taking them from him. "Thanks, Keiryn."

Giving his emotions a moment to settle, he followed closely behind her as she walked to the water's edge. "So what's the plan?"

"I thought we might travel by boat for a while so our physical scent goes off their radar," she replied, placing the sticks on the water's surface.

The boys watched in amazement as she transformed them into a simple wooden boat with two oars. The boat was fourteen feet long, five and a half feet wide and deep enough for them to lie down to get beneath the current breeze.

The three climbed in and made their way along the river to Lake Powell. Once safely there, Taryn held the small boat idle in the center of the lake, allowing them all to get some much needed rest.

ဆပ္သဆပ္သ

As nighttime gave way to the day, Taryn woke, finding herself sandwiched between the two boys. Careful not to wake them, she moved to the back of the boat and listened for any hint of Farren's voice in the breeze. The only sound she heard was the growling coming from their stomachs. She was relieved that Farren remained silent, but she also knew they would have to go find food very soon, and that meant going back onto land where they would leave a trail that the werewolves could pick up.

While the boys slept, she soaked up what she could of the sun's rays as it fought to peak through the clouds. A quiet giggle slipped past her lips when Larkin rolled over, slinging his arm across Keiryn's chest.

While the boys cuddled, her thoughts began to turn to the memories that Andalyn had shared with her. She recalled how much fear and pain the child had experienced in her tragically short life. Her heart broke all over again for the precious little girl and Andyn, causing her to reconsider if the punishment she had bestowed upon Ardyn had been severe enough.

"Taryn?" Larkin placed his hand cautiously on her knee.

Jerking out of the sad reality, she looked at him. "Larkin?"

"Is everything alright?" He inclined his head in the direction of the water churning violently around them.

Not realizing that she had let her emotions get so out of control, she reeled them back in, restoring calm to the water and settling the boat. "I'm sorry," she whispered, looking into his eyes, seeking refuge from the emotional storm still churning inside of her.

"You have nothing to be sorry for." He took her hand, placing it over his heart. "I love you, Taryn."

"And I love you." She focused on the steady beat of his heart beneath her hand.

"And we all love each other, blah, blah, blah," Keiryn teased, still lying down. Standing, he stretched and took a look around. His stomach growled loudly with hunger pangs. "I don't suppose you could somehow animate fried chicken, potato salad and homemade rolls?"

"I could grow us a fruit tree, but considering that we are in the middle of a lake not to mention the power signature that it would leave, I think we need to find another alternative."

"We are going to have to find something to eat, and soon," Larkin stated, noticing the grumbles and growls from his own stomach.

"Do either of you know if there is a marina nearby?"

"There are few back in Wahweap Bay," Keiryn remembered from his trips there with his father.

"Good! Maybe we can find something to eat on one of the boats there."

"It's worth a shot," Larkin agreed.

They made their way back to Wahweap Marina. Due to the cooler weather in the winter season, there wasn't another person in sight as they searched through the numerous boats moored there.

They hit pay dirt on one of the larger cruisers where they found a cache of canned food and bottled water.

Taking time to satiate their growling tummies, they began loading their boat with the food and supplies before heading back through the water ways up Lake Powell. She used her gifts to navigate the rapidly changing territory through the Green River until they had no other choice but to start walking on land.

After stuffing the bags they had taken with the remaining supplies, they pushed northward through the Flaming Gorge National Park into Wyoming, traveling via water whenever possible to help mask their scent. The rugged terrain was both treacherous and beautiful, causing each one of them to get caught up in the splendor of it all, nearly forgetting why they were there and what they were running from. Thankfully, they had one another to stay rooted in reality.

After three days on the run, they made their way into Yellowstone National Park. Physically and mentally exhausted, they came across a deserted Ranger's cabin and decided it would be the safest place to spend the night. Larkin started a fire in the fireplace while Taryn and Keiryn laid out blankets for them to sleep on.

Sitting comfortably in front of the crackling fire, she feasted on a can of peas while the boys finished off the remaining cans of tuna.

Scrapping the inside with his fork, Keiryn looked at her. There was dirt smudged across her cheek from where she had swiped her hair back from her face after clawing her way up a steep hill earlier in the day. Sitting there in her dirty, torn and tattered jeans and pale pink t-shirt, her hair an absolute mess, she still looked beautiful to him.

"Taryn?" He set his can to the side.

"Yeah?"

He was no longer able to keep his curiosity at bay. "How did you figure out what Ardyn and that woman were doing to the kid and his sister?"

For a moment, it grew very quiet inside the cabin. Larkin scooted closer to her, eager to hear her explanation as well.

Her chest rose and fell as she exhaled heavily, considering how crazy she was going to sound when she told them the truth. "Do you remember how I told you I saw someone the day you nearly died, and again at the hospital elevators?"

"Yeah," Larkin nodded, moving in even closer.

"He wasn't some figment of my imagination, he was real. At the dinner in honor of Andalyn, I saw him again." She glanced to them both, trying to gauge their reaction. When neither boy took their eyes off of her, she continued. "I followed after him."

"But we were watching you the entire time," Larkin interrupted.

"I know."

"Let her speak." Keiryn interjected.

"I'm sorry, Taryn. Please, go on."

"His name is Farren. People can't usually see him, but I can. He has an immense responsibility resting upon his shoulders, and for whatever reason, I can see and walk beside him."

"So this Farren...he told you what they were doing?" Larkin asked.

"Not exactly. He played a huge part in it, but in the end it was Andalyn who opened my eyes to the horrors that she and Andyn suffered at the hands of those monsters." Both boys now wore a look of confusion upon their faces. Confusion was something she could relate to herself. After swiping away the tears that swelled in her eyes, thinking about what the little girl had shown her, she

~ 433 ~

continued. "The entire time, I could see Karvyn for who she really was, but I had no idea that she wasn't the real Lilyan Mitchell."

"But you were suspicious of her," Keiryn commented.

"I was. But if it wasn't for Farren bringing Andalyn back to show me the truth, I'm not certain that I would have figured things out in time to save her brother…my brother."

"Farren can communicate with the dead?"

"You could say that," she replied vaguely, afraid the complete truth would be too much for them. "I owe him a debt of gratitude for what he's done for us over the past few days. I heard him whispering to me in the canyon. If not for him, we'd probably be dead right now."

"I remember, you shouted his name when we were near the edge," Larkin recalled.

"He whispered to you in the wind?" Keiryn wondered if it was Farren who had spoken to him the day they had saved her life.

"You've heard him too?"

"I think so. The day when we almost lost you."

"Here I thought you were crazy, just talking to yourself," Larkin shrugged, still processing it all.

"Did he tell you why he's helping us?"

"No, he didn't." She now wondered to herself why Death would help her cheat him so many times.

"Whatever his reasons, I'm grateful." Larkin kissed her on top of the head. He noticed a few bits of dirt and dried leaves in her hair. "Don't take offense, Taryn, but you could use a bath."

"And you couldn't benefit from one of your own?"

"There's a tub in the bathroom. If you want, Keiryn and I can grab the buckets from outside and fill it up with the river water. Then you could do that thing you do and heat it up."

"A bath sounds nice, but what about the two of you?"

"We can each take one after you. It's nothing to fetch fresh water if you will heat it up for us," Keiryn offered.

"Of course."

After the boys filled up the tub for her, she swiped her fingers across the surface of the chilly water, tempering it perfectly to her liking, before slipping into it. As she scrubbed the grime of the last several days away, she sighed in contentment. Once clean, she wrapped herself in one of the blankets, dreading the thought of putting her dirty clothes back on.

While Larkin and Keiryn each took their turns bathing, Taryn took their dirty clothes to the river and scrubbed them against the rocks, cleaning them as well as she could. Once she was done, she draped them over the low hanging branches of nearby trees, blushing when she touched their underwear.

Concentrating, she kicked up the wind to a fever pitch, drying the wet clothes in a matter of minutes. Keiryn and Larkin stood on the porch of the cabin wrapped in blankets of their own, watching her in fascination as her hair whipped around.

Larkin smiled as the wind died down and she turned to face him, blushing when she realized she had an audience. Pulling her blanket more securely around her, she gathered up the dry clothes and carried them back to the cabin.

"You are an incredible girl, Taryn Malone." He leaned in and planted a soft kiss on her lips as she handed him his clothes.

Feeling incredibly vulnerable dressed only in a blanket she blushed again before handing Keiryn his clothes and stepping inside to change. Once everyone was dressed, they laid the blankets back out on the floor. She settled down between the two boys, lying her head on Larkin's arm as he slipped it underneath her. Giving in to sheer exhaustion, she drifted quickly to sleep.

In the dead of night, Larkin was awakened by the sound of a twig snapping outside. As his heart thundered in his chest, he listened closely. Closing his eyes, he searched for any hint of power coming from the other side of the door. Finding nothing, he sighed in relief. Glancing around, he saw Taryn snuggled up in a ball with Keiryn's arm flung around her. Though a part of him knew he should be jealous, he was strangely unaffected. She was his, of that he had no doubt. He knew Keiryn had strong feelings for her, but he had promised not to come between them and he knew that he could trust his brother's word. Deciding no harm would come from the innocent contact, Larkin closed his eyes and drifted back to sleep.

CHAPTER FIFTEEN

"Taryn Malone," a strange voice thundered from the other side of the cabin door, waking the trio from their slumber as dawn broke.

"Who is that?" Keiryn jumped to his feet.

"I don't know, but he's not alone." Larkin peered out the window, sensing several werewolves in the area.

"They can't come in. I'm blocking their entry." She listened closely for any sign of Farren while glancing at the man.

"Good, you're awake," the man stated, catching a glimpse of her in the window.

"What do you want?" Larkin shouted.

"The Elder Council has decided to allow you the opportunity to dispute the claims made against you." His tone was void of any emotion.

Taryn opened the door to look him in the eye. "Who are you?" He was tall and slender, with wavy black hair and dark gray eyes. His face showed the signs of someone in their late thirties or early forties. Though his build did not appear imposing, there was something in the way he stood that made him unnerving to look at.

"I am Nelmaryc, a representative of the Elder Council. I have been tasked with convincing you to turn yourselves in and face trial for your crimes."

"Supposed crimes," Larkin corrected, standing behind her with darkened eyes.

"Ah, yes...supposed crimes." Nelmaryc studied the teen, noticing the distinct color change in his irises. Inclining his head, he nodded slightly.

"And if we choose not to go with you?" Keiryn asked, standing next to Larkin.

"Then your families, as well as numerous members of your community will stand trial in your place. And just so we are all on the same page, I brought a friend of yours along to inspire cooperation."

"Jonesy," Taryn gasped, sensing his presence. "I want to see him."

"Very well, then." He turned, looking over his shoulder. "Bring me the boy."

A moment later, several wolves appeared as they escorted their friend into sight. Jonesy appeared to be physically unharmed, but fear showed deep in his eyes.

"Are you alright?" Taryn asked him.

"Yes," he nodded hesitantly as one of the werewolves snarled in his direction.

Larkin and Keiryn each grabbed hold of her arms, holding her in place, knowing she would jump to protect him.

"Let go of me."

"No, Taryn. That's what the Council wants. If you do something, they can say they acted in self-defense," Larkin whispered to her.

Turning back to Nelmaryc, she stated, "I'll go with you, but they stay here." She motioned to Keiryn and Larkin with a nod of her head.

"I'm afraid that won't be possible. The Council insists that you all come before them," he answered, his voice still void of emotion.

"That's good, because we would insist on going," Larkin growled, drawing a curious look from the Council's mouth piece and a disapproving look from Taryn.

"Very well then." She nodded for the man to step aside. Once he was out of the way, she stepped outside, leaving Larkin and Keiryn still locked behind her protective shield, much to their dismay. She walked over to where Jonesy stood, still surrounded by the giant beasts. Several snarls and low growls could be heard, but she remained unphased. "Jonesy, are you alright?" She took his hand in her own.

"Ye, ye, yes," he stammered, looking down at the ground.

The beast who had growled at her friend earlier, did so again. She stepped to him, locking eyes with the auburn colored animal. He brought his snout within millimeters of her face and growled again, sending Larkin into an absolute frenzy behind the shield. She did not flinch as his humid and stinky breath caressed her cheeks.

"I think this one could benefit from a breath mint," she smirked with a twinkle in her eye, eliciting a response.

Just as he raised his arm to strike her, two other werewolves bounded, taking him to the ground. She stood, feet planted, watching their response. Satisfied, at least for the moment, that they were safe from harm, she lowered the shield that had prevented Larkin and Keiryn from exiting the cabin.

"What the hell, Taryn?" Larkin growled, letting her know his discord with what she had just done.

"I had to be sure they didn't mean to harm us the second I let my guard down."

"Then next time let me be the one to go enrage the werewolf."

"Are we ready now?" Nelmaryc inquired, appearing to grow tired of waiting.

"Yes, we're ready," she answered, holding tightly to Jonesy's hand while Larkin and Keiryn followed closely behind them.

Once they came to a small clearing Nelmaryc held out his hand. Before him appeared a large, arched gateway of sorts.

"What is that?" she asked.

"It's an Adora Gateway," Jonesy whispered.

"It can transport you from one plane to another by simply walking through it," Larkin offered, knowing she still had no idea what it was by name alone.

"A Gaias by the name of Adora James discovered how to bend her powers to open a portal to allow travel between the various planes of the Earth. Most people didn't believe that other planes exist. Adora did, and she spent years trying to prove it. When she finally made the discovery, she opened whole new worlds to others of our kind. Still to this day, very few Gaias have the ability to open an Adora Gateway. It's a very rare gift. The Elder Council has claimed one of the many planes for their own. They call it Hypatia. That means highest or supreme in ancient Greek," Jonesy rambled, giving her specific details as he struggled with his nerves.

"Well that's original." She rolled her eyes, eliciting a growl from the nearest werewolf. "Thanks, Jonesy." She smiled, squeezing his hand, easing his worry with her gift of Influence.

Flanked now by werewolves standing on either side of them, they walked through the gateway. As Taryn emerged, she immediately noticed how very similar this plane was to the one they had just left. Directly in front of them, a stone building stood tall and formidable against the pale blue sky. It was flanked on either side by large trees towering several hundred feet in the air.

Following Nelmaryc, they ascended the stone steps of the building until they reached a heavy set of black wooden doors with ornately carved symbols decorating them. With a slight flick of his wrist, the doors opened and he led them down a long hall that boasted tiled floors and gleaming gold ceilings. At the end of the hall stood another doorway, this one arched and in shiny gold.

When the door was opened, they stepped into the large room, very similar to the secret room behind Gastyn's classroom. Taryn gasped as she saw nearly every member of their community seated in chairs along one side of the room, while her mother, Gastyn, Maxym and Teigan sat on the other. She held her head high as she gave each of them a nod of acknowledgement. Several feet away, Ardyn, Karvyn and Andyn stood with werewolves guarding them.

Forgetting about where they were, she ran to him, wrapping her arms tightly around the boy. "Andyn, are you okay?" She checked him over thoroughly.

"Yes." He glanced over to his father and Karvyn.

Something about Ardyn caught Taryn's eye. The man who used to stand with his shoulders back, exuding arrogance, now stood, head bowed, body jerking with a steady stream of drool running from the corner of his mouth.

"Taryn Malone," a new voice called out, one that was dark and menacing.

"Yes?"

"Step forward, Child," the mysterious voice commanded.

She did as directed, hesitating before leaving Andyn standing by the monsters that had tortured him and his sister. Larkin and Keiryn filled in protectively behind her while Jonesy took a seat next to Jayma, on the side with the rest of the community. His aunt grabbed hold of him, taking him into a fierce hug.

In grand fashion, the farthest end of the room that had been concealed in darkness lightened, revealing the thirteen members of the Elder Council. Each member was seated upon a large wooden throne with blood red velvet cushions beneath them. They were dressed in peculiar fashion, almost as if they had not yet realized it was the twenty-first century. The twelve men on the council wore dark black trousers and shirts, with long black blazers over them. Their shoes were shiny black, and polished to perfection. The lone woman wore a sedate black dress with long sleeves that flared out at the wrists. It tapered in at her waist with a glittering gold belt before flaring out again at her hips.

Taryn studied them, committing each face to memory. The man in the middle snapped his fingers. A young boy, appearing no older than seven, came forward carrying a dark stick. He sat it on the floor in front of the thrones and walked away as quickly as he could. With a flick of his wrist, the man in the middle turned the stick into a long black table that contained name plaques for each council member.

She fought hard not to laugh at the absurdity of the gesture. It reminded her so much of the way council meetings were portrayed on television.

The lone woman on the council was Siobhyn. Her fiery red hair made her flesh as pale as the winter snow, setting off her vibrant green eyes. Seated next to her was Lucien. He had long blonde hair that was pulled back from his stark features in a ponytail that hung half way down his back. His eyes were violet in color and void of emotion, much like Nelmaryc's.

Taryn could sense the fear from her friends and family as it spread like wild fire, filling the air. Trying not to let it deter her, she continued her perusal of the council. Emryck sat next to Lucien. He appeared to be extremely tall with brown hair that was shaved close to his head. His brown eyes almost perfectly matched his caramel-colored skin.

Next to Emryck sat Conus, who was a rotund man with laugh lines around his mouth. His long nose and pointy chin made him look as if he had been drawn as a caricature of his normal self. Sitting next to him, was Julius. His hair was a vibrant shade of ginger and his green eyes sparkled with kindness, something that seemed to be lacking in the others.

Seated beside Julius, was his cousin, Nodryck. His beady black eyes bored into hers as she studied his face. He could be classified as handsome with his jet black wavy hair and strong features if it weren't for those creepy eyes. Turning away from his piercing stare, she found Odyn looking at her curiously.

Odyn held the prominent middle spot. He appeared to be the oldest member of the council with his gray hair, beard and bushy eyebrows. Though he had a keenness in his eyes, he also had a great weariness about him, as if time had finally caught up with him.

Oleg sat to Odyn's left. Though he had been the one to animate the table into existence, his respect for Odyn was obvious, leading her to believe that he was second in command. Much like Nodryck, his dark brown eyes bored into her, as if they were searching deep within her very soul for something. She wanted to cringe from the weight of his stare, but she stood firm, showing no fear. He wore his hair long and straight, in a muted shade of brown.

Grandyn and Dravyn sat to Oleg's left. They appeared to be brothers, if not twins. Both had jet black hair and light gray eyes and were of Asian descent. Their attention seemed to be focused somewhere other than her. Glancing around, she realized they were studying Ardyn with intense scrutiny.

Barclay sat to the left of Dravyn, tapping his elongated fingernails on the table. He had golden hair with dark eyes that stared distantly through her, almost as if he were somewhere else. Paydyn and Hermyn rounded out the council. Both had unassuming features of mousy brown hair and dull brown eyes. They stared at her pointedly, trying to look intimidating, but she found them to be anything but.

"Taryn Malone, do you know why you have been brought before this council?" Oleg's deep voice thundered.

Taking a step forward, she held her head high and looked at him. "To stand trial for saving the life of my brother, Andyn Malone." Her voice was unwavering and unapologetic.

A smirk emerged on the face of Nodryck as he muttered something beneath his breath, drawing her attention. He looked down at her with his dark eyes. She watched as his normally attractive face turned hideous, covered with large boils and sores, before transforming back to its original complexion.

"You have been accused of stealing the powers of another for your own gain. In addition, you and your friends attacked a member of the Council's Guard. How do you plead?" Oleg continued.

"Not guilty on both counts."

"Are we bothering you, Child?" Emeryck inquired, sensing her annoyance.

"To be quiet honest, yes." She drew looks of contempt from the majority of the council members and curiosity from the others. "You sent your 'guard' to kill me for something that is untrue."

"So you deny stealing Ardyn Mitchell's powers?" Nodryck chided.

"Yes. I did not steal his powers. I only locked them deep inside where he can no longer access them."

"Lies," Conus countered. "We've studied him closely and there isn't any sign of power residing within him."

"There is if you know where to look," she retorted.

"Silence," Odyn, the eldest member of the council bellowed. "I'm interested in hearing more about why you felt the need to save this boy." He pointed in Andyn's direction.

"I discovered that his sister died at the hands of that monster and his witch, and I knew that he was going to do the same to my brother, Andyn."

"And how, exactly, is it that you knew this, Child?"

"Because his sister showed me."

"She told you this before she died?" Julius inquired, leaning forward in his throne.

Taryn swallowed hard, knowing her answer would cause those present to doubt the credibility of her story. "No, after she had already passed."

Grumbles resonated throughout the council and a mischievous gleam came into Nodryck's eyes as he practically bounced in his seat with excitement.

"Rishyn, step forward," Odyn called out.

From the shadows behind them, a beautiful woman with white hair, porcelain skin and pale grey eyes stepped forward. She was dressed in a blood-red, silk gown. "Yes, Odyn?" she bowed.

"I would like to resolve this matter quickly. Read her mind and tell us if she speaks the truth."

With her hips pushed forward, the woman stalked towards Taryn. "You're hand," she declared, holding out her own.

"What are you?" Taryn could sense something strange inside of her, a great power she had never felt before.

"I am a Seer. My gift is to see into the minds of others. If you are telling the truth, you have nothing to fear. But if you're lying, I will know, as will they," she answered, her tone hollow.

Taryn glanced back to Larkin and Keiryn. She could see the trepidation written plainly on their beautiful faces. Flashing them a small smile, she turned back to face Rishyn.

She held out her hand for the woman, surprised at the strength in which she took it. Locking her eyes with Taryn's, she began searching inside her head for the truth. She fought the chills that so desperately wanted to come as she forced herself to allow this stranger's powers to trail through her thoughts and memories, though she remained cautious not to allow the woman to see anything that could be seen as a violation to the council's rules and codes.

When Rishyn found what she was looking for she closed her eyes and began taking in every minute detail of the memory. Her body jerked violently as she held onto Taryn's hand, causing alarm amongst the council. Soon it was over and Rishyn quickly withdrew her powers and her hand. When her eyes opened, they were full of tears. Taryn knew they were from witnessing Andalyn's death. The woman staggered away from her, still reeling from what she had seen and felt from the vision.

"Well?" Odyn demanded of her.

"The child speaks the truth. Ardyn Mitchell murdered his wife, stole his daughter's essence and planned to do the same to the boy and to her," she spoke, never taking her eyes off Taryn.

He could tell the Seer was holding something back. "And how is she able to know such things?"

"Because she walks and talks with…Death." The room filled with audible gasps from everyone present.

Much of the council shifted uncomfortably back and forth in their seats as they studied this strange girl. Never had they heard of such a thing being possible. Death could only be seen when he came to claim a soul. How could this girl see him and speak with him when she was very well amongst the living.

Taryn looked over her shoulder to Larkin and Keiryn. She could see that they now fully understood what it was that she had omitted when telling them about Farren.

Larkin stepped to her and wrapped his arms protectively around her. "I'm sorry," he breathed, regretting every moment that he had doubted her.

"You're mistaken, Rishyn. That is impossible," Nodryck hissed, slamming his hand against the arm of his throne, breaking it into a thousand little splinters. Jealousy spurred inside of him as he stared darkly at the young girl.

"I see only truth," Rishyn bowed, falling onto her knees in front of him. "Death allowed the little girl to show her their suffering."

"Bring the boy and his parents forward," Nodryck thundered to the guards. He gestured for them to bring Ardyn even closer so that he could search him once more for any sign of power residing within.

Nodryck, Siobhyn, Lucien, Julius and Odyn held their hands against Ardyn's chest. After several minutes, a smile of delight formed upon Julius's face.

"I can feel it," he marveled, turning to look at Taryn. "His power is there, deep inside. It's very hard to find," he stated, almost to himself. "Search deep, Sister, Brothers. It is there." Turning to Taryn with rapt curiosity he asked, "How did you manage to pull off such a feat, Child?"

"I had to do whatever I could to save my brother," she answered, continuing to make her feelings for Andyn known. "I am not Mortari. I don't take another's powers to prolong my own life."

"I don't feel anything," Nodryck remarked, rolling his eyes at the praise his cousin had bestowed upon the girl.

Odyn squinted in concentration. She watched as a glorious smile lit up on his face. "Wait…yes…it's there." Soon Lucien and Siobhyn nodded in agreement, burning Nodryck to his core.

Growling in disgust, he bellowed, "If you are all so certain that this girl has done no wrong, then let's move on to sentencing this family."

"Very well," Odyn agreed, motioning for the guard to pull Ardyn back. "Before we do, I have a question for young Taryn. Why is it that you chose this to be his fate after all that he has done? Why not death?"

"I felt that this punishment would be far worse than death for someone like him. Anyone who could harm a child, let alone a child of their own, deserves to suffer in madness." Her words held a distinct bite. Seeing the current state of Ardyn, she knew, without a doubt, that he was slowly going mad from not being able to touch the power that he could still feel churning inside of him.

Odyn nodded to her, before turning back to the council. In a flash, the lights above them dimmed, leaving only the guards, their family and members of their community visible.

Taryn looked to her mother and saw relief flood her eyes, providing her with comfort that only a parent could to their child. "I love you," Ilya mouthed to her.

"I love you, too, Mom."

Feeling a weight lifted from her shoulders, she turned her focus back to Andyn. "Soon we'll be back home, and this will all be a distant nightmare."

"I love you, Taryn."

The lights brightened and the Elder Council came into view once again. Odyn began speaking, reading the charges against Ardyn and Karvyn.

⁋⁙⁄⁙⁄⁋

"Prepare yourself, Taryn," Farren whispered, standing beside her as she watched over Andyn protectively from twenty feet back.

"What are you doing here?" she gasped, knowing what his presence meant.

"You know why I'm here. I am everywhere that death lingers," he replied in his silky smooth tone.

"Are they going to kill me?"

"I'm not here for you." He motioned in Andyn's direction.

"No!"

⁋⁙⁄⁙⁄⁋

The moment she stopped screaming, she found herself back in the present, listening to Odyn reading the sentence.

"A determination has been made that the best way to protect our kind is to execute all three of these individuals. The crime of one shall be the crime of all."

"I won't let you," Taryn thundered, as she rushed towards Andyn.

Nodryck, who was elated by her response, motioned for the five werewolves standing closest to attack. Before he had finished giving the order, Larkin's protective instincts kicked in and he shifted into werewolf form, leaping into battle, desperate to save her.

The werewolf standing closest to Andyn slipped past him and reached Taryn. Lunging, he caught her, biting forcefully into her right shoulder. The second his canine fangs pierced her flesh, he felt a searing pain. Unable to tolerate the merciless burn ravaging him from the inside out, he released her, yelping as he fell to the floor, his body wracked with convulsions as he shifted back into his human form.

The screams of their fallen brother caused the other werewolves to stop their fighting momentarily, allowing Larkin to send them all to the ground in one crashing blow. Immediately he went to Taryn's side, standing protectively over her as the other werewolves moved in closer, trying to catch a glimpse of their brother.

Keiryn rushed over, fearful that she would try to undo the suffering that the man was experiencing. "You can't Taryn. They'll kill us all," he whispered, wrapping both her and Andyn in his arms protectively.

"I know, but I have to at least ease his suffering."

"Ease it, don't cure it," he reiterated, before letting her go.

"I'm sorry," she cried, watching him writhing in pain. Reaching out she placed her hand against his forehead and used her gift of Influence to remove him from the suffering of his body. "It's alright, go with him. You will find peace and happiness," she nodded to Farren, who was now standing on the other side of his body. She watched as the man's spirit stood and walked beside him, disappearing into the darkness.

The council members watched in confusion, uncertain of exactly what had just happened to their guard.

"He's gone," she whimpered, running her fingers gently along his cheek.

Still in werewolf form, Larkin motioned for Keiryn to move her away from the soulless body. For a moment, he glanced to where the members of his community were seated and saw the shock present on their faces. He could only assume that part of the shock was due to their discovery that he was a seventeen-year-old werewolf.

"Heel," a man dressed in black commanded as he unleashed a whip much like the one that Ardyn had used against Taryn onto Larkin, causing him to yelp with pain.

Already having moved to her feet, Taryn turned and held her hand out to him, crushing the power-whip into dust. "Don't you dare strike him," she seethed, stepping directly between the man and her love with both hands held out in front of her, keeping part of her attention focused on making her wounds bleed.

"He's a werewolf, and therefore property of the Elder Council."

"He belongs to no one."

"Taryn," Odyn addressed her, his voice sorrowful.

"Yes?" she replied, not turning her back on the man dressed in black.

"Please, look at me." With fire still raging behind her brilliant eyes, she did as he asked. "Listen to me, Dear Girl. We see that you're only trying to protect those who you care deeply for, but we have ruled in the best interest for all of our kind. This boy has no other family and we cannot take a chance that he will turn into the monster his father so desperately wanted to become."

"I'm his family," she countered.

"Just because you say it, or want it to be, doesn't make it so, Little One."

Watching from the side, Gastyn caught sight of something on Taryn's shoulder through the tears in the fabric of her shirt. "Wait," he shouted, after understanding what it was he was seeing.

"What's the meaning of this interruption?" Oleg frowned.

"If you would please indulge me, I only need a few moments of the Council's time."

"Very well," he nodded, motioning for the guards to allow him to come closer.

Once close enough, Gastyn took another look at her shoulder, getting lost in the detailed image he could now clearly see.

"Well?" Nodryck demanded, bringing him back from distraction.

"You said that the reason to destroy the boy was due to the fact that he doesn't have any family?"

"Yes, without the guidance of a pack or family, the boy poses too great of a risk," Odyn answered.

"But if he belonged to a pack, would the boy's sentence be rescinded?"

"Yes, but he doesn't belong to any pack. He is twelve, and therefore too young to be a member of an official pack."

"But if he did…you would allow him to live?"

"Yes, yes, yes," Nodryck hissed, growing irritated by the redundant questions.

"Andyn, please remove your shirt and show the members of the council your right shoulder," Gastyn directed, praying his hunch was correct.

The boy did as his teacher had instructed. When the council gazed upon him they saw the unmistakable mark upon his shoulder. The intricate tattoo was unmistakable in the light of the chamber. An exquisite ancient looking tree stood alone in the middle of a grassy meadow as a dark cloud hovered above with a brilliant bolt of lightning angling down to strike the center.

"To which pack leader does this boy belong?" Nodryck questioned, fury raging behind his eyes as he scanned the room for possible candidates.

"My brother belongs with me," Taryn declared.

Immediately, she drew laughs from most of the members of the council and the guards who were present. The only four not laughing were Siobhyn, Odyn, Emryck and Julius.

"Show us your shoulder, Girl," Siobhyn demanded.

"No woman, let alone some teenage girl, has ever been a pack leader," Nodryck interrupted.

"Then you will allow her to show us her right shoulder, Brother," Siobhyn countered, her tone biting. Once he sat back in his throne and conceded, she turned her attention back to Taryn. "Now, show us your shoulder."

She turned around and pulled what remained of that side of her shirt off her shoulder.

"There's nothing more than blood and her wounds," Nodryck cackled.

"Look beyond the blood," Gastyn persisted, drawing a look of contempt from Nodryck, Conus and Barclay.

Julius rose from his throne and walked down to take a closer look. Even through the blood, he could clearly see the larger tattoo of a pack leader present upon her shoulder. He took his finger, holding it just above her flesh and traced its outline with amazement, before pulling away and covering his mouth with his hand.

He continued to look her up and down thoroughly. As he began to circle her, Larkin released a low growl of warning. Julius paused for a moment and looked to the werewolf with softened eyes. He sensed the beast would protect this girl even if it cost him his own life, a quality that he admired in such a young person. Turning his attention back to Taryn, he finally stopped to stand directly in front of her. "You are something quite unique," he whispered, his tone comforting.

"What is it, Cousin?" Nodryck asked curiously, standing again.

Julius reached up just shy of touching her cheek and flashed a brief smile before answering his ill-tempered cousin. "This young girl, she is a first for our kind. She is, indeed, the pack leader to this boy."

"But she isn't even eighteen years of age," Lucien mused.

"Regardless, she bears the symbol of a pack leader, and the boy's marking shows their connection to be true and irrefutable," Julius proclaimed.

"Come, Julius. We must convene," Odyn directed.

He took a final look at the girl before stepping around her to rejoin the rest of the council. As he took his seat, the lights above them dimmed and they disappeared once more.

During the council's absence, Taryn grabbed hold of Andyn's hand and kept him by her side while Larkin shifted back into human form. She, Gastyn and the three boys stepped aside, allowing the werewolves to claim the corpse of their fallen comrade from the grand room.

"I am deeply sorry for what my blood did to him."

In a surprising move, the largest of the werewolves stepped towards her. Larkin immediately moved between them, but Taryn shook her head and he hesitantly stepped aside.

The caramel colored beast shifted into human form, revealing his tanned skin and blue-green colored eyes. His hair was blonde, as if the sun itself had kissed the top of his head. He towered over her by almost a foot. Though she should have been afraid from his sheer size alone, the kindness she could detect in his eyes put her at ease. "You spared his suffering and showed mercy. For that, we are grateful." He bowed his head to her for a brief moment. Straightening, he gave her one last curious look before shifting back into the form of a beast and walking away.

"Taryn," Gastyn stated, placing his hand on her shoulder. "I'm sorry that I couldn't see through Karvyn's veil. But I am more sorry that I continued to doubt you once I had."

"It's alright, Gastyn. I understand that it's not always easy to see what I do. Besides, what you did for Andyn…you may have just saved us all."

She walked over to where her mother, Maxym and Teigan stood, still holding onto Andyn. "Looks like our little family has grown." Ilya choked back her tears as she gazed upon the boy who would now be her son.

"So do I call you, Mom?" Andyn asked, looking to Ilya with hope in his eyes.

"If it's alright with Taryn, I'd be honored, Andyn." She cupped his cheeks with her hands and placed a tender kiss on the boy's forehead.

"Sis?"

"Definitely."

The young boy's face lit with the most brilliant of smiles as he looked at his new family.

"Hey," Kellan shouted from the other side where everyone else in the community was being held.

Taryn looked to her mother, Maxym and Teigan with nothing but love in her eyes for them all. "We'd better go say hi."

"We'll be home soon," Ilya exhaled, watching them walk away as she leaned against Maxym with relief.

"My man, the legit pack member, let's take a look at your ink," Kellan grinned as they approached.

Eagerly and with pride, Andyn turned his shoulder exposing his tattoo to Kellan and the rest of the pack members.

"Awesome," Kellan exclaimed, hugging him tightly. While he couldn't help but feel a hint of jealousy over the kid's ink, he was elated that his young friend was safe because of it.

"You're more of a badass than any of us ever knew, Kansas," Nalani smiled, reaching over and bestowing a monstrous hug upon her. "Hey, Kid, that doesn't mean you get to take my place as this badass girl's best friend."

"You can be her best friend, Lani. She's my sister now."

Hava and Beldyn Love cautiously approached the teens. "Taryn," Beldyn spoke.

"Hello," she greeted them warmly, sensing their apprehension. Before Beldyn could speak again, she continued. "Mr. and Mrs. Love, I want to apologize to you, your children and the rest of the community for being drug here in front of the council because of me." She glanced around them to the other adults and parents who looked on with worry in their eyes.

"Taryn, you dear girl, our entire community owes you an apology as well as a debt of thanks," Hava replied, reaching her hand out and cupping Andyn's cheek. "You saved this sweet boy when no one else could." She fought to hold back her tears.

"Taryn's the best," Andyn chimed in, wrapping his arms around her.

"She is rather incredible," Beldyn agreed, looking down with great admiration in his eyes.

"The Council is ready to speak." Nelmaryc emerged from the darkness, directing everyone back to their seats and insisting that Taryn, Larkin, Keiryn, Andyn and Gastyn come forward once more.

As Taryn walked past the length of the galley in which her community sat, she saw two figures that she hadn't noticed earlier. Agustin and Adalia Moore sat quietly at the back of the group with their heads bowed, avoiding looking directly at her. A small fire erupted in the pit of her stomach as she recalled Larkin telling her that it was Agustin who had initially contacted the council. She could feel the disdain that father and daughter harbored for her and her friends. Deciding this wasn't the appropriate time to address their numerous issues, she pushed her feelings to the back of her mind. There would be time yet to deal with them, but for now she would just let them think her anger had been swept under the rug.

Taryn joined Andyn and the rest where they stood, waiting for the council's return. Just as before, the lights brightened and the council appeared once again, as if out of thin air. This time she noticed something different in each member's demeanor, however, it was Nodryck that caught her attention the most. His handsome face was once again marred by the boils and lesions that she had seen earlier in the day, but this time it did not transform back. A chill ran through her spine as she waited for one of them to speak.

"Today, we have witnessed a historical event. For the first time in our great history, a young woman has joined the ranks as pack leader," Oleg announced, his voice lacking any real emotion. The council, as a whole, bowed their heads for a brief moment in acknowledgement and acceptance of the historic event. "In addition, this is the first time that anyone under the age of eighteen has formally been considered part of a pack," he continued, referring to both Taryn and Andyn and the tattoos that had appeared on each of their shoulders, an unmistakable and irrefutable sign that they were truly a pack. Again, the council bowed their heads for a moment showing their acknowledgement and acceptance. She could feel Nodryck's eyes burning through her as he barely inclined his head in the bow. Oleg nodded to his brother then settled back into his throne.

"In what we, the Council, would see as an act of good faith, we ask that our Seer be allowed to search the minds of your two great protectors," Odyn stated, waving Rishyn forward.

"For what purpose?" Taryn asked, sensing something more than good faith was at play.

"Not that we owe you explanation, Child," Conus hissed. "But there are a few amongst us that would feel more comfortable if we knew their intentions were pure, since they have shown a willingness to die to protect you."

"It's okay, Taryn," Larkin stated, sensing her desire to protect them.

She smiled up at him before turning to Keiryn. "Are you good with this?"

"Yeah, Taryn, it'll be fine."

Rishyn stepped first to Larkin and took his hand between her own. She peered deep into his eyes as she searched his mind. When she had finished, a smirk formed across her face, placing Taryn on the defensive. What had she seen that was so amusing?

The woman walked past and smiled wildly at her. Taryn, still holding protectively onto Andyn's hand, guided the boy to stand behind her, as far away from the Seer as she could get him. Next, Rishyn took Keiryn's hand between her own and probed deep inside his head. After less than a minute it appeared that she had found what she was searching for. A wicked smile formed across her face as she turned and looked directly at Taryn.

"My, my, my, what an interesting trio," she smirked, backing away from the teens.

Nodryck leaned forward in his throne, curiosity mixed with an evil gleam, written on his face. "What is it that you found?"

"Does he know?" She focused her attention back on Taryn while nodding in Larkin's direction.

"Know what?" Conus thundered.

"Yes," Taryn echoed, "Perhaps you could be more specific and stop playing coy."

"As you wish, Child," Rishyn smiled, putting emphasis on the word child. "Does he know that his best friend is in love with you? That you consume his every thought?"

"We're family," Larkin growled at the insinuation. "Love comes with being a part of a close knit family."

"That may be true, but jealousy is not," she stated, her eyes glittering with elation. "Are you aware, Little Wolf, that your best friend is jealous of your relationship with this girl? He begrudges the bond you have with her and wants her for his own."

Larkin didn't answer, instead he glanced at Keiryn and immediately saw the look of shame in his best friend's eyes. Fire flared inside of him as he realized the Seer was right. His best friend had harbored even greater feelings for his love than he had ever imagined. How could he have been so blind as to not see what was so clearly written on his friend's face?

"That's not all, is it, Taryn?" Rishyn questioned.

"What does she mean," Larkin fumed, looking to Taryn for an answer.

She glared at the woman, knowing exactly what this request was truly about. Anger raged inside of her but she pushed it back down, knowing she had to allow the council this one thing in order to appease their needs.

"No, it's not," she admitted, hating that she had to hurt Larkin in order to play their game. "You are waiting for me to say that I love Keiryn, too. Well, I do." Larkin's eyes echoed the pain of a thousand blades being plunged deep into his heart, breaking her own. She wanted so badly to reach out and use her gift of Influence to wash it away, but she knew if she did, the council would seek their satisfaction in some other way.

"No, you don't. You can't."

Her eyes begged him to understand, but she kept her voice clear. "I do love him." She fought hard to hold back her emotions.

He bowed his head, his shoulders rising and falling with every breath he made as he struggled to control his anger and humiliation. It was too late. A deep seeded hatred festered inside of him, causing him to rush towards Keiryn, who had remained silent while the Seer had played her brutal game of truths, embarrassed that his secrets had come out in such a public way.

Grabbing him by the shirt, Larkin lifted his feet off the ground. "You're supposed to be my best friend."

In the background, Maxym and Teigan pushed against the guards in an attempt to get to their children. It proved futile against the numerous werewolves that stood blocking their efforts.

"I am your best friend, Larkin."

"None of this was about protecting her, was it? This whole time you have been waiting for the perfect opportunity to make your move."

"It wasn't like that. I swear! I promised you that I wouldn't interfere with your relationship, and I haven't," he reasoned as Larkin's eyes lit with rage.

"Let him go, Larkin," Taryn ordered.

"No, I want to hear him say it. I want to hear him tell me the truth."

Nodryck, Conus and a few other council members watched in delight as the tight trio quickly unraveled before their eyes. Rishyn glanced back at Nodryck, who gave her an approving nod.

Knowing there was no way to salvage what had been, Keiryn relented. "It's true. I do love her. And no, I don't think that you're good enough for her."

"And you are?"

"Stop this, now," Taryn shouted, pulling on Larkin's arm until he finally looked at her. "This isn't the time or the place," she whispered, nodding in the direction of the council, who continued to watch eagerly.

Though he wasn't exactly happy with her, he knew that she was right. Releasing his hold on Keiryn, he shoved him away before walking off.

"Taryn," Keiryn murmured.

"Not now." She placed a hand on his shoulder. Exhaling forcefully, he nodded, accepting her request. Turning, she stepped back to face the council. "Is there anything further?" she asked, fighting to subdue the anger churning inside of her.

Odyn tilted his head, studying the girl for a moment. He could see the displeasure from what just occurred shining through her eyes, but he knew their business was not concluded just yet. "We ask at this time that Gastyn Wylder step forward."

"Yes?" Gastyn took a step forward, unsure of what to expect.

"You are the teacher of this girl?" Odyn asked.

"That is correct."

"Then we make a simple request of you. We ask that you swear an Oath that she will never use her powers in such a way as she had done with Ardyn Mitchell, regardless of the circumstances. Such disciplinary matters must be left to the Council."

Knowing that Taryn would not do anything to place her friends and family in harm's way, he spoke. "I do. I make this solemn oath to you, Brothers and Sister, that Taryn Malone…"

With the wheels inside her head spinning in a hundred different directions, Taryn zoned out momentarily. As she heard Gastyn speak her name, she found Farren standing at her side. "Not now," she bit at him while searching inside herself for understanding of how Gastyn's promise could affect them all. Death would have to wait. She could not allow her teacher to make such a grievous error.

She listened as Gastyn started to speak the oath. "No, no, no," she interrupted, shaking her head.

"Is something wrong, Child?" Julius leaned forward.

Still shaking her head back and forth she grabbed hold of Gastyn's arm. "I'm sorry, Gastyn, but I can't allow you to speak for me, knowing it would be a lie."

"Taryn?" He placed his hand briefly over hers.

"I'll take my chances and tell them the truth." She pulled away from him to face the council.

"What is it?" Oleg demanded.

"You asked this great man to make a promise on my behalf. I cannot allow him to do so when I know that it is a promise that I would break, if need be. No one, not my mother, my teacher nor my friends, speak for me."

Julius looked to his cousin and smirked as she continued, pleased to see that she was every bit the person he believed her to be.

"You ask the impossible. My community…they are my family." She walked back to where they sat in the galley, looking at each member, excluding the Moore's, with great love shining in her eyes. "I can't promise what you ask, because I will use every bit of power that resides within me to defend each and every member of my family from anyone, or anything that should ever pose a threat to them. This is the solemn Oath that I can give to you. My family, my community, my home," she swore, placing her hands over her heart, her tone reflected the sincerity in her words.

As silence filled the great room, Taryn stepped forward, taking Andyn's hand back in her own. Nodryck looked down with a glaring hatred in his eyes.

"Is this meant to be some sort of threat?" he posed, in an attempt to rile other members of the council.

"No, Cousin. Young Taryn was merely pointing out how far she is willing to go to protect those she cares about," Julius answered with a warm smile.

"I agree. There was no threat made here today," Siobhyn concurred, though her face showed her apprehension for the girl.

"Very well, then. If there is nothing further..." Odyn stated, preparing to dismiss the council.

"Actually, I have one request of this just Council," Taryn interrupted, drawing a variety of looks from the members.

"Go on," Odyn directed her, not missing the use of her word just in describing the council.

"There are two present here today that I view to be a threat to our great community of Williams. They have never belonged and they never will." Taryn pointed to Agustin and Adalia Moore. "I believe my family will agree that they have been a poison in our society, one that will spread if left unchecked."

"What is it that you are asking, Child?" Julius asked, wondering if she would show mercy to the man and daughter who had set much of the day's events into motion.

"I'm not asking," Taryn stated matter-of-factly, a heated gleam in her eyes. "I'm giving them twenty-four hours to vacate their property and leave Williams, never to return." Her face was blank and her voice unwavering. It took all the fight she held inside to refrain from unleashing a hellish rant against the father and daughter who had so callously put everyone she loved and cared for in such grave danger.

"I think that sounds more than reasonable. We will send a few members of the guard to help clear out their home to ensure that everything goes smoothly and help expedite the process," Nodryck replied, catching everyone by surprise, including the members of the council.

"Is this acceptable?" Odyn inquired of her.

"Yes, thank you," she nodded, showing her gratitude.

"Very well then, this concludes today's events," Odyn stated quickly before anyone else had a chance to speak. The second he finished, the lights dimmed and the council was gone once more.

Cheers erupted from the galley as her community sighed with relief. She watched as Agustin and Adalia Moore were removed by two enormous werewolves, a shared look of fear on both their faces.

Nelmaryc held his hand out, opening a large Adora Gateway in the council room for Taryn and her extended family to return through. Still hesitant to believe that the Elder Council was going to let them go so easily, she insisted that everyone go before her. Once they were all safely through, she took her turn with a sullen Larkin and Keiryn flanking her.

Glancing back over her shoulder, she noticed Nelmaryc nod his head in her direction, wearing what appeared to be a half-smile upon his usually neutral face. She paused for a moment, nodding her head in acknowledgement then turned and walked the rest of the way through the gateway.

EPILOGUE

Nodryck angrily paced the floor behind his brothers and sister in the Elder Council's private chamber as they continued to discuss Taryn.

"She's a clever one, that little girl," Oleg chuckled, finding himself amused by all that she had accomplished. "She hid Ardyn's powers inside of him, evaded our guards for more than three days, jumped the Grand Canyon and faced us without showing an ounce of fear. She's a strong Imperium, but also possesses great control as an Influential."

"We should never have allowed her to leave here today," Conus argued, shifting in his seat, seeing things far differently than his brother.

"Don't be ridiculous. She showed more character than any one of us expected of someone so young," Siobhyn countered, sipping her warm tea.

"It was agreed that if she failed your last test, she would be put down. But she passed, and you must find a way to accept that," Odyn stated, having grown tired by the day's events.

"She was this close to letting him speak for her," Nodryck grumbled beneath his breath, holding his fingers only millimeters apart to show how close she had come to facing death.

"We agreed that if she proved to be influenced by, or willing to follow another, that she would be destroyed. She did neither," Oleg pointed out.

"What happens when she does fall under the wrong person's influence? What then?" Grandyn inquired.

"Were you watching the same girl that I was?" Lucien laughed. "That child showed not even a hint of fear as she stood before us facing certain death. When we observed her in the forest through the Helix Orb she didn't so much as bat an eye when she challenged the mutt and he prepared to strike her down."

"All the more reason why we should have destroyed her today," Conus growled.

"Did anyone else feel the power pulsing from her as she crushed the Handler's power-whip?" Dravyn mused.

"We can't allow her to control a member of our guard. And the boy, Larkin…is no one else concerned that he is only seventeen, yet he has the affliction? He is enamored with the girl. That makes them dangerous and they should both be destroyed." Conus asserted.

Julius shook his head in disagreement.

Nodryck looked at him and paused in his pacing. "What would you have us do, Cousin? Invite all of our kind to throw a parade in her honor?"

"A parade, what a splendid idea," Julius mocked.

"Careful, Cousin."

Choosing to ignore him, as he often did, he addressed the rest of the council members. "This girl possesses something truly special, and I'm not just speaking of her gifts. She showed forethought and compassion for the guards as they chased them through the canyon, putting up an invisible shield to prevent them from falling to what would have been certain death. Even when the guard attacked her earlier, she eased his suffering when not one of us acted to do so. Her heart is pure and we should embrace her, not seek reasons to end her."

"What happens when the Mortari discovers what she did to our guard today? They'll seek her out in an attempt to use her against us. The werewolves are our only defense against them. What will happen when they find out her blood is poison to them?" Hermyn pointed out.

"Have you not listened to anything that I have said?"

"I heard you, Julius, but her blood burned through our guard like acid, and that is something the Mortari will try to use against us, whether she is willing or not."

"She would never allow that to happen."

A knock at the chamber door drew their attention. "Come in," Oleg stated, flipping his wrist from the comfort of his seat and opening the door.

"I apologize for the intrusion," Rishyn bowed.

"What is it you need?" Odyn yawned, wanting nothing more than to get away from his brothers and sister to rest his weary bones.

"She's here at my request," Nodryck stated blankly, walking to her and glancing around the room before escorting her out by the elbow. Once the door closed behind them, he stopped and faced her. "Is it done?"

"Yes. Father and daughter are detained, waiting for you to interrogate them. However, I think you will find Adalia to be quite eager to dish all that she knows about the girl."

"And what of Ardyn and Karvyn?"

"The trade has been made and your payment secured."

"Excellent," he grinned wickedly. "You may earn your freedom yet, Seer."

###

Thank you for reading.

ABOUT THE AUTHOR

Karlie Mavre is the shared alter-ego for co-authors, Karin Reeve and Leslie Marvin, two fun-loving, mid-west girls who share a passion for writing and who believe no one is ever too old to follow their dreams. A chance meeting four years ago quickly blossomed into a lasting friendship and the eventual creation of the epic young adult fantasy series, The Oath Saga. The duo has a tremendous talent for weaving intricate stories with complex characters and vivid imagery. Taking this journey together has been rewarding, challenging, and unbelievably amazing.

They are currently hard at work on *Volume Three, Reign of Fire*, but would love for you to visit with them on their website, www.karliemavre.com or on their Facebook author page at www.facebook.com/karlie.mavre. You can also catch them on Twitter at www.twitter.com/Karliemavre.

Coming November 2014
THE OATH SAGA: WINTER'S FROST
VOLUME TWO

Made in the USA
Lexington, KY
20 November 2015